SWEET TEMPTATION

"But you're enchanting!" he exclaimed.

She put out her hands quickly to hold him off. "No!"

He caught her wrists and swept them behind her, clipping them in the small of her back and so holding her chest to chest. Her heart beat fast; she felt breathless, but not afraid.

"Yes!" he said, still mocking. "You should have run away, my golden girl, while you had the chance to do it!"

Also by Georgette Heyer
from *Jove*

GEORGETTE HEYER
VENETIA

A JOVE BOOK

This Jove book contains the complete
text of the original hardcover edition.
It has been completely reset in a typeface
designed for easy reading, and was printed
from new film.

VENETIA

A Jove Book / published by arrangement with
G.P. Putnam's Sons

PRINTING HISTORY
G.P. Putnam's Sons edition published 1958

Five previous paperback printings
Jove edition / February 1981
Second printing / December 1982

ISBN: 0-515-06878-0

Jove books are published by Jove Publications,
Inc., 200 Madison Avenue, New York, N.Y. 10016.
The words "A JOVE BOOK" and the "J" with sunburst
are trademarks belonging to Jove Publications, Inc.

PRINTED IN THE UNITED STATES OF AMERICA

1

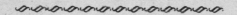

"A fox got in amongst the hens last night, and ravished our best layer," remarked Miss Lanyon. "A great-grandmother, too! You'd think he would be ashamed!" Receiving no answer, she continued, in an altered voice: "Indeed, you would! It is a great deal too bad. What is to be done?"

His attention caught, her companion raised his eyes from the book which lay open beside him on the table and directed them upon her in a look of aloof enquiry. "What's that? Did you say something to me, Venetia?"

"Yes, love," responded his sister cheerfully, "but it wasn't of the least consequence, and in any event I answered for you. You would be astonished, I daresay, if you knew what interesting conversations I enjoy with myself."

"I was reading."

"So you were—and have let your coffee grow cold, besides abandoning that slice of bread-and-butter. Do eat it up! I'm persuaded I ought not to permit you to read at table."

"Oh, the *breakfast*-table!" he said disparagingly. "Try if you can stop me!"

"I can't, of course. What is it?" she returned, glancing at the volume. "Ah, Greek! Some improving tale, I don't doubt."

"The *Medea*," he said repressively. "Porson's edition, which Mr. Appersett lent to me."

"*I* know! She was the delightful creature who cut up her brother, and cast the pieces in her papa's way, wasn't she? I daresay perfectly amiable when one came to know her."

1

He hunched an impatient shoulder, and replied contemptuously: "You don't understand, and it's a waste of time to try to make you."

Her eyes twinkled at him. "But I promise you I do! Yes, and sympathize with her, besides wishing I had her resolution! Though I think I should rather have buried *your* remains tidily in the garden, my dear!"

This sally drew a grin from him, but he merely said, before turning back to his book, that to order her to do so would certainly have been all the heed their parent would have paid.

Inured to his habits, his sister made no further attempt to engage his attention. The slice of bread-and-butter, which was all the food he would accept that morning, lay half-eaten on his plate, but to expostulate would be a waste of time, and to venture on an enquiry about the state of his health would serve only to set up his hackles.

He was a thin boy, rather undersized, by no means ill-looking, but with a countenance sharpened and lined beyond his years. A stranger would have found these hard to compute, his body's immaturity being oddly belied by his face and his manners. In point of fact he had not long entered on his seventeenth year, but physical suffering had dug the lines in his face, and association with none but his seniors, coupled with an intellect at once scholarly and powerful, had made him precocious. A disease of the hip-joint had kept him away from Eton, where his brother Conway, his senior by six years, had been educated, and this (or, as his sister sometimes thought, the various treatments to which he had been subjected) had resulted in a shortening of one leg. When he walked it was with a pronounced and ugly limp; and although the disease was said to have been arrested the joint still pained him in inclement weather, or when he had over-exerted himself. Such sports as his brother delighted in were denied him, but he was a gallant rider, and a fair shot, and only he knew, and Venetia guessed, how bitterly he loathed his infirmity.

A boyhood of enforced physical inertia had strengthened a natural turn for scholarship. By the time he was fourteen if he had not outstripped his tutor in learning he had done so in understanding; and it was recognized by the worthy man that more advanced coaching than he felt himself able to supply was needed. Fortunately, the means of obtaining it were at hand. The incumbent of the parish was a notable scholar, and had for long observed with a sort of wistful delight Aubrey Lanyon's progress. He offered to prepare the boy for Cambridge; Sir Francis Lanyon, relieved to be spared the necessity of admitting a new tutor into his household, acquiesced in the arrangement; and Aubrey, by that time able to bestride a horse, thereafter spent the better part of his days at the Parsonage, poring over texts in the Reverend Julius Appersett's dim bookroom, eagerly absorbing his gentle preceptor's wide lore, and filling him with an ever-increasing belief in his ability to excel. He was entered already at Trinity College, where he would be admitted at Michaelmas in the following year; and Mr. Appersett had little doubt that young though he would still be he would soon be elected a scholar.

Neither his sister nor his elder brother cherished doubts on this head. Venetia knew his intellect to be superior; and Conway, himself a splendidly robust young sportsman to whom the writing of a letter was an intolerable labour, regarded him with as much awe as compassion. To win a Fellowship seemed to Conway a strange ambition, but he sincerely hoped Aubrey would achieve it, for what else (he once said to Venetia) could the poor little lad do but stick to his books?

For her part, Venetia thought he stuck too closely to them, and was showing at an alarmingly early age every sign of becoming just such an obstinate recluse as their father had been. He was supposed, at the moment, to be enjoying a holiday, for Mr. Appersett was in Bath, recuperating from a severe illness, a cousin, with whom he had fortunately been able to exchange, performing his duties for him. Any other boy would have thrust his books on to a shelf and equipped himself instead with his rod. Aubrey brought books even to the breakfast-table, and let his coffee grow cold while he sat propping his broad, delicate brow on his hand, his eyes bent on the printed page, his brain so much concentrated on what he read that one might speak his name a dozen times and still win no response. It did not occur to him that such absorption made him a poor companion. It occurred forcibly to Venetia, but since she had long since recognized that

3

he was quite as selfish as his father or his brother she was able to accept his odd ways with perfect equanimity, and to go on holding him in affection without suffering any of the pangs of disillusionment.

She was nine years his senior, the eldest of the three surviving children of a Yorkshire landowner of long lineage, comfortable fortune, and eccentric habits. The loss of his wife before Aubrey was out of short coats had caused Sir Francis to immure himself in the fastness of his manor, some fifteen miles from York, and to remain there, sublimely indifferent to the welfare of his offspring, abjuring the society of his fellows. Venetia could only suppose that the trend of his nature must always have been towards solitude, for she was quite unable to believe that such extravagant conduct had arisen from a broken heart. Sir Francis had been a man of rigid pride, but never one of sensibility, and that his marriage had been one of unmixed bliss was an amiable fiction his clear-sighted daughter was quite unable to believe. Her memories of her mother were vague, but they included the echoes of bitter quarrels, slammed doors, and painful fits of hysteria. She could remember being admitted to her mother's scented bed-chamber to see her dressed for a ball at Castle Howard; she could remember a beautiful discontented face; a welter of expensive dresses; a French maid; but not one recollection could she summon up of maternal concern or affection. It was certain that Lady Lanyon had not shared her husband's love of country life. Every spring had seen the ill-assorted pair in London; early summer took them to Brighton; when they returned to Undershaw it was not long before her ladyship became moped; and when winter closed down on Yorkshire she was unable to support the rigours of the climate, and was off with her reluctant spouse to visit friends. No one could think that such a butterfly's existence suited Sir Francis, yet when a sudden illness had carried her off he had come home a stricken man, unable to bear the sight of her portrait on the wall, or to hear her name mentioned.

His children grew up in the desert of his creating, only Conway, sent to Eton and passing thence into the Foot, escaping into a larger world. Neither Venetia nor Aubrey had been farther from Undershaw than Scarborough, and their acquaintance was limited to the few families living

4

within reach of the Manor. Neither repined, Aubrey because he shrank from going amongst strangers, Venetia because it was not in her nature to do so. She had only once been disconsolate: that was when she was seventeen, and Sir Francis had refused to let her go to his sister, in London, to be presented, and brought out into Society. It had seemed hard, and some tears had been shed. However, a very little reflection had sufficed to convince her that the scheme was really quite impractical. She could not leave Aubrey, a sickly eight-year-old, to Nurse's sole care: that excellent creature's devotion would have driven him into a madhouse. So she had dried her eyes, and made the best of things. Papa, after all, was not unreasonable: though he would not consent to a London Season he raised no objection to her attending the Assemblies in York, or even in Harrogate, whenever Lady Denny, or Mrs. Yardley, invited her to go with them, which they quite frequently did, the one from kindness, the other under compulsion from her determined son. Nor was Papa at all mean; he never questioned her household expenditure, bestowed a handsome allowance on her, and somewhat to her surprise, left her, at his death, a very respectable competence.

This event had occurred three years previously, within a month of the glorious victory at Waterloo, and quite unexpectedly, of a fatal stroke. It had been a shock to his children, but not a grief. "In fact," said Venetia, scandalizing kind Lady Denny, "we go on very much better without him."

"My dear!" gasped her ladyship, who had come to the Manor prepared to clasp the orphans to her sentimental bosom. "You are overwrought!"

"Indeed I'm not!" Venetia replied, laughing. "Why, ma'am, how many times have you declared him to have been the most unnatural parent?"

"But he's *dead*, Venetia!"

"Yes, but I don't suppose he has any more fondness for us now than he had when he was alive, ma'am. He never made the least push to engage our affections, you know, so he really *cannot* expect us to grieve for him."

Finding this unanswerable Lady Denny merely begged her not to say such things, and made haste to ask what she now meant to do. Venetia had said that it all depended

5

on Conway. Until he came home to take up his inheritance there was nothing she could do but continue in the old way. "Except, of course, that I shall now be able to entertain our friends at the Manor, which will be very much more comfortable than it was when Papa would allow none but Edward Yardley and Dr. Bentworth to cross the threshold."

Three years later Venetia was still awaiting Conway s return, and Lady Denny had almost ceased to inveigh against his selfishness in leaving the burden of his affairs on her shoulders. No one had been surprised that he had at first found it impossible to return to England, for no doubt everything must have been at sixes and sevens in Belgium and France, and all our regiments sadly depleted after so sanguinary a battle as Waterloo. But as the months slid by, and all the news that was to be had of Conway came in a brief scrawl to his sister assuring her that he had every confidence in her ability to do just as she ought at Undershaw, and would write to her again when he had more time to devote to the task, it began to be generally felt that his continued absence arose less from a sense of duty than from reluctance to abandon a life that seemed (from accounts gleaned from visitors to the Army of Occupation) to consist largely of cricket-matches and balls. When last heard of, Conway had had the good fortune to be appointed to Lord Hill's staff, and was stationed at Cambray. He had been unable to write at much length to Venetia because the Great Man was expected, and there was to be a Review, followed by a dinner-party, which meant that the staff was kept busy. He knew she would understand exactly how it was, and he remained her affectionate brother Conway. *P.S. I don't know which field you mean—you had best do what Powick thinks right.*

"And for anything he cares she may live all her days at Undershaw, and die an old maid!" tearfully declared Lady Denny.

"She is more likely to marry Edward Yardley," responded her lord prosaically.

"I have nothing to say against Edward Yardley,—indeed, I believe him to be a truly estimable person!—but I have always said, and I always *shall* say, that it would be throwing herself away! If only our own dear Oswald were ten years older, Sir John!"

But here the conversation took an abrupt turn, Sir John's evil genius prompting him to exclaim that he hoped such a fine-looking girl had more sense than to look twice at the silliest puppy in the country. As he added a rider to the effect that it was high time his wife stopped encouraging Oswald to make a cake of himself with his play-acting ways, Venetia was forgotten in a pretty spirited interchange of conflicting opinions.

None would have denied that Venetia was a fine-looking girl; most would not have hesitated to call her beautiful. Amongst the pick of the debutants at Almack's she must have attracted attention; in the more restricted society in which she dwelt she was a nonpareil. It was not only the size and brilliance of her eyes which excited admiration, or the glory of her shining guinea-gold hair, or even the enchanting arch of her pretty mouth: there was something very taking in her face which owed nothing to the excellence of her features: an expression of sweetness, a sparkle of irrepressible fun, an unusually open look, quite devoid of selfconsciousness.

The humorous gleam sprang to her eyes as she glanced at Aubrey, still lost in antiquity. She said: "Aubrey! Dear, *odious* Aubrey! Do lend me your ears! Just *one* of your ears, love!"

He looked up, an answering gleam in his own eyes. "Not if it is something I particularly dislike!"

"No, I promise you it isn't!" she replied, laughing. "Only, if you mean to ride out presently will you be so very obliging as to call at the Receiving Office, and enquire if there has been a parcel delivered there for me from York? Quite a *small* parcel, dear Aubrey! not in the *least* unwieldy, upon my honour!"

"Yes, I'll do that—if it's not fish! If it is, you may send Puxton for it, m'dear."

"No, it's muslin—unexceptionable!"

He had risen, and walked over to the window with his awkward, dragging step. "It's too hot to go out at all, I think, but I will—Oh, I most *certainly* will, and at once! M'dear, *both* your suitors are come to pay us a morning-visit!"

"Oh, no!" exclaimed Venetia imploringly. "Not again!"

"Riding up the avenue," he assured her. "Oswald is looking as sulky as a bear, too."

"Now, Aubrey, pray don't say so! It is his *gloomy* look.

7

He is brooding over nameless crimes, I daresay, and only think how disheartening to have his dark thoughts mistaken for a fit of the sulks!"

"What nameless crimes?"

"My dear, how should I know—or he either? Poor boy! it is all Byron's fault! Oswald can't decide whether it is his lordship whom he resembles or his lordship's *Corsair*. In either event it is very disturbing for poor Lady Denny. She is persuaded he is suffering from a disorder of the blood, and has been begging him to take James's Powders."

"Byron!" Aubrey ejaculated, with one of his impatient shrugs. "I don't know how you can read such stuff!"

"Of course you don't, love—and I must own I wish Oswald had found himself unable to do so. I wonder what excuse Edward will offer us for this visit? Surely there cannot have been *another* Royal marriage, or General Election?"

"Or that he should think we care for such trash." Aubrey turned away from the window. "Are you going to marry him?" he asked.

"No—oh, I don't know! I am sure he would be a kind husband, but try as I will I can't hold him in anything but esteem," she replied, in a comically despairing tone.

"Why do you try?"

"Well, I must marry someone, you know! Conway will certainly do so, and then what is to become of me? It wouldn't suit me to continue living here, dwindling into an aunt—and I daresay it wouldn't suit my unknown sister either!"

"Oh, you may live with me! *I* shan't be married, and I shouldn't at all object to it: you never trouble me!"

Her eyes danced, but she assured him gravely that she was very much obliged to him.

"You would like it better than to be married to Edward."

"Poor Edward! Do you dislike him so much?"

He replied, with a twisted smile: "I never forget, when he's with us, that I'm a cripple, m'dear."

A voice was heard to say, beyond the door: "In the breakfast-parlour, are they? Oh, you need not announce me: I know my way!"

Aubrey added: "And I dislike his knowing his way!"

8

"So do I, indeed! There is no escape!" she agreed, turning to greet the visitors.

Two gentlemen of marked dissimilarity came into the room, the elder, a solid looking man in his thirtieth year, leading the way, as one who did not doubt his welcome; the younger, a youth of nineteen, with a want of assurance imperfectly concealed by a slight, nonchalant swagger.

"Good-morning, Venetia! Well, Aubrey!" said Mr. Edward Yardley, shaking hands. "What a pair of slugabeds, to be sure! I was afraid I shouldn't find you in on such a day, but came on the chance that Aubrey might care to try his luck with the carp in my lake. What do you say, Aubrey? You may fish from the boat, you know, and not suffer any fatigue."

"Thank you, but I shouldn't expect to get a rise in such weather."

"It would do you good, however, and you may drive your gig to within only a few yards of the lake, you know."

It was kindly said, but there was a suggestion of gritted teeth in Aubrey's reiterated refusal. Mr. Yardley noticed this and supposed, compassionately, that his hip was paining him.

Meanwhile, young Mr. Denny was informing his hostess, rather more impressively than the occasion seemed to warrant, that he had come to see her. He added, in a low, vibrant voice, that he could not keep away. He then scowled at Aubrey, who was looking at him with derision in his eyes, and relapsed into blushful silence. He was nearly three years older than Aubrey, and had seen much more of the world, but Aubrey could always put him out of countenance, as much by his dispassionate gaze as by the use of his adder's tongue. He could not be at ease in the boy's presence, for besides being no match for him in a battle of wits he had a healthy young animal's dislike of physical deformity, and considered, moreover, that Aubrey traded on this in a very shabby way. But for that halting left leg he could have been speedily taught what civility was due to his elders. He knows himself to be safe from me, thought Oswald, and curled his lip.

Upon being invited to sit down he had assumed a careless pose upon a small sofa. He now found that his fellow-guest was steadfastly regarding him, and with unmistakeable reprobation, and he was at once torn between

9

hope that he presented a romantic figure and fear that he had a trifle overdone the nonchalant attitude. He sat up, and Edward Yardley transferred his gaze to Venetia's face.

Mr. Yardley, with no wish to appear romantic, would never have been guilty of lounging in a lady's presence. Nor would he have paid a morning visit dressed in a shooting-jacket, and with a silk handkerchief knotted round his throat, its ends untidily worn outside his coat. He was dressed with neatness and propriety in a sober riding-coat and buckskins, and so far from training a lock of hair to droop over one brow he wore his hair rather closer cropped than was fashionable. He might have served as a model for a country gentleman of solid worth and modest ambition; certainly no stranger would have guessed that it was he, and not Oswald, who was the only child of a doting and widowed mother.

His father having died before Edward had reached his tenth birthday he had at a very early age come into the possession of his fortune. This was respectable rather than handsome, large enough to enable a prudent man to command the elegancies of life and still contrive to be beforehand with the world. A sprig of fashion, bent on cutting a dash, would have thought it penury, but Edward had no extravagant tastes. His estate, which was situated rather less than ten miles from Undershaw, was neither so extensive nor so important as Undershaw, but it was generally considered to be a snug property, and conferred upon its owner the acknowledged standing in the North Riding which was the summit of his ambition. Of a naturally serious disposition he was also endowed with a strong sense of duty. Frustrating all the efforts of his mama to ruin his character by excessive indulgence he early assumed the conduct of his affairs, and rapidly grew into a grave young man of uniform virtues. If he had neither liveliness nor wit he had a great deal of commonsense; and if his masterful nature made him rather too autocratic in his household his firm rule over his mama and his dependants was always actuated by a sincere belief in his ability to decide what would be best for them to do on all occasions.

Venetia, feeling that it behoved her to atone for Aubrey's scant civility, said: "How kind in you to have thought of Aubrey! But you shouldn't have put yourself to so much trouble: I daresay you must have a thousand things to do."

"Not quite a *thousand*," he responded, smiling. "Not even a *hundred*, though in general I am pretty busy, I own. But you must not suppose me to be neglecting any urgent duty: I hope I needn't charge myself with that! What was pressing I was able to attend to when you, I'll wager, were still asleep. With a little management one can always find time, you know. I have another reason for coming to see you, too: I've brought you my copy of Tuesday's *Morning Post*, which I believe you will be glad to have. I have marked the passage: you will see that it is concerned with the Army of Occupation. It seems certain that the feeling of the French against our soldiers' continuing there is growing very strong. One cannot wonder at it, though when one remembers—however, that is of less interest to you than the prospect of welcoming Conway home! I believe you may have him with you before the year is out."

Venetia took the newspaper, thanking him in a voice that quivered on the edge of laughter, and taking care not to meet Aubrey's eye. Ever since Edward had discovered that the Lanyons were dependent for news on the weekly *Liverpool Mercury* he had made the sharing with them of his own London daily paper an excuse for his frequent visits to Undershaw. He had begun by coming only when some startling piece of intelligence, such as the death of the old King of Sweden and the election to the throne of Marshal Bernadotte, was announced; and during the spring months the journals served him nobly, with a spate of royal marriages. First there had been the really astonishing news that the Princess Elizabeth, though somewhat stricken in years, was betrothed to the Prince of Hesse Homburg; and hardly had the descriptions of her bridal raiment and the panegyrics on her skill as an artist ceased than no fewer than three of her middle-aged brothers followed her example. That, of course, was because of the Heiress of England, poor Princess Charlotte, had lately died in childbed, and her infant with her. Even Edward owned that it was diverting, for two of the Royal Dukes were over fifty, and looked it; and everyone knew that the eldest of the three was the father of a large family of hopeful bastards. But since Clarence's nuptials, in July,

11

Edward had been hard put to it to discover any item in the journals which was at all likely to interest the Lanyons; and had been obliged more than once to fall back on reports that the Queen's health was giving the Royal physicians cause for despondency, or that dissension had reared its head amongst the Whigs over Tierney's continued leadership of the party. Not the most confirmed optimist could have supposed that the Lanyons would be interested in such rumours as these, but it was reasonable to expect them to hail the prospect of Conway's homecoming as news of real value.

But Venetia only said that she would believe that Conway had sold out when she saw him walk in at the door; and Aubrey, after giving the matter frowning consideration, added, on a regrettably optimistic note, that there was no need to despair, since Conway would probably find another excuse for remaining in the Army.

"*I* should!" said Oswald. He then realized that this was decidedly uncomplimentary to his hostess, fell into an agony, and stammered: "That is, I don't mean—that is, I mean I should if I were Sir Conway! He'll find it so devilish slow here. One does, when one has seen the world."

"You find it slow after a trip to the West Indies, don't you?" said Aubrey.

That drew a laugh from Edward, and Oswald, who had meant to ignore Aubrey's malice, said with unnecessary emphasis: "I've seen more of the world than you have, at all events! You've no notion—you'd be amazed if I told you how different it all is in Jamaica!"

"Yes, we were," agreed Aubrey, beginning to pull himself up from his chair.

Edward with the solicitude so little appreciated at once went to his assistance. Unable to shake off the sustaining grip on his elbow Aubrey submitted to it, but his thank you was icily uttered, and he made no attempt to stir from where he was standing until Edward removed his hand. He then smoothed his sleeve, and said, addressing himself to his sister: "I'll be off to collect that package, m'dear. I wish you will write to Taplow, when you have a moment to yourself, and desire him to send us one of the London daily journals in future. I think we ought to have one, don't you?"

"No need for that," said Edward. "I promise you I am only too happy to share mine with you."

Aubrey paused in the doorway to look back, and to say, with dulcet softness: "But if we had our own you wouldn't be obliged to ride over to us so often, would you?"

"If I had known you wished for it I would have ridden over *every day*, with my father's copy!" said Oswald earnestly.

"Nonsense!" said Edward, annoyed by this as he had not been by Aubrey's overt ill-will. "I fancy Sir John might have something to say to that scheme! Venetia knows she can depend on me."

This snubbing remark goaded Oswald into saying that Venetia could depend on him for the performance of far more dangerous services than the delivery of a newspaper. At least, that was the gist of what he meant to say, but the speech, which had sounded well enough in imagination, underwent an unhappy transformation when uttered. It became hopelessly involved, sounded lame even to its author, and petered out under the tolerant scorn in Edward's eye.

A diversion was just then created by the Lanyon's old nurse, who came into the room looking for Venetia. Finding that Mr. Yardley, of whom she approved, was with her young mistress she at once begged pardon, said that her business could wait, and withdrew again. But Venetia, preferring a domestic interlude, even if she were obliged to inspect worn sheets or listen to complaints of the younger servants' idleness, to the company of her ill-assorted admirers, rose to her feet, and in the kindest possible way dismissed them, saying that she would find herself in disgrace with Nurse if she kept her waiting.

"I have been neglecting my duties, and if I don't take care shall be subjected to a dreadful scold," she said, smiling, and holding out her hand to Oswald. "So I must send you both away. Don't be vexed! you are such old friends that I don't stand on ceremony with you."

Not even Edward's presence could deter Oswald from raising her hand to his lips, and pressing a fervent kiss upon it. She received this with unruffled equanimity, and upon recovering her hand held it out to Edward. But he only smiled, and said: "In a moment!" and held open the door for her. She went past him into the hall, and he followed her, firmly shutting his rival into the breakfast-parlour. "You should not encourage that stupid boy to dangle after you," he remarked.

"Do I encourage him?" she said, looking surprised. "I thought I behaved to him as I do to Aubrey. That's how I regard him—except," she added thoughtfully, "that Aubrey doesn't want for sense, and seems much older than poor Oswald."

"My dear Venetia, I do not accuse you of *flirting* with him!" he replied, with an indulgent smile. "Nor am I jealous, if that's what you are thinking!"

"Well, it isn't," she said. "You have no reason to be jealous and no right either, you know."

"Certainly no *reason*. As for *right*, we are agreed, are we not? that it would be improper to say more on that head until Conway comes home. You may guess with what interest *I* perused that column in the newspaper!"

This was said with an arch look which provoked her to exclaim: "Edward! Pray don't refine too much upon Conway's homecoming! You've fallen into a way of speaking of it as if *that* would make me ready to fall into your arms, and I wish you will not!"

"I hope—indeed, I am quite sure—that I have never expressed myself in such terms," he responded gravely.

"No, never!" she agreed, a mischievous smile hovering round her lips. "Edward, do—do ask yourself, before I become so bored with Conway that I shall be ready to snap at *any* offer, if you *really* wish to marry me! For I don't think you do!"

He looked taken aback, even rather shocked, but after a moment he smiled, and said: "I know your love of funning! You are always diverting, and if your sportiveness leads you now and then to say some odd things I fancy I am too well-acquainted with you to believe you mean them."

"Edward, pray—*pray* make at least a push to disabuse your mind of illusions!" begged Venetia earnestly. "You can't know me in the least, if that's what you think, and what a dreadful shock it will be to you when you discover that I *do* mean the odd things I say!"

He replied playfully, yet with no diminution of his confidence: "Perhaps I know you better than you know yourself! It is a trick you've caught from Aubrey. *You* do

14

not in general go beyond the line of what is pleasing, but when you talk of Conway it is as if you did not hold him in affection."

"No, I don't," she said frankly.

"Venetia! Think what you are saying!"

"But it is perfectly true!" she insisted. "Oh, don't look so shocked! I don't dislike him—though I daresay I may, if I am obliged to be with him a great deal, for besides not caring a straw for anyone's comfort but his own he is quite *dismally* commonplace!"

"You should not say so," he replied repressively. "If you talk of your brother with so little moderation it is not to be wondered at that Aubrey shouldn't scruple to speak of his homecoming as he did just now."

"My dear Edward, a moment since you said that *I* had caught the trick from *him!*" she rallied him. His countenance did not relax, and she added, in some amusement: "The truth is—if you would but realize it!—that we haven't any tricks, we only say what we think. And I must own that it is astonishing how often we have the same thoughts, for we are not, I believe, much alike—certainly not in our tastes!"

He was silent for a minute, and then said: "It is allowable for you to feel a little resentment, perhaps. I have felt it for you. Your situation here since your father's death, has been uncomfortable, and Conway has not scrupled to lay his burdens—indeed, his *duties!*—upon your shoulders. But with Aubrey it is otherwise. I was tempted to give him a sharp set-down when I heard him speak as he did of his brother. Whatever Conway's faults may be he is very good-natured, and has always been kind to Aubrey."

"Yes, but Aubrey doesn't like people because they are kind," she said.

"Now you are talking nonsensically!"

"Oh, no! When Aubrey likes people it isn't for anything they do: it's for what they have in their minds, I think."

"It will be a very good thing for Aubrey when Conway does come home!" he interrupted. "If the only people he is foolish enough to think he can like are classical scholars, it's high time—"

"What a stupid thing to say, when you must know that he likes me!"

He said stiffly: "I beg your pardon! No doubt I misunderstood you."

"Indeed you did! You misunderstood what I said about Conway, too. I promise you I don't feel the least *resentment*, and as for my situation—oh, how absurd you are! Of course it's not uncomfortable!" She saw that he was looking offended, and exclaimed: "Now I have vexed you! Well, it's too hot a day for quarrelling, so we won't argue any more, if you please! In any event, I must go up to see what it is Nurse wants. Goodbye!—and thank you for being so kind as to bring us your newspaper!"

2

Escaping from Nurse, who, besides worn sheets, displayed for her reprobation two of Aubrey's shirts, with wrist-bands torn by careless mangling, Venetia fell into the clutches of the housekeeper. Mrs. Gurnard's ostensible purpose was to remind her that now or never was the time for making bramble-jelly; her real object, arrived at only after much divagation, was to defend the new laundry-maid, her own niece, from Nurse's accusations. Since these two elderly retainers had lived for some twenty-six years on terms of mutual jealousy, Venetia knew that the alleged shortcomings of the laundry-maid would inevitably lead to the recital of a number of other grievances against Nurse; after which Nurse, rendered suspicious by the length of her visit to the housekeeper's room, would pounce on her to discover by rigorous questioning what malicious lies had been told her; so, with an adroitness born of long practice, she swiftly brought the conversation back to bramble-jelly, diverting Mrs. Gurnard's mind by a promise to bring her a basketful of blackberries that very day, and slipping away to her bedchamber before that redoubtable dame could recollect any more of Nurse's iniquities.

Shedding the French cambric dress she was wearing, Venetia pulled out an old dimity from her wardrobe. It was rather outmoded, and its original blue had faded to an indeterminate gray, but it was quite good enough for blackberrying, and not even Nurse would cry out censoriously if it became stained. A rather stouter pair of shoes and a sunbonnet completed her toilet; and, armed with a large basket, she presently left the house, sped on her way by the intelligence, conveyed to her by Ribble, the butler, that Mr. Denny, having ridden away to Thirsk, where he had business to transact, rather thought he should call again at Undershaw on his homeward journey, in case Miss Lanyon might wish to charge him with a message for his mama.

Her sole companion on this expedition was an amiable if vacuous spaniel, bestowed on her by Aubrey, when he had discovered that besides being of an excitable disposition the pup was incurably gun-shy. As escort to a lady on her solitary walks he was by no means ideal, for, his unfortunate weakness notwithstanding, he was much addicted to sport, and after impeding her progress for a few hundred yards by gambolling round her, jumping up at her with hysterical yelps, and in general enacting the role of a dog rarely released from his chain, he would dash off, deaf to all remonstrance, and reappear only at intervals, with his tongue hanging out, and an air of having snatched a moment from urgent private affairs to assure himself that all was well with her.

Like most country-bred girls of her generation Venetia was an energetic walker; unlike most of her gently-born contemporaries she never scrupled to walk alone. It was a custom developed in her schoolroom days, when her object was to escape from her governess. An hour spent in strolling about the paths in the shrubbery was thought by Miss Poddemore to be sufficient exercise for any lady; and on the rare occasions when circumstance or persuasion induced her to set forth on the mile-long walk to the nearest village her decorous pace was as exasperating to her pupil as was her habit of beguiling the way with instructive discourse. Although not so highly accomplished as Miss Selina Trimmer, whom she had once met and ever afterwards venerated, she was well-educated. Unfortunately she possessed neither Miss Trimmer's force of character nor her ability to inspire her pupils with affection. By the time she was seventeen Venetia was so heartily bored by her that she marked her emergence from the schoolroom into young ladyhood by informing her father that since she was now grown-up and perfectly able to manage the household they could dispense with Miss Poddemore's services. From that date she had had no other chaperon than Nurse, but, as she pointed out to Lady Denny, since she neither went into society nor received guests at Undershaw it was hard to see what use a chaperon would be to her. Unable to say that there was any impropriety in a girl's living unchaperoned in her father's house, Lady Denny was obliged to abandon that argument, and to implore Venetia instead not to roam about the countryside unattended even by a maid. But Venetia had only laughed, and told her playfully that she was as bad as Miss Poddemore, who had never wearied of citing the example of Lady Harriet Cavendish (one of the pupils of the distinguished Miss Trimmer), who, when staying at Castle Douglas before her marriage, had never ventured beyond the gardens without her footman to attend her. Not being a duke's daughter she did not feel it incumbent on her to take Lady Harriet for her model. "Besides, ma'am, that must have been ten years ago at least! And to drag one of the maids with me, when she would rather be doing anything else in the world, I daresay, would destroy all my pleasure. No, no, I didn't rid myself of Miss Poddemore for *that!* Why, what should happen to me here, where everyone knows who I am?"

Lady Denny, sighing, had had to be content with a promise that her independent young protegee would never go unescorted into York, or Thirsk. When Sir Francis had died she had renewed her entreaties, but without much hope of being attended to. It distressed her that Venetia should say she had outgrown her girlhood, but she could not deny it: Venetia was then twenty-two, perilously near to being on the shelf.

"Without ever having been *off* it, Sir John—though that's not precisely what I mean, only that it is a wicked shame, so beautiful as she is, and so full of liveliness, besides having the best disposition imaginable! For my part, I hold that aunt of hers pretty cheap! She never made a real push to persuade Sir Francis to let Venetia go to London for a season when the poor child first came out, and if she has urged her to go now that he's dead *I* have heard nothing of it! I believe her to be as selfish as her brother was, and if it were not for the expense, and our own girls to bring out—for even if anything *should* come of that attachment between Clara and Conway, which I don't at all reckon on, I am determined that all five must and shall be presented at Court!—well, as I say, if it were not for that I should be strongly tempted to take her to

London myself, and I shouldn't wonder at it if she made a very respectable marriage, even though she isn't in the first blush of youth! Only, you may depend upon it she would refuse to leave Aubrey," she added in a despondent tone. "And soon it will be too late, if only she knew it!"

Venetia did know it, but since she could see no remedy while Conway remained obstinately abroad she continued to make the best of things. Lady Denny would have been astonished had she been allowed to know with what misgiving Venetia regarded the future.

For any female in her position it was bleak indeed, and seemed to offer her no choice between marriage with Edward Yardley or the life of an ageing, and probably unwanted, spinster in her brother's household. Mistress of an easy competence, it was convention and not dependence that would force her to remain at Undershaw. Single ladies did not live alone. Sisters, past the marriageable age, might do it; years and years ago the Lady Eleanor Butler and her dear friend, Miss Sarah Ponsonby, had done it, but in the teeth of parental opposition. They had fled to a cottage somewhere in Wales, renouncing the world just as if they had been nuns; and since they were still living there and had never, so far as anyone knew, stirred from their retreat, it was to be inferred that they were content. But Venetia was no eccentric, and even had she possessed a bosom friend she would not for an instant have entertained the thought of setting up house with her: marriage to Edward would be preferable to such a menage. And without indulging her fancy with girlish dreams of a noble and handsome suitor Venetia felt that marriage with another than Edward would be the most agreeable solution to her difficulties.

She had never been in love; and at five-and-twenty her expectations were not high. Her only acquaintance with romance lay between the covers of the books she had read; and if she had once awaited with confidence the arrival on her scene of a Sir Charles Grandison it had not been long before commonsense banished such optimism. In the days when she had now and then attended the Assemblies in York she had attracted a great deal of admiration, and more than one promising young gentleman, first struck by her beauty and then captivated by her frank manners and the charm of her smiling eyes, would have been very happy to have followed up a mere ball-room acquaintanceship. Unfortunately there was no possibility of following it up in the accepted mode, and although several susceptible gentlemen inveighed bitterly against the barbarity of a parent who would permit no visitor to enter his house none of them was so deeply heart-smitten after standing up with the lovely Miss Lanyon for one country-dance as to cast aside every canon of propriety (as well as to the horrid dread of making a great cake of himself) and ride out of York to Undershaw, either to hang about the gates of the Manor in the hope of achieving a clandestine meeting with Venetia, or to force his way into the house.

Only Edward Yardley, Sir Francis's godson, had been accorded tacit permission to cross his threshold. He was not made welcome, Sir Francis rarely emerging from his bookroom during his visits, but since he was permitted to walk, talk, and ride with Venetia it was generally believed that an offer from him for her hand would be accepted by her morose parent.

No one could have described him as an impatient lover. Venetia was the magnet which drew him to Undershaw, but it was four years before he declared himself, and she could almost have believed then that he did it against his better judgment. She had no hesitation in declining his offer, for however much she might value his good qualities, and however grateful she might be for the various services he performed for her, she could not love him. She would have been glad to have continued on the old terms of friendship with him, but Edward, having at last made up his mind, was apparently as determined as he was confident. He was not at all cast down by her refusal; he ascribed it variously to shyness, maiden modesty, surprise, and even to devotion to her widowed father; assured her kindly that he perfectly understood such sentiments and was content to wait until she knew her own heart; and began from that day to develop a possessive manner towards her which provoked her very frequently to run directly counter to his advice, and to say whatever occurred to her as being most likely to shock him. It did not answer. His disapproval was often patent, but it was softened by indulgence. Her liveliness fascinated him, and he did not doubt his ability to mould her

21

(once she was his own) to his complete liking.

When Sir Francis died, Edward repeated his offer. It was again refused. This time he was more persistent, which Venetia had expected. What she did not expect was that he should suddenly suppose that her continued reluctance to accept him sprang from what he called the peculiar delicacy of her situation. He said that he honoured her for scruples which she privately thought absurd, and would forbear to press her for another answer until Conway, her natural protector, came home. What should have put such a notion into his head she was at a loss to discover, only two possible solutions presenting themselves to her puzzled mind: the first, that while he was strongly attracted to her he was by no means convinced that as his wife she would add to his comfort; the second, that his mother had suggested it to him. Mrs. Yardley was a colourless little woman, always submissive to his will, and kindling to mild warmth only in his presence. She had never been other than civil to Venetia, but Venetia was quite sure that she did not want Edward to marry her.

With the news that there was a very real hope that the Army of Occupation would soon be withdrawn from France the problem of the future had drawn suddenly close to Venetia. As she walked through Undershaw's small park she turned it over and over in her mind, but to no good purpose, as she ruefully acknowledged to herself. So much rested upon conjecture, or, at the best, possibility, the only certainty being that when Conway returned Edward would expect a favourable answer to his suit, and would not easily be persuaded to accept any other. That was her own fault, of course, for having been too ready to seize the respite offered by his peculiar notion of propriety; and to agree, even if only tacitly, that nothing could be decided until Conway came home. Edward could hardly be expected to understand that her answer must depend largely on what Conway meant to do. There had been a rather sentimental girl-and-boy attachment between Conway and Clara Denny before he joined, to which Clara at least seemed to attach importance. If Conway attached an equal importance to it she would find herself with a sister-in-law all too ready to resign the conduct of her household into the hands of one

22

whom she had all her life regarded with humble admiration. That, thought Venetia, would be very bad for her, and very bad for me too, but I don't think I *could* play second fiddle to poor little Clara at Undershaw!

Marriage to Edward would be safe and comfortable. He would be a kind husband, and he would certainly shield her from inclement winds. But Venetia had been born with a zest for life which was unknown to him, and a high courage that enabled her to look hazards in the face and not shrink from encountering them. Because she did not repine over her enforced seclusion Edward believed her to be content, as he himself was content, to pass all her days under the shadow of the Cleveden Hills. So far from being content she had never imagined that this could be her ultimate destiny. She wanted to see what the rest of the world was like: marriage only interested her as the sole means of escape for a gently-born maiden.

In fact, thought Venetia, as she emerged from the park on to a narrow lane which separated it from the neighbouring estate of Elliston Priory, my case is clearly past remedy, and I've nothing to do but decide whether to be an aunt to Conway's children, or a mother to Edward's— and I have a lowering presentiment that Edward's children will be dreadfully dull, poor little things! Where's that wretched dog? "Flurry! *Flurry!*"

After she had been calling for several minutes, in growing exasperation, her canine friend came galloping up, full of amiability, his flanks heaving, and his tongue lolling. Being considerably out of breath he was so obliging as to remain within her sight until, a few hundred yards down the lane, she entered the grounds of the Priory through a turnstile set beside a heavy farm-gate. This gave access to an ancient right of way, but Venetia, on excellent terms with Lord Damerel's bailiff, was at liberty to roam where she liked on his domain, as Flurry well knew. Refreshed by the brief interlude on the lane he raced ahead, in the direction of the woods which straggled down a gentle declivity to the stream which wound through the Priory's grounds. Beyond the stream lay the Priory itself, a rambling house built in Tudor times upon the foundations of the original structure, subsequently enlarged, and said to be replete with a wealth of panelling, and a great many inconveniences. With the house Venetia was not concerned, but the grounds had for years been the favourite haunt of the three young Lanyons. Sir Francis's vagaries had not led him to neglect his estate, which he kept in excellent order. His children preferred to seek adventure in less neat surroundings. The Priory woods, which partook of the nature of a wilderness, exactly suited youthful ideas of what was delightful; and if Venetia, grown to maturity, felt it to be a pity that the place should be neglected, it still held its charm for her, and she frequently walked there, and, since its owner rarely came near it, could allow the disobedient Flurry to range at will, chasing rabbits and flushing pheasants without danger of drawing wrath down upon his head. The Wicked Baron, as she had long ago christened Lord Damerel, would neither know nor care: the only party he had ever brought to the Priory had certainly not been a shooting-party.

His family was an old and a distinguished one but the present holder of the title was considered by the respectable to be the neighbourhood's only blot. It was almost a social solecism to mention his name to polite company. Innocent enquiries by the children, who wanted to know why Lord Damerel never came to live at the Priory, were repressed. They were told that they were too young to understand, and that there was no need for them to think about him, much less talk about him: it was to be feared that his lordship was not a *good* man; and now that was quite enough, and they might run away and play.

That was what Miss Poddemore told Venetia and Conway, and they naturally speculated on the possible (and often impossible) nature of his lordship's crimes, rapidly creating a figure of lurid romance out of Miss Poddemore's mysterious utterances. It was years before Venetia discovered that Damerel's villainy included nothing as startling as murder, treason, piracy, or highroad robbery, and was more sordid than romantic. The only child of rather elderly parents, he had no sooner embarked on a diplomatic career than he fell head over ears in love with a married lady of title, and absconded with her, thus wrecking his own future, breaking his mama's heart, and causing his papa to suffer a paralytic stroke, from which he never entirely recovered. Indeed, as it was succeeded,

24

three years later, by a second and fatal stroke it was not too much to say that the shocking affair had actually killed him. All mention of his heir had been forbidden in his household; and after his death his relict, who seemed to Venetia to have had a marked affinity with Sir Francis Lanyon, lived in semi-seclusion in London, visiting the Yorkshire estates only at rare intervals. As for the new Lord Damerel, though many were the rumours about his subsequent actions no one really knew what had happened to him, for his scandalous behaviour had coincided with the short-lived Peace of Amiens, and he had spirited his stolen lady out of the country. All that was thereafter known about her was that her husband had refused to divorce her. For how long she had remained with her lover, where they had fled when the war broke out again, and what had been her ultimate fate were problems about which there were many conjectures. The most popular of these was that she had been cast off by her lover, and left to fall prey to Bonaparte's ravening soldiers; which, as the villagers did not fail to point out to their erring daughters, was what she deserved, and the sort of thing that was bound to befall any girl careless of her virtue.

Whatever the truth might be, one thing was sure: the lady was not with Damerel when he returned to England, some years later. Since that date he appeared (if only half the stories told of him were true) to have devoted himself to the pursuit of all the more extravagant forms of diversion, going a considerable way towards dissipating what had once been a handsome fortune, and neglecting no opportunity that offered to convince his critics that he was every bit as black as he had been painted. Until the previous year his occasional visits to the Priory had been too brief to allow any of his neighbours to do more than catch sight of him, and very few had even done that. But he had spent one whole week at the Priory in August, under perfectly outrageous circumstances. He had not come alone; he had brought a party of guests with him— and *such* a party! They had come for the races, of course: Damerel had had a horse running in one of them. Poor Imber, the butler who had been caretaker at the Priory for years, had been thrown into the greatest affliction, for never had such a fast, ramshackle set of persons been entertained at the Priory! As for Mrs. Imber, when she

25

had discovered that she was expected to cook for several rackety bucks and for three females whom she recognized at a glance for what they were, she had declared her intention of leaving the priory rather than so demean herself. Only her devotion to the Family had induced her to relent, and bitterly did she regret it, when (as might have been expected) none of the villagers would permit their daughters to go to work in what was little better than a Corinth, and it had been necessary to hire in York three far from respectable wenches to wait on the raffish company. As for the amusements of these dashing blades and their convenients, his late lordship, declared Imber, must have turned in his grave to see such lewd goings-on in his ancestral home. If the guests were not indulging in vulgar rompings, such as playing Hunt the Squirrel, with those shameless lightskirts squealing fit to bring the rafters down, and egging on the gentlemen to behave in a very scandalous way, they were turning the house into a gaming-hell, and drinking the cellar dry. Not one but had had to be put to bed by his valet, and that my Lord Utterby (a loose-screw, if ever Imber had seen one!) had not burnt the Priory to the ground was due only to the chance that had carried the smell of burning to the nostrils of Mr. Ansford's peculiar, who had not scrupled to track it to its source though she had been clad only in her nightgown—not but what that was a more decent cloak to her opulent form than the dress she had worn earlier in the day!—and had torn down the smouldering bed-curtains, screeching all the time at the top of her very ungenteel voice.

These orgies had lasted for seven days, but they had provided the neighbouring countryside with food for gossip that lasted for months.

However, nothing further had been heard of Damerel. He had not come north for York Races this year, and unless he meant to come later for the pheasant-shooting, which (from the neglected state of his preserves) seemed unlikely, the North Riding might consider itself free from his contaminating presence for another year. It came, therefore, as a surprise to Venetia, serenely filling her basket with his blackberries, when she discovered that he was much nearer at hand than anyone had supposed.

She had been making her way round the outskirts of the wood, and had paused to disentangle her dress from a particularly clinging trail of bramble when an amused voice said: *"Oh, how full of briars is this working-day world!"*

Startled, she turned her head, and found that she was being observed by a tall man mounted on a handsome gray horse. He was a stranger, but his voice and his habit proclaimed his condition, and it did not take her more than a very few moments to guess that she must be confronting the Wicked Baron. She regarded him with candid interest, unconsciously affording him an excellent view of her enchanting countenance. His brows rose, and he swung himself out of the saddle, and came towards her, with long, easy strides. She was unacquainted with any men of mode, but although he was dressed like any country gentleman a subtle difference hung about his buckskins and his coat of dandy gray russet. No provincial tailor had fashioned them, and no country beau could have worn them with such careless elegance. He was taller than Venetia had at first supposed, rather loose-limbed, and he bore himself with a faint suggestion of swashbuckling arrogance. As he advanced upon her Venetia perceived that he was dark, his countenance lean and rather swarthy, marked with lines of dissipation. A smile was curling his lips, but Venetia thought she had never seen eyes so cynically bored.

"Well, fair trespasser, you are justly served, aren't you?" he said. "Stand still!"

She remained obediently motionless while he disentangled her skirt from the brambles. As he straightened himself, he said: "There you are! But I always exact a forfeit from those who rob me of my blackberries. Let me look at you!"

Before she had recovered from her astonishment at being addressed in such a style he had an arm round her, and with his free hand had pushed back her sunbonnet. In more anger than fright she tried to thrust him away, uttering a furious protest. He paid no heed at all; only his arm tightened round her, something that was not boredom gleamed in his eyes, and he ejaculated: *"But beauty's self she is...!"*

27

Venetia then found herself being ruthlessly kissed. Her cheeks much flushed, her eyes blazing, she fought strenuously to break free from a stronger hold than she had ever known, but her efforts only made Damerel laugh, and she owed her deliverance to Flurry. The spaniel, emerging from the undergrowth to find his mistress struggling in the arms of a stranger, was cast into great mental perturbation. Instinct urged him to fly to her rescue, but dimly understood precept forbade him to bite anything that walked on two legs. He tried compromise, barking hysterically. It did not answer, and instinct won the day.

Since Damerel was wearing topboots Flurry's heroic assault drew no blood, but it did cause him to glance down at the spaniel, relaxing his hold on Venetia just enough to enable her to wrench herself away.

"*Sit!*" commanded Damerel.

Flurry, recognizing the voice of a Master, promptly abased himself, ears dipped, and tail deprecatingly wagging.

"What the devil do you mean by it, eh?" said Damerel, catching him by the lower jaw, and forcing up his head.

Flurry recognized that voice too, and, much relieved, did his best to explain that the regrettable incident had arisen from a misunderstanding. Venetia, who, instead of seizing the opportunity to run away, had been angrily retieing the strings of her sunbonnet, exclaimed: "Oh, have you *no* discrimination, you idiotic animal?"

Damerel, who was patting the repentant Flurry, looked up, his eyes narrowing.

"And as for you, sir," said Venetia, meeting that searching stare with a flaming look, "your quotations don't make your advances a whit more acceptable to me—and they don't deceive me into thinking you anything but a *pestilent, complete knave!*"

He burst out laughing. "Bravo! Where did you find that?"

Venetia who had suddenly remembered the rest of the quotation, replied: "If you don't know, I certainly shan't tell you. *That* phrase is apt enough, but the context won't do."

"Oho! My curiosity is now thoroughly roused! I recognize the hand, and see that I must carefully study my Shakespeare."

"I should think you had seldom employed your time more worthily!"

"Who are you?" he demanded abruptly. "I took you for a village maiden—probably one of my tenants."

"Did you indeed? Well, if that is the way you mean to conduct yourself amongst the village maidens you won't win much liking here!"

"No, no, the danger is that I might win too much!" he retorted. "Who are you? Or should I first present myself to you? I'm Damerel, you know."

"Yes, so I supposed, at the outset of our delightful acquaintance. Later, of course, I was sure of it."

"Oh, oh—! *My reputation, Iago, my reputation!*" he exclaimed, laughing again. "Fair Fatality, you are the most unusual female I have encountered in all my thirty-eight years!"

"You can't think how deeply flattered I am!" she assured him. "I daresay my head would be quite turned if I didn't suspect that amongst so many a dozen or so may have slipped from your memory."

"More like a hundred! Am I never to learn your name? I shall, you know, whether you tell me or no!"

"Without the least difficulty! I am very much better known in this country than you, for I'm a Lanyon of Undershaw!"

"Impressive! Undershaw? Oh, yes! your land marches with mine, doesn't it? Are you in the habit of walking abroad quite unattended, Miss Lanyon?"

"Yes—except, of course, when I have had warning that you are at the Priory!"

"Spiteful little cat!" he said appreciatively. "How the devil was I to recognize Miss Lanyon of Undershaw in a crumpled gown and a sunbonnet, and without even the chaperonage of her maid?"

"Oh, am I to understand, then, that if you had known my quality you wouldn't have molested me? How chivalrous!"

"No, no, I'm not chivalrous!" he said, mocking her. "The presence of your maid would have checkmated me, not your quality, *I'm* not complaining, but I wonder at such a little beauty's venturing to roam about the country alone. Or don't you know how beautiful you are?"

"Yes," replied Venetia, taking the wind out of his sails.

"Item, two lips, indifferent red—"

"Oh, no, you're quite out, and have gone to the wrong poet besides! *They look like rosebuds filled with snow!*"

"Is that from *Cherry-ripe?*" she demanded. He nodded, much entertained by her suddenly intent look. Her eyes sparkled with triumph; she uttered a tiny gurgle of laughter; and retorted: "Then I know what comes next! *Yet them no peer nor prince can buy, Till Cherry-ripe* themselves *do cry!* So let *that* be a lesson to you to take care what poets *you* choose!"

"But you're enchanting!" he exclaimed.

She put out her hands quickly to hold him off. "No!"

He caught her wrists, and swept them behind her, clipping them in the small of her back, and so holding her chest to chest. Her heart beat fast; she felt breathless, but not afraid.

"Yes!" he said, still mocking. "You should have run away, my golden girl, while you had the chance to do it!"

"I know I should, and I can't think why I did not," she replied, incurably candid.

"I could hazard a guess."

She shook her head. "No. Not if you mean it was because I wanted you to kiss me again, for I don't. I can't prevent you, for my strength is so much less than yours. You needn't even fear to be called to account for it. My brother is a schoolboy, and—very lame. Perhaps you already know that?"

"No, and I'm much obliged to you for telling me! I need have no scruples, I see."

She looked up at him searchingly, trying to read his mind, for although he jeered she thought his voice had a bitter edge. Then, as she stared into his eyes she saw them smiling yet fierce, and a line of Byron's flashed into her head: *There was a laughing devil in his sneer.* Oh, *do* let me go!" she begged. "I've suddenly had the most diverting thought! Oh, dear! *Poor* Oswald!"

He was quite taken aback, as much by the genuine amusement in her face as by what she had said, and he did let her go. "You've suddenly had the most diverting thought?" he repeated blankly.

"Thank you!" said Venetia, giving her crushed dress a little shake. "Yes, indeed I have, though I daresay you might not think it a very good joke, but that's because you don't know Oswald."

"Well, who the devil is he? Your brother?"

"Good God, no! He is Sir John Denny's son, and the top of his desire is to be mistaken for the *Corsair.* He combs his hair into wild curls, knots silken handkerchiefs round his neck, and broods over the dark passions in his soul."

"Does he, indeed? And what has this puppy to say to anything?"

She picked up her basket. "Only that if ever he meets you he will be quite *green* with jealousy, for you are precisely what he thinks *he* would like to be—even though you don't study the picturesque in your attire."

He looked thunderstruck for a moment, and ejaculated: "A Byronic hero—! Oh, my God! Why, you abominable—" He broke off, as a cock pheasant exploded out of the wood, and said irritably: "*Must* that worthless dog of yours make my birds as wild as be-damned?"

"Yes, because my brother doesn't like him to do so at Undershaw, which is why I brought him with me today. Putting up game is what he particularly enjoys doing, and as he's quite useless as a gun-dog, poor fellow, he gets very few opportunities to do it. Do you object? I can't see why you should, when you never come here to shoot!"

"I never *have* done so!" he retorted. "*This* year is quite another matter, however! I own I had not meant to stay in Yorkshire above a few days, but that was before I made your acquaintance. I am going to remain at the Priory for the present!"

"How splendid!" said Venetia affably. "In general it is a trifle dull here, but *that* will be quite at an end if you are to remain amongst us!" She caught sight of Flurry, called him to heel, and dropped a slight curtsy. "Good-bye!"

"Oh, not goodbye!" he protested. "I mean to know you better, Miss Lanyon of Undershaw!"

"To be sure, it *does* seem a pity you should not, after such a promising start, but life you know, is full of disappointments, and that, I must warn you, is likely to prove one of them."

He fell into step beside her, as she made her way

31

towards the turnstile. "Afraid?" he asked provocatively.

"Well, what a stupid question!" she said. "I should have supposed you must have known yourself to be the ogre who would infallibly pounce on every naughty child in the district!"

"As bad as that?" he said, rather startled. "Had I better try to retrieve my shocking reputation, do you think?"

They had reached the turnstile, and she passed through it. "Oh no, we should have nothing to talk about any more!"

"Vixen!" he remarked. "Well—! Tell your lame brother how shamefully I used you, and fear nothing! I won't pounce on him."

Venetia went home with her thoughts in quite unaccustomed disorder. Feeling that after such an agitating experience a period of calm reflection was necessary she walked slowly, thinking over all the circumstances of her first encounter with a rake; but after dwelling on the impropriety of Damerel's conduct, and telling herself how fortunate she had been to have escaped a worse fate, it rather horrifyingly occurred to her that she had shown herself to be lacking in sensibility. A delicately nurtured female (unless all the books lied) would have swooned from the shock of being kissed by a strange man, or at the very least would have been cast into the greatest affliction, her peace cut up, her spirits wholly overpowered. What she would not have done was to have stayed to bandy words with her wolfish assailant. Nor would she have been conscious of a feeling of exhilaration. Venetia was very conscious of it. She had not enjoyed being so ruthlessly handled, but for one crazy instant she had known an impulse to respond, and through the haze of her own wrath she had caught a glimpse of what life might be. Not, of course, that she wished to be mauled by strangers. But if Edward had ever kissed her thus! The thought drew a smile from her, for the vision of Edward swept out of his rigid propriety was improbable to the point of absurdity. Edward was sternly master of his passions; she wondered, for the first time, if these were very strong, or whether he was, in fact, rather coldblooded.

The question, being of no particular moment, remained unanswered; Damerel, entering rudely on to the scene, instantly dominated it, and whether he was the villain or merely a minor character it was useless to deny that he had infused life into a dull play.

Venetia found it hard to make up her mind what to tell Aubrey. If she disclosed her meeting with Damerel he might ask her questions she would find it difficult to answer; on the other hand, if she said nothing, and Damerel did succeed in improving his acquaintance with her, he would certainly make Aubrey's acquaintance too; and although he could scarcely be so shameless as to refer to the nature of his previous encounter with her he might well mention that he had met her before, which would surely make Aubrey think it odd of her not to have told him of so unprecedented an event. Then she thought that the likeliest chance was that Damerel had no real intention of remaining at the Priory, and decided to keep her own counsel.

As matters turned out she was heartily glad of it. It was Aubrey who first spoke of Damerel's return, but as he had very little interest in his neighbours and none at all in a man he had never laid eyes on, he did so quite casually, saying as he sat down to dinner that day: "Oh, by the by! I heard in the village that Damerel's back again—but without Paphians! Alone, in fact."

"What, no scandal-broth brewing? That won't please the quizzy ones! I wonder what brings him?"

"Business, I should think," replied Aubrey indifferently. "High time he did look into his affairs here."

She agreed, but did not pursue the topic. It was to be raised again, though not by Aubrey. Such an exciting piece of news naturally spread rapidly over the district, and before nightfall both Nurse and Mrs. Gurnard, forced into temporary alliance, had impressed upon Venetia the need for her to behave with the greatest circumspection. On no account must she step beyond the garden without an escort. There was no telling what might happen to her if she didn't do as she was bid, said Nurse darkly.

Venetia soothed the alarms of these two well-wishers; but when Edward Yardley came to Undershaw on the following day she was never nearer losing her temper with him.

"I daresay he won't remain at the Priory above a day or two, but while he is here it will be best for you to discontinue your solitary walks," Edward said, with a calm assumption of authority which she found so irritating that she was obliged to choke down a hasty retort. "You

34

know," he added, with a wry smile, "that I have never liked that custom of yours."

Oswald Denny visited her too, but the form his solicitude took was a dramatic assurance that if Damerel should dare to molest her he would know how to answer "the fellow". The significant laying of his hand upon an imaginary sword-hilt was too much for Venetia's gravity: she went into a peal of laughter, which provoked him to exclaim: "You laugh, but I've lived where they hold life cheap! I promise you I should have no compunction in calling this fellow out, were he to offer you the smallest affront!"

After this Venetia was not at all surprised when, two days later, the Dennys' barouche-landau disgorged Lady Denny at Undershaw. But it soon transpired that her ladyship's object was not so much to warn her young friend to beware of encountering a notorious rake as to enjoy a comfortable gossip about him. She had actually spoken to him! Well, more than that: Sir John, meeting him by chance, had seized the opportunity to try if he could not win his support over some matter of parish business; and finding him perfectly amiable, had brought him back to Ebbersley, further to discuss the affair, and had ended by inviting him to eat luncheon there.

"You may imagine my amazement when in they both walked! I must own, my love, that I was not quite pleased, for Clara and Emily were both sitting with me, and although Clara is not, I fancy, very likely to have her head turned, Emily is at just that age when girls fall in love with the most ineligible men. However, there's no fear of that, as it turns out: the girls both declared there was never anything more disappointing, for he is quite old, and not at all handsome!"

"*Old?*" Venetia exclaimed involuntarily.

"Well, so he seemed to the girls," Lady Denny explained. "He can't be above forty, I suppose, if he's as much as that. I am not perfectly sure—when he was a child he was scarcely ever at the Priory, you know, because Lady Damerel had the greatest dislike of Yorkshire, and never would come here, except when they had parties for the races. You wouldn't remember, my dear, but she was a very proud, disagreeable woman—and I *will* say this for her son: he seems not to be at all top-lofty—not,

35

of course, that he has the least occasion to hold up his nose! Except that the Damerels are a very old family, and this man's father, though always perfectly civil, was said to have a great deal of self-consequence. There was nothing of *that* to be seen—indeed, I thought his lordship had too little particularity! I don't mean to say that his manners gave me a disgust of him, but he has an odd, abrupt way that is a trifle too careless to please *me!* As for the girls, they rated him very cheap—though I daresay they would not if he had behaved more prettily to them. He hardly spoke above a dozen words to them—the merest commonplace, too!"

"How shabby!" said Venetia. "He is—I mean, he sounds to me quite *odious!*"

"Yes, but I was thankful for it!" said her ladyship earnestly. "Only think what my feelings must have been had he proved to be a man of insinuating address! And for Sir John to declare that dearest Clara has not enough beauty to engage the interest of such a man as Damerel is not at all to the point, besides being a most unnatural thing to say of his own daughter! He would have been well-served if Damerel *had* thrown out lures to Clara, bringing him in upon us as he did! But all he will say is that he doesn't choose to live on bad terms with his neighbours, and that it is a great piece of nonsense in me to suppose that Damerel is so ramshackle as to behave improperly to any female in Clara's situation. Very pretty talking, when everyone knows he didn't scruple to seduce a lady under her husband's very nose!"

"Who was she?" interrupted Venetia curiously. "What became of her?"

"I don't know that, but she was one of the Rendlesham girls—there were three of them, and *all* great beauties, which was fortunate, because Rendlesham was as poor as a church mouse, and *yet* they all made good marriages! Not that I mean to say *that* one prospered, and for my part I shouldn't have liked it for one of my daughters, even if Sir John were as monstrously in the wind as they say Rendlesham was. Well, for one thing he had the most peculiar name: *Vobster!* I believe he came into the world hosed and shod, as the saying is, but his father was a shocking mushroom, and as for his grandfather I'm sure no one ever knew who *he* was! The *on-dit* was that he owned a two-to-one shop—at least, so my brother George was used to say!—but I daresay that was nothing but a Banbury story. At all events, Gregory Vobster was as rich as Midas, which was what made him acceptable to Lord Rendlesham. He was used to play off all the airs of an exquisite, I recall, but when the pinch came he was not at all up to the rig. Nothing would prevail upon him to consent to a divorce! He behaved very shabbily, just wishing to be revenged, you know, and if he hadn't broken his neck, overturning his curricle on the Newmarket road, that wretched female would be still married to him! But the thing is, my dear, that that happened not three years after the break-up of the marriage, and though I don't know *why*, I *do* know that she didn't marry Damerel, which everyone expected she would, of course. Which gives me a very poor notion of him, and makes me excessively reluctant to receive him in my house! What's more, if he hoped, by abandoning Lady Sophia, to become reconciled with his own family he was well-served, for they utterly cast him off, and it wasn't until Lady Damerel died that he came back to England. Indeed, if it hadn't been for his having inherited an independence from old Matthew Stone—he was his godfather, and what they call a chicken-nabob—I daresay he must have been reduced to absolute penury—let alone not being able to run off with Lady Sophia in the first place! Which all goes to show what folly it is to endow young men with fortunes."

"Cast him off!" Venetia exclaimed. "They would have done better to have cast themselves off!"

"Cast themselves off?" repeated Lady Denny.

"Yes, for having done so ill by him as to let him make a cake of himself over this Lady Sophia! It happened when he was twenty-two, didn't it? Well, then! I dare swear she was older than he, too. Was she?"

"She was a few years older, I fancy, but—"

"Then you may depend upon it that it was a great deal more her fault than his, ma'am! And although I suppose he ought to have married her in the end I can't help thinking that she only came by her deserts when he didn't. In fact, I begin to feel almost sorry for the Wicked Baron. Does he mean to make a long stay in Yorkshire? Shall we be obliged to recognize him?"

"*I* must do so, if we should chance to meet, but I am

determined it shan't go beyond a civil bow; and as for inviting him to dine with us in a formal way, I have begged Sir John not to ask it of me! 'And, pray, which of our acquaintance would you have me invite to meet him?' I said. 'The Yardleys? the Traynes? Poor Mrs. Motcomb? Or have you our sweet Venetia in your mind?' I am happy to say that he saw that it would be quite improper. It is a fortunate circumstance, since I don't mean to be drawn into the slightest intimacy, that Damerel is a bachelor. If the gentlemen choose to visit him they may do so: he cannot invite ladies to his parties."

On this triumphant conclusion Lady Denny departed, leaving her young friend to await events with such mixed feelings that she could not have told whether she wished Damerel to find some way of seeing her again, or whether she would be glad to know that he had left the Priory. It was certainly a bore to be confined within the bounds of the park, and that, she had decided, must be her fate, unless she rode with Aubrey, for however little heed she paid to Nurse's dark warnings she was fully alive to the possibility of Damerel's lying in wait for her, and had no doubt that if he were to find her walking by herself he would believe her to be courting his advances. On the whole, she thought, she would be glad to know that he had gone away. He was dangerous; his conduct had been inexcusable; and to meet him again might be demoralizing to one who had led so cloistered a life as hers had been.

But when a week crept by without a sign from him she was piqued. He was still at the Priory, but he was making no effort whatsoever to become acquainted with his neighbours. The village gossips, much astonished, reported that he was actually interesting himself in the business of the estate; and Croyde, his long-suffering bailiff, permitted for the first time to lay before him all the crying needs that were never filled, was indulging a flicker of optimism: though his lordship had not yet authorized expenditure he was at least listening to advice, and seeing with his own eyes the slow decay of good land under bad husbandry. Edward, a sceptic, said that the only thing that might induce Damerel to spend a groat on repairs or improvements would be the hope that he might wring back from the state a greater yield to squander on his amusements. Venetia would have suspected that his sudden interest in his inheritance was nothing more than an excuse for remaining at the Priory had he made some attempt to seek her out. She thought it would not have been difficult for him to have found a pretext for calling at Undershaw; and being far too innocent to realize that Damerel, an expert in the art of dalliance, was employing tactics which none knew better than he to be tantalizing, she was forced to conclude that he had not been as strongly attracted to her as she had supposed. There was nothing in store at Undershaw for his lordship but a setdown, but it was disappointing to be granted no opportunity to deliver this. She found herself imagining a second encounter; and, between disgust at herself and resentment at Damerel for holding her so cheap, became so nearly cross that Aubrey asked her if she felt quite the thing.

And in the end it was neither she who brought about a second meeting, nor Damerel, but Aubrey.

Damerel was riding home with Croyde after one of his tours of inspection when a faint cry for help made him break off what he was saying, and look round. The cry was repeated, and Croyde, standing in his stirrups, so that he could see over the hedge that straggled beside the lane, exclaimed: "Good God, it's Mr. Aubrey! Ay, I thought as much!—that nappy young chestnut of his has come down with him, like I always said he would! If your lordship will excuse me, I'll have to attend to him."

"Yes, of course. Is there a gate, or do we push through the hedge?"

There was a gate a little farther along the lane, and in a very few moments both men had dismounted, and Croyde was kneeling beside Aubrey, who was lying just clear of the ditch which, with the hedge above it, separated the stubblefield from a stretch of pasturage. At a little distance his horse was standing; and when he moved nervously away from Damerel's advance it was seen that he was dead lame.

Aubrey was sickly white, and in considerable pain. He said faintly: "I came down on my weak leg. I can't get up. Think I must have stunned myself. Where's Rufus? Jumped off his fore. I hope to God he didn't break his knees!"

"Never you mind about that clumsy brute, sir!" Croyde said, in a scolding tone. "What have *you* broken, that's what I want to know?"

"Nothing. For God's sake, don't maul me about, or I shall go off again! I've twisted my other ankle—that's the devil of it!" He struggled on to his elbow, turning ashen as he did it, and biting his lip. Croyde supported him, and after a moment he managed to say: "I shall do—in a minute. My horse—?"

"Your horse has a badly sprained fetlock," said Damerel. "You can't ride him, but he hasn't broken his leg. The question is, are you quite sure you've not broken your own?"

Aubrey looked rather hazily up at him. "It's not broken. It is only my hip. I have—a weak hip. It will be better directly, I daresay. If a message could be sent to Undershaw they'll bring the carriage."

"It's young Mr. Lanyon, my lord," explained Croyde. "I was thinking it would be best if I was to fetch the chaise from the Priory, for it's six miles and a way-bit to Undershaw."

"And a devilish rough road to be jolted over," said Damerel, looking thoughtfully down at Aubrey. "We'll take him to the Priory. Tell 'em to make up a bed, and bring Nidd back with you to take charge of the horses. Here, put this under the boy's head!" He stripped off his coat as he spoke, rolled it up, and handed it to Croyde, adding, after a glance at Aubrey's face: "Bring some brandy as well—and bustle, will you?"

He took Croyde's place beside Aubrey, and began to loosen the boy's neckcloth. Aubrey opened his eyes. "What—Oh! Thank you. Are you Lord Damerel, sir?"

"Yes, I'm Damerel, but never mind talking to me!"

"Why not?"

"Well, I fancy you had a slight concussion, and would do better to lie quiet."

"I don't know. Or even how long I've been here. I did come round once, and then I suppose I went off again. I was trying to get up. You see, I can't."

Damerel caught the bitter note, but all he said was: "No, and with a weak hip and a sprained ankle you were a damned young fool to try, weren't you?"

Aubrey grinned feebly, and shut his eyes again. He

40

did not open them until Croyde came back with the chaise, but Damerel knew from the frown between his brows and a certain rigidity about his mouth that he was neither asleep nor unconscious. He muttered something about being able to walk with a little help when he was lifted, but upon being commanded to put his arm round Damerel's neck he obeyed, and thereafter devoted his energies to the really rather formidable task of maintaining a decent fortitude. Carrying so slight and thin a boy across the field presented no difficulties, but it was impossible to lift him into the chaise without subjecting him to a good deal of pain, and although little more than a mile had to be covered before the Priory was reached the road was so rough that the journey became a severe trial. No complaint was uttered, but when he was lifted down from the chaise Aubrey fainted again.

"Just as well!" said Damerel cheerfully, carrying him into the house. "No, no, take those smelling-salts away, Mrs. Imber! We'll have his boots off before we try to bring him round again, poor lad! Get a razor, Marston!"

The removal of his boots brought Aubrey to his senses again, but it was not until he had been stripped of his clothing and put into one of his host's nightshirts that he was able to collect his dazed wits. The relief to his swollen right ankle afforded by a cold compress seemed to mitigate the grinding ache that radiated from his left hip-joint, and the sal volatile which was tilted down his throat enabled him, after a fit of choking, to take stock of his surroundings. He frowned unrecognizingly upon Damerel and his valet, but when his eyes wandered to Mrs. Imber's concerned face his memory returned, and he exclaimed thickly: "Oh, I remember now! I took a toss. Hell and the devil confound it! Riding like a damned *roadster!*"

"Oh, the best of us take tosses!" said Damerel. "Don't fret yourself into a fever over that!"

Aubrey turned his head on the pillow to look up at him. A surge of colour came into his cheeks; he said stiffly: "I'm very much obliged to you, sir. I beg your pardon! Making such a bother of myself for nothing worse than a tumble! You must think me a poor creature."

"On the contrary, I think you've excellent bottom. More bottom than sense! you silly gudgeon! You know you ride a feather! What made you suppose you could hold such a heady young 'un as that chestnut of yours?"

"He didn't get away with me!" Aubrey said, firing up. "I let him rush it—I was riding carelessly—but there isn't a horse in the stable I can't back!"

"*Much* more bottom than sense!" said Damerel, quizzing him, but with such an understanding smile in his eyes that Aubrey forbore to take offence. "And I suppose a few worse gudgeons, like that bailiff of mine, told you the horse was too strong for you, which was all that was needed to set you careering over the countryside! I own I should have done the same, so I won't comb your hair for it. Where am I to find the sawbones who doctors you when you've knocked yourself up?"

"Nowhere! I mean, I don't want him: he will only pull me about, and make it ten times worse! It's nothing—it will go off if I lie still for a while!"

"Now, Mr. Aubrey, you know Miss Lanyon would have the doctor to you, and no argle-bargle about it!" interposed Mrs. Imber. "And as for making you worse, why, what a way to talk when everyone knows he's as good as any grand London doctor, and very likely better! It's Dr. Bentworth, my lord, and if it hadn't been for Croyde taking Nidd off with him like he did I would have sent him to York straight!"

"Well, if he has brought the horses in by now he can set off as soon as I've written a note for the doctor. Meanwhile—"

"I wish you will not!" Aubrey said fretfully. "I'm persuaded I shall be well enough to go home long before he can come all this way. If you would but leave me alone—! I won't have a grand fuss made over me! I hate it beyond anything!"

This ungracious speech made Mrs. Imber look very much shocked, but Damerel replied coolly: "Yes, abominable! No one shall make a fuss over you any longer. You shall try instead if you can go to sleep."

To Aubrey, who was feeling as if his every limb had been racked, this suggestion seemed so insensate that it was with difficulty that he refrained from snapping back an acid retort. He was left to solitude, and to his own reflections, but these, do what he would, could not be diverted for long from his body's aches and ails, and soon resolved themselves into a nagging dread that the fall had injured his hip badly enough to turn him into an out-and-out cripple, or at the very least to keep him tied to a sofa for months. However, before he had had time to make himself sick with worry Damerel came back into the room with a glass in his hand. After one keen look at Aubrey, he said: "Pretty uncomfortable, eh? Drink this!"

"It's of no consequence: I can bear it," Aubrey muttered. "If it's laudanum I don't want it—thank you!"

"Remind me to ask you what you want, if ever I should wish to know!" said Damerel. "At the moment I don't! Come along, do as I tell you, or a worse fate may befall you!"

"It couldn't," sighed Aubrey, reluctantly taking the glass.

"Don't be too sure of that! I've no patience, and no bowels of mercy either. Can it be that you don't know you are in the ogre's den?"

That made Aubrey smile, but he said, looking distastefully at his potion: "I don't take this stuff unless I am absolutely obliged. I'm not a weakling, you know—even if I do ride a feather!"

"You're an obstinate whelp. And who is making the grand fuss now, I should like to know? All for nothing more than a composer to make you more comfortable until your doctor can set you to rights! Drink it at once, and let me have no more nonsense!"

Wholly unused to receiving peremptory commands, Aubrey stiffened a little; but after staring at Damerel for a moment out of dangerously narrowed eyes he capitulated, saying with his twisted smile: "Oh, very well!"

"That's better," said Damerel, taking the empty glass from him. Something in Aubrey's thin, set face made him add: "I've a strong notion there's nothing much amiss with you but bruises and blue devils. You'd be in worse pain if you had done yourself a serious mischief, so come out of the dismals, young paperskull!"

Aubrey's eyes turned quickly towards him. "Yes. Yes, I should! I hadn't thought of that. Thank you—I'm very much obliged to you! I didn't mean to be uncivil—at least, I did, but—but I beg pardon, sir!"

"Oh, pooh! go to sleep!"

"Yes, very likely I shall, after drinking that vile stuff," Aubrey agreed, with a shy grin that made him look suddenly younger. "Only my sister will be a trifle anxious, I daresay. Do you think—"

"Have no fear! I have already sent one of the stable-boys to Undershaw with a letter for her."

"Oh! Thank you! You didn't tell her anything to alarm her, did you?"

"No, why should I? I told her precisely what I told you, and merely requested her to put up what you need in the way of nightshirts and tooth-brushes for the boy to bring back with him."

"That's right!" Aubrey said, relieved. "They can't fly into a pucker over *that!*"

4

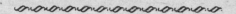

The letter which reached Venetia had been written in the most elegant of formal terms, and in a spirit of unholy amusement. Damerel took pains over it, wondering what its effect on her would be. He addressed her as a stranger, but she was unlikely to be deceived into thinking that he did not remember very well who she was. Though he was careful not to pen a word that might betray to her his enjoyment of the situation, she would certainly perceive how maliciously fate had played into his hands. That might bring her to the Priory in a mood of seething resentment, but he did not think it would keep her away from a delicate young brother who seemed to be in her sole charge; and he did not doubt his ability to gentle her into laying her ruffled plumage. He ended his letter with a prim *Yours etc*, and wished, as he sealed it with a wafer, that he could watch her face when she read it.

In point of fact not one of the thoughts he had imagined for her so much as crossed her mind. By the time the letter reached Undershaw she was much more anxious than she cared to betray to Nurse, who had been prophesying disaster ever since the discovery that Aubrey had not come home to share a nuncheon with his sister. That circumstance had not alarmed her; he had not told her where he was going, and for anything she knew it might have been to Thirsk, or even to York, where there was a bookshop that enjoyed his patronage. But by four o'clock she had reached the nerve-racking stage of wondering whether to send out the menservants to scour the countryside, or whether in so doing she would be indulging a fit of extravagant folly which would infuriate Aubrey. So when Ribble brought the letter to her, with Nurse wringing her hands in his wake, and declaring that she had known it all along, and there was her sainted lamb, picked up for dead, and lying at the Priory with every bone in his body broken, there was no room in her head for any thought of Damerel. Her fingers trembled as she broke open the letter; she felt quite sick with dread; and in her anxiety to learn the worst never even noticed the ironic formality over which such pains had been spent. Running her eyes rapidly down the single sheet she exclaimed thankfully: "No, no, he's not badly hurt! Rufus came down with him, but there are no bones broken. A sprained ankle—considerable bruising—in case of any injury to the left hip—oh, how *very* kind of him! Listen, Nurse! Lord Damerel has sent to York already to fetch Dr. Bentworth to Aubrey! He writes however that although Aubrey believes himself to have fallen on that leg, he thinks, from the spraining of his right ankle, that it was not so and he has done no more than jar the weak joint. I do *pray* he may be right! He thought it better to convey Aubrey to the Priory than to subject him to the torment of the longer journey to his own home—*indeed* it was! And if I will be so good as to put up Aubrey's necessities the bearer will carry them back to the Priory. As though I shouldn't go to Aubrey myself!"

"That you will not!" declared Nurse. "The Lord may see fit to turn an old woman over into the hands of the wicked, but it says in the Good Book that many are the afflictions of the righteous, and, what's more, that they shall be upheld, which I do trust I shall be, though never did I think to be forced to stand in the way of sinners! But as for letting you set foot in that ungodly mansion, Miss Venetia, never!"

Recognizing from the sudden Biblical turn of the conversation that her guardian was strongly moved, Venetia applied herself for the next twenty minutes to the task of soothing her agitation, pointing out to her that they had more reason to liken Damerel to the Good Samaritan than to the wicked, and coaxing her to accept her own determination to go to Aubrey as something as harmless as it was inevitable. In all of this she was only partially successful, for although Nurse knew that once Miss Venetia had made up her mind she was powerless to prevent her doing whatever she liked, and was obliged to admit some

46

faint resemblance in Damerel to the Good Samaritan, she persisted in referring to him as The Ungodly, and in ascribing his charitable behaviour to some obscure but evil motive.

She came closer to the truth than she knew, or could have brought Venetia to believe. Venetia had no guile, and no affectations; she knew the world only by the books she had read; experience had never taught her to doubt the sincerity of anyone who did her a kindness. So when Damerel, seeing the approach of a carriage round a bend in the avenue, strolled out to meet his guest it was neither a wrathful goddess nor a young lady on her dignity who sprang down from the vehicle and gave him both her hands, but a beautiful, ingenuous creature with no consciousness in her frank eyes, but only a glow of warm gratitude. She exclaimed, as he took her hands: "I am so much obliged to you! I *wish* I could tell you, but there seems to be nothing to say but *thank you*." She added, shyly smiling: "You wrote me such a comfortable letter, too! That was so very kind: did you guess I must be quite sick with apprehension? Oh, pray tell me that it was true, and he didn't injure himself badly?"

It was several moments before he answered her or released her hands. In a faded old gown, with her hair untidy under a sunbonnet, and her countenance flushed with indignation he had thought her an uncommonly pretty girl; she was dressed now simply but charmingly in jonquil muslin, with a hat of unbleached straw whose high-poke front made a frame for a lovely face that was neither flushed nor indignant, but smiling up at him with unshadowed friendliness, and she took his breath away. Hardly aware that he was still holding her hands, and in far too strong a grasp, he stood staring down at her until Nurse recalled him to his senses by clearing her throat in a marked and an intimidating manner. He recovered himself quickly then, saying: "Why, yes, Miss Lanyon! to the best of my belief it was perfectly true, but although I have some experience of broken bones I know nothing of the trouble that makes your brother lame, and so thought it imperative to send for his doctor. I hope it may not be long before he arrives. Meanwhile, you must, I'm persuaded, be impatient to see the boy. I'll take you to him at once."

"Thank you! I've brought our Nurse, as you see, and she means to stay to look after him, if she may do so?"

"Oh, that's capital!" he said, smiling in appreciative amusement as he encountered a glare from the rigid moralist's hostile eyes. "You will know just what to do for him, and to have you will make him feel very much more at home."

"Is it paining him very badly?" Venetia asked anxiously, as Damerel led her into the house.

"No, not now. I gave him some laudanum, and he seems tolerably comfortable—but I fear you'll find him pretty drowsy."

"Gave him laudanum?" Venetia exclaimed. "Oh, if he would swallow *that* he must have been suffering dreadfully! He will never take drugs—not even the mildest opiate, only to make him sleep when his hip has been aching!"

"Oh, he didn't swallow it at all willingly, I promise you!" he replied, taking her across the flagged hall to the staircase. "I respect his reluctance, but to be allowing him to play the Spartan youth, when he was suffering (unless I mistake the matter) as much from fear that he may have crippled himself as from his bruised bones, would have been folly. Or so I thought!"

"You were very right!" she agreed. "But unless you forced it down his throat, which I do hope you didn't, I can't imagine how you persuaded him to take it, for I never knew anyone so obstinate!"

He laughed. "No, no, I wasn't obliged to resort to violence!" He opened the door into Aubrey's room as he spoke, and stood aside for her to go in.

Aubrey, lying in the middle of a big four-poster bed and wearing a nightshirt many sizes too large for him, looked the merest wisp of a boy, but he had recovered his complexion a little. Roused by his sister's fingers laid over his wrist he opened his eyes, smiled sleepily at her, and murmured: "Stoopid! I've only bruised myself, m'dear: nothing to signify! I think I crammed him. Rufus, I mean."

"Cawker!" she said lovingly.

"I know. Damerel said, more bottom than sense." His gaze focused itself on Nurse, who, having set down a bulging portmanteau, was divesting herself of her bonnet

48

with all the air of one determined to remain at his side whatever might be the consequences. He uttered thickly: "Oh, *no*, my God—! How *could* you, Venetia? Take her away! I'm damned if I'll have her fussing and fuming over me as if I were a baby!"

"Ungrateful brat!" remarked Damerel. "You'd be well-served if your nurse took you at your word, and left you to my mercies! I should certainly beat you."

Considerably to Venetia's surprise this intervention, so far from offending him, made Aubrey give a tiny spurt of laughter. Turning his head on the pillow so that he could look at Damerel, he said: "Well, how would *you* like it, sir?"

"Very much indeed! You are more fortunate than you know."

Aubrey pulled a face; but when Damerel had left the room he said: "I like him, don't you? You'll say everything that's proper, won't you? I don't think I did, and I ought."

She replied soothingly, and he shut his eyes again. He was soon asleep, so that there was nothing for Venetia to do but to sit down to await the arrival of Dr. Bentworth, while Nurse unpacked the portmanteau, her lips tightly folded in disapproval, except when she opened them to whisper warnings to Venetia against falling into the snares of the wicked. She was presently drawn into the adjoining dressing-room by Mrs. Imber, and Venetia was left to while away the time as best she might. There was nothing to occupy her save her thoughts, and nothing to be seen from the window but a neglected garden bathed in autumn sunshine. Having mentally weeded this, stocked its flower-beds with her favourite plants, and set a couple of men to scythe the lawn, she wondered how long she would be obliged to sit idle. She feared it might be for a considerable period, for York was twelve miles distant, and it was more than probable that a busy practitioner might not be found at liberty to come immediately to Aubrey's bedside.

When Nurse came back into the room Venetia was glad to see that her countenance had slightly relaxed its expression of uncompromising severity. Her opinion of Damerel's morals, and her conviction that his end would be a lesson to other sinners, remained unchanged, but she was to some degree mollified by the discovery that

49

he had ordered Mrs. Imber not only to make up a bed for her in the dressingroom, but to obey whatever injunctions she might see fit to lay upon her. Furthermore, his valet was not, as might have been supposed, a saucy jacka-napes, but a very respectable man who had behaved with great civility to her, deferring to her superior judgment, and begging, as a favour, to be allowed to share with her the duties of waiting on the invalid. It appeared that Nurse had graciously conferred this honour upon him, but whether she had done so because she was won over by his tact, or because she knew that Aubrey would stren-uously resist any attempt to reduce him to nursery status, remained undisclosed. She was representing to Venetia in persuasive terms how unnecessary it was for her to remain at the Priory another instant when Aubrey woke up, rather cross, and complaining that he was hot, thirsty, and uncomfortable. Nurse thought this an excellent op-portunity to change Damerel's contaminating nightshirt for one of his own, so she summoned Marston to her assistance, and was pretty well occupied when Damerel walked into the room to invite Venetia to partake of dinner in his company. Before Nurse had grasped the scandalous nature of his errand the invitation had been accepted, and Damerel was bowing Venetia out of the room.

"Thank you!" Venetia said, as he shut the door. "You came in at precisely the right moment, you know, when poor Nurse was too much taken up with scolding Aubrey for being so tiresome to think what *I* might be doing!"

"Yes, I didn't think I should clear that fence without a check," he agreed. "Would you have attended to her protests?"

"No, but she is being strongly moved by the spirit, and the chances are it would have moved her to say something impolite to you, which would have covered me with mor-tification."

"Oh, don't let that trouble you!" he said, laughing. "Only tell me how I should address her!"

"Well, *we* have always called her Nurse."

"No doubt! But it won't do for me to copy you. What is her name?"

"Priddy. The underservants call her *Mrs*. Priddy, though I can't think why, for she has never been married."

"Mrs. Priddy she shall be. You won't tell me I rank

above the underservants in her esteem!" An irrepressible chuckle made him glance down at her; he saw the brimming merriment in her eyes, and demanded: "Now what? Do I rank above them?"

"I don't *think* so," she answered cautiously. "At least, I never heard her say, even of the laundrymaid, that she would be eaten by frogs!"

He gave a shout of laughter. "Good God, does that fate await me?"

Encouraged by the discovery that he shared her enjoyment of the absurd she laughed back at him, saying: "Yes, and also that your increase will be delivered to the caterpillar."

"Oh, I've no objection to that! The caterpillar is welcome to my increase!"

"No, how can you be so unnatural? Increase *must* mean your children!"

"Undoubtedly! Any side-slips of mine the caterpillar may have with my good-will," he retorted.

"Poor little things!" she said, adding thoughtfully, after a moment: "Not that it is at all easy to perceive what harm one caterpillar could do them."

"Do you know that you are a very strange girl?" he asked abruptly.

"Why? Have I said something I ought not?" she said rather anxiously.

"On the contrary: I'm afraid it was I who did that."

"Did you?" She wrinkled her brow. "Side-slips? Well, that was quite my fault for mentioning your children at all, when I know you are not married. *Have* you—No."

His lips twitched, but he said gravely: "Not to my knowledge."

That drew a responsive twinkle from her. "Yes, I *was* going to ask you that," she admitted. "I beg your pardon! The thing is, you see, that I so seldom talk to anyone but Aubrey that I forget to take care what I say when I go into company."

"Don't set a guard on your tongue on my account!" he said, ushering her into the dining-room. "I like your frankness—and detest damsels who blush and bridle!"

She took the chair Imber was holding for her. "Well, I don't think I did that, even in my salad days."

"A long time ago!" he said, quizzing her.

51

"Well, it is, for I'm five-and-twenty, you know."

"I must take your word for that, but do enlighten me! Do you hold my sex in dislike, or have you taken a vow of celibacy?"

"I wish you won't make me laugh just as I am drinking soup! You nearly made me choke! Of course not!"

"What a set of slow-tops the Yorkshire bucks must be! This soup seems to be made entirely of onions. I don't wonder at your choking. And as far as I can see," he said, levelling his quizzing-glass at the various dishes set out on the table, "there is worse to come. What the devil is *that* mess, Imber?"

"Veal, my lord, with a sauce Bechermell—Mrs. Imber not being prepared for company," replied Imber apologetically. "But there is the raised mutton pie, and a brace of partridges for the second course, with French beans and mushrooms, and—and a dish of fruit, which Mrs. Imber hopes you will pardon, miss, for his lordship not being partial to sweetmeats she hadn't a cream nor a jelly ready to serve, and, as you know, miss, such things take time."

"I am astonished poor Mrs. Imber should have been able to dress *half* as many dishes," instantly responded Venetia. "With such an upset in the house she can't have had a moment to spare! Pray tell her that I am particularly partial to veal, and quite detest jellies!"

Damerel was regarding her with a smile in his eyes. He said, as Imber bore off the empty soup-plates: "Everything handsome about you!—your face, your name, and your manners! Tell me about your life! Why did I never see you before? Do you never come to London?"

She shook her head. "No, though perhaps I shall when Aubrey goes to Cambridge next year. As for telling you about my life—why, there's only one answer to that, and it's *A blank, my lord!*"

"Am I to understand that you pine in thought? I hope you don't mean to tell me you have a green and yellow melancholy, for that I'll swear you have not!"

"Good gracious, no! Only that I have no history! I have passed all my life at Undershaw, and done nothing worth the telling. I wish you will tell me some of the things *you* have done!"

He looked up quickly from the dish he was serving,

his eyes hardening. She met that searching stare with a little enquiring lift to her brows, and saw his lips curl into the sneer which had made her liken him to the *Corsair*. "I think not," he said dryly.

"I said *some* of the things you have done!" she exclaimed indignantly. "You can't have spent your whole life getting into idiotish scrapes!"

The ugly look vanished as he burst out laughing. "Most of it, I assure you! What is it you wish to know?"

"I should like to know about the places you have been to. You have travelled a great deal, haven't you?"

"Oh, yes!"

"I envy you that. It is a thing I always longed to do. I daresay I never shall, because single females are so horridly restricted, but I still indulge myself with planning tours to all the strange places I've only read about."

"No, no, don't do it!" he begged. "Such dreams, believe me, are the seeds from which the eccentric springs! You would end, like that ramshackle Stanhope woman, queening it over hordes of evil-smelling Bedouins!"

"I promise you I should not! It sounds very disagreeable—and quite as boring as the life I've known! You refer, I collect, to Lady Hester: did you ever meet her?"

"Yes, at Palmyra, in—oh, I forget!—'13? '14? It doesn't signify."

"Have you visited Greece, as well as the Levant?" she interrupted.

"I have. Why? Can it be that you are a classical scholar?"

"No, I am not, but Aubrey is. Do, pray tell him about the things you must have seen in Athens! He has only Mr. Appersett to talk to about what he most cares for, and although Mr. Appersett—he is the Vicar, you know!—is a fine scholar he has not *seen*, with his own eyes, as you have!"

"I'll tell Aubrey anything he may want to know—if you, mysterious Miss Lanyon, will tell me what I want to know!"

"Well, I will," she replied handsomely. "Though what there is to tell you, or why you should call me mysterious has me in a puzzle!"

"I call you mysterious because—" he paused, amused

by the look of innocent expectancy in her eyes—"Oh, because you are five-and-twenty, unwed, and, so far as I can discover, unsought!"

"On the contrary!" retorted Venetia, entering into the spirit of this. "I have *two* admirers! One of them is excessively romantic, and the other is—"

"Well?" he prompted, as she hesitated.

"Worthy!" she produced, and went into a peal of mirth as he dropped his head into his hands.

"And you a nonpareil!"

"No, am I? The truth is that there is no mystery at all: my father was a recluse."

"That sounds to me like a *non sequitur*."

"No, it's the very hub of the matter."

"But, good God, did he shut you up as well as himself?"

"Not precisely, though I have frequently suspected that he would have liked to have done so. My mother died, you see. He must have loved her quite desperately, I suppose, for he fell into the most deplorable lethargy, and became exactly like Henry I: never smiled again! I can't tell how it was, because he would never have her name mentioned; and, besides that, I was only ten years old at the time, and not at all acquainted with either of them. In fact, I can scarcely remember what she looked like, except that I am sure she was pretty, and wore beautiful dresses. At all events, Papa was utterly thrown into gloom by her death, and until I was seventeen I think I never exchanged a word with anyone beyond our own household."

"Good God! Was he mad?"

"Oh no! Merely eccentric!" she replied. "I never knew him to care for anyone's comfort but his own, but I fancy eccentrics don't. However, when I grew up he permitted Lady Denny and Mrs. Yardley to take me now and then to the Assemblies in York; and once he actually consented to my spending a week in Harrogate, with my Aunt Hendred! I did hope that he would consent also to let me visit her in London, so that she might bring me out in the regular way. She offered to do so, but he wouldn't have it, and I daresay she didn't very much wish to do it, for she didn't press it."

"Poor Venetia!"

If she noticed his use of her name she gave no sign of having done so, only smiling, and saying: "I own I was sadly dashed down at the time, but after all, you know, I don't think I could have gone, even had Papa been willing, for Aubrey was still tied to a sofa, and I couldn't have left him."

"So you have never been farther afield than Harrogate! No wonder you dream of travel! How have you endured such intolerable tyranny?"

"Oh, it was only on that one subject Papa was adamant! For the rest I might do as I chose. I wasn't unhappy—did you think I had been? Not a bit! I might now and then be *bored*, but in general I have had enough to keep me occupied, with the house to manage, and Aubrey to take care of."

"When did your father die? Surely some years ago? Why do you stay here? Is habit so strong?"

"No, but circumstance is! My elder brother is a member of Lord Hill's staff, you see, and until he chooses to sell out *someone* must look after Undershaw. There's Aubrey, too. I don't think he would consent to go away, because that would mean he could not read with Mr. Appersett any more; and it wouldn't do to leave him alone."

"I can well believe that he would miss you, but—"

She laughed. "Aubrey? Oh, no! Aubrey likes books more than people. The thing is that I am afraid Nurse would drive him crazy, trying to wrap him in cottonwool, which is a thing he can't bear." Her brow creased. "I only wish she may not vex him to death while he is here! I was obliged to bring her, because if I had not she would have trudged all the way. Then, too, she does know what to do when he is ailing, and I couldn't leave him quite on your hands. Perhaps Dr. Bentworth will say he may come home."

But when the doctor arrived, although he was able to allay any fears that Aubrey had seriously injured his hip he returned a flat negative to Nurse's suggestion that he would be better in his own home. The quieter he was kept, said Dr. Bentworth, the more quickly would the torn ligaments heal. This verdict was accepted reluctantly

55

by Nurse, and by Aubrey, whose endurance had been tried pretty high by the doctor's examination, with profound relief.

With a tact born of experience Venetia had not accompanied the doctor to the sickroom. She had asked Damerel to go with him in her stead, and he had nodded, and had said in his curt way: "Yes, I'll go. Don't worry!" It was several minutes before it occurred to her that she had turned to him as to a friend of many years' standing. Then, a little wonderingly, she thought over that protracted dinner, and of how they had sat talking long after Imber had removed the covers, Damerel leaning back in his carved chair, a glass of port held between his long fingers, she with her elbows on the table and a half-eaten apple in one hand; and the dusk creeping into the room unheeded, until Imber brought in candles, in tall, tarnished chandeliers, and set them on the table, furnishing a pool of light in which they sat while the shadows darkened beyond it. Trying to recall what they had talked of during that comfortable hour, it seemed to Venetia that they had talked of everything, or perhaps of nothing: she did not know which, but only that she had found a friend.

When the doctor told her that he could not advise her to remove Aubrey from the Priory he seemed to be both surprised and relieved by her tranquil acceptance of his verdict. The note of apology in his voice at first puzzled her, but after she had thought it over she saw what he must have meant when he spoke of embarrassment and awkward situations; and when Damerel came back into the room, after escorting the doctor to his carriage, she looked rather anxiously up at him, and said with a little difficulty: "I am afraid—I hadn't thought—Will it be troublesome to you to keep Aubrey until he is better?"

"Not a bit!" he replied, with reassuring alacrity. "What put such a daffish notion as that into your head?"

"Well, it was Dr. Bentworth's saying how sorry he was to be obliged to put me in an awkward situation," she disclosed. "He meant, of course, that it is quite shocking to foist poor Aubrey on to you, and he was perfectly right! I can't think why it should not have occurred to me before, but I daresay—"

"He meant nothing of the sort," Damerel interrupted

ruthlessly. "His solicitude is not on my behalf, but on yours. He perceived the impropriety of thrusting you into acquaintanceship with a man of libertine propensities. Morals and medicine warred within his breast, and medicine won the day—but I daresay morals may give him a sleepless night!"

"Is *that* all?" she exclaimed, her brow clearing.

"That's all," he answered gravely. "Unless, of course, he fears I may corrupt Aubrey. Evil communications, you know!"

"I shouldn't think you could," she said, dispassionately considering the matter. She saw his lips quiver, and her own gravity vanished. "Oh, I don't mean that you would make the attempt! You know very well I don't! The thing is that even if you were to hold an *orgy* here the chances are he would only think it pretty tame, compared with the Romans, not to mention the Bacchae, who, from anything I can discover, were precisely the sort of females one would wish a boy *not* to know about!"

This view of the matter was almost too much for his self-control; it was a moment before he could command his voice enough to say: "I promise you I won't hold any orgies while Aubrey is under my roof!"

"Oh, no, I know you would not! Though I must say," she added, a gleam of fun in her eyes, "it would be worth it, only to see Nurse's face!"

He laughed out at that, flinging back his head in wholehearted enjoyment, gasping: "Why, oh *why* did I never know you until now?"

"It does seem a pity," she agreed. "I have been thinking so myself, for I always wished for a friend to laugh with."

"To laugh with!" he repeated slowly.

"Perhaps you have friends already who laugh when you do," she said diffidently. "I haven't, and it's important, I think—more important than sympathy in affliction, which you might easily find in someone you positively disliked."

"But to share a sense of the ridiculous prohibits dislike—yes, that's true. And rare! My God, how rare! Do they stare at you, our worthy neighbours, when you laugh?"

"Yes! or ask me what I mean when I'm joking!" She glanced at the clock above the empty fireplace. "I must go."

"Yes, you must go. I have sent a message down to the stables. There is still light enough for your coachman to make out the way, but it will be dark in another hour, or even less." He took her hands, and putting them palm to palm held them so between his own. "You'll come again tomorrow—to visit Aubrey! Don't let them dissuade you, our worthy neighbours! Beyond my gates I make you no promises; don't trust me! Within them—" He paused, his smile twisting into something not quite a sneer yet derisive. "Oh, within them," he said in brittle self-mockery, "I'll remember that I was *bred* a gentleman!"

5

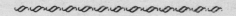

Venetia opened her eyes to sunlight, dimmed by the chintz blinds across her windows. She lay for a few minutes between sleep and waking, aware, at first vaguely and then with sharpening intensity, of a sense of well-being and of expectation, as when, in childhood, she had waked to the knowledge that the day of a promised treat had dawned. Somewhere in the garden a thrush was singing, the joyous sweetness of its note so much in harmony with her mood that it seemed a part of her happiness. She was content for some moments to listen, not questioning the source of their happiness; but presently she came to full consciousness, and remembered that she had found a friend.

At once the blood seemed to quicken in her veins; her body felt light and urgent; and a strange excitement, flooding her whole being like an elixir, made it impossible for her to be still. No sound but bird-song came to her ears; quiet enfolded the house. She thought it must be very early, and, turning her head on the pillow, tried to recapture sleep. It eluded her; the sunlight, blotched by the pattern on the chintz, teased her eyelids: she lifted them, yielding to a prompting more insistent than that of reason. A new day, fresh with new promise, set her tingling; the thrush's trill became a lure and a command; she slid from the smothering softness of her feather-bed, and went with a swift, springing step to the window, sweeping back the blinds, and thrusting open the casement.

A cock pheasant, pacing across the lawn, froze into an instant's immobility, his head high on the end of his shimmering neck, and then, as though he knew himself safe for yet a few weeks, resumed his stately progress. The autumn mist was lifting from the hollows; heavy dew sparkled on the grass; and, above, the sky was hazy with lingering vapour. There was a chill in the air which made the flesh shudder even in the sun's warmth, but it was going to be another hot day, with no hint of rain, and not enough to bring the turning leaves fluttering down from the trees.

Beyond the park, across the lane that skirted Undershaw to the east, beyond its own spreading plantations, lay the Priory: not very far as the crow flew, but a five-mile drive by road. Venetia thought of Aubrey, whether he had slept during the night, whether there were many hours to while away before she could set forth to visit him. Then she knew that it was not anxiety for Aubrey, her first concern for so many years, which made her impatient to reach the Priory, but the desire to be with her friend. It was his image, ousting Aubrey's from her mind's sight, which brought such a glow of warmth to her. She wondered if he too was conscious of it; if he was wakeful, perhaps looking out of his window, as she from hers; thinking about her; hoping that she would soon be with him again. She tried to remember what they had talked of, but she could not; she remembered only that she had felt perfectly at home, as though she had known him all her life. It seemed impossible that he should not have felt as strongly as she the tug of sympathy between them; but when she had thought for a little she recalled how widely different were their circumstances, and recognized that what to her had been a new experience might well have meant nothing more to him than a variation on an old theme. He had had many loves; perhaps he had many friends too, with minds more closely attuned to his than she believed her own to be. These troubled her as his loves did not. With his loves she was as little concerned as with his first encounter with herself. That had angered her, but it had neither shocked nor disgusted her. Men—witness all the histories!—were subject to sudden lusts and violences, affairs that seemed strangely divorced from heart or head, and often more strangely still from what were surely their true characters. For them chastity was not a prime virtue: she remembered her amazement when she had discovered that so correct a gentleman and kind a husband as Sir John Denny had not always been faithful to his lady. Had Lady Denny cared? A little, perhaps, but she had not allowed it to blight her marriage. "Men, my love, are different from us," she had said once, "even the best of them! I tell you this because I hold it to be very wrong to rear girls in the belief that the face men show to the females they respect is their only one. I daresay, if we were to see them watching some horrid, vulgar prize-fight, or in company with women of a certain class, we shouldn't recognize our own husbands and brothers. I am very sure we should think them disgusting! Which, in some ways, they *are*, only it would be unjust to blame them for what they can't help. One ought rather to be thankful that any affairs they may have amongst what they call the muslin company don't change their *true* affection in the least. Indeed, I fancy affection plays no part in such adventures. So odd!—for *we*, you know, could scarcely indulge in them with no more effect on our lives than if we had been choosing a new hat. But so it is with men! Which is why it has been *most* truly said that while your husband continues to show you tenderness you have no cause for complaint, and would be a zany to fall into despair only because of what to him was a mere peccadillo. 'Never seek to pry into what does not concern you, but rather look in the opposite direction!' was what my dear mother told me, and very good advice I have found it. She spoke, of course, of gentlemen of character and breeding, as I do now—for with the demi-beaux and the loose-screws females of our order, I am glad to say, have nothing to do: they do not come in our way."

But Damerel had come in their way, and although he was not a demi-beau he was certainly a loose-screw. Lady Denny had been obliged to receive him with the appearance at least of complaisance, but she was not going to pursue so undesirable an acquaintance; and there could be little doubt that she would be horrified when she discovered that her young protegee was not only on the best of terms with him but was also committing the gross impropriety of visiting his house. Could she be made to understand that he, like those nameless, aberrant husbands, had two sides to his character? Venetia thought not. The best to be hoped was that she would understand

61

that while Aubrey lay at the Priory his sister would go to him though Damerel were a Caliban.

The clatter of shutters being folded back in the parlour beneath her room roused her from these doubtful reflections. If the servants were stirring it was not so very early after all: probably about six o'clock. Seeking an excuse for rising an hour before her usual time she remembered the several but very pressing duties which had been left undone on the previous day, and decided to perform them immediately.

She was no bustling housewife, but by the time she came into the breakfast-parlour she had visited the dairy and the stables; discussed winter-sowing with the bailiff; delivered to the poultry-woman, in a slightly expurgated form, a remonstrance from Mrs. Gurnard; listened in return to a Jeremiad on the general and particular perversity of hens; and directed an aged and obstinate gardener to tie up the dahlias. It seemed improbable that he would do so, for he regarded them as upstarts and intruders, which in his young days had never been heard of, and always became distressingly deaf whenever Venetia mentioned them.

Mrs. Gurnard, to Venetia's relief, took it for granted that she would drive over to see poor Master Aubrey, but was thrown into dignified sulks by Venetia's refusal to carry with her a sizeable hamper packed as full as it would hold with enough cooked food for a banquet. When asked, in a rallying tone, if she supposed Aubrey to be living on a desert island she replied that there were many who would consider him to be better off on a desert island than abandoned to the rigours of Mrs. Imber's cookery. Mrs. Imber, said Mrs. Gurnard, besides being feckless, inching, and unhandy, was one whom she could never bring herself to trust. "I've not forgotten the pullets, miss, if you have, and what's more I never shall, not if I live to be a hundred!"

"Pullets?" said Venetia, bewildered.

"Cockerels!" uttered Mrs. Gurnard, her eyes kindling. "Cockerels every one, miss!"

But as Venetia could perceive no connection between cockerels and Mrs. Imber's cookery she remained adamant, and went off to collect the various items which Nurse, in the agitation of the moment, had omitted to pack. These included the shirt she was making for Aubrey, and her tatting, both to be found in her sewing-basket, together with needles, thread, scissors, her silver thimble, and a lump of wax. Venetia was to wrap all these things up neatly in a napkin, and to be sure not to forget any of them; but as Venetia knew that the only certainty was of being told that she had brought the wrong thread and the very scissors Nurse had not wanted she preferred, in spite of its formidable dimensions, to take the basket itself to the Priory.

Fulfilling Aubrey's behests was an even more difficult task, for he wanted not only such simple matters as a supply of paper and several pencils, but a number of books as well. He had told her that she would find his *Phaedo* on the desk in the library, and so she did; but *Guy Mannering* was only found after an exhausting search, a zealous housemaid, to whom the sight of a book lying open on a chair was an offence, having wedged it, upside-down, into a shelf devoted to text-books and lexicons. Virgil presented no problem: Aubrey had certainly asked for the *Aeneid*; but Horace blandly offered a choice of several volumes, and Venetia was quite unable to remember whether Aubrey wanted *Odes*, or *Satires*, or even *Epistles*. In the end, she added all three to her collection, and Ribble bore off the pile to the waiting tilbury, where Fingle, the middle-aged groom, received them from him with the cheerful prognostication that the next thing any-one would know was that Master Aubrey had studied himself into a brain-fever.

Feeling that she had acquitted herself in a manner worthy of a scholar's sister, Venetia then drove off to the Priory, where any hopes she might have cherished of earning encomium were speedily dashed. "Oh, you need not have brought them after all!" said Aubrey. "Damerel has a capital library—a first-rate affair, large enough for a catalogue! He found it for me last night, and brought me up the books I particularly wanted. I warned him, when I saw what a splendid collection it is, that he would find it hard to be rid of me, but he says I may always borrow any volumes I choose. Oh, is that you, Fingle? Good-morning: have you taken a look at Rufus? Lord Damerel's groom has him in charge, but I daresay you'll wish to see that foreleg for yourself. No, don't set those books down: I find I don't want 'em!"

"Odious, odious boy!" Venetia said, bending over him

to drop a kiss on his brow. "When it took me half-an-hour to find *Guy Mannering*, and I brought *all* your Horace, because I couldn't remember which volume you wanted!"

"Stoopid!" he said, smiling up at her. "I'll keep *Guy Mannering*, though, in case I want something to read in the night."

She withdrew it from the pile Fingle was still holding, nodded dismissal to him, a twinkle in her eyes which caused him to cast up his own expressively, and ventured to ask Aubrey how he had slept.

"Oh—tolerably well!" he replied.

"There is no truth in you, love. I collect that you spurned the syrup of poppies Nurse was so careful to bring with her?"

"After the laudanum Damerel gave me! I should rather think I did! He agreed I should be better without it, too, so Nurse went off to bed in a miff, which I was heartily glad of. Damerel brought up a chessboard, and we had a game or two. He's an excellent player: I won only once. Then we fell to talking—oh, till past midnight! Did you know he had read classics? He went to Oxford—says he has forgotten all he ever knew, but that's humbug! I should think he had been a pretty good scholar. He has visited Greece, too, and was able to describe things to me—things worth describing! Not like that fellow who stayed with the Appersetts last year, and had nothing more to say of Greece than that he couldn't drink the wine because of the resin in it, and had been eaten alive by bed-bugs!"

"So you enjoyed your evening?"

"Yes—but for my curst leg! However, if I hadn't taken a toss I daresay I might never have met Damerel, so I don't regret it."

"It must be very agreeable to be able to talk with someone who enters into the things you care for most," she agreed.

"It is," he said frankly. "What's more he knows better than to ask me, a dozen times in an hour, how I feel, or if I wouldn't like another pillow! I don't mean that *you* do so, but Nurse is enough to throw a saint into a pelter! I wish you had not brought her: Marston can do all I need—and without putting me in a bad skin!" he added, with his rueful, twisted smile.

"My dear, I couldn't have kept her away from you! Tell me *once* how you find yourself this morning, and then I promise—word of a Lanyon!—I won't ask you again!"

"Oh, I'm well enough!" he replied shortly. She said nothing, and after a moment he relented, and grinned at her. "If you *must* know, I feel devilish—as though I had dislocated every joint in my body! But Bentworth assures me it's no such thing, so my aches are of no consequence, and will soon go off, I daresay. Let us play piquet—that is, if you mean to stay for a while? You'll find some cards somewhere—on that table, I think."

She was fairly well satisfied, although upon first entering the room she had thought he looked pale and drawn. It was not to be expected, however, that a boy of such frail physique should not have been badly shaken by his fall; that he was not in one of his testy, unapproachable moods encouraged her to hope that he had not suffered any very serious set-back. When Nurse presently came in, to put a fresh compress round his swollen ankle, Venetia saw, at a glance, that she too was taking an optimistic view of his situation, and was still more cheered. Nurse might show a lamentable want of tact in her management of Aubrey, but she knew his constitution better than anyone, and if she, with years of experience at her back, saw more cause for scolding than for solicitude an anxious sister could banish foreboding.

Upon Marston's coming into the room with a glass of milk for the invalid Venetia drew Nurse into the adjoining dressing-room, saying, as she shut the door: "You know what he is! If he thought *we* cared whether he drank it or no he would refuse to touch it, just to teach us not to treat him as though he were a baby!"

"Oh, yes," said Nurse bitterly. "Anything Marston or his lordship tells him he'll do, just as if it was them that had looked after him from the day he was born! For all the use *I* am I might as well be back at home—not that I mean to leave this house until he does, nor ever did, so his lordship could have spared his breath!"

"Why, did he try to send you away?" Venetia asked, surprised.

"No, and I should hope he knew better than to think he could! It was me saying to Master Aubrey that if he preferred to have Marston to wait on him I'd as lief pack up and go—well, miss, he was so twitty and troublesome last night that anyone might be excused for being put out! But as for meaning it, his lordship should have known better, and no need at all for him to remind me that it wouldn't do for you to visit here without I'm in the house! I know that well enough, and better you shouldn't come at all, Miss Venetia! It's my belief Master Aubrey wouldn't care if neither of us came next or nigh him, not while he can clutter up his bed with a lot of unchristian books, and lie there talking to his lordship about his nasty heathen gods!"

"He would very soon wish for you if he were to be really ill," Venetia said soothingly. "I think too that he is just at the age when he's not a child, but not quite a man either, and excessively jealous of his dignity. Do you remember how uncivil Conway was to you at very much the same age? But when he came home from Spain he didn't care how much you cosseted and scolded him!"

Since Conway held the chief place in her heart Nurse would by no means admit that he had ever conducted himself in any way that fell short of perfection, but she disclosed that his lordship had said much the same thing as had Venetia about Master Aubrey. She added that no one understood better than she Master Aubrey's hatred of his disability, and his passionate desire to show himself as hearty and as independent as his more fortunate contemporaries: an unprecedented announcement which furnished Venetia with a pretty accurate notion of his lordship's skill in handling hostile and elderly females.

There could be no doubt that he had succeeded in considerably mollifying Nurse. She might resent Aubrey's preference for his society, but she could not wholly condemn anyone who, besides showing so proper a regard for Aubrey's well-being, managed to keep him in cheerful spirits under conditions calculated to cast him into a state of irritable gloom.

"I'm not one to condone sin, Miss Venetia," she said austerely, "but nor I'm not one to deny anyone their due neither, and this I will say: he couldn't behave kinder to Master Aubrey, not if he was the Reverend himself." She added, after an inward struggle: "And for all he'd no need to tell me what my duty is to you, Miss Venetia, it was a sign of grace I didn't think to see in him, and there's no saying that the Lord won't have mercy on him, if he was to forsake his way—not but what salvation is far from the wicked, as I've told you often and often, miss."

This lapse into pessimism notwithstanding, Venetia was encouraged to think that Nurse was fairly well reconciled to her sojourn under an unhallowed roof. Aubrey, when regaled with the passage, said that her change of heart could only have arisen from Damerel's having ridden off to Thirsk for the express purpose of buying a roll of lint.

"As a matter of fact, it was no such thing: he went on some business of his own, but when Nurse started grumbling, about the lint—it's for my ankle, you know!—he said he would procure some, and she took it into her head he was going to Thirsk for no other reason. Up till then she wasn't talking about his kindness, I promise you! She said he roared in the congregation."

"She didn't!" Venetia exclaimed, awed.

"Yes, she did. Do you know where it comes? We could not find it, though we looked in all the likeliest places."

"So you repeated it to Damerel!"

"Of course I did! I knew he wouldn't care a rush for what Nurse said of him."

"I expect he enjoyed it," Venetia said, smiling. "When did he set out for Thirsk?"

"Oh, quite early! Now you put me in mind of it he gave me a message for you: something about being obliged to go to Thirsk, and hoping you'd pardon him. I forget! It was of no consequence: just doing the civil! I told him there was not the least need. He said he thought he should be back again by noon—oh, yes! and that he trusted you wouldn't have gone away by then. Venetia, pray look on that table, and see if Tytler is there! Nurse must have moved it when she bandaged my ankle, for I had been reading it, and only laid it down when you came in. She can't come near me without meddling! *Essay on the Principles of Translation*—yes, that's it: thank you!"

"I think, if you should not object *very* much to my leaving you, that I'll take a turn in the garden," said Venetia, handing him the book, and watching him in some amusement as he found his place in it.

"Yes do!" said Aubrey absently. "They will be plaguing me to eat a nuncheon soon, and I want to finish this."

She laughed, and was about to leave him when a gentle tap on the door was followed by the entrance of Imber, announcing Mr. Yardley.

"*What?*" ejaculated Aubrey, in anything but a gratified tone. Edward came in, treading cautiously, and wearing his most disapproving face. "Well, Aubrey!" he said heavily. "I am glad to see you looking stouter than I had expected." He added, in a lower voice, as he clasped Venetia's hand: "This is unfortunate indeed! I knew nothing of what had happened until Ribble told me of it half-an-hour ago! I was never more shocked in my life!"

"Shocked because I took a toss?" said Aubrey. "Lord, Edward, don't be such a slow-top!"

Edward's contenance did not relax; rather it seemed to grow more rigid. He had not exaggerated his state of mind; he was profoundly shocked. He had ridden to Undershaw in happy ignorance, to be met with the alarming tidings that Aubrey had had a bad accident, which had made him instantly fear the worst; and hardly had Ribble reassured him on this head than he was stunned by the further news that Aubrey was lying under Damerel's roof, with not only Nurse in attendance on him but his sister also. The impropriety of such an arrangement really appalled him; and even when he was made to understand that Venetia was not sleeping at the Priory he could not forbear the thought that any disaster (short of Aubrey's death, perhaps) would have been less harmful than the chance that had pitchforked her into the company of a libertine whose way of life had for years scandalized the North Riding. The evils of her situation were, in Edward's view, incalculable; and foremost amongst them was the probability that such a man as Damerel would mistake the inexperience which led her to behave so rashly for the boldness of a born Cytherean, and offer her an intolerable insult.

A level-headed man, Edward did not suppose that Damerel was either so foolhardy or so steeped in villainy as to attempt the seduction of a girl of virtue and quality; but he was very much afraid that Venetia's open, confiding manners, which he had always deplored, might encourage him to believe that she would welcome his advances; while the peculiar circumstances under which she lived would certainly lead him to think that she had no other protector than a crippled schoolboy.

Edward saw his duty clear; he saw too that the performance of it was more than likely to involve him in consequences repugnant to a man of taste and sensibility; but he did not shrink from it: he set his jaw, and rode off to the Priory, not in such a spirit of knighterrantry as Oswald Denny would have brought to the task, but inspired by a sober man's determination to protect the reputation of the lady whom he had chosen to be his bride. At the best, he hoped to bring her to a sense of her impropriety; at the worst, he must bring Damerel to a precise understanding of Venetia's true circumstances. This task could not be other than distasteful to one who prided himself on his correct and well-regulated life; and it might, if Damerel were as careless of public opinion as he was said to be, plunge him into just the sort of scandal his disposition urged him to avoid. He was by no means deficient in courage, but he had not the smallest wish, whatever Damerel's offences might be, to find himself confronting his lordship early one morning with a pistol in his hand and twenty yards of cold earth between them. If it came to that it would be because Aubrey's recklessness and Venetia's incorrigible imprudence had forced him into a position from which, as a man of honour, he could not draw back, even when he considered her to have courted whatever ill might befall her by stepping beyond the barriers of strict propriety, and so giving such men as Damerel a false notion of her character.

It was therefore not with romantic ardour that he rode from Undershaw to the Priory but with a sense of outrage and an exacerbated temper rather hardened than mollified by being kept under rigid control.

His arrival almost coincided with that of Damerel, from Thirsk. As he dismounted, Damerel came striding round the corner of the house from the stables, a package tucked, with his riding-whip, under one arm while he pulled off his gloves. At sight of Edward he checked, in surprise, and for a few moments they stood looking one another over in silence, hard suspicion in one pair of eyes, and in the other a gathering amusement. Then Damerel lifted an enquiring eyebrow, and Edward said stiffly: "Lord Damerel, I believe?"

They were the only rehearsed words he was destined to utter. From then on the meeting proceeded on lines quite unlike any for which he had prepared himself. Damerel strolled forward, saying: "Yes, I'm Damerel, but you have the advantage of me, I fear. I can guess that you must be a friend of young Lanyon's, however. How do you do?"

He smiled as he spoke, and held out his hand. Edward was obliged to shake hands with him, a friendly gesture which forced him to abandon the formality he had decided to adopt.

"How do you do?" he responded with civility, if not with warmth. "Your lordship has guessed correctly: I am a friend of Aubrey Lanyon—I may say a lifelong friend of his *family!* I cannot suppose that my name is known to you, but it is Yardley—Edward Yardley of Netherfold."

He was mistaken. After a frowning moment Damerel's brow cleared, he said: "Does your land lie some few miles beyond my south-western boundary? Yes, I thought so." He added, with his swift smile: "I flatter myself I am making progress in my knowledge of the neighbourhood! Have you been visiting Aubrey?"

"I have only this instant arrived, my lord—from Undershaw, where I was informed by the butler of this very unfortunate accident—he told me also that Miss Lanyon was here."

"Is she?" said Damerel indifferently. "I've been out all the morning, but it's very probable. If she's here she will be with her brother: do you care to go up?"

"Thank you!" Edward said, with a slight bow. "I should like to do so, if Aubrey is sufficiently well to receive a visitor."

"I daresay it won't do him any harm," replied Damerel, leading the way through the open door into the house. "He's not much hurt, you know: no bones broken! I sent for his doctor to come to him last night, but I don't think I should have done so if he hadn't told me that he had a diseased hip-joint. He is none too comfortable, but Bentworth seems to be satisfied that if only he can be kept quiet for a time no evil consequences need be anticipated. Once he had discovered the existence of my library I saw that there would not be the least difficulty about *that.*"

There was a laugh in his voice; none at all in Edward's as he answered: "He always has his head in a book."

Damerel had moved to where a frayed bell-pull hung beside the stone fireplace; as he tugged at it he shot a swift, appraising glance at Edward. The gleam of amusement in his eyes was pronounced, but he said only: "*You*, I apprehend, are too well-acquainted with him to be astonished by the scope and power of his quite remarkable intelligence, *I*, on the other hand, after sitting with him for some hours last night, my forgetful and, alas! indolent brain at full stretch to bear me up through arguments which ranged from disputed texts to percipient mind, retired from the lists persuaded that what threatened the boy was not a crippled leg but an addled brain!"

"Do you think him so clever?" asked Edward, rather surprised. "For my part I have often thought him lacking even in commonsense. But I myself am not at all bookish."

"Oh, I shouldn't think he has any commonsense at all!" returned Damerel.

"I confess I consider it a pity he had not enough to refrain from riding a horse he could not master," said Edward, with a slight smile. "I warned him how it would be when I first set eyes on that chestnut. Indeed, I begged him most earnestly not to make the attempt."

"Did you?" said Damerel appreciatively. "And he didn't heed you? You astonish me!"

"He has been very much indulged. That, of course, was made inevitable, to some degree, by his sickliness; but he has been allowed to have his own way beyond what is proper, from the circumstances attached to his upbringing," said Edward, painstakingly explaining the Lanyons. "His father, the late Sir Francis Lanyon, though in many respects a most estimable man, was eccentric."

"So Miss Lanyon informed me. I should suppose him to have been a curst rum touch, myself, but we won't quarrel over terms!"

"One hesitates to speak ill of the dead," persevered Edward, "but towards his children he displayed an almost total want of interest or consideration. One would have expected him to have provided his daughter with a chaperon, for instance, but such was not the case. You may have wondered, I daresay, at the *freedom* of Miss Lanyon's manners, and, not knowing the circumstances, have thought it odd that she should be permitted to go abroad quite unattended."

"No doubt I should, had I met her when she was a girl," responded Damerel coolly. He turned his head, as Imber came into the hall. "Imber, here is Mr. Yardley, who has come to visit our invalid! Take him up—and see that Mrs. Priddy has that bundle of lint, will you?" He nodded to Edward to follow the butler, and himself walked off to one of the saloons that led from the hall.

Edward trod up the broad, shallow staircase in Imber's wake, his feelings almost equally divided between relief at finding Damerel apparently indifferent to Venetia, and annoyance at the casual way he had been dismissed.

In general he ignored Aubrey's frequent rudeness, but that scornful adjuration to him not to be a slow-top vexed him so much that he was obliged to suppress a sharp retort. He never allowed himself to speak hastily, and it was therefore in a measured tone that he said, after a moment: "Let me point out to you, Aubrey, that if *you* would not try to be quite such a hard-goer this unfortunate accident would never have occurred."

"It was not, after all, so very unfortunate," intervened Venetia. "How kind in you to have come to see how he does!"

"I must regard as unfortunate—to put it no higher!— an accident that places *you* in an awkward situation," he said.

"Well, pray don't tease yourself over that!" she said soothingly. "To be sure, I had rather Aubrey were at home, but I am able to visit him every day, you know, and *he*, I am persuaded, has not the least wish to be at home. I must tell you, Edward, that nothing could be greater than Damerel's kindness to Aubrey, or his good nature in allowing Nurse to order everything precisely as she chooses here. You know her way!"

"You are very much obliged to his lordship," he replied gravely. "I do not deny it, but you will scarcely expect me to think your indebtedness anything but an evil, the consequences of which may, I fear, be far-reaching."

"*What* consequences? I hope you mean to tell me what you mean, for I promise you I don't know! The only consequence I perceive is that we have made an agreeable new acquaintance—and find the Wicked Baron to be very much less black than rumour has painted him!"

"I make every allowance for your ignorance of the world, Venetia, but surely you cannot be unaware of the evil that attaches to acquaintance with a man of Lord Damerel's reputation! I should not wish to make a friend of him myself, and in *your* case—which is one of particular delicacy—every feeling revolts against such an acquaintance!"

"*Quousque tandem abutere, Catilina, patientia nostra?*" muttered Aubrey savagely.

Edward glanced at him. "If you wish me to understand you, Aubrey, I fear you will be forced to speak in English. I do not pretend to be a scholar."

"Then I'll give you a tag well within your power to translate! *Non amo te, Sabidi!*"

"No, Aubrey, *pray* don't!" begged Venetia. "It is mere nonsense, and to be flying into a rage over it is the most nonsensical thing of all! Edward is only in one of his fusses over propriety—and so, let me tell you, is Damerel! For when you vexed poor Nurse so much that she threatened to leave you, my love, what must he do but tell her she must remain here to safeguard my reputation? Anyone might think I was a chit just emerged from the schoolroom!"

Edward's countenance relaxed a little; he said, with a slight smile: "Instead of a staid and middle-aged woman? His lordship was very right, and I don't hesitate to say that it gives me a better opinion of him. But I wish you will discontinue your visits to Aubrey. He is not so badly hurt as to make your attendance on him necessary, and if you come only to entertain him—well, I must say, however much you may resent it, Aubrey, that I think you deserve to be left to entertain yourself! Had you but listened to older and wiser counsel none of this awkwardness would have arisen. No one has more sympathy than I for the disability which makes it imprudent—indeed, I am afraid I must say *foolhardy!*—for you to attempt to ride such a headstrong animal as that chestnut of yours. I told you so at the outset, but—"

"Are you imagining that Rufus bolted with me?" interrupted Aubrey, his eyes glittering with cold dislike. "You're mistaken! The plain truth is that I crammed him!

A piece of bad horsemanship which had nothing to do with my disability! I'm well aware of it—don't need to have it thrust down my throat!"

"That is certainly an admission!" said Edward with an indulgent little laugh. "Neck-or-nothing, eh? Well, I don't mean to give you a scold. We must hope your tumble has taught you the lesson you wouldn't learn from me."

"Much more likely!" Aubrey said swiftly. "I never dared learn of you, Edward: as well as your caution I might have acquired your hands—*quod avertat Deus!*"

It was at this moment that Damerel entered the room, saying cheerfully: "May I come in? Ah, your servant, Miss Lanyon!" He met her eyes for a brief instant, and continued in the easiest style: "I've told Marston to bring up a nuncheon for you to eat with Aubrey, and my errand is to discover whether you like to drink tea with it—and also to carry off your visitor to share *my* nuncheon." He smiled at Edward. "Come and bear me company, Yardley!"

"Your lordship is very obliging, but I never eat at this hour," Edward said stiffly.

"Then come and drink a glass of sherry," replied Damerel, with unimpaired affability. "We will leave our graceless invalid to the ministrations of his sister and his nurse—indeed, we must! for Mrs. Priddy, having now a large stock of lint at her disposal, is about to descend upon him, armed with salves, compresses, and lotions, and you and I, my dear sir, will not be welcome here!"

Edward looked vexed, but as he could scarcely refuse to be dislodged there was nothing to be done but to take his leave. Nor did he receive any encouragement to stay from Venetia, who said frankly: "Yes, pray do go away, Edward! I know you mean it kindly, but I *cannot* have Aubrey put into a passion! He is not at all the thing yet, and Dr. Bentworth particularly charged me to keep him quiet."

He began to say that he had not meant to put Aubrey in a passion; but the moralizing strain in him made it impossible for him to refrain from pointing out how wrong it was of Aubrey to fly into a rage only because one who had his interests sincerely to heart thought it his duty to reprove him. Before he was more than halfway through this speech, however, Venetia, seeing Aubrey raising

74

himself painfully on his elbow interrupted, saying hastily: "Yes, yes, but never mind! Just go away!"

She pushed him towards the door, which Damerel was holding open. He had intended to offer to escort her back to Undershaw, but before he could do so he had been irresistibly shepherded out of the room, and Damerel was shutting the door behind him, saying in a consolatory tone: "The boy is pretty well knocked-up, you know."

"One can only hope it may be a lesson to him!"

"I daresay it will be."

Edward gave a short laugh. "Ay! if one could but make him realize that he owes his aches to his own folly in persisting in his determination to ride horses he can't control! For my part I consider it the height of imprudence in him to jump at all, for with that weak leg, you know—"

"But what a pudding-hearted creature he would be if he didn't do so!" said Damerel. "Did you ever know a halfling who deemed prudence a virtue?"

"I should have supposed that when he knows what the consequences of a fall might be—However, it is always the same with him! he will never brook criticism—flies into a miff at the merest hint of it! I don't envy you the charge of him!"

"Oh, I shan't criticize him!" replied Damerel. "I have not the least right to do so, after all!"

Edward made no answer to this, merely saying, as he descended the stairs: "I do not know when Miss Lanyon means to return to Undershaw. I should be pleased to escort her, and had meant to have offered it."

There was a decidedly peevish note in his voice. Damerel's lips twitched, but he replied gravely: "I am afraid I don't know either. Would you wish me to discover for you?"

"Oh, it is of no consequence, thank you! I daresay she won't leave Aubrey until she has coaxed him out of his sullens—though it would be better for him if she did!"

"My dear sir, if you feel her groom to be an insufficient escort, do, I beg of you, make yourself at home here for as long as you choose!" said Damerel. "I would offer to go with her in your stead, but I might not be at hand, you know, and, I own, I should not have thought it at all necessary. However, if you feel—"

75

"No, no! it was merely—But if she has her groom there is of course no need for me to remain. Your lordship is very good, but I have a great deal of business to attend to, and have wasted too much of my time already."

He then took formal leave, refusing all offers of refreshment, but expressing, in punctilious terms, his sense of obligation for the kindness shown to Aubrey, and his hope that it would soon be possible to relieve his lordship of so unwanted a burden.

To all of this Damerel listened politely, but with a disquieting twinkle in his eye. He said, in the careless way which had previously offended Edward: "Oh, Aubrey won't worry me!" and having waved farewell almost before Edward's foot was in the stirrup turned back into the house, and went up to Aubrey's room again.

6

He entered to find Aubrey still seething with annoyance, his eyes overbright and his thin cheeks flushed, and said, in an amused voice: "Well, you do accord your visitors Turkish treatment, don't you?"

"Where is he?" demanded Aubrey.

"*Abit, excessit...*"

"What, already? *Vae victis!* Did you kick him out?"

"On the contrary! I invited him to treat the house as his own."

"Oh, my God, no!"

"No, that's very much what he thought—though he didn't phrase it so. I fancy he doesn't like me above half—but nothing could have exceeded his civility." He turned his laughing eyes towards Venetia. "*Worthy* was exactly the right epithet!"

She laughed back at him. "Oh, did you guess?"

"Of course I did! Poor man, I was heartily sorry for him!"

"Sorry for that—that windsucker?" exploded Aubrey. "Wait till you see how little need you had to give him leave to treat your house as his own! He has been doing so with ours ever since my father died! Meddling and moralizing! I tell you to your head, Venetia, if you do marry him I'll have nothing more to do with you!"

"Well, I don't mean to marry him, so stop fidgeting yourself into a stew!"

He stirred restlessly, wincing a little. "I'd as lief live with Conway! No, by Jove, I'd *prefer* Conway to that bumptious, prosing piece of self-consequence that never crossed anything but a slug in his life! *He* to talk of giving me lessons—! Why, he has the worst seat and the worst

77

hands of any man in the county, and will go half a mile out of his way to find a gap in a hedge his horse might have taken in his stride! You'd take him for a pad-groom! And as for his curst presumption, walking in here to scold and moralize, you may tell him, Venetia, that I might take that from Conway, but from no one else!"

"Good God, he'll be demanding satisfaction of me next!" exclaimed Damerel. "Mr. Lanyon, allow me to offer you my most humble apologies!"

Aubrey turned his head on the pillow, and looked at him in some impatience and a good deal of suspicion. "Are you roasting me?"

"I shouldn't dare! I am begging your pardon for having had the curst presumption to scold you. How I can have had so little conduct—!"

"Gammon!" snapped Aubrey crossly, but with the hint of a reluctant grin. "All you said was that I was a damned young fool, and had more bottom than sense, and I don't care for *that!*"

"No, indeed! *Quite* unexceptionable!" approved Venetia. "I *knew* his lordship must have said everything that was kind and civil to have put you so much in charity with him!"

"Well, he didn't moralize over me!" retorted Aubrey, trying not to laugh. "But as for being in charity with him, when he let that Jack-pudding come up here—"

"Why, you ungrateful brat, who rescued you from him? If I hadn't come in with a hoaxing tale about your Nurse and a roll of lint he would be here yet! Take care I don't turn that into a true story! I will, if you don't stop taking snuff."

"Yes," Aubrey said, with a sharp sigh. "I beg pardon! I didn't mean—oh, lord, I don't know why the devil I lost my temper with such a gudgeon! I don't do so in general."

His angry flush began to subside. By the time Marston brought in a tray of cold chicken, and fruit, and tea he had recovered his equanimity; and although he rejected the chicken he was persuaded without much difficulty to drink some tea, and to eat a slice of bread-and-butter. Damerel went away when the nuncheon was brought in, but he came back just as Nurse was preparing to change the compress round Aubrey's ankle, and to anoint his several bruises with a sovereign remedy of her own, and invited Venetia to take a turn in the garden with him.

She was very willing, but hardly expected to escape without meeting opposition from Nurse. All Nurse said, however, was that she was not to go out without her hat, which was as surprising as her apparent failure to notice that Aubrey was looking exhausted. This was a circumstance which would ordinarily have drawn from her exclamations, rebukes, searching questions, and a comprehensive scold, but although she had eyed him narrowly she had made no comment.

For this abstention Aubrey had his host to thank, Damerel had waylaid Nurse on her way up to his room, and had told her of the disastrous results of Edward's visit.

Edward, as a respectable candidate for Venetia's hand, had hitherto enjoyed Nurse's favour, but no man who had caused Aubrey to suffer a set-back could hope to maintain his place in her esteem. When she learned that he had been reading Aubrey a lecture her eyes snapped with wrath, for reading lectures to Aubrey was a privilege she reserved exclusively to herself. Had she been present Edward should have had a piece of her mind to digest. She had not been present, but in her absence Damerel (though a sinner) had acted with a promptness and a propriety that won her instant approval. So deserving had he shown himself to be that she listened to his advice, and even agreed that it would be imprudent to mention the episode to Aubrey. Damerel thought that if he were to be left alone Aubrey would fall asleep, to which end he proposed to remove his sister from his side for a while. Perhaps she would like to stroll about the garden: what did Mrs. Priddy think?

Gratified, but suspicious, Nurse said that there was no need for Venetia to remain at the Priory any longer, at which Damerel smiled, and said: "None at all, but we could never persuade her to go home until she sees her brother on the mend again."

That was true, and since his lordship's manner was far more that of a civil but slightly bored host than of a ravisher of innocent females Nurse raised no further objection to his scheme.

"How in the world," demanded Venetia, accompanying Damerel down the stairs, "did you contrive to turn Nurse up so sweet?"

79

He glanced quizzingly down at her. "Did you think I couldn't?"

"Well, I know you can cajole *young* females—at least, you are generally believed to do so!—but I am persuaded it would never answer to try to flirt with Nurse."

"So flirting is all you give me credit for! You underrate my talents, Miss Lanyon! Having created a breach in her defences by showing solicitude for Aubrey and a proper respect for her judgment in all matters concerning him, I got within her outer walls at least by the exercise of devilish strategy. In fact, I sacrificed your worthy suitor, and stormed the fortifications over his fallen carcase. She was so pleased with me for having rid Aubrey of him that she not only allowed herself to be flummeried into giving her consent to this very perilous expedition, but even agreed *not* to raise any more dust by commenting on Aubrey's hagged look."

"Nurse was pleased with you for getting rid of Edward?" Venetia exclaimed incredulously. "But he is a prime favourite with her!"

"*Is* he? Well, if he has sufficient address (which I doubt), he may succeed in winning back to that position, but not, if she is to be believed, until she has rung a rare peal over him! And certainly not until Aubrey has left the shelter of my roof: I'll see to that! A truly estimable young man—and one with whom I find I have nothing in common. I gave him leave to come and go as he chooses— and mean to contrive, by judicious fanning of the flames of your admirable Nurse's wrath, to ensure that he doesn't avail himself of my *carte blanche*. I regret infinitely, Miss Lanyon, but I find that a taste of your worthy suitor constitutes a surfeit!"

"Well, you need not say it as though you supposed *I* wished him to come!" said Venetia indignantly. "I was never more thankful for anything than the chance that brought you into the room at just that moment!"

"Chance, indeed! I came for no other purpose than to remove him before he had driven Aubrey into a raging fever!"

"You shouldn't have permitted him to come up at all," said Venetia severely.

"I know I shouldn't. Unfortunately I said he might do so before I had his measure. By the time Imber came to conduct him upstairs, however, I had it!"

She laughed, but said in rather a worried voice: "I am afraid Aubrey was more hurt by that fall than I had thought. He doesn't like Edward, but I never knew him to fly out at him before."

"Perhaps he has never before encountered him after a bad shakeup and a sleepless night," suggested Damerel, holding open the door for her to pass into the garden. "To judge by the very improving discourse with which he favoured me, he said precisely what anyone with a grain of tact would have left unsaid."

"Yes, he did. As though he had been Aubrey's father!"

"Or his elder brother. He appears to think himself that already, for he thanked me for what he called my kindness to Aubrey."

"*He* thanked you—? Now, *that*," said Venetia, her eyes kindling, "is coming it very much too strong! In fact, it is a great piece of impertinence, for the only person who ever said I should marry him was my father, and he can't possibly suppose that I should be guided by Papa's wishes! Well, it is my own fault for having allowed him to suppose that when my brother Conway returns I shall accept him. I *did* tell him it was no such thing, but he didn't believe me, and *now* see what comes of it!"

"From what I have seen of that young man I should think persuading him to believe anything he did not choose to believe a labour of Hercules," he remarked.

"Yes, but the truth is that I didn't try very hard to convince him," she said frankly.

"Are you telling me that you ever entertained for as long as five minutes the thought of accepting such a clod-pole?" he demanded. "Good God, the fellow's a dead bore!"

"He is, of course, but there's no saying he wouldn't be a good husband, for he is very kind, and honourable, and—and respectable, which I believe are excellent qualities in a husband."

"No doubt! But not in *your* husband!"

"No, I believe we should tease one another to death. The thing was, you see, that because he was Papa's god-son Papa permitted him to visit us, and so we grew to know him very well, and when he wished to marry me I did wonder (though it was not at all what I wanted) whether perhaps it might not be better for me to do so than to grow into an old maid, hanging on Conway's sleeve. However, if Aubrey dislikes him as much as *that* it won't do. Oh dear, you have allowed your garden to grow into a wilderness! Only look at those rose-trees! They can't have been pruned for years!"

"Very likely not. Shall I set a man on to attend to them? I will, if it would please you."

She laughed. "Not at this season! But later I wish you will: it might be such a delightful garden! Where are you taking me?"

"Down to the stream. There's a seat in the shade, and we can watch the trout rising."

"Oh, yes, let us do that! Have you fished the stream this year? Aubrey once caught a three-pounder in it."

"Oh, he did, did he?"

"Yes, but he wasn't poaching, I assure you! Croyde gave him leave—he does so every year. You don't fish it yourself, after all!"

"*Now* I know why I've had such poor sport each time I've taken my rod out! What a couple you are! First my blackberries, and now my trout!" he said.

The laughing devil was in his eyes, but she was not looking at him, and replied without a trace of embarrassment: "What a long time ago that seems!"

"And how angry you were!"

"I should rather think I was! Well, of all the abominable things to have done!"

"*I* didn't find it so!"

She turned her head at that, looking up at him in a considering way, as though she were trying to read the answer to a problem in his face. "No, I suppose not. How very odd, to be sure!"

"What is?"

She walked on, her brow a little furrowed. "Wishing to kiss someone you never saw before in your life. It seems quite madbrained to me, besides showing a sad want of particularity." She added charitably: "However, I daresay it is one of those peculiarities of gentlemen even of the first respectability which one cannot hope to understand, so I don't refine too much upon it."

He gave one of his sudden shouts of laughter. "Oh, not of the *first* respectability!"

They had emerged by this time from the rose-garden through an archway cut in the hedge on to the undulating lawns which ran down to the stream. Venetia paused, exclaiming: "Ah, this is a delightful prospect! Looking at the Priory from the other side of the river, one can't tell that you have that distant view. I have never been here before."

"I've seldom been here myself. But I prefer the nearer prospect."

"Do you? Just green trees?"

"No, a green girl. That is why I've remained here. Had you forgotten?"

"I don't think I am green. It's true I only know what I've read in books, but I've read a great many books—and I think you are *flirting* with me."

"Alas, no! only trying to flirt with you!"

"Well, I wish you will not. I conjecture that you came into Yorkshire to ruralize. Isn't that what they call it, when you find yourself *cleaned-out?*"

"*Not* so very green!" he said, laughing. "That's it, fair fatality!"

"If but one half the stories told about you are true you must be *very* expensive," she observed reflectively. "Do you indeed keep your own horses on all the main post-roads?"

"I had need to be a Dives to do that! Only on the Brighton and Newmarket roads, I fear. What other stories do they tell of me? Or are they unrepeatable?"

She allowed him to guide her to a stone bench, under an elm tree, and sat down on it, clasping her hands loosely in her lap. "Oh, no! None that were told me, of course." She turned her face towards him, her eyes brimming with mischief. "It was always *We could an if we would* whenever we tried—Conway and I—to discover why you were the Wicked Baron. That was our name for you! But no one would tell us, so we were obliged to resort to imagination. You wouldn't believe the crimes we saddled you with! Nothing short of piracy would do for us until Conway, who was always less romantic than I, decided that that must be impossible. I would then have turned you into a highwayman, but even that wouldn't do for him. He said you had probably killed someone in a duel, and had been forced to flee the country."

He had been listening to her in amusement, but at that his expression altered. He was still smiling, but not pleasantly, and although he spoke lightly there was a hard note in his voice. "But how acute of Conway! I did kill someone, though not in a duel. My father."

She was deeply shocked, and demanded: "Who said that to you?" Then, as he merely shrugged, she said: "It was an infamous thing to have said! Idiotish, too!"

"Far from it. The news of my elopement caused him to suffer a stroke, from which he never recovered. Didn't you know that?"

"Everyone knows it! And also that he died nearly three years later, of a second stroke. Were you accountable for *that?* To be sure, it was unfortunate you didn't know he was likely to suffer a stroke, and so were the unwitting cause of it, but if you think he would not have succumbed to it sooner or later you can know very little about the matter! My father had a stroke too: *his* was fatal. It was not brought about by any shock, and it couldn't have been averted." She laid an impulsive hand on one of his, saying earnestly: "I *assure* you!"

He looked at her, queerly smiling, but whether he mocked himself or her she could not tell. "It doesn't keep me awake o'nights, my dear. Not much love was lost between us at the best of times."

"I didn't love mine either. In fact, I disliked him. You can't think how comfortable it is to be able to say that and not fear to be told that I cannot mean it, or that it was my duty to love him! Such nonsense, when he never pretended to care a button for any one of us!"

"Yours seems to have given you little reason to love him, certainly," he remarked. "Honesty compels me to say, however, that mine had a poor bargain in his only son."

"Well, if I had an only son—or a dozen sons, for that matter!—I would find something better to do for him when he was in a scrape than cast him off!" declared Venetia. "Would not *you?*"

"Oh, lord, yes! Who am I to throw stones? I might even make a push to stop him getting into the scrape—though if he were to be half as infatuated as I was I daresay I should fail," he said reflectively.

After a short pause, during which he seemed to her to be looking back across the years, and with no great pleasure, she ventured to ask: "Did she die?"

His eyes came back to her face, a little startled. "Who?

Sophia? Not that I know of. What put that into your head?"

"Only that no one seems to know—and you didn't marry her—did you?"

"Oh, no!" He saw the troubled look, and grimaced. "You want to know why, do you? Well, if such ancient history interests you, she was not, at the time of Vobster's death, living under my protection. Oh, don't look so dismayed!"

"Not dismayed—not that!" she stammered.

"Ah, you feel compassionate? Wasted, my dear! Our mutual passion was violent while it lasted, but soon wore itself out. Fortunately we were saved from dwindling into a state of mutual boredom by the timely appearance on our scene of an accomplished Venetian."

"An accomplished Venetian!"

"Oh, of the first stare! Handsome, too, and all in print. Air and address were quite beyond my touch!"

"And fortune?" she interpolated.

"That, too. It enabled him to indulge the nattiest of whims! He drove and rode only gray horses, never wore any but black coats, and always, summer or winter, with a white camellia in his buttonhole."

"Good God, what a quiz! How could she—Lady Sophia—have liked him?"

"Oh, make no mistake! he was a charming fellow! Besides, poor girl, she had become so devilish bored! Who could blame her for preferring an experienced Tulip to the callow tuft I was in those days? For the life of me I can't conceive how she contrived to bear with my ardours and jealousies for as long as she did. There were no bounds to my folly: if you can picture Aubrey tail over top in love, I imagine I must have been in much the same style. Chuckfull of scholarship, and with no more commonsense than to bore her to screaming point with classical allusions! I even tried to teach her a little Latin, but the only lesson she learned of me was the art of elopement. She put that into practice before we had reached the stage of murdering one another—for which piece of prudence I've lived to thank her. She had her reward, too, for Vobster was so obliging as to break his neck before custom had staled her variety, and her Venetian was induced to marry her. I daresay she threatened to leave him, and he may well have despaired of finding another who would have blended so admirably with his taste for

85

black and white. She had a milky complexion and black hair—raven's wing black!—and eyes so dark as to *appear* black at least. A little plump beauty! I'm told she was never afterwards seen abroad except in white gowns and black cloaks, and I'll swear the effect must have been prodigious!"

The note of derision was marked, but she was not deceived by it. Unable to trust her voice she said nothing, and afraid of showing in her face the indignation that swelled within her she kept her eyes lowered. She made the rather horrifying discovery that the slim fingers of a lady could curl into claws, and quickly straightened them. But perhaps she had not done so quickly enough; or perhaps her silence betrayed her; for after a moment Damerel said, more derisively still: "Did you fancy a tragedy to lie behind me? Nothing so romantic, I fear: it was a farce—not one of the ingredients lacking, down to the inevitable heroic meeting at dawn, with both combatants coming off scatheless—for which I am heartily obliged to my rival! He added superb marksmanship to his other accomplishments, and might have put a bullet through me at double the range, I daresay. In fact, he deloped—fired in the air!"

He had told her now as much as she would ever wish to know. He might jeer at the memory of his younger self, but as keenly as though she had been the sufferer did she feel the wound a light woman and a practised man-of-the-town had dealt his pride. She had brothers, and knew that in his pride a boy was most vulnerable. She thought she could see him quite clearly as he must have been: surely a fine young man, tall, straight, and big-shouldered as he was now, but with a face unlined, and eyes full of eagerness, not boredom. He must have been rash, ardent, and perhaps he had been desperately in earnest. Experience had made him a cynic, but he had not been cynical in his fiery youth. He had not then, she knew, been able even to smile at his own folly.

Everything he had done since he had seen himself as a laughing-stock (and she neither knew nor cared to what depths he might have sunk) she perceived to be part of a pattern made inevitable by a wanton's betrayal. Had they supposed, his righteous parents, that he would return to enact the role of the prodigal son? They should have known better! He might have returned, wedded to his wanton, outfacing the censorious, not, though he ruined

86

himself past recovery, as a cuckolded lover. Ishmael his family had declared him to be, and Ishmael he had chosen to remain, taking a perverse pleasure, she guessed, in providing the interested with rich evidence of his depravity. And all for a little, plump, black-eyed slut, older than himself, whose marriage-ring and noble degree hid the soul of a courtesan!

"Too bad, wasn't it?" Damerel said. "Instead of dying heroically for love I was left disconsolate—though not, I must admit, for long!"

She raised her eyes at that, and said warmly: "I am excessively glad to hear that, and I do *hope* your next mistress was entertaining as well as pretty!"

The sneer vanished from his face; the smile that lit his eyes was one of pure amusement. "A charming little lady-bird!" he assured her.

"Good! What a fortunate escape you had, to be sure! I daresay it may not have occurred to you, but I have little doubt that by this time Lady Sophia has grown sadly fat. They do, you know, little plump women! I believe the Italians use a great deal of oil in their cookery, too, which would be *fatal!* I only wish she may not be quite gross!" She added, as his shoulders began to shake: "You may laugh, but I assure you it's more than likely. What's more, if your father had warned you of it, instead of behaving in a very foolish and extravagant way, exactly like a Shakespearian father, it would have been very much more to the purpose! Pray, what good did it do old Capulet to fly into a ridiculous passion? Or Lear, or Hermia's absurd father! But perhaps Lord Damerel was not addicted to Shakespeare?"

His head was down on his hands; he gasped: "It seems he cannot have been!"

Recollecting herself, she said apologetically: "I shouldn't have said that. It is quite the worst of my bad habits—Aubrey's too! We say precisely what we happen to be thinking, without pausing to reflect. I beg your pardon!"

He raised his head, still choking with laughter, and said: "Oh, no, no! *Sweet Mind, then speak your-self...!*"

She wrinkled her brow, and then directed a look of enquiry at him.

"What, lurched, O well-read Miss Lanyon?" he said

provocatively. "It was written by Ben Jonson, of another Venetia. I turned it up last night, after you had left me."

"No, is it indeed so?" she exclaimed, surprised and pleased. "I never heard it before! In fact, I didn't know there had been any poems written to a Venetia. What was she like?"

"Like yourself, if John Aubrey is to be believed: *a beautiful desirable creature!*"

Quite unmoved by this tribute, she replied seriously: "I wish you won't fall into flowery commonplace! It makes you sound like a would-be beau at the York Assemblies!"

"You little wretch!" he exclaimed.

"That's much better—between friends!" she approved, laughing at him.

"So you think I'm offering you Spanish coin, do you? I can't imagine why you should, for you know how beautiful you are! You told me so!"

"I?" she gasped. "I never said such a thing!"

"But you did! You were picking blackberries at the time—my blackberries!"

"*Oh!* Well, that was only to give you a set-down!" she said, blushing a little.

"Good God, girl, and you said you had a mirror!"

"So I have, and it tells me that I am well-enough. I believe I take after my mother in some degree—at least, Nurse told me once, when I was indulging a fit of vanity, that I should never be equal to her."

"She was mistaken."

"Oh, did you know her?" she asked quickly. "She died when I was only ten years old, you know, and I can scarcely remember her. We saw so little of her: she and Papa were always away, and her likeness was never taken. Or, if it was, Papa destroyed it when she died. He could not bear even to hear her name spoken—forbade the least mention of her! And no one ever did mention her at Undershaw, except Nurse, on that one occasion. I think it an odd way of showing one's devotion, but then he *was* odd. Do I resemble her at all?"

"I suppose some might think so. Her features—as I recall—were more perfect than yours, but your hair is a richer gold, your eyes a deeper blue, and your smile is by far the sweeter."

"Oh dear, now you are back in your nonsensical vein! You cannot possibly remember at this distance of time how blue her eyes were, or how gold her hair, so stop hoaxing me!"

"Yes, ma'am," he said meekly. "I had far rather talk of *your* eyes, or even of your pretty lips, which you quite wrongly described as *indifferent red*."

"I cannot conceive," she interrupted, with some severity, "why you will persist in recalling an episode which you would do better to forget!"

"Can't you?" He put out his hand, and took her chin in his long fingers, tilting it up. "Perhaps to remind you, my dear, that although I am obliged at this present to behave with all the propriety of a host it's only a veneer— and God knows why I should tell you so!"

She removed his hand, but said with a chuckle: "I don't think your notion of propriety would *take* in the first circles! And furthermore, my dear friend, it is high time you stopped trying to make everyone believe you are much blacker than you have been painted. That's a habit you fell into when you were young and foolish, and *perfectly* understandable in the circumstances. Though also very like Conway, when he used to boast to me of the shocking pranks he played at Eton. Banbury stories, most of them."

"Thank you! But I have never done that: there has been no need for Banbury stories. With what improbable virtues are you trying to endow me? An exquisite sensibility? Delicacy of principle?"

"Oh, no, nothing of that nature!" she replied, getting up. "I allow you all the vices you choose to claim—indeed, I know you for a gamester, and a shocking rake, and a man of sadly unsteady character!—but I'm not so green that I don't recognize in you one virtue at least, and one quality."

"What, is *that* all? How disappointing! What are they?"

"A well-informed mind, and a great deal of kindness," she said, laying her hand on his arm, and beginning to stroll with him back to the house.

Edward Yardley returned to Netherfold in a mood of dissatisfaction but with no apprehension that Damerel might prove to be his rival. He had not liked him, and could perceive nothing either in his manners or his appearance that might reasonably be supposed to take Venetia's fancy. Punctilious himself in every expression of civility, Edward considered that Damerel's easy carelessness was unbecoming in a man of rank; while his rather abrupt way of talking could only disgust. As for his appearance, it was no great thing, afterall: his figure was good, but his countenance was harsh, with features by no means regular, and a swarthy complexion; and there was nothing particularly modish about his raiment. Females, Edward believed, were often dazzled by an air of fashion; and had Damerel worn yellow pantaloons, Hessians of mirror-like gloss, a tightly waisted coat, a monstrous neckcloth, exaggerated shirt-points, rings on his fingers, and fobs dangling at his waist it might have occurred to Edward that he was a dangerous fellow. But Damerel wore a plain riding-coat and buckskin breeches, quite a modest neckcloth, and no other ornaments than a heavy signet ring, and a quizzing-glass: he was no Pink of fashion; he was not even a very down-the-road looking man, though report made him a first-rate driver: quite a top-sawyer, in fact. Edward, who had expected a Corinthian, was disposed to rate him pretty cheap: more squeak than wool, he thought, remembering some of the exotic stories which had filtered back to Yorkshire. He flattered himself that he had never believed the half of them: that noble Roman lady, for instance, who was said to have deserted husband and children to cruise with Damerel in the Mediterranean aboard the yacht which he had had the effrontery to christen *Corinth*; or the dazzling high-flyer, whose meteoric progress across liberated Europe under his protection had been rendered memorable by the quantities of fresh rose-petals he had caused to be strewn on the floors of her various apartments, and the sea of pink champagne provided for her refreshment. Edward, solemnly trying to compute the cost of this extravagant freak, had certainly not believed that tale; and now that he had met Damerel face to face he wholly discredited it. He had not really been afraid that a sensible female would succumb to the lure of such trumpery magnificence, but when he rode away from the Priory there was an unacknowledged relief in his breast. Damerel might try to make Venetia the object of his gallantry (though he had not seemed to be much impressed by her beauty), but Edward, who knew his own worth, could not feel that he stood in danger of being eclipsed in her eyes by such a brusque, bracket-faced fellow. Females were naturally lacking in judgment, but Edward considered Venetia's understanding to be superior to that of the generality of her sex, and although she had met few men, the three whom she knew well—her father, Conway, and himself—must have provided her with a standard of manners and propriety by which she had enough sense to measure Damerel.

The worst feature of the affair, Edward decided, was the damage that would be done to her reputation if her daily visits to the Priory became known; and this possibility teased him so much that he told his mother the whole story.

A meek little woman, Mrs. Yardley, so colourless that no one would have suspected how deep and jealous was her adoration of her only child. Her skin was parchment, with thin, bloodless lips, and eyes of a shallow, faded blue; and her hair, which she wore neatly banded under a widow's cap, was of an indeterminate hue, between sand and gray. She was not a talker, and she listened to Edward without comment, and almost without expression. Only when he told her, a trifle too casually, that Venetia was visiting Aubrey daily at the Priory did a flicker of emotion show in her eyes, and then it was no more than a darting, lizard-like look, gone as quickly as it had appeared. He did not notice it, but went on explaining all the circumstances to her, not asking her opinion, but rather instructing her, as his habit was. When he paused she said: "Yes," in the flat voice that offered no clue to her thoughts. In general he would have been perfectly satisfied with this meagre response, but on this occasion he found it insufficient, because in telling her how unexceptionable it was for Venetia to visit the Priory when she had Nurse for a chaperon he had been arguing against his own convictions, and wanted reassurance.

"One couldn't expect her not to do so," he said. "You know how devoted she is to Aubrey!"

"Yes, indeed. He is very much obliged to her. I have always said so," she replied.

"Oh, as to that—! I should be glad to think it, but he is one who takes all for granted. The thing is that there is no harm in Venetia's visiting him."

"Oh, no!"

"Under the circumstances, you know, and with Nurse there—and it is not as if she were a young girl, after all. I do not see that there is anything in it to set people talking, do you?"

"Oh, no! I am persuaded they will not."

"Of course, I cannot like her being thrown into acquaintanceship with such a man, but I fancy I made it plain to him how the matter stands—just hinted him away, you know, in case he had some notion of trying to attach her. Not that I have any great apprehension of it: I believe I am a pretty good judge, and it did not seem to me that he was at all struck by her."

"I expect she is not in his style."

His countenance lightened. "No, very likely she is not! No doubt he is bored by virtuous females. And *she*, you know, doesn't want for sense. Under that sportive playfulness she has true delicacy of character, and the tone of her mind is too nice to allow of her encouraging his lordship in any encroaching fancy."

"Oh, no! I am persuaded she would not do so."

He looked relieved; but after fidgeting with the blind-cord for a few moments he said in a vexed tone: "It is an awkward situation, however! I should be excessively reluctant to be obliged to be on terms of intimacy with Lord Damerel, even if we lived near enough to the Priory to make frequent visits to his house possible. In that event

I should feel it to be my duty, perhaps—But to be riding thirty miles every day—there and back, you know!—is out of the question."

"Oh, yes, dear, you are very right! I don't think you should go there at all. I daresay Aubrey will be well enough to go home in a day or two, and it is not to be supposed that Lord Damerel will continue at the Priory for long. He never does so, does he?"

This placid view of the matter did much to allay his uneasiness; and he was further relieved by the discovery, on the following evening, when he escorted his mother to a dinner-party at Ebbersley, that his hostess regarded it as a matter of no particular moment.

In this he was mistaken, but Lady Denny did not like sententious young men, and she took care to conceal the dismay she had felt ever since Sir John had broken the news to her. Sir John had had it from Damerel, whom he had encountered in Thirsk, and had communicated it to her in the most casual way imaginable. When she had exclaimed in horror, he had stared at her with his brows raised; and when she had demanded what was to be done he had first required her to explain what she meant, and then, when he had received a pretty forthright explanation, he had continued to stare at her for a full minute, as though she had been talking gibberish; and had finally retired again into his book with a dryly uttered recommendation to her not to be so foolish.

But it was not she who was foolish, as she immediately pointed out to him. He might say what he liked (a generous permission of which he showed no disposition to avail himself) but she knew very well what was likely to come of throwing an inexperienced girl into the arms of a notorious libertine. There was no need for Sir John to tell her that Damerel would make no improper advances to a lady in Venetia's situation: very likely he would not—though there could be no guessing what a man with such a reputation might do—but, pray, had he considered how extremely likely it was that he would induce the poor innocent to fall in love with him, and then go off, leaving her with a broken heart?

Thus straitly questioned Sir John said No, he had not considered this. He did not think Venetia a poor innocent: she was five-and-twenty, a woman of superior sense, and calm disposition; and in his opinion she was very well able to take care of herself. He added that he trusted that her ladyship would refrain alike from making a great piece of work about nothing, and from meddling in what was no concern of hers.

This stupid sort of indifference could not be allowed to pass without rebuke; but after Lady Denny had dealt with it as it deserved she began to think it might contain perhaps a grain of truth, and that nothing very dreadful, after all, would come of Venetia's acquaintance with a rake. In any event she did not mean to encourage Edward Yardley's pretensions, so when he said, in a grave tone, that doubtless she had heard of Aubrey's unfortunate accident she made light of the whole affair, even going so far as to say that she was thankful that a happy chance had taken Damerel to the spot, and that he had had the good sense to send immediately for Dr. Bentworth.

This was going too far, and Edward's countenance assumed an expression of severity. Lady Denny turned from him to greet Mr. and Mrs. Trayne, but the scion of the house, observing his lengthening upper lip, eyed him scornfully, and uttered in a sinister undervoice: "No need to put yourself about: Miss Lanyon knows she can rely on *me!*"

Since propriety forbade him to give young Mr. Denny a set-down Edward was obliged to pretend he had not heard this speech. His temper was ruffled, and his doubts returned; but during the course of the evening he derived a certain amount of consolation from Miss Denny, who confided to him that she sincerely pitied Venetia. In her eyes, which were filled with the sentimental vision of a blonde and handsome soldier, Damerel was horridly ugly, quite old, and not at all conversable. "Poor Venetia!" said gentle Clara. "She will be worn-out with civility, and bored to tears, I daresay! He hardly spoke to Emily or me when Papa brought him home once, and to Mama he talked the merest commonplace. That will never do for Venetia, will it? For she is so lively, and she is used, besides, to converse with you, and Aubrey. You are all of you so very clever!"

Edward was pleased, but he replied with an indulgent smile at feminine simplicity: "I hope my conversation is *rational*, but I don't pretend to scholarship, you know. In that line I fear I am quite outshone by Aubrey!"

"Of course he is very bookish, isn't he?" agreed Clara.

"That is how *I* should describe him, I own, but Lord Damerel, I apprehend, considers his intellect to be remarkable."

"Does he? Yes, I expect it is, for I am sure I don't understand above half the things he says. But you are very well-informed too, and you express yourself much more clearly, so that I am able to follow your arguments, even if I am not clever enough to take part in them."

He had too great a regard for the truth to reassure her on this head, but he told her very kindly that he had no great liking for blue-stockings, and amused her with a paradox: that the *wisest* of her sex did not aspire to be *clever*. She laughed heartily at this, exclaiming: "There! That is precisely what I meant when I said that Venetia would find Lord Damerel a bore! I daresay he would never think of saying anything as witty!"

So, while Lady Denny was trying to persuade herself that Venetia had too much commonsense to fall in love with a rake, Edward went home cheered by the vision of her being bored by Damerel's lack of conversation. And since neither of them set eyes on her for a considerable period this peaceful complacency remained undisturbed by any knowledge of the glow of happiness which was giving an added bloom to the lovely Miss Lanyon's beauty.

Aubrey remained for ten days at the Priory, and even the weather conspired to make them halcyon days for his sister. There was only one wet and chilly day in all the ten, and then the gold of the mellowing landscape crept into the house, for Damerel had a fire kindled in the library, and its light, flickering over the tooled backs of the volumes that lined the room from wainscot to cornice, made them glow like turning leaves. He carried Aubrey down, and laid him on a sofa, and they played three-handed cribbage, pored over books of engravings, discovered rare treasures on the crowded shelves, and argued hotly on every imaginable subject, from the *esse* of material things to the proposition that a black horse with no spot of white upon him must necessarily be full of mischief and misfortunes. Then Damerel brought out his Grecian sketch-book, setting Aubrey in a blaze; and

Nurse, established by the window with her interminable tatting, looked over her spectacles at the group by the fire, and was satisfied. The Lanyons had their heads together over a book of pictures, Venetia on the floor beside the sofa, and Aubrey explaining them to her, and the pair of them looking up every now and then at his lordship and pelting him with questions as he stood leaning over the back of the sofa. Nurse saw them as children, and Damerel as an adult person, like herself good-naturedly allowing them to tease him with their questions. Perhaps it was wrong to let them form the habit of such easy intercourse with a sinner, but although the Scriptures warned one that the wicked were like a troubled sea, whose waters cast up mire and dirt, they also yielded some pretty pungent warnings against backbiters and unrighteous witnesses. *Every neighbour will walk with slanders*, said the prophet Jeremiah, and one had only to cast an eye over the district to know how true that was. Nurse was much inclined to think that his lordship had been a victim of false report. If anyone were to ask her, all she could say was that she took people as she found them, and she had found him just what any gentleman of his age ought to be, behaving more like an uncle to Miss Venetia and Mr. Aubrey than a seducer, and understanding much better than most gentlemen how hard a task it was to take care of such a headstrong couple. If it was true that he had once run off with a married lady—well, it had happened a great many years ago, and Nurse knew what to think of such ladies: hussies, that's what they were, and heaven help the young man they got their claws into! And if it were true that there had been nasty goings-on at the Priory only one year ago—well, the Scriptures adjured the wicked to forsake his way, and perhaps that was what his lordship had done. There were no nasty goings-on now, that was all Nurse knew.

It had taken Damerel three days to bring Nurse round his thumb: cutting a wheedle, Aubrey called it, when he had almost brought the trap down on him by going into stifled laughter at hearing Damerel agreeing with her that it was of no use to muffle all the furniture in holland covers, and hope to keep the moth away by such means; that indeed the chairs and the tables and the cabinets in the disused saloons ought to be well polished; that he would be only too glad if the whole house could be set in order. That had been quite enough for Nurse, never permitted at Undershaw to encroach on Mrs. Gurnard's ground. But Mrs. Imber was a feckless, humble creature, who did as she was bid, and was grateful for advice and instruction. Nurse, who had gone to the Priory with the utmost reluctance, was enjoying herself enormously, and did not mean to leave it until, with the assistance of the Imbers, the gardener's wife, and a Stout Girl from the village, she had (as Imber resentfully phrased it) turned the house out of doors. For the first time since the days when she had reigned over the nursery at Undershaw she held undisputed sway, and just as soon as she had decided that there was nothing to be feared from Damerel she relaxed her vigilance, and trotted about the great, rambling house, harrying her slaves, so deeply absorbed in housewifery that she neither noticed the glow in Venetia's eyes nor suspected that when she supposed her to have gone home she was with Damerel, perhaps sitting in the garden, perhaps strolling along the river-bank, or allowing him to escort her back to Undershaw by the longest possible route.

Damerel's groom and his valet both knew, but Nidd did not tell Nurse how many hours were spent in the Priory stables by Venetia's mare, or the cob she drove in the gig; and Marston did not tell her, when she asked him if Venetia had gone home, that she had done so in his master's company.

Nidd thought it was a queer set-out, but when he said as much to Marston he won no other response than a blank stare. But Marston thought it queer too, because it wasn't like his lordship to throw out lures to innocent young ladies, much less sit in their pockets. He was loose in the haft, but not as loose as that. Or maybe he was too fly to the time of day to meddle with virgins of quality: Marston did not know, but he did know that in all the years he had served his lordship he had never seen him dangling after such a lady as Miss Lanyon. He had never seen him behave to any of his loves as he was behaving to her, either; or known him to stay so quiet and sober. He had not been as much as half-sprung since the day he carried Mr. Aubrey into the house, and that was a sure sign that he wasn't bored, or in one of his black moods.

He wasn't even restless, yet he hadn't meant to remain at the Priory above a day or two. They had been on their way to Lord Flavell's shooting-lodge, but they were not going there after all: he had told Marston that he had written to cry off. Were they going back to London, then, when Mr. Aubrey had left the Priory? His lordship had made no plans, but thought he should remain in Yorkshire for a while.

It might be that he was amusing himself with a new kind of flirtation, but in any other man it would have looked remarkably like courtship. If that was it, Marston wondered whether Miss Lanyon knew what sort of a life his lordship had led, and what that elder brother of hers would have to say to such a match.

He would have been shocked had he guessed how much Venetia knew, and how much she was entertained by some of Damerel's more repeatable adventures; and he would have been considerably astonished had he known on what terms of easy camaraderie this very odd couple stood.

They were fast friends: a stranger might have supposed them to be related, so frank and unceremonious were their interchanges, and so far removed from mere dalliance. Accepting, as a matter of tactics in the game few knew better than he how to play, the role of *fidus Achates* thrust upon him, Damerel soon found himself advising Venetia on knotty problems arising out of her stewardship of her elder brother's estates, or discussing with her the peculiar difficulties presented by her younger brother's apparent determination to allow his powerful mind to wear out his frail constitution. He gave her better advice than he had ever put into practice, but told her bluntly that there was little she could do to divert Aubrey from his devouring passion. "He has been too much alone. If it had been possible to have sent him to Eton he would no doubt have formed friendships there, but as it is he seems to have only two friends: yourself, and his old grinder—this parson he talks about: I forget his name. What he needs is to rub shoulders with springs of his own age and tastes—and to overcome his dread of being pitied or despised."

She gave him a speaking glance. "Do you know, you are the first person ever to have perceived that he hates

98

his lameness in *that* way? Even Dr. Bentworth doesn't properly understand, and I can only guess, because he doesn't speak of it. But he has talked to you, hasn't he? He told me the thing you said to him—that if you were offered the choice between a splendid body or a splendid mind you would choose the mind, because it would long outlast the body. I know he was a good deal struck, for he would not else have told me about it, and I was so grateful I could have embraced you!"

"By all means!" he said promptly. "Do!"

She laughed, but shook her head. "No, I'm not funning. You see, it was exactly the right thing to have said, and that he talked to you at all about it showed me how much he likes you. In general, you know, he is very stiff with strangers, and when people like Lady Denny enquire after his health, or Edward helps him to get up out of his chair, he becomes quite *rigid* with fury."

"I should imagine he might! Is that what that gudgeon does?"

"Yes, and say what I will to him he persists! It is all kindness, I know, but—"

"Much that graceless scamp cares for kindness!"

"That's what I told Edward, but he thought it nonsensical. And your sort of kindness he *does* care for: I don't mean entering into what interests him only, but roasting him, and calling him rude names, and threatening to do the most brutal things to him if he won't swallow that horrid valerian!"

"Is that your notion of kindness?" he asked, in some amusement.

"Yes, and yours too, or you wouldn't do it. I expect it makes Aubrey feel that he is just the same as any other boy—or, at any rate, that you don't care a rush for his lame leg. It has done him a great deal of good to be with you—more good than I could ever do him, because I'm only a female. A sister, too, which makes it even harder."

"You are a good sister. I hope you may have your reward—but strongly doubt it. Don't let him hurt you! He's fond of you, but he's an egotist, my dear."

"Oh, I know that!" she said cheerfully. "But he's not as bad as Papa was, I assure you, *or* Conway! Aubrey would very likely put himself out to oblige me, if he ever thought of it, but Papa would not, and as for Conway, I don't think he *can* think of anyone but himself!"

It was such remarks as this, delivered perfectly seriously, that kept him in a state of chuckling enjoyment, and made him call her his dear delight. She accepted the title with equanimity, but told him to take care not to say it within tongue-shot of Nurse. "For it would be very mortifying for you to see your cajolery wasted, besides destroying all our comfort."

"I'll lay you odds she wouldn't come the ugly. She believes me to be in a state of grace."

"No, only *approaching* it—and that was merely because you supported her against Imber! You may not know it, but you suffered a set-back yesterday, when you wouldn't permit her to have the carpet in the library taken up to be beaten. She began to say things about the ungodly again, and Aubrey swears she told him that one sinner destroys much good."

"Since then, however, I have expressed my admiration of her tatting, and my credit is now high with her!" he retorted.

"I wish it might be high enough for her to give it to you! There must be *miles* of it, for she has been tatting ever since I can remember, and very rarely gives any of it away. The dreadful thing is that she means it for whichever of us is the first to be married. The most lowering reflection!"

"Perhaps," he said thoughtfully, "I had better not make my credit *too* high! What do you advise? Shall I hold an orgy, ill-use Aubrey, or—just call you my dear delight within her hearing?"

"That would lower your credit too much. Tell her that when you gave her to understand thay you came into Yorkshire to redress your tenants' grievances—which I am very sure you did, for who else would have put such a preposterous notion into her head?—it was nothing but a fudge! Perhaps you had better not tell her, however, that you came because of that thing at Tattersall's, for she thinks racing very ungodly!"

"*What* thing at Tattersall's?" he demanded. "I haven't yet been floored by the hammer, if that's what you mean!"

"No, no! At least, I don't know what it signifies, but it wasn't *that!* Conway spoke of it once—oh, *Black Monday!*"

"Settling-day! No, I won't tell her that. I am always more or less in Dun territory, but this visit of mine isn't an attempt to shoot the crow! I am escaping from my aunts."

"Why, what are they doing to you? Are you roasting me?"

"Not at all. They are bent on re-establishing me. There are three of 'em, and they are all antidotes. Two are unmarried, and live together—one's fubsy-faced, and t'other's a squeeze-crab; and the eldest is a widow, and the most intimidating female you ever beheld. She lives in a mausoleum in Grosvenor Square, rarely stirs out of it, but holds receptions, very like the Queen's Drawing-Rooms. She's clutch-fisted, dresses like a quiz, has neither wit nor amiability, and yet by means unknown to me—unless it be by force of character, and I'll allow she has that!—has persuaded the *ton* that she is a second Lady Cork, to whose *salons* it is an honour to be invited."

"She sounds very disagreeable!"

"She *is* very disagreeable. A veritable dragon!"

"But why does she wish to re-establish you?"

"Oh, for two reasons! The first is that however black my sins may be I'm the head of the family, a circumstance by which she sets great store; and the second is that having issued a royal command to my cousin Alfred, who is also my heir, to present himself in Grosvenor Square for inspection, she made the shocking discovery that he was a member of the dandy-set—indeed, the pinkest of Pinks, a swell of the first stare! Not having the least guess that the old lady holds every Bond Street beau in the utmost abhorrence, the silly pigeon rigged himself out as fine as fivepence, and trotted round to Grosvenor Square looking precise to a pin: Inexpressibles of the most delicate shade of primrose, coat by Stulz, Hessians by Hoby, hat—the *Bang-up*—by Baxter, neckcloth—the Oriental, which is remarkable for its height—by himself. Add to all this a Barcelona handkerchief, a buttonhole as large as a cabbage, a strong aroma of Circassian hair-oil, the deportment of a dancing-master, and a lisp it took him years to bring to perfection, and you will perceive that Alfred is not just in the ordinary style!"

"I wish I might see him!" she said, laughing. "Did *you*, or is this make-believe?"

"Certainly not! I didn't see him, but what he didn't describe to me my aunt did. Poor fellow! he was only bent on doing the pretty, but all his hopes were cut up! The breach was to have been healed—oh, I didn't mention, did I, that my aunts had quarrelled with his mother? I believe she offended them on the occasion of my uncle's obsequies, but as I was not present I don't know what crime she committed, though I wouldn't bet against the chance that she didn't render proper respect to their consequence. In any event, Alfred obeyed my Aunt Augusta's summons, confident that the exercise of a little address—coupled, of course, with his exquisite appearance—would decide not only her, but my Aunts Jane and Eliza as well, to make him their heir—which is a matter of very much more interest to him than his being *my* heir, *pour cause!* But alas! faced with the choice between a fop and a rip they preferred the rip—or they would, if I'd be conformable!"

"Behave with propriety?"

"Worse! Marry a butter-toothed female with a pug-nose and a deplorable figure!"

She laughed. "Well, I daresay they wish you to be married, because that would be the most respectable thing you *could* do, and also, of course, on account of children, so that your cousin would be quite cut out—but I see no reason why she should be pug-nosed, or butter-toothed!"

"Nor I, but she's both, I promise you. What's more, she's been an ape-leader for ten years at least. Do you wonder that I fled?"

"No, but I *do* wonder that your aunts should have been so gooseish as to have proposed such a match to you! They must be quite addle-brained to suppose that you would look twice at any but the most ravishing females, for you have been used only to be in love with beauties for years and years! It is most unreasonable to expect people to change their habits in the twinkling of an eye."

"Very true!" he agreed, admirably preserving his countenance. "And Miss Amelia Ubley's eye has as much twinkle as may be seen in the eye of a fish."

"Then on *no* account must you offer for her!" she said earnestly. "I am excessively sorry for her, poor thing, but she would be far happier as an old maid than as your wife!

I shouldn't wonder at it if you made off with someone else before the bride-visits had all been paid, and only think how mortifying for her. How came your aunts to hit upon such an unsuitable female for you? They must have a great deal more hair than wit!"

His lips twitched, but he replied gravely: "I fancy they consider me to be past the age of romantic indiscretions. My Aunt Eliza, at all events, tells me that it is now time I *settled-down*. She drew for me a very moving picture of the advantages of becoming regularly established."

"I can see she did. It moved you all the way to Yorkshire! Pray, what are Miss Ubley's virtues?"

"Well—virtue!"

"That won't do in the least. Not if you mean that she's strait-laced, and she sounds to me as if she would be."

"That's what she both sounded and looked like to me. However, my aunts informed me that besides being of the first respectability she has superior sense, propriety of taste, and can be trusted to behave always just as she ought. Her fortune is as good as I have any right to expect; and I must remember that if she were not above thirty years of age, and an antidote, neither she nor her parents would entertain my proposal for a minute."

"What moonshine!" exclaimed Venetia indignantly.

There was a good deal of the sneer in the half smile he threw her. "No, that was true enough. I imagine I must rank high on the list of ineligible bachelors—which has this advantage: that there is no need for me to take care lest I fall a prey to a match-making mama. It is she who warns her daughter that if she should chance to find herself in company with me she must keep a proper distance."

"Then you do go to parties?" she asked. "I am very ignorant about society, and what you call the *ton*, and when you said you were a social outcast I thought perhaps it meant you didn't go into polite circles at all."

"Oh, it isn't as bad as that!" he assured her. "I'm certainly not invited to run tame in houses where the daughters are of marriageable age, and I can think of nothing more unlikely than of being permitted to cross the sacred threshold of Almack's—unless, of course, I reformed my way of life, married Miss Ubley, and was sponsored by my Aunt Augusta into that holy of holies—but only the very highest sticklers go to the length of cutting my acquaintance! If anything were wanting to make me flee from Miss Ubley's vicinity it would be the dread of being dragged into precisely those circles from which I am most happy to be excluded!"

"I must say, from all Lady Denny has told me I should suppose the Assemblies at Almack's to be amazingly dull," she observed. "When I was a girl it used to be the top of ambition to attend them, but I think now that I should find them insipid."

But this he would not allow. He scolded her for speaking of her girlhood as a thing of the past, and said: "When your brother comes home you'll go on a visit to that aunt of yours, and you will enjoy yourself very much. You will be gay to dissipation, my dear delight, going to all the fashionable squeezes, breaking a great many hearts, and finding every day too short for all the pleasuring you wish to cram into it."

"Oh, when that day dawns I shall very likely be in my dotage!" she retorted.

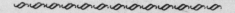

Edward Yardley, secure in the knowledge of his own worth, might rate Damerel cheap, but young Mr. Denny, by no means so self-confident as he tried to appear, recognized in him both a model and a menace. Like Edward, he rode over to the Priory to enquire how Aubrey did; unlike Edward, he no sooner clapped eyes on Damerel than he became possessed of a deep and envious hatred.

Imber ushered him into the library, where Damerel and Aubrey were playing chess, with Venetia seated on a stool by the sofa, watching the game. This cosy scene afforded him no pleasure at all; and when Damerel rose, and he saw how tall he was, with what careless grace he moved, and how much lazy mockery lurked in his eyes, he knew that his sisters had grossly misled him: they had thought his lordship dull and middleaged; Oswald perceived at one glance that he was a dangerous marauder.

His visit was not of long duration, but it lasted for quite long enough to enable him to see on what easy terms of intimacy the Lanyons were with their host. They were not only perfectly at home in his house, but they behaved as though they had known him all their lives. Aubrey even called him Jasper; and although Venetia did not go to such outrageous lengths as that she used no formality when she spoke to him. As for Damerel, Nurse might think his attitude avuncular, but Oswald, his perception sharpened by jealousy, was not deceived. When his eyes rested on Venetia there was an expression in them very far from avuncular, and when he addressed her there was a caress in his voice. Oswald glared at him, and tried in vain to think of some adroit way of getting himself and Venetia out of the room. None occurred to him, so he was forced to employ direct tactics, saying rather throatily, and with reddening cheeks, as he shook hands in farewell: "May I speak to you for a moment?"

"Yes, of course you may!" Venetia replied kindly. "What is it?"

"Don't be gooseish, m'dear!" recommended Aubrey, inspiring Oswald with a longing to wring his neck.

"You have a message for her from Lady Denny, which you would prefer to deliver in private, haven't you?" suggested Damerel helpfully, but with an unholy twinkle.

In a nobler age one could have answered such impertinence by jostling his lordship as he stood holding open the door, so that he would have been obliged to demand a meeting. Or did one, even in that age, refrain from jostling people in doorways when a lady was present?

Before he had decided this point he had followed Venetia into the hall, and Damerel had shut the door on them. He uttered tensely: "If I know myself, there will be a reckoning between us one day!"

Venetia was accustomed to his dramatic outbursts, but she found this one surprising. "Between us?" she asked. "Now, what in the world have I done to put you in a miff, Oswald?"

"You! Never!" he declared. "It's no matter—I should not have spoken, but there are times when a man's feelings may not be suppressed!" He eyed her hungrily. "Only give me the right to call you mine!" he invited.

"What, is that why you wanted to talk to me alone?" she exclaimed. "Of all the ridiculous starts—! I wish you will believe that when I say No, No is precisely what I mean! How can you be so absurd? I am more than six years older than you! Besides, you don't really wish to marry me in the least!"

"N-not *w-wish* to marry you?" he stammered, thunderstruck.

Her eyes danced. "Of course you don't. Only think what a bore it would be to be obliged to settle down as a respectably married man before you have had a great many adventures!"

He had never before looked at the matter in this light, and he could not help feeling secretly rather struck. However, he was too earnest in the pursuit of his calf-love to acknowledge the good sense of her observation. "I ask no greater felicity than to win you!" he assured her.

Her lips quivered irresistibly, but she managed to keep from laughing. Only if one was very cruel did one laugh at a boy in the throes of his first love. She said: "Well, it is excessively kind of you, Oswald, and indeed I am flattered, even if I can't return your sentiments. Pray don't talk about it any more! Tell me, is Lady Denny well? And your sisters?"

He ignored this, but said in a gloomy tone: "I shall say no more, except to beg you to believe that my devotion is unalterable. I didn't come for that purpose, but to tell you that you may count upon me. *I* am not afraid of a consequential prig, like Yardley! *I* am not afraid of going against etiquette—in fact I don't care a straw for such stuff, but then, *I* have seen more of the world than—"

"Oswald, what *are* you talking about?" Venetia interrupted. "If it is Edward who has put you in this passion—"

"That skirter!" he ejaculated, with awful contempt. "Let him busy himself with his roots, and his cattle: it is all he is fit for!"

"Well, you must own that he is very fit for that!" said Venetia reasonably. "I daresay his land is in better heart than any you would find in half a day's journey. Even Powick, you know, doesn't disdain his advice when it is a matter of farming."

"I didn't come to talk about Yardley!" said Oswald. "I merely mentioned—well, it's no odds! Venetia, if that fellow should offer you an insult, *send me word!*"

"*Edward* offer me—Oh, good God, do you mean Damerel? You absurd creature, go home, and try if you can be interested in roots, or cattle, or anything you please as long as it is not me! Lord Damerel is our very good friend, and it vexes me very much to hear you talk in that foolish style about him."

"You are too innocent, too divinely pure, to be able to read the mind of a man of his stamp," he told her, his brow darkling. "He may deceive Yardley, but I knew him for what he is the instant I clapped eyes on him! A Man of the Town! It is a-a desecration to think of his so much as touching your hand! When I saw how he looked at you—By God, I was within ames-ace of planting him a facer!"

At that she did laugh. "I wish I might see you make the attempt! No, no, don't make me any more protestations! What you have said, you know, is the outside of enough! Indeed, it is most improper! Lord Damerel is a gentleman, and if he were not, I am not so innocent that I'm not very well able to take care of myself. Besides, it's all fustian! Your papa would say you were enacting a Cheltenham tragedy, and that's precisely what you *are* doing! If you choose to play-act it is quite your own concern, but you shall not do so at my expense. Goodbye!— Give my fond love to Lady Denny, if you please, and tell her that Aubrey is going on so well that I hope Dr. Bentworth will say, when next he visits him, that I may take him home."

With these bracing words, she nodded dismissal, and went back into the library before he could form any adequate answer.

He rode home to Ebbersley a prey to mixed emotions, his self-esteem so much wounded by Venetia's parting speech that for at least a mile he was occupied with extensive plans for renouncing his allegiance, abjuring the society of her sex or perhaps cultivating it in a very cynical way, causing its members to attempt by every art known to them to discover what dark secret was hidden behind his marble front and sardonic sneer. This scheme, though not unattractive, was attended, however, by certain difficulties, chief amongst them being the degradingly conventional standard of behaviour prevailing at Ebbersley, and a marked tendency on Lady Denny's part to press a Blue Pill on anyone suffering torment of the soul. Nor did the North Riding afford the right background for a mysterious and sinister stranger. For one thing the country in which Ebbersley was situated was sparsely populated; and for another, he was too well-known to the gentry there, and even in York itself, to have the least hope of figuring as a stranger, much less a mysterious and sinister stranger. He would be obliged to attend the Assemblies, with his mama and his elder sister, because if he refused to go they would raise such a dust that the matter would come to Papa's ears, and nothing was more certain than that Papa would command him to do as he was bid. As for standing romantically aloof at these functions, and declining all the offers of the Master of Ceremonies to present him to desirable patrons, there was no hope of doing that either. The ballroom would be full of girls with whom he had been acquainted all his life, and if he did not ask them to stand up with him, Mama would not only scold him for incivility but was quite capable of excusing his behavior to her friends on the score that he was bilious, or had the toothache. In a better regulated world the father of any young gentleman no longer at school would be compelled to supply his son with an allowance sufficiently handsome to enable him to set up for himself in London, and cut a dash in the fashionable world; but the world was ill-regulated, and Sir John so unenlightened a parent that he thought (and stated) that after sending his heir on a visit to his uncle in Jamaica he had a right to expect him to settle down at home, and learn all the business of managing the considerable estate which would, in due course, be his own.

Fortunately, before he had dwelled for long on his bleak prospects Oswald remembered that in one of the nobler ages that had preceded the present drab century knights and troubadours had apparently been inspired by scornful mistresses to perform heroic deeds. The more disdainful, not to say insulting, the ladies, the greater their devotion had been, and the greater their ultimate triumph when their exploits had convinced the favoured fair ones of their true qualities.

The vision thus conjured up of winning Venetia's admiration was agreeable enough to make him abandon any immediate intention of becoming a misogynist, and brought him back to Ebbersley in a sunny mood, which lasted until the recollection that whatever glory the future might hold in store the present was overcast by the shadow of Lord Damerel unluckily coincided with a request from Sir John that he should change his Belcher handkerchief for a more seemly neckcloth before sitting down to dinner with his mother and sisters. These two circumstances naturally threw him back into gloom, and had it not been for the happy chance that had made Lady Denny order a turkey with truffles for dinner his low spirits would have made it impossible for him to fancy anything that was set before him. However, his fainting appetite revived at sight of the turkey, and he made a very good meal. A tendency to relapse into brooding melancholy was frustrated by Sir John, who challenged him to a game of billiards. He had not heart for such idle sport, but in the excitement of beating his father, running out with the longest break he had ever achieved, he forgot his troubles, and became animated and loquacious, particularly when describing his glorious victory to his mama and his sisters later in the evening. Such was his elation that he went up to bed much inclined to think that he had allowed himself to be needlessly disturbed by Lord Damerel's menacing presence in the district. As soon as Aubrey returned to Undershaw his lordship would no doubt leave the Priory, and be no more seen in Yorkshire for at least a twelvemonth.

Two days later the welcome tidings that Aubrey was at home again came in a note from Venetia to Lady Denny; and, as though Providence had suddenly decided to bestow favours upon young Mr. Denny with a lavish hand, this was almost immediately followed by the news that Edward Yardley, who had been feeling poorly for several days, was in bed, with the chickenpox. Oswald, seeing his path clear of rivals, rode over to Undershaw to make good his opportunity, and arrived there to find Venetia walking in the shrubbery with Damerel.

It was a severe blow, and still worse was the discovery that Damerel had no immediate intention of leaving the Priory. His ostensible reason for prolonging his stay there might be, as his bailiff hoped, to repair some of the ravages which years of neglect had wrought upon his lands, but his real object was insolently patent: Venetia was his quarry, and he was hunting her remorselessly, intent, Oswald was persuaded, on nothing but the gratification of his own evanescent lust. Report credited him with hundreds of lovely victims, and Oswald saw no reason to doubt either its truth, or that no twinge of compunction and no respect for public opinion would check him in the pursuit of his desire. A man whose career had begun with the abduction of a married lady of quality, and included traffic with such trollops as had turned the Priory into a bordello only a year before, was capable of committing any infamy and Damerel had shown years ago how little he cared for public opinion. If his past actions had not betrayed him, one glance at him, Oswald thought, was enough to inform any but such clods as Edward Yardley that he was a reckless freebooter, who would not hesitate, if he could ensnare her in his toils, to bear Venetia off to foreign lands, just as he had borne off his first mistress; and later, when her sweetness no longer pleased his jaded palate, to abandon her. He had already more than half bewitched her; as those who talked comfortably of her calm good sense must surely realize if they did but see the look in her eyes when she raised them to his. Such smiling eyes they were, but never had they smiled so tenderly as they did now. For a disturbing moment Oswald felt that she had suddenly become quite a different person and was reminded of some story, probably one of Aubrey's, about a statue brought to life by some goddess or other. Not that Venetia had ever been at all like a statue, but underlying her liveliness she had been cool and rational, affectionate but never blinded by affection, regarding even Aubrey, whom she loved, with amusement, and offering to no one else more than friendliness. This temperate disposition pleased Edward Yardley, because he believed it to be a sign of modesty and good breeding; it had pleased Oswald too, but on quite another count: it transformed her from the prettiest lady in the district into a princess of fairyland whose hand could only be won by the bravest and noblest and most handsome of her many suitors. In his more romantic moments Oswald had frequently imagined himself in this role, either kindling love in her by wit and charm, or by rescuing her (while Edward Yardley stood by, not daring to risk his life in the attempt) from burning houses, runaway steeds, or brutal ravishers. In these dreams she at once fell passionately in love with him, Edward slunk away, shamed and discomfited, and all who had previously treated young Mr. Denny as though he had been a schoolboy thereafter looked up to him in awe, spoke of him with respect, and thought it an honour to entertain him at their parties. They were agreeable dreams, but only dreams. He had never expected them to come true. It was extremely unlikely that Venetia would be trapped in a blazing house, and still more unlikely that in such a contingency he would be at hand to rescue her; she was an accomplished horse-woman; and the sudden intrusion into the peaceful and law-abiding neighbourhood of a brutal ravisher had seemed, even in the dream, to be rather too far-fetched.

Yet that was what had happened, for Damerel, though

111

not precisely corresponding to the creature of the dream, was certainly a ravisher. But instead of seeking protection from his loathsome advances Venetia, utterly deceived by the mask he wore, was positively encouraging them. Like the statue, she had been brought to life, but not by a goddess, not even by her heroic young adorer, but by her would-be seducer.

As he watched the meeting of their eyes, and listened to their light, funning talk, some hardly recognized perception of the affinity between them made Oswald feel so sick with hatred of Damerel that he could not bring himself to respond to any of the attempts made to draw him into the conversation, but answered only in a manner that sounded boorish even in his own ears, and soon took an abrupt leave of his hostess. This hatred, so much more intense than the dislike he felt for Edward Yardley, or the jealousy with which he would have regarded any other rival, sprang from his unacknowledged recognition in Damerel of the romantic figure he himself longed to become. He was the devil-may-care outlaw who roamed the world, dark secrets locked in his bosom, nameless crimes littering his past; and had Venetia not existed Oswald would almost certainly have copied his style of dress, his unconventional manners, and would have done his best to have acquired his air of unconcerned assurance. These were all things which a youth chafing against the restrictions of a polite age admired: but when he met them in a rival he bitterly resented them, because he knew himself to be at a disadvantage, playing the *Corsair's* role in front of the *Corsair* himself.

Had Sir John been privileged to know what emotions were raging in his son's breast he might have regretted his decision not to send him up to Oxford or Cambridge, but he was too well accustomed to Oswald's moodiness to attach any significance to what he thought a fit of the sullens, arising out of the boy's calf-love for Venetia. He merely trusted that this phase would be as short-lived as it was violent, and paid no other heed to it than to recommend Oswald not to make a fool of himself. Lady Denny would have shown more sympathy had she had the leisure to study him, but Edward Yardley, not content (she said) with contracting chicken-pox himself, had communicated it to Anne, the youngest of the Denny family, whom he had met out walking with the rest of the school-room party on the very day he later took to his bed. He was so kind as to indulge her with a ride on his horse, for he was very fond of children, and that was when the mischief must have been done. Anne had lost no time in passing it on to her next sister, Louisa, and to the nursery-maid; and Lady Denny lived in hourly expectation of seeing a rash break out on Elizabeth as well, and had no eyes for her only son's spiritual ills.

Having no particular friend in the neighbourhood, and despising the company of his sisters, Oswald had very little to do but brood over the disastrous effect of Damerel's continued residence at the Priory; and it was not long before he had persuaded himself that before Damerel's arrival on the scene he had been in a fair way to winning Venetia. He recalled every instance of her past kindness, and by magnifying these, minimizing her occasional snubs, and contrasting both with her present attitude he soon became convinced that Damerel had deliberately cut him out, and occupied most of his waking hours trying to think how best to win her back.

He had arrived at no satisfactory answer to this problem when he became an unsuspected witness of an episode which brought all his festering resentment to a head. Having ridden to Undershaw on the flimsiest excuse, the first sight to meet his eyes, as he dismounted in the stableyard, was Damerel's big gray being led into the stable by Aubrey's groom. Fingle said, with the hint of a dour smile, that his lordship had ridden in not five minutes earlier, bringing with him a book for Mr. Aubrey. Oswald vouchsafed no reply to this, but he looked so thunderous that the hinted smile grew into a broad grin, as Fingle watched him stride off towards the house.

Ribble, opening the door to Oswald, rather thought that Miss Venetia was in the garden; but when Oswald asked ominously after Lord Damerel he shook his head. He had not seen his lordship that day.

"Oh, indeed?" said Oswald. "Yet his horse is in the stables!"

Ribble did not seem to be surprised, but he looked a little worried, and replied after a moment's pause that his lordship very often walked up to the house through the garden, entering it by way of the door Sir Francis had had made in the ante-room which led to his library. Ribble added, as Oswald gave a snort of indignation: "His lordship frequently brings Mr. Aubrey books, sir, and stays talking with him for quite a while—about his studies, I understand."

There was a troubled note in his voice, but Oswald did not hear it, or realize that Ribble was trying to reassure himself. He thought him a gullible old fool, and turned on his heel, saying that if Miss Lanyon was in the garden he would look for her there, since he had come to visit her, not Mr. Aubrey. He strode off, seething with anger. Even Edward Yardley, who had been permitted to enter Undershaw for years, never did so except through the front door, yet this buccaneering stranger was apparently free to walk in whenever he chose, and without the least ceremony.

There was no sign of Venetia either in the garden or the shrubbery, but just as Oswald was about to follow Damerel's example, and go into the house through the ante-room door, he bethought him of the orchard. She was not there either, but Oswald heard her voice, raised in laughing protest, and coming from an old barn, which had once housed cattle, and had been used of late years as a storehouse for the gardener's tools and a workshop for Aubrey, who occasionally amused himself with carpentry. There was no mistaking the voice that spoke in answer to hers, and when he heard it Oswald fell into such a fever of suspicious rage that without so much as considering the impropriety of his conduct he went stealthily up to the barn, and paused beside the big double-door, out of sight, but well within hearing of whatever might be going on inside the barn. A cautious peep revealed no glimpse of Venetia, but it did show him Damerel's backview, as he stood in the middle of the floor with his head tilted back, as though Venetia were some way above him.

This puzzled Oswald, unfamiliar with the barn, but, in fact, Venetia had mounted by means of a short ladder into the open loft which covered half the barn, to rescue a litter of hungry kittens, whose parent, absent from her duties for a day and a night, was presumed to have met with an untimely end. Damerel had located her by the simple expedient of calling her name, and had been in-

114

stantly summoned to her assistance. "For that ladder is not at all steady, and I had as lief not climb down it carrying the kittens," she explained.

"Is that what you have in that basket?" he asked. "How the deuce did they get up there?"

"Oh, they were born here! It's the kitchen-cat: she always comes here to have her kittens. But I'm afraid something must have happened to her this time, and the poor little things are starving. That I *cannot* bear, though if they can't lap yet I suppose they will have to be drowned."

"Well, that fate will be preferable to starvation," he said. "Hand over the orphans!"

She knelt on the edge of the loft, and reached the basket down to his upstretched hand. He grasped it, and set it down on the floor, and looked up again, rather wickedly smiling. "Shall I hold the ladder for you, my dear delight?"

"Certainly not!" said Venetia firmly.

"But you said it was unsteady!"

"It is, but if I could come up it I can come down it."

"Do!" he said cordially. "I shall have a stiff neck if I'm obliged to converse with you at that level. Or shall I come up?"

She looked down at him with laughter in her eyes, but said severely: "No, you will *not* come up! Odious creature! You know very well I can't come down that ladder while you stand there watching me!"

"Can't you? Oh, that's easily remedied!" he retorted, and removed the ladder, and laid it down.

It was this impish action which drew the protest from her which Oswald heard. "Fiend!" she said. "Do put it back, and go away!"

"Not I!" he replied, grinning up at her.

"But it is most unchivalrous of you!" she complained.

"No, no, on the contrary! The ladder is clearly unsafe."

She tried to make her mouth prim, but failed. "Do you know, my dear friend, that besides being most ungentlemanly you are shockingly untruthful?" she enquired.

"No, am I? Do *you* know how entrancing your face is when seen from this angle?"

She was still kneeling, resting her hands on the edge of the loft, and looking directly down at him. "Upside down? Well, of all the unhandsome things to say! Now, Damerel, will you be so very obliging as to stop behaving like a horrid schoolboy, and set the ladder up again?"

"No, dear torment, I will not!"

"Wretch! Do you mean to keep me a prisoner up here? I warn you, the instant your back is turned I shall jump down!"

"Oh, don't wait for that! Jump now!" he said. "I'll catch you!"

"Thank you, I had as lief not be caught!"

"What, are you afraid I'll let you fall? Little craven! And you a Lanyon of Undershaw!"

"Pooh!" said Venetia, making a face at him. She then altered her position, drew her flounced skirt tightly round her ankles, swung her legs over the edge of the loft, and slid down into Damerel's arms.

He caught her, and held her in a strong grip, but whatever might have been his next intention was frustrated by Oswald, who at this moment revealed his presence, starting forward with a wrathful imprecation.

His purpose was to command Damerel to unhand Venetia, and, if necessary, to wrest her from his grasp, but as Damerel, without showing the smallest sign of surprise, much less of discomfiture, had already set her on her feet, and released her, there was no need to do this. He was unable, on the spur of the moment, to think of anything else to say, and stood glaring at Damerel instead.

Venetia had been startled by his sudden appearance, but she betrayed no more discomfiture than Damerel, merely saying: "Oh, is it you, Oswald? What a pity you should not have arrived just one minute earlier! You might have played the knight-errant to my damsel in distress. Would you believe it?—finding me engaged on an errand of mercy up there, Lord Damerel threacherously removed the ladder!" She laughed at Damerel. "In fact, you remind me strongly of my brother Conway!"

"And worse you cannot say of anyone, I collect!" His lazy yet penetrating gaze rested on Oswald's flushed countenance for a moment. There was a good deal of amusement in his eyes, but some not unkindly understanding as well. "I shall go and seek comfort of Aubrey," he said.

Oswald, standing in the doorway still, hesitated, but

after a moment's indecision, moved reluctantly aside to allow him to pass.

Venetia bent to pick up her basket. "I must take these unfortunate kittens up to the house. At least their eyes are open, so perhaps they will be able to lap."

"Wait!" uttered Oswald.

She looked enquiringly at him. "Why?"

"I must and will speak to you! That fellow—!"

"If you mean Damerel, as I conclude you must, I wish you will say so, and not call him *that fellow!* It is not at all becoming in you to speak in such a way of a man so much older than you are, and particularly when you've no cause to do so."

"No cause!" he exclaimed hotly. "When I find him here, f-forcing his improper attentions upon you!"

"Fiddle!"

He flushed. "How can you say that? When I saw—and heard—"

"You neither saw nor heard him forcing anything upon me. And you won't," she added calmly.

"You don't understand! You—"

"Yes I do."

He stared at her, rather nonplussed. "You know nothing about men of his stamp! You've let him hoax you with his curst cajolery into thinking he means no harm, but if you knew what his reputation is—"

"Well, I do know, better than you, I daresay."

"The fellow's a rake! No female is safe with him!"

She gave an involuntary laugh. "How very dreadful! Oswald, do, pray, stop talking fustian! You can't think how absurd it is!"

"It's *true!*" he said earnestly.

"Yes, it's true that he's a rake, but I assure you there is no need to worry over my safety. I expect you mean it kindly, but I shall be very much obliged to you if you will say no more!"

He stared at her fiercely, and ejaculated: "You're bewitched!"

The oddest little smile flickered in her eyes. "Am I? Well, never mind! It is quite my own affair, after all. Now I must take these kittens up to the kitchen, and see what can be done for them."

He resolutely barred the way. "You shall hear me!" he

declared. "You hope to fob me off, but it will not do!"

She looked at him for a measuring instant, and then sat down on Aubrey's bench, and folded her hands in her lap, saying, with resignation: "Very well: say what you wish, if nothing else will do for you!"

It was not very encouraging, but there was so much that Oswald was burning to say, and had, indeed, several times rehearsed, that he was not at all daunted. He plunged, stammering a little, into a speech that began as worldly-wise advice from a man of wide experience to a singularly innocent and gullible girl, but very soon changed to a diatribe against Damerel, and an impassioned declaration of undying love for Venetia. It lasted for quite a considerable time, and Venetia made no attempt to check it. Nor did she laugh, for it was apparent to her that her youthful admirer had worked himself into a dangerously over-wrought condition, and believed himself to be far more violently in love with her than she had guessed. She gathered from one or two of his utterances that he was persuaded that she had been in a fair way to returning his love until Damerel had cast his spell over her; and although she knew that she had never given him the smallest encouragement she was vexed with herself for not having perceived that a turbulent boy with a yearning for romance and a marked turn for dramatizing himself was quite capable of exaggerating mere elder-sisterly kindness into something far warmer. So she let him talk himself out uninterrupted, thinking that since so many wild and tangled emotions had been festering in his bosom he would probably feel much better for being allowed to pour them forth, and even a little ashamed of himself. However, when he reached the stage of urging her to marry him, and outlining in a rapture of fantasy, a wedding-trip that included the more remote parts of the globe, and would, at the lowest computation, take quite three years to accomplish, she judged it to be time to intervene, and to administer a damper calculated to make him fall out of love with her as suddenly as he had fallen into it.

As soon as he paused, eagerly scanning her face to see what effect his eloquence had had on her, she rose, and said, as she picked up her basket: "Well, now, Oswald, if you have finished talking nonsense, you may listen to what I have to say, and after that you may go home! You have been quite amazingly impertinent, but I don't mean to scold you for that, because I can see that you've hoaxed yourself into thinking I was as good as promised to you before Damerel came to the Priory. How you can be so conceited as to suppose I should have a *tendre* for a boy not very much older than Aubrey I can't think! I wish you will try to cure yourself of make-believe, and learn to be a little more sensible! It seems to me that you imagine so much that it gets to be quite real to you, which leads you, you know, to say the most absurd things! Only consider, for instance, what would happen if I were as silly as you, and agreed to marry you! Do you soberly suppose that Sir John and Lady Denny would have nothing to say to such a ridiculous match?"

"Nothing they could say would turn me from my purpose!" he averred.

"Oh, wouldn't it?" she retorted. "We should just fly to the Border, I collect, since you're not of age, and be married over the anvil! I *should* cut a pretty figure! What next should we do? Set forth on this wonderful journey of yours?—which sounds to me excessively uncomfortable, and, indeed, would be more than uncomfortable, because we should soon find ourselves without a feather to fly with. Or have you bamboozled yourself into believing that Sir John will be so obliging as to put you in command of a handsome independence?" She paused, and could not help smiling at the sudden change in his expression. A baffled and angry scowl, which made him look like a thwarted schoolboy, was now being bent upon her, and seemed to indicate that he was already more than half out of love. She moved forward, saying: "You see how foolish it is, don't you? Don't let us say any more about it! When you are as old as I am I expect you will be very much in love, no play-acting, with a girl who is at this present sewing samplers in the schoolroom, and if you remember me at all, which you very likely won't, you'll wonder how you came to make such a cake of yourself! Go home now— and no more dangling after me, if you please!"

By this time Oswald was hating her quite as much as he had adored her, but not being prone in his most equable moods to consider what was the true state of his feelings he was quite incapable of performing this feat when a prey to emotion. In the jumble of hurt, and fury, and chagrin into which Venetia's cool mockery had plunged him he saw only one thing clearly, and that was that she looked on him as a schoolboy. He said in a voice that shook with anger: "You think I'm too young to love, do you? Well, you're *wrong!*"

With these bitter words, and before she had had time to realize his intention, he seized her, and managed, though not very expertly, to get his arms round her.

Venetia, more concerned for the unhappy kittens, which were very nearly tilted out of the basket by this sudden onslaught, than for herself, cried sharply: "Take care! You idiotish boy, let me go at once!"

But Oswald, who had never before held a girl in his arms, was in the grip of a novel and exciting sensation, and he hugged her rather more tightly, and kissed first her ear, then her eyebrow, and then her cheekbone in several dogged attempts to reach her lips. Between these assaults he said in a breathless, exultant voice: "A child, am I? *I'll* show you!"

"Oswald, *stop!* How *dare* you—oh, thank goodness!"

If Oswald wondered what had drawn this unexpected exclamation from her, or why she suddenly ceased struggling, he was not left for more than a very few seconds in doubt. A hand was thrust roughly into his neckband, and closed like a vice, nearly choking him, and its fellow grasped the seat of his riding-breeches; he was plucked bodily away from Venetia, jerked round, propelled irresistibly to the doorway, and sent sprawling through it.

9

Having disposed in this rough and ready fashion of Oswald, Damerel turned to direct a quizzical look at Venetia. "What the deuce have you been doing to cast the boy into this frenzy?" he enquired.

"You may well wonder!" she replied, very much incensed, and considerably dishevelled. "Trying to cure him of his silly fancy for me!"

"Oh, that was it, was it?" he said, amused. He glanced towards Oswald, who was picking himself up. "Well, you had best remain discreetly out of sight now, fair disaster, because if I know anything of the matter your hot-headed swain is about to make a spirited attempt to send me to grass."

"Oh, no, he is not!" declared Venetia, a martial light in her eye. "You may leave this to me, Damerel! In fact, I *order* you to do so!"

She swept past him, just as Oswald, having managed to overcome the effects of semi-strangulation, started towards Damerel with his fists clenched. Finding Venetia in his path, he was obliged to check himself, and before he could thrust her aside, which, in his blind rage, he had every intention of doing, she had spoken words that fell on him like a cold douche. "Are you now proposing to begin a vulgar brawl for my entertainment? I give you fair warning, Oswald, that if I have to endure any more of your unmannerly behaviour I shall tell your papa just what has occurred, and with what a total lack of good breeding or propriety you have conducted yourself! I am excessively reluctant to inflict such a mortification upon him, or to distress your mama, so if you wish to make me amends for your rudeness don't make it necessary for me to do so!"

Scarlet-faced, he stammered: "I'm sorry—it wasn't—I didn't mean—"

"Very well, you need say no more," she interrupted. "I shall not speak of it to anyone, and nor, you may be sure, will Lord Damerel. You had best go home now."

To his credit, he managed, though the effort nearly choked him, to swallow the various scathing retorts which rose to his tongue, and even to achieve a stiff bow. "Pray—pray accept my humble apologies, and believe that I shall not again trouble you, ma'am!" he said. He then turned his smouldering gaze on to Damerel, and suffered a slight lapse from his stateliness. "And as for *you*," he said fiercely, "I'll—" He gave a gasp, and ended on a note of paralysing formality: "Your lordship shall hear from me!"

He then executed another bow, and strode away.

"*Alas, poor Yorick!*" remarked Damerel. "My withers are slightly wrong, you know."

"Yes, so too are mine," Venetia agreed, a worried frown between her brows. "I can't but feel that I am to blame for not having given him a heavy set-down as soon as he began to dangle after me. If I had had the least notion that he was suffering from anything more than a fit of calf-love which would very soon wear itself out I would have done so, of course."

"He wasn't. Unless I am much mistaken, it's I who am responsible for today's outburst, not you. The silly young nodcock has been wanting to murder me from the moment he first clapped eyes on me."

She turned her eyes towards him. "Yes, he has. Oh dear, I do trust he won't do anything foolish!"

He smiled. "That's past praying for, but it isn't his own life he is planning to end! Don't look so concerned! From what I have seen of him I'd wager a handsome sum on the certainty that before he reaches Ebbersley the worst of his present pangs will be over, and he will be deriving great satisfaction from a vision of my lifeless corpse stretched on the ground—at a distance of twenty yards. Or even of his own. Lord, yes, of course his own! That would ensure a lifetime of remorse for you, my cruel fair, and for me the execration of all. I should be obliged to fly the country, and serve me right! Even my seconds would shun me, for if I didn't fire before the drop of the handkerchief, or something equally dastardly, you may

122

depend upon it that I should in some way or other cut a very contemptible figure, while *he* won their pity and admiration by his unshakeable calm and noble bearing."

She could not help laughing, but she said rather anxiously: "I know that's what he meant, when he said you should hear from him, but *surely* he wouldn't do anything as silly as that? For when he thinks it over—No, that's just what he *won't* do! If he sends you a challenge, *must* you accept it?"

"What, accept a challenge from a whelp who hasn't yet cut his milk teeth? No, you absurd girl! I most emphatically must *not!*"

"Well, thank goodness for that!" she said, relieved. "Not but what he deserves a sharp lesson! He very nearly made me drop these unfortunate kittens, mauling me about in that detestable way! There is *nothing* I dislike more!"

"I agree that he needs a lesson. I should rather suppose it to have been his first attempt. He ought, of course, to have got rid of the livestock," said Damerel, taking the basket out of her hand, and setting it down, "for while you were preoccupied with their safety what could he expect but a rebuff? Once they were disposed of he should have taken you in his arms, like *this*, and not as though he were a bear, bent on hugging you to death. Nor am I in favour of dabbing kisses all over a girl's face. If you cannot persuade her, by a ruse, to look up, you should make her do so, with a hand under her chin—*thus*, my dear delight!"

She had offered no resistance, and she lifted her face now without the urge of his hand. She was blushing a little, but she looked up into his eyes very willingly, her own shyly smiling.

He too was smiling, but as he stared down at her she saw the smile fade, and an intent, searching look take its place. He was still holding her, but he seemed to stiffen. She heard the sharp intake of his breath, and, the next instant, Aubrey's voice, shouting his name, and then she was no longer in his arms, and he had turned away to answer Aubrey's call. She looked doubtfully at him, for it had seemed to her that it had not been Aubrey's voice which had made him refrain from kissing her but some change in his own mind.

Aubrey came limping between the trees towards them. "What the deuce are you doing here?" he asked. "Ribble said you had been asking for me."

"Very true, but as he thought you were in the library and I knew you were not I abandoned the quest. I only wanted to give you Reid's *Intellectual Powers*, and I left it on your desk."

"Oh, good! Thank you! I was in the gunroom, as Ribble might have guessed, if he ever took the trouble to think. By the by, I found that passage: it *was* Virgil, but in the *Georgics*, not the fourth *Eclogue*. Come up to the house, and I'll show you!"

"I'll take your word for it. I can't stay now. I have an uneasy feeling, moreover, that if I linger I may be called upon to drown a litter of kittens and I prefer to leave that task to you!"

"Is that what brought you here?" enquired Aubrey, of his sister. "Yes, I remember now: you said something about it at breakfast, didn't you?" He cast a cursory glance at the orphans, and added: "Give 'em to Fingle: he'll drown 'em for you."

"For shame! Have you *no* sensibility?" Damerel said lightly. He held out his hand to Venetia. "I must go. He's right, you know: you'll never rear them!" He kept her hand in his for a moment, and then, as though yielding to compulsion, raised it to his lips and kissed it. Their eyes met only fleetingly, but she saw in his the answer to the question in her heart, and the tiny doubt that had disturbed her happiness vanished.

It struck Fingle, however, covertly observing Damerel as he saddled up for him, that his lordship was looking uncommonly grim. He had generally a pleasant word and a smile for anyone who performed a service for him, but he seemed to have nothing to say on this occasion beyond a curt Thank you when he took the bridle in his hand, and swung himself into the saddle. He did not forget to bestow his usual *douceur* upon Fingle, but no smile went with it: he seemed to be thinking of something else, and nothing so very agreeable either, to judge by the frown on his face, thought Fingle.

Damerel rode slowly back to the Priory, for a considerable part of the way with a slack rein, allowing the gray to walk. The frown did not lift from his brow: rather it deepened: and it was not until Crusader, startled by the sudden uprising of a pheasant, stopped dead, throwing up his head and snorting that he was jerked out of his abstraction. He admonished Crusader, but leaned forward to pat his neck as well, because he knew the fault was his. "Old fool!" he said. "Like your master—who is something worse than a fool. *Would she could make of me a saint, or I of her a sinner*—Who the devil wrote that? You don't know, and I've forgotten, and in any event it's of no consequence. For the first part it's too late, old friend, too late! And for the second—it was precisely my intention, and a rare moment this is to discover that if I could I would not! *Come* up!"

Crusader broke into a trot, and was kept to it, until, rounding a bend in the lane that brought the main gates of the Priory within view, Damerel saw a solitary horseman, walking his horse, and ejaculated: "Damn the boy!"

Young Mr. Denny, looking over his shoulder, braced himself, and wheeled about, and took up a position in the centre of the lane with the evident intention of disputing the right of way if his quarry should try to elude him. The set of his jaw was pugnacious, but he also looked to be suffering a considerable degree of embarrassment, which, indeed, he was.

Impetuosity had betrayed him into a false position from which he could see no way of extricating himself with credit. Leaving Undershaw on the crest of his fury he had indulged for a time in very much the sort of imaginings which Damerel had described to Venetia; but even such wrath as his could not be maintained at fever-heat for long. Thanks to Damerel's dawdling return to the Priory his had subsided into resentment some time before the gray horse came into sight, and for a full half hour he had been trying to make up his mind what to do, and without once allowing it to wander into the realm of fancy. From the moment when it occurred to him that the humiliation he had suffered was the direct result of his own misconduct the affair had been too serious for grandiose dreams. He suddenly perceived that Damerel had played the part he had imagined for himself: it was the villain who had rescued the lady from the hero. So appalling was this realization that for several minutes he could see no other solution to his troubles than instant flight from Yorkshire, and a future spent in obscurity, preferably at the other end of the world. His next and more rational impulse was to abandon his plan of challenging Damerel to a duel; and he had actually started for home when another hideous thought entered his head: he had addressed fatal words to Damerel, and if he did not make them good Damerel would believe that he had failed to do so because he was afraid. So he turned back again, because whatever else Damerel might say of him he was determined he should never be able to say that he had no more pluck than a dunghill cock. The challenge must be delivered, but try as he would Oswald could not recapture his eagerness. An uneasy suspicion that persons more familiar with the Code of Honour than himself would condemn his action as grossly improper nagged at him; and when he placed himself in Damerel's path he would have given everything he possessed to have been a hundred miles away.

Damerel pulled the gray up, and surveyed his youthful foe sardonically. "All that is needed to complete the picture is a mask and a pair of horse-pistols," he remarked.

"I have been waiting for you, my lord!" said Oswald, gritting his teeth.

"I see you have."

"I imagine your lordship must know why! I said—I told you that you should hear from me!"

"You did, but you've had time enough to think better of it. Try for a little wisdom, and go home!"

"Do you think I'm afraid of you?" Oswald demanded fiercely. "I'm not, my lord!"

"I can see no reason why you should be," said Damerel. "You must know that there's not the least possibility of my accepting a challenge from you."

Oswald flushed. "I know nothing of the sort! If you mean to say I'm unworthy of your sword I'll take leave to tell you, sir, that I'm as well-born as you!"

"Don't rant! How old are you?"

Oswald glared at him. There was a derisive gleam in the eyes which scanned him so indifferently, and it filled him with a primitive longing to smash his fist between them. "My age is of no consequence!" he snapped.

"On the contrary: it is of the first consequence."

"*Here* it may be! I don't regard that, and you need not

126

either! I have been about the world a little, and visted places where—" He stopped, suddenly recollecting that he was talking to a man who had traveled widely.

"If you have visited places where men of my years accept challenges from boys who might well be their sons you must have strayed into some pretty queer company," remarked Damerel.

"Well, anyway, I'm reckoned to be a fair shot!" said Oswald.

"You terrify me. On what grounds do you mean to issue this challenge?"

The angry young eyes held his for an instant longer, and then looked away.

"I won't press you for an answer," said Damerel.

"Wait!" Oswald blurted out, as Crusader moved forward. "You shan't fob me off like that! I know I ought not to have—I never meant—I don't know how I came to— But there was no need for *you* to—"

"Go on!" said Damerel encouragingly, as Oswald broke off. "No need for me to rescue Miss Lanyon from a situation which she was plainly not enjoying? Is that what you mean?"

"Damn you, no!" Oswald sought for words to express the hopeless tangle of his thoughts; none came to him, only the age-old cry of youth: "You don't understand!"

"You may ascribe the astonishing guard I have so far kept over my temper to the fact that I do," was the rather unexpected reply. "Patience, however, was never numbered amongst my few virtues, so the sooner we part the better. I am very sorry for you, but there's nothing I can do to help you recover from these pangs, and your inability to open your mouth without going off into rodomontade does rather alienate my sympathy, you know."

"I don't want your damned sympathy!" Oswald flung at him, intolerably stung. "*One* thing you can do, my lord! You can stop trying to give Venetia a slip on the shoulder!" He saw the flash in Damerel's eyes, and hurried on recklessly: "W-walking into her house as though it were your own, cajoling her with your man-of-the-town ways, c-cutting a wheedle with her because she's too innocent to know it's all a rig, and you're bamboozling her. T-talking to me as if *I* was the loose-screw! I m-may have lost my head but *I* mean honestly by her! And you needn't think I don't know it's uncivil to say things like this to you, because I do, and I don't care a rush, and if you choose to nab the rust you may do so—in fact, I hope you *will!*—And I don't care if you tell my father I've been uncivil to you *either!*"

Damerel had been looking a little ugly, but this sudden anticlimax dispelled his wrath, and made him laugh. "Oh, I won't proceed to such extreme measures as that!" he said. "If there were a horse-pond at hand—! But there isn't, and at least you've made me a speech without any high-flown bombast attached to it. But unless you have a fancy for eating your dinner with your plate on the mantelpiece for the next few days don't make me any more such speeches!"

Oswald gave a gasp of outrage. "Only dismount, and we'll try that!" he begged.

"My deluded youth, that is being *more childish valourous than manly wise*: I'm sure you're full of pluck, and equally sure that it would be bellows to mend with you in rather less than two minutes. I'm not a novice, you see. No, keep your mouth shut! It is now my turn to make a speech! It will be quite short, and, I trust, quite plain! I've borne with you because I haven't forgotten the agonies of first love, or what a fool *I* made of myself at your age; and also because I perfectly understand your desire to murder me. But when you have the infernal impudence to tell me I can stop trying to seduce Miss Lanyon you've gone very far beyond the line of what I'll take from you! Only her brother has the right to question my intentions. If he chooses to do it I'll answer him, but the only answer I have for you is contained in the toe of my boot!"

"Her brother isn't here!" Oswald retorted swiftly. "If he were it would be a different matter!"

"What the devil—Oh, you're talking of her elder brother, are you? I wasn't."

"*Aubrey?*" exclaimed Oswald incredulously. "That scrubby little ape? Much good he could do—even if he tried! What does he know about anything but his fusty classics? If he thought about it at all he wouldn't have the least notion what sort of a game you're playing!"

Damerel gathered up his bridle, saying dryly: "Don't despise him on that head! Neither have you the least notion."

"I know you don't mean marriage!" Oswald retorted.

Damerel looked at him for a moment, an oddly disquieting smile in his eyes. "Do you?" he said.

"Yes, by God I do!" As Crusader moved forward, Oswald wrenched his own horse round, staring after Damerel in sudden dismay. He stammered: *"Marriage?* You and Venetia? She wouldn't— she *couldn't!"*

There was undisguised revulsion in his voice, but the only response it drew from Damerel was a laugh, as he turned Crusader in through the gateway of the Priory, and cantered away down the long weed-grown avenue.

Oswald could hardly have been more shocked had Damerel openly declared the most dishonourable of intentions. He was left a prey to doubt and disbelief, and with no other course open to him than to ride tamely home to Ebbersley. It was a long, dull ride, and with only the most humiliating reflections to occupy his mind he very soon became so sunk in gloom that not even the knowledge that his last words at least had flicked Damerel on the raw would have done much to elevate his spirits.

Marston, gathering up Damerel's discarded coat and breeches, looked thoughtfully at him, but offered no comment, either then or much later, when he found Imber, an expression of long-suffering on his face, decanting a bottle of brandy.

"On the cut!" said Imber. "I thought it wouldn't be long before he was making indentures. He's finished the Diabolino, what's more, so if he doesn't relish what was always good enough for his late lordship it's no manner of use for him to blame me. I told him a se'en-night past how it was."

"I'll take it to him," Marston said.

Imber sniffed, but raised no demur. He was an old man, and his feet hurt him. He always accepted Marston's services, but thought poorly of him for undertaking tasks which lay outside his province. Quite menial tasks, some of them: he made nothing of fetching in logs for the fires, or even of sawing them up; and had been known, when Nidd was absent, to unsaddle his master's horse, and rub him down. You wouldn't have caught the late lord's valet so demeaning himself, thought Imber, contrasting him unfavourably with that most correct of gentlemen's gentlemen. Like master like man, he thought. Stiff-rumped the late lord had been; he knew what was due to his consequence, and always kept a proper distance. No one ever dared to take any liberties with him, any more than he ever talked to his servants in the familiar way the present lord used. As for arriving at the Priory without a word of warning, and accompanied only by his valet and his groom, and taking up a protracted residence there with more than half the rooms shut up, and not so much as a single footman to lend respectability to the household, imagination boggled at the very idea of his late lordship behaving so improperly. It all came of living in foreign parts, amongst people who like as not were little better than savages. That was what his present lordship had said, when he had ventured to give him a hint that the terms he stood on with Marston were unseemly in a gentleman of his position. "Marston and I are old friends," he said. "We've been in too many tight corners together to stand on ceremony." It was no wonder that Marston thought himself above his company, and was too top-lofty to indulge in comfortable gossip about his lordship. He was pleasant enough, in his quiet way, but close as wax, and with a trick of seeming not to hear what he didn't choose to answer. If he was so out of reason fond of his lordship why didn't he speak up for him? instead of looking like a wooden image? thought Imber resentfully, watching him pick up the salver, and carry it away, down the stone-flagged passage that led to the front hall.

Damerel did not keep town-hours at the Priory; he allowed the Imbers to serve dinner at six o'clock; and, since Aubrey's arrival, he had abandoned his tiresome habit of lingering in the dining room over his port, but had carried it up to Aubrey's room while Aubrey was confined to bed, and later had fallen into the way of drinking it in the library. Tonight, however, he had shown no disposition to leave the table, but sat lounging in his great, carved chair as though he meant to stay there all night.

Marston cast a measuring look at him before moving out of the shadowed doorway into the light of the candles on the table. He was staring fixedly ahead, lost in a brown study, the pupils of his eyes slightly blurred. He gave no sign that he had noticed Marston's entrance, but that one look had sufficed to satisfy Marston that Imber had exaggerated. He had been dipping rather deep, perhaps, but he wasn't as much as half-sprung: just a trifle concerned, certainly not castaway. It was only on very rare occasions that he was really shot in the neck, for he was one who could see them all out, as the saying went.

Marston set the decanter down, and went over to the big, open fireplace, and set another log on the sinking embers. The fine weather was still holding, but when the sun went down a creeping chill made one glad to see the curtains drawn across the windows and a fire burning in the hearth.

Marston swept the wood-ash into a pile, and rose from his knees. One of the candles had begun to gutter, and he snuffed it. Damerel lifted his eyes. "Oh, it's you, is it?" he said. "What's happened to Imber? Fallen down the cellar stairs?"

Marston's impassive countenance relaxed into a faint smile. "No, my lord."

"Did he tell you I was dead-beat?" enquired Damerel, taking the stopper out of the decanter, and pouring some brandy into his glass. "He's got his Friday-face on: enough to give one a fit of the blue devils!"

"He's old, my lord," Marston said, trimming another overlong wick. "If you were meaning to remain here it would be necessary to hire some servants."

He spoke in his usual expressionless manner, but Damerel looked up from his glass, which he was holding cupped between his hands.

"But I daresay we shan't return here after the Second Autumn Meeting," Marston continued, his attention still on the candles. "Which reminds me, my lord, that it would be as well for me to write to inform Hanbury at what date you mean to arrive at the Lodge, and whether you will be bringing company with you."

"I haven't thought about it."

"No, my lord. With the weather so remarkably warm one hardly realizes that we shall soon be into November," agreed Marston. "And the Autumn Meeting, I fancy—"

"I'm not going to Newmarket." Damerel drank some of the brandy in his glass, and after a moment gave a short laugh, and said: "You're not gammoning me, you know. Think I ought to go, don't you?"

"I rather supposed that you would go, sir—when you have a horse running."

131

"I've two horses entered, and precious few hopes of either." Damerel drank again, draining his glass. His mouth curled, but in a sneer rather than a smile. "Any more plans for me?" he asked. "Newmarket—Leicestershire—then what?" Marston looked down at him at that, but said nothing. "Shall we go to Brook Street, or shall we embark on a journey to some place we haven't yet seen? We can be as easily bored by either scheme."

"Not if I know your lordship!" replied Marston, with a gleam of humour. "I don't think I ever went anywhere with you but what you got into some kind of hobble, and, speaking for myself, I never found the time for being bored. When I wasn't expecting to be shipwrecked I was either hoping to God we could convince a lot of murderous heathen that we were friendly, or wondering how long it would be before I found myself sewn up in a sack and being thrown into the Bosphorus!"

"I think that was the nearest I ever came to being nailed," said Damerel, grinning at the recollection. "I've got you into a lot of scrapes in my time—But one grows older Marston."

"Yes, my lord, but not so old that you won't get me into a good few more, I daresay."

"Or myself?" Damerel said. "You think I'm in one now, don't you? You may be right: I'm damned if I know!" He stretched out his hand for the decanter, and tilted it over his glass, slopping the brandy over the table. "Oh, lord! Mop it up, or Imber will be sure I'm tap-hackled! I'm not: merely careless!" He slouched back again in his chair, relapsing for several minutes into brooding silence, while Marston found an excuse for lingering in carefully aligning the several pieces of plate set out on the sideboard. He contrived to watch Damerel under his eyelids, misliking the look in his face, and a little puzzled by it. He was taking this affair hard, and that was not like him, for he was an easy lover, engaging lightly in his numerous adventures, foreseeing at the start of each its end, and quite indiscriminating in his choice. He was a charming protector; he would indulge the most exacting of his mistresses to the top of her bent; but no one who had seen his unconcern at parting, or his cynical acceptance of falsity, could doubt that he held women cheap. This look of bitter melancholy was strange to Marston, and disturbing.

Damerel lifted his glass again, and sipped meditatively. "The King of Babylon, or an Ethiopian?" he said. "Which, Marston? Which?"

"I can't tell you that, sir, not being familiar with the King of Babylon."

"Aren't you? He stood at the parting of the way, but which way he took or what befell him, I haven't the smallest notion. We need Mrs. Priddy to set us right. Not that I think she would take a hopeful view of my case, or think that there was the least chance that the years that the locust has eaten could yet be restored to me. She would be more likely to depress me with pithy sayings about pits and whirlwinds, or to remind me that whatsoever a man soweth that shall he also reap. Would you care to reap any crop of my sowing, Marston? I'm damned if I would!" He tossed off the rest of his brandy, and set the glass down, thrusting it away. "To hell with it! I'm becoming ape-drunk. I can give you a better line than any you'll get from Mrs. Priddy! *Learn that the present hour alone is man's*—and don't ask me when I mean to leave Yorkshire! I can't tell you. My intention is to remain until Sir Conway Lanyon comes home, but who knows? I might fall out of love as easily as I fell into it: that wouldn't amaze you, would it?"

"I don't know, sir," Marston said.

"You'd best pray I may do so!" Damerel said. "Even if I could set my house in order—How far have I gone into Dun territory? Do I owe *you* any blunt, Marston?"

"Nothing worth the mention, my lord—since Amaranthus won at Nottingham."

Damerel burst out laughing, and got up. "You're a fool to stay with me, you know. What makes you do it? Habit?"

"Not entirely," Marston replied, with one of his rare smiles. "Serving you, my lord, has its drawbacks, but also its advantages."

"I'm damned if I know what they are!" said Damerel frankly.

"Unless you count being paid at irregular intervals and finding yourself in scrapes not of your making as advantages?"

"No," said Marston, moving to the door, and holding it open. "But sooner or later you do pay me, and if you lead me into scrapes you don't forget to rescue me from

133

them—on one or two occasions at considerable risk to yourself. There is a nice fire in the library, my lord, and Nidd brought back the London papers from York half an hour ago."

10

The intelligence that her son was at daggers drawn with
Lord Damerel, and Venetia Lanyon head over ears in love
with him, reached Lady Denny at third hand, and from
the lips of her eldest daughter. Clara was a very sensible
girl, no more addicted to exaggeration than her father, but
not even her temperate account of what Oswald had confided to Emily, and Emily had repeated to her, could
make her disclosures anything but disquieting in the extreme.

It had been Oswald's intention to have maintained an
impenetrable silence on the events that had shattered his
faith in women and transformed him, at one blow, from
an ardent lover into an incurable misogynist; and had his
parents, or even his two oldest sisters, had enough sensibility to enable them to perceive that the care-free youth
who had ridden away from his home before noon returned
at dinner-time an embittered cynic he would have refused
to answer any of their anxious questions, but would have
fobbed them off instead in a manner calculcated to convince them that he had passed through a soul-searing
experience. Unfortunately the sensibilities of all four
were so blunted that they noticed nothing unusual in his
haggard mien and monosyllabic utterances, but talked
throughout dinner of commonplaces, and in a cheerful
style which could not but make him wonder how he came
to be born into such an insensate family. His refusal to
partake of any of the dishes that made up the second
course did draw comment from his mama, but as she ascribed his loss of appetite to a surfeit of sugarplums, he
could only be sorry that she had noticed his abstention.

It was not until the following day that a chance remark

made by Emily proved too much for his resolution. With all the tactlessness of her fifteen years she marvelled that he had not ridden off to visit Venetia, which goaded him into giving a bitter laugh, and saying that never again would he cross the threshold of Undershaw. As he added a warning to her to ask him no questions she at once begged him to tell her what had happened.

He had no intention of telling her anything, but she was the most spirtually akin to him of all his family, and it was not long before he had confided some part at least of his troubles into her sympathetic ears, in a series of elliptical remarks which, while they conveyed no very accurate idea to her of the previous day's events, appealed strongly to her romantic heart. She drank in all he said, filled in the gaps with the aid of an imagination quite as dramatic as his, and ended by recounting the whole to Clara, under the seal of secrecy.

"But although I daresay it is all fustian, Mama, I felt obliged to say that I couldn't think it right not to tell you," said Clara.

"No, indeed!" exclaimed Lady Denny, quite aghast. "Challenging Lord Damerel to a duel? Good God! he must be out of his mind! I never heard anything to equal it, and what your father will say I tremble to think of! Oh, it can't be true! Ten to one it's one of Emily's Canterbury tales!"

"I think it is not wholly that, Mama," said Clara conscientiously. "I fear there can be no doubt that Oswald has *quarrelled* with Lord Damerel, though whether he challenged him to a duel is another matter. You know how he and Emily exaggerate! I should have supposed it to have been impossible, but if it's true that Lord Damerel is pursuing poor Venetia with his attentions it *might* be. Which is why I thought it my duty to tell you, because Oswald is certainly in one of his extravagant puckers, and when that happens one can't depend on his behaving rationally. And if he should be so imprudent as to force a quarrel on Lord Damerel—"

"Don't speak of such a thing!" begged Lady Denny, shuddering. "Oh dear, oh dear, why had that detestable man to come here? Setting us all in an uproar! Pursuing Venetia—Did you say he goes *every day* to Undershaw?"

"Well, Mama, so Oswald told Emily, but I didn't refine very much upon that, because he said also that Venetia

136

is quite besotted, and encourages Lord Damerel to behave with the greatest impropriety, and that *must* be nonsense, mustn't it?"

But Lady Denny, far from being reassured, turned
quite pale, and ejaculated: "I might have known what
would happen! And what must Edward Yardley do at this
of all moments but fall sick with chicken-pox! Not that I
think he would be of the least use, but he might have
prevented Damerel from living in Venetia's pocket, instead of letting his mother send for Mr. Huntspill every
time she fancies his pulse is too rapid, and making as
much fuss as if he had the small-pox!"

"Oh, Mama!" protested Clara, distressed by this severity. "You know Mr. Huntspill told us that Edward's
papa had a consumptive habit, so that it was not to be
wondered at that Mrs. Yardley should be anxious! And he
said that Edward was quite knocked up, much more so
than my sisters!"

"What Mr. Huntspill said," retorted Lady Denny
grimly, "was that people like Edward Yardley, who have
excellent constitutions and scarcely know what it is to be
out of sorts, are the worst of patients, because they fancy
themselves at death's door if they only have a touch of
the colic! Don't talk to me of Edward! I must speak to
your father immediately, for, however angry he may be,
Oswald is his son, and it is his duty to *do* something about
this dreadful business!"

But Sir John, when the story was first disclosed to him,
was not disposed to attach much weight to it, and beyond
saying that he was out of all patience with Oswald's childish play-acting he showed no sign of flying into a rage.
It was not until he had questioned Clara himself that he
began to see that there might be more truth in the tale
than he had supposed. Even then he seemed to be more
vexed than dismayed, but after he had thought the matter
over he said that if Oswald had no more sense than to
make a pea-goose of himself over Venetia there was only
one thing to be done, and that was to pack him off to
another part of the country until he had recovered his
wits.

"He had better go to your brother George," he told
Lady Denny. "That will give him something other to
think about than this folly!"

"Go to George? But—"

"I'm not going to run the risk of his kicking up some infernal rumpus here. I don't know how much to believe of the story, but if he's as jealous as Clara thinks there's no saying what he might do, and I tell you to your head, my dear, that I won't have the young cub annoying Damerel, or anyone else!"

"No, no! Only think how dreadful it would be if he forced a quarrel on to that man!"

"Well, he won't do that, so you may be easy on that score. If he did try to do so yesterday I sincerely hope Damerel clouted him over the head for his impudence! There's nothing for it but to send him off to your brother's place."

She said doubtfully: "Yes, but perhaps it might not suit them to have him at Crossley at this season. To be sure, George is very good-natured, and Elinor too, but I daresay they will have a houseful of guests, for they always do when the hunting begins."

"No need to worry over that. I said nothing about it at the time, because I don't above half like sending Oswald into that fashionable set, but I had a letter from George last week saying that they would be glad to have him on a visit, if I cared to let him go. Well, I don't, but I'd rather send him there than keep him here. I only hope he may keep the line!"

"George will see he does so," said Lady Denny confidently. "Depend upon it, Sir John, it would be the very thing for Oswald, and nothing could do him more good than to be with his cousins. Only how to persuade him to go?"

"*Persuade* him?" repeated Sir John. "*Persuade* him to accept an invitation to stay in the heart of the Cottesmore country? In a house where he knows he'll find himself amongst the Corinthian set? No, no, my love, *that* won't be necessary!"

She was by no means convinced, but Sir John was quite right. When the invitation was conveyed to Oswald its effect on him was almost ludicrous, so suddenly and so completely did it transform him from a sulky martyr into an excited boy in whom gratification, ecstatic anticipation, and some slight trepidation left no room for such minor matters as Venetia's faithlessness, Damerel's villainy, or his own broken heart. Stunned by the magnificence of the offered treat, he was at first unable to do more than stammer: "L-like to g-go to Crossley? I should th-think I *would!*" After that he sat throughout the rest of dinner in a sort of trance, from which he later emerged in so sunny a mood that not even his father's warning that he must conduct himself with propriety if he were permitted to go to Crossley roused umbrage in his breast. "Oh, yes, *of course* I will!" he earnestly promised Sir John. He then spent a happy evening discussing with him such anxious matters as what he should bestow in vails at Crossley, how best to convey his hunters there, and whether he would be expected to wear kneebreeches in the evening. Sir John reassured him on this head, but seized the opportunity to enter an embargo against the sporting of coloured and loosely knotted handkerchiefs in place of neatly arranged neck-cloths. But as the dizzy prospect of entering into Corinthian circles had banished from Oswald's mind any desire to study the picturesque in his attire this was unnecessary, and Sir John soon found himself obliged instead to forbid the purchase of a pair of riding boots with white uppers. Oswald was disappointed, but so unwontedly docile that Sir John was encouraged to offer him some very sensible advice on the modest demeanour to be adopted by a novice who wished to win the approval of those hardened sportsmen who ranked as Top-of-the-Trees in the world of the *haut ton*. As he prefixed his rather damping homily by saying that if he had not been satisfied that he had nothing to blush for in his son's horsemanship he would not for a moment have entertained the thought of permitting him to go to Crossley, Oswald was able to swallow the whole with a good grace. Sir John had not been so much in charity with his only son for many months, as he later informed Lady Denny, adding, as he snuffed his bedside candle, that if the boy behaved as prettily at Crossley he had no doubt that his uncle and aunt would be very well pleased with him.

Her mind relieved of its weightiest care, Lady Denny was able to turn it to the consideration of a secondary anxiety. Sir John having rejected in unequivocal terms a tentative suggestion that he should hint Damerel away from Undershaw, she decided that notwithstanding the claims of her invalid children it was her duty to drive over to Undershaw, to see for herself how much truth there was in Oswald's allegations, and, if necessary, to take such steps as would bring to an end a very dangerous situation. What steps it would be possible for her to take she did not know, or very seriously consider, for the more she thought about the matter the more hopeful did she become that she would find that the alarming story was nothing but a product of Oswald's fevered imagination.

But when she arrived at Undershaw on the following day she saw at one glance that she had been indulging a groundless optimism. Venetia was radiant, lovelier than ever before, with happiness shining in her eyes, and a new bloom in her cheeks.

She greeted her motherly friend with her usual affection, and every expression of pleasure at receiving a visit from her, but Lady Denny was not deceived: she was living in a halcyon world of her own; and although she enquired after the invalids at Ebbersley, listened with sympathy to an account of their progress, laughed at a description of Mrs. Yardley's daily alarms, and appeared to be genuinely interested in these and several other such topics, her civilities were only surface deep.

Lady Denny, trying, while she maintained a comfortable flow of small-talk, to discover some way of introducing the real purpose of her visit without too obviously disclosing what this was, had seldom found herself at such a loss. She had decided that the most natural approach would be through discussion of Aubrey's accident, but although she got as far as to say that it had placed Venetia in an awkward situation this promising gambit failed. Venetia smiled mischievously at her, and replied: "Dear ma'am, that makes you sound like Edward! I beg your pardon, but I can't help laughing! It wasn't in the least awkward."

Lady Denny tried her best. "Well, my dear, I am happy to know that, but I think you don't quite understand that the situation was one of particular delicacy."

"No," agreed Venetia disconcertingly. "I can understand, of course, that it *might* have been awkward, though at the outset I was too anxious about Aubrey to think about that, and later it would have been absurd to think about it. The Priory seemed like my own home, and Damerel—oh, a friend whom I had known all my life! I don't

140

think either Aubrey or I ever spent ten days more happily. Even Nurse, I fancy, was secretly sorry to leave the Priory!"

Taken aback by the unexpected openness of this reply Lady Denny could think of nothing whatsoever to say. Before she had collected her wits again Venetia was entertaining her with a lively account of Nurse's behaviour at the Priory. The hope of being offered an opportunity to discharge her mission steadily receded, and vanished altogether when Venetia told her how kind Damerel was to Aubrey, and how much Aubrey had benefited from his friendship. She was no fool, and she saw clearly that to suggest to Venetia that Damerel was using Aubrey as a tool would serve no other purpose than to estrange her. Her spirits sank; she began to be seriously alarmed, feeling Venetia to be beyond her reach, and so bedazzled that no dependence could be placed on the calm good sense which had previously characterized her.

All at once the door opened, and Aubrey looked into the room, saying: "Venetia, I'm going into York with Jasper. Have you any—" He broke off, seeing Lady Denny, and limped across the room, to shake hands with her. "I beg pardon, ma'am. How do you do?"

She saw Damerel on the threshold, and while she asked Aubrey if he had quite recovered from the effects of his fall managed to keep both him and Venetia under observation. If either of them had shown a trace of embarrassment she would have been less dismayed. Neither did; and had anything been wanting to convince her that Oswald had not exaggerated when he said that Damerel visited Undershaw daily it would have been supplied by the entire absence of ceremony shown him by Venetia. Instead of rising, as a hostess should, and shaking hands, she only turned her head and smiled at him. Lady Denny saw that smile, and, glancing swiftly at Damerel, saw the smile that answered it. As well might they have kissed! she thought, suddenly aware of a hitherto unsuspected danger.

"I've no need to introduce you to Lady Denny, have I?" Venetia was saying.

"No, I have already had that honour," Damerel replied, advancing with what her ladyship felt to be brazen effrontery to shake hands with her. "How do you do?"

141

She responded civilly, because she was a woman of breeding, but her palm itched to slap that harsh-featured, coolly smiling face. She fancied she could detect mockery in his eyes, as though, well aware of her disapproval, he was daring her to try whether she could come between him and Venetia, and it was with a real effort that she answered his polite enquiry after her husband.

"Do you want me to bring you anything from York?" Aubrey asked his sister. "That's what I came to ask you."

"Did you, love?" she retorted, quizzing him. "I am so *very* much obliged to you! And so much moved to think that such a notion came into your head!"

He grinned at her, not at all abashed. "It didn't!"

"What a graceless scamp you are!" remarked Damerel. "You might at least have *assumed* that virtue!"

"Why should I, when she knows I have it not?" said Aubrey, over his shoulder, as he went to take leave of Lady Denny. "Goodbye, ma'am: you don't think it uncivil of me to go, do you? No, for you came to see Venetia, I know. I won't keep you waiting above a minute, Jasper, only I can't go to York in these slippers, can I?"

"Not in my company, at all events," said Damerel. He looked at Venetia as the door shut behind Aubrey, and again Lady Denny saw the smile that passed between them. It was so slight as to be almost imperceptible: hardly more than a softening of expression, a tenderness in the eyes. She realized that it was involuntary, and knew the affair to be more serious than she had dreamed it could be, for Damerel, whatever his intentions might be, was not amusing himself with a desperate flirtation: he was as much in earnest as Venetia. He was speaking to her now, only about Aubrey, but in a way that betrayed how intimate they had become. "I won't let him stand for hours with his nose in a book," he was saying. "The drive won't hurt him."

"No, on the contrary. What good angel prompted you to this? *I* couldn't lure him away from the library! It was close on midnight when I heard him come to bed last night, and when I ventured to remonstrate this morning he informed me that he had wasted a great deal of time since his accident, and must now *seriously* apply himself to study! I thought that was what he *had* been doing!"

"Oh, no!" Damerel said sardonically. "He was absorbed in *light* reading while in my house—as provided by Berkley and Hume—with excursions into Dugald Stewart. Mere relaxation!" He glanced at the clock on the wall. "If I am to restore him to you by dinner-time I had best go and see what he's doing. Would you lay me odds I don't find him with a boot on one foot, a slipper on the other, and his nose in a lexicon, because he has suddenly remembered that he was about to track some obscure word to its source when I broke rudely in upon him?"

He turned from her to take leave of Lady Denny, and, that done, shook hands briefly with Venetia, saying: "*Do* you want anything brought from York?"

"No—not even fish, in a rush basket, which is Aubrey's chief loathing!"

He laughed, and went away. Venetia said, in her frank way: "I am glad he should have chanced to come in while you were with me, ma'am."

"Are you, my dear? Why?" asked Lady Denny.

"Oh—! Because I could see that you wondered at my liking him, for *you* did not, when you met him before, did you?"

Lady Denny hesitated, and then said: "I perfectly understand why you like him, Venetia. Indeed, I should have been astonished if he had failed to make you do so, for men of his—his *stamp* know how to make themselves charming to women."

"Yes," Venetia agreed. "They must have had a great deal of practice, though I don't think it can be wholly due to practice, do you? I never met a rake before, or thought much about it, but I should suppose that a man could scarcely become one—well, not a very *successful* one, at all events—if he were not naturally engaging."

"Very true!" said Lady Denny, rather faintly. "It is what makes them particularly dangerous. *You*, I am persuaded, have too much good sense and elegance of mind to be taken-in, but I wish you will be a little on your guard, my love. No doubt you find Lord Damerel's company agreeable, and feel yourself to be very much obliged to him, but I own—and you must not take it amiss that I should tell you this, for I know the world as you do not—I own that I did not quite like to find him so very much at home here. It is not the thing, you know, for an unmarried lady of your age to be entertaining gentlemen."

143

Venetia gave a little chuckle. "I wish you will tell Edward so!" she begged. "He hasn't a notion of it! He even *dines* here, if he can contrive to linger until I am forced, for the sake of common civility, to invite him to do so."

"Well, my dear—well, that is another matter!" said Lady Denny, trying to rally her forces. "Your friendship is of such long standing that—Besides, your papa liked him!"

"No, no, ma'am, how can you do Papa such an injustice?" protested Venetia. "When you must *know* he liked no one! However, I know what you mean to say: he thought that Edward would do very well for me!"

"Now, Venetia—!"

Venetia laughed. "I beg your pardon! I *could* not resist! But there is not the least need for uneasiness, because Damerel sees the matter exactly as you do. I daresay you may have noticed that I didn't ask him if he would stay to dine, when he said he would bring Aubrey back by dinner-time? I know it to be useless: he will never do so. He tells me that while he does no more than pay us morning visits the quizzy people will say that he is dangling after me, but if he *dined* here they would say that I was encouraging his very improper advances. Does that make you easy, dear ma'am?"

It had a reverse effect on her kind friend, and it was a very troubled lady who was driven back to Ebbersley, and who presently gave Sir John an account of her visit. Had her mind been less preoccupied the expression on her son's face, at once guilty and apprehensive, when she looked into the room where he was sitting with Sir John and asked Sir John to come to her dressing-room, might have given rise to further anxieties. Fortunately, however, she did not look at Oswald; and he, after a nerve-racking period during which he imagined her to be divulging to his father his shocking conduct in Aubrey's carpentry-barn, realized, when his father rejoined him, that Venetia had not after all betrayed him, and was so profoundly relieved that he resolved to write a very civil apology to her before he left Ebbersley for Crossley.

Sir John looked grave when he listened to what his lady had to tell him, but he remained firm in his refusal to meddle. Lady Denny, who considered this poor-spirited, said in an accusing tone: "Pray, would you *hesitate* to speak to Lord Damerel if it was your daughter who was in question?"

"No, certainly not, but Venetia is not my daughter," he replied. "Nor, my dear, is she eighteen years of age. She is five-and-twenty, and her own mistress. If she has indeed fallen in love with Damerel I am sorry for it, because it will cause her to suffer a heartache, I fear. But if you are apprehensive of her committing any very serious imprudence I am persuaded you are permitting your anxiety to overcome your reason. For my part I believe Venetia to be a girl of excellent principles and a good understanding; and I cannot suppose that Damerel, who, whatever his principles may be, is certainly not deficient in commonsense, has anything more in mind than flirtation." He saw Lady Denny shake her head, and added with a little asperity: "Do, my love, allow me to know a little better than you how such a man as Damerel may be expected to conduct himself towards a girl in Venetia's situation! He is a libertine: I don't deny that, but the case is that you are too prejudiced. Whatever his follies may be he is a man of breeding, and no common degree of worldly knowledge, and you may depend upon it he has nothing more in his head than an agreeable flirtation with a very pretty female. It is wrong, very mischievous, for he will forget her within a week of leaving the Priory, and very likely she will suffer a great deal of pain, but if you are right in thinking that she has a *tendre* for him, that cannot be cured by any meddling on my part, or—I must add—by any attempt on yours to warn her that Damerel is merely trifling with her."

"Oh, Sir John, there is no need to tell me that!" she exclaimed. "I am not such a ninnyhammer that I didn't see in a trice that it was useless to talk to her! But you mistake! I own that when I set out this morning—But when I saw him, the look in his eyes everytime they rested on her, the most dreadful apprehension seized me! One thing you may be sure of: he is not trifling, he is as much in love with her as she with him! Sir John, if nothing is done to protect her from him she will *marry* him!"

"Good God!" he ejaculated. "Do you mean to tell me— No, I don't credit it! He has no intention of marrying Venetia, or any other woman! He is every day of eight-

and-thirty, and his way of life is fixed: *that* he has clearly shown the world! If he had meant to marry, for the sake of an heir, perhaps, he would scarcely have pursued so ruinous a course during all these years. If the estates had not been entailed I don't doubt he would have disposed of them, just as he had wasted a very handsome fortune, and we may judge by that how little he cares who may succeed him. As for the open scandals which attend his progress, one might almost suppose he meant to render himself a most ineligible *parti!*"

"All that you say is no doubt very true, and has nothing to do with the case!" retorted her ladyship. "Whatever may have been his *intention* you may as well put out of your mind, my dear, for he has certainly put it out of his! I know how a man looks when he is flirting, and how he speaks, and you may believe that that is not what I saw today! He is very much in love with her, and if he doesn't offer her a *carte blanche*—or she is not so besotted as to listen to so shocking a suggestion!—he will ask her to marry him, and she will accept him!" She had the doubtful satisfaction of seeing from the change in Sir John's expression that she had succeeded in convincing him that her alarms were not the products of a disordered mind, and demanded; "*Now* will you speak to Damerel?"

But he remained adamant. "Certainly not! Pray, what would you wish me to say to him? My acquaintance with him is of the slightest; Venetia is neither related to me nor accountable to me for her actions. Any such intervention would be a piece of gross impertinence, ma'am! If you cannot prevail upon her to understand how disastrous such a marriage would be there is nothing to be done in the matter."

Recognizing the note of finality in his voice she abandoned the attempt to bring him to her own way of thinking, merely saying that something *must* be done, since it was nonsensical to suppose that because Venetia was five-and-twenty she could be trusted to manage her own affairs. No one could be less trusted to do so than a girl who could count on the fingers of one hand the bachelors of her acquaintance, and so might be depended on to fall in love with the first man of practised address who crossed her path. "And you know what people would say, Sir John! But she is *not* like her mother, however much she may resemble her in countenance, and she *shan't* be allowed to ruin her life! If only Aubrey took the least interest in anything outside his books—But you may depend upon it he doesn't even see what is going on under his nose, and wouldn't believe me if I told him!"

In this she was mistaken. Aubrey had not only seen, but was taking a detached interest in the affair, as he disclosed to his sister a day or two later. He had been so obliging as to drive her to Thirsk, where she had shopping to do; and on the way home, when Damerel's name had cropped up, as it frequently did, he startled her by asking quite casually: "Are you going to marry him, m'dear?"

She was a good deal taken aback, for he was in general so indifferent to what lay beyond his own concerns that she had supposed, like Lady Denny, that it had not occurred to him that Damerel's visits to Undershaw might be due to a desire to see her rather than himself. She hesitated for a moment, and he added: "Should I not ask you? You needn't answer, if you don't choose."

"Well, I *can't* answer," she said frankly. "He hasn't made me an offer!"

"I know that, stoopid! You must have told me, if you had become engaged to him! Shall you accept him when he does offer for you?"

"Aubrey, who set you on to ask me that?" she demanded. "It cannot have been Lady Denny! Was it Nurse?"

"Lord, no! No one did. Why should anyone?"

"I thought someone might have told you to try whether you could persuade me not to allow Damerel to come to Undershaw."

"Much heed I should have paid! Does Lady Denny know? Why should she wish you not to see Jasper? Don't she like him?"

"No—that is, she does not know him, but only his reputation, and I fancy she thinks I might be taken-in."

"Oh!" He frowned ahead, checking his horses a little as they approached the lodge-gates. "I don't know much about such things, but I shouldn't think you would be. Ought I to ask Jasper what his intentions are?"

She could not help laughing. "I beg you will not!"

"Well, I'd as lief not," he owned. "Besides, I see no sense in it: he couldn't tell me he meant to seduce you, even if he did, and, anyway, what a totty-headed notion that is! Why, when I wanted to get rid of Nurse he said she must stay at the Priory to play propriety! I never thought much about the stories people told of him, but I daresay they weren't true. In any event, you probably know more about 'em than I do, and if you don't care why should I?"

They had passed through the gates by this time, and were bowling up the avenue that wound through the park. Venetia said: "I don't know why anyone should care, but they all seem to think that because I've lived my whole life in this one place I must be a silly innocent with much more hair than wit. I'm glad you don't, love. I can't tell what may happen, but—if Damerel did wish to marry me—you at least wouldn't dislike it, would you?"

"No, I think I should be glad of it," he replied. "I shall be going up to Cambridge, of course, next year, but there will be the vacations, you know, and I'd rather by far spend them in Damerel's house than in Conway's."

This view of the matter made her smile, but no more was said, for at that moment the last bend in the avenue brought the house into sight, and she was surprised to see that a laden post-chaise-and-four was drawn up at the door.

"Hallo, what's this?" exclaimed Aubrey. "Good God, it must be Conway!"

"No, it isn't," Venetia said, catching sight of a feathered bonnet. "It's a female! But who in the world—oh, can it be Aunt Hendred?"

But when Aubrey pulled his horses up behind the chaise and the visitor turned, Venetia found herself staring down at a complete stranger. She was still more astonished by the discovery that the stranger was apparently superintending the removal from the chaise of a formidable quantity of portmanteaux and bandboxes. She turned her bewildered gaze towards Ribble, her brows lifting in a mute question; but he was looking quite stunned, and before she could ask for an explanation the stranger, who was a middle-aged lady, dressed in the height of fashion, stepped forward; saying with an air of affable assurance: "Miss Venetia Lanyon? But I need not ask! And the poor little lame boy? *I* am Mrs. Scorrier, which you have perhaps guessed—though the butler seems not to have been informed of our expected arrival!"

"I beg your pardon, ma'am," said Venetia, descending from the phaeton, "but there must be some mistake! I am afraid I don't understand!"

Mrs. Scorrier stared at her for a moment, an expression far removed from affability in her face. "Do you mean to tell me that what that man said is true, and you have *not* received a letter from—I might have known it! oh, I should certainly have guessed as much when I discovered in London that no notice had been sent to the *Gazette!*"

"Notice?" repeated Venetia. "*Gazette?*"

Recovering her affability, Mrs. Scorrier said, with a little laugh: "So naughty and forgetful of him! I shall give him a tremendous scold, I promise you! I daresay you must be quite at a loss. Well, I have brought you a surprise, but not, I hope, an unpleasant one! Charlotte, my pet!"

In response to this call, which was directed towards the open door, a very fair girl, with large, apprehensive eyes of a light blue, a quantity of flaxen ringlets, and a soft, oversensitive mouth, emerged from the house, saying in a nervous breathless voice: "Yes, Mama?"

"Come here, my love!" invited Mrs. Scorrier. "Dear child! You have been so anxious to meet your new sister, and your little lame brother, have you not? Here they both are! Yes, Miss Lanyon: this is *Lady* Lanyon!"

11

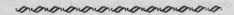

The shock held Venetia silent for several moments, which was perhaps fortunate, since the first thought to leap to her mind was that the announcement could not be true. She realized immediately that it must be true; and, as the extraordinary nature of the situation came home to her, began to laugh. "Oh, how *outrageous* of Conway, and how *like* him!" she exclaimed. She put out her hand to Charlotte. "How do you do? What a shocking welcome you have had to your new home! You must forgive us, for indeed we had not the least notion that we were to have this pleasure! I collect that Conway is not with you? Where— Oh, you will tell us all about it presently, but first I must see Mrs. Gurnard—our housekeeper, and tell her which rooms to prepare. Pray let me take you in! I daresay you must both be tired after your journey."

She led the way into the house, and to the drawing-room, where a fire had recently been lit, and begged the two ladies to be seated. Charlotte, who seemed to be too shy to raise her eyes for more than an instant, murmured something about kindness, and being so very sorry, to which Venetia replied smilingly: "Now that we have each of us begged pardon of the other I think we should unite in abusing the real culprit, don't you? I believe Conway would do almost anything rather than write a letter—to him a Herculean labour!—but it is certainly too bad of him to have failed on *this* occasion! Won't you take off your hat, and your pelisse? I am sure you will be glad of some refreshment after your journey: do you like tea? You shall have some directly, and then I'll take you upstairs."

"Thank you! So very kind! If it is not a trouble!"

Mrs. Scorrier, who had been looking appraisingly

about her, laughed at this, and exclaimed: "You will make Miss Lanyon think you quite a goose, my love, if you talk like that! You must remember that you are in your own house, must she not, dear Miss Lanyon? Some tea would be very welcome, though I do not in general indulge in that luxury at this hour. But Charlotte, I just tell you, is in a delicate situation, and although we lay at Doncaster last night I daresay she is quite done-up."

"In a delicate situation!" Venetia looked in some amazement at Charlotte. "You have been married for some time, then!"

"July," whispered Charlotte, blushing. "Conway was on furlough, you see—in Paris."

"I don't wonder you should look amazed, Miss Lanyon!" said Mrs. Scorrier, disposing herself on a sofa beside the fire, and drawing off her gloves. "I promise you I was so much amazed that I let Sir Conway sweep me quite off my feet. Such a whirlwind-romance as it was! A case of love at first sight, and nothing would do for Sir Conway but to carry his treasure back to Headquarters with him. Indeed, I believe if I had refused my consent to the marriage he would positively have eloped with her!"

"Oh, Mama!" faintly protested Charlotte.

"But—you were not previously acquainted? I had supposed—Well, that was certainly a romance! I shall look forward to your telling me about it—when you have had some tea!"

She excused herself gracefully, and went away to confer with Mrs. Gurnard. She had seen her standing at the foot of the stairs when she had entered the house, and had known, without venturing to meet her speaking eye, that she was far from pleased. She had now acquired reinforcements, in the persons of Nurse and Ribble, and no more than a glance at these three devoted retainers was enough to inform Venetia that trouble lay ahead. No time was lost in disclosing its root: upon being desired to send in a teatray to the new arrivals Mrs. Gurnard replied in icy accents: "I have already ordered it to be done, Miss Venetia—her ladyship's mama having desired me to do so. Not," she added carefully, "that it was necessary for her to have spoken to me on the matter, for it was on the tip of my tongue to have asked her ladyship if she would take some tea, or a glass of wine, to refresh her after her journey."

"Miss Venetia!" broke in Nurse. "In my very hearing that Mrs. Scorrier, or whatever she calls herself, told Mrs. Gurnard to be sure the beds were well-aired! If she had had the audacity to say such a thing to *me* I'd have told her to her head that this is a gentleman's seat, and not a common inn!"

"I would not so demean myself, Nurse," said Mrs. Gurnard loftily. "But when it come to her saying that the best bedchamber must be prepared instantly for her ladyship—"

"*and* informing us that until her fine London abigail arrives here one of the housemaids must wait on her ladyship!" interpolated Nurse.

"—I felt obliged to say, miss, that no doubt you would give me whatever orders you thought proper."

"That's just what *I* said, ma'am!" nodded Ribble approvingly. "The lady seemed to feel, Miss Venetia, that without she attended to the matter herself no one here would think to send in to York tomorrow to meet the young woman, who, I understand, will be coming by the stage. I trust I was able to set her mind at rest. I assured her, miss, that I shouldn't fail to ask you what you wish done."

With a sinking heart Venetia applied herself to the task of soothing these ruffled sensibilities. With only one of the indignant parties did she achieve a modicum of success: Nurse, learning that the bride was already in the family way, showed by the fanatical light in her eyes that this circumstance did much to reconcile her to Charlotte. Though lamentably unworthy of the position she had been called upon to fill she could (and, indeed, must) be tolerated for the sake of the infant over whom Nurse had every intention of exercising the fullest control. Mrs. Gurnard, foreseeing that the happy event would elevate Nurse once more to her vacated throne, spoke ominously of her advancing years and inability to accustom herself to new ways; and Ribble, not presuming to comment upon an affair of such delicacy, added a still more sinister note to the symposium by begging leave to enquire whether Mrs. Scorrier would be making a prolonged stay at Undershaw.

Having succeeded in slightly mollifying these important members of the household Venetia prepared to grapple with the far more difficult task of persuading Aubrey to behave at least with propriety towards his sister-in-law and her mama. He had driven off to the stables, without having uttered one word, and Venetia had thought it prudent to retrain from making any attempt to detain him. She guessed that he must have come into the house through the garden-door, and went to look for him in the library, reflecting, as she walked down the broad passage that led to it from the front hall, that a very little of Mrs. Scorrier's somewhat overpowering personality would suffice to turn Aubrey into as obstinate a recluse as ever his father had been. As she had expected, he was in the library. He had obviously been waiting her appearance with a good deal of impatience, for he demanded almost before she had shut the door into the ante-room: "What have you done with them. Do you believe such a tale?"

"That was my own thought," she admitted. "But it won't do, love: it *must* be true! A horrid shock, wasn't it? I don't yet know how we are to make the best of it, but that's what we must do."

"Don't you know? Then I'll tell you! We'll set up house for ourselves—exactly as you planned to do in this event!"

"Yes, of course, but we can't do so immediately, my dear! You must perceive how impossible it would be! Until Conway returns I'm responsible for Undershaw."

"And failing you, Mytchett!" he said swiftly. "Conway empowered both of you to act for him. I remember Mytchett's coming here to discuss the terms of the power of attorney with you before he sent it to Conway to be signed!"

"To be sure he did, but that was because he knew he was very much fitter than I to take care of the invested capital, and, of course, any legal business that might arise. He did not bargain to have all the everyday affairs of the estate thrust upon him as well. Besides, Aubrey, we could not leave Undershaw the instant Conway's wife entered it! It would be most improper, and unkind as well."

"As improper and as unkind as to have foisted her on to us without one word of warning?"

"Well, I fancy that wasn't her fault. In fact, I'm sure of it. Poor creature, she is so much mortified she dare hardly speak above a whisper! I am very sorry for her.

153

And I don't find her in the least objectionable, love: she seems to be a gentle, shy sort of a girl, and I daresay we shall soon grow to be very much attached to her."

"*Do* you? And as for her mother, I collect we shall positively *dote* on her!"

She laughed. "For my part, no! A detestable woman— she has set up the servants' backs already, and mine too, a little! But I don't mean to show her anything but civility, and I beg you won't either!"

He looked at her out of narrowed eyes, but said nothing. The most she could wring from him was a promise that he would say nothing uncivil to Mrs. Scorrier unless she offered him provocation, and with this she had to try at least to be satisfied. But as what Aubrey might regard as provocation depended to a large extent upon his mood her expectations were not high; and it was with considerable foreboding that she took him to the drawing-room to be formally introduced.

They found the two ladies discussing tea and macaroons. Mrs. Scorrier welcomed Venetia into the room with a gracious smile, saying: "Such delicious tea, dear Miss Lanyon! I must really ask the housekeeper where she procures it." She then saw that Aubrey had entered the room in his sister's wake, and included him in her welcome. He bowed rather stiffly, and shook hands with her before turning to Charlotte, and saying: "How do you do? How did you leave my brother! Will he soon be following you?"

"I don't know—I hope—I did not like to leave him, but Mama thought—"

"Mama thought that her daughter would be very much better away from the hurly-burly of Cambray!" interrupted Mrs. Scorrier, with the laugh that was already beginning to irritate Venetia. "Your brother will certainly be at home by the end of the year, for the Duke means to begin removing the Army at the beginning of next month. Miss Lanyon, I have been saying to Charlotte what a pretty room this is! Quite chàrming, indeed, and wants nothing but fresh hangings to make it as elegant a saloon as any I have seen."

Venetia was a little taken aback by this, but replied with composure, and, in the hope that if she could engage Mrs. Scorrier in conversation Aubrey and Charlotte might become acquainted, sat down beside her on the sofa.

Mrs. Scorrier was perfectly ready to talk, and soon showed that she possessed the ability to maintain more than her share of one conversation while interpolating remarks every now and then into another. Whatever was addressed to her daughter she answered, and whatever Charlotte said she either corrected or amplified. Her manner was good-humoured, she smiled almost continuously, but it was not long before Venetia became convinced that she was being regarded with suspicious hostility. Mrs. Scorrier was lavish in paying her compliments, but contrived at the same time to disparage; and Venetia, who had never before encountered her like, was puzzled to account for her attitude. She seemed to be determined to see in her daughter's sister-in-law a foe whom it was necessary to overcome; and by talking about the changes Charlotte would no doubt inaugurate at Undershaw, and assuring Venetia how well she understood what must be her feelings at being obliged to hand over the reins of government to another, she made it plain that she was very jealous of Charlotte's rights, and very ready to do battle in defence of them.

At the end of nearly an hour, when Mrs. Gurnard came in, at her most stately, to offer to conduct the two ladies to their respective bedchambers, Venetia knew that the comfort of Undershaw was over, and that the immediate future promised nothing but strife and vexation. In addition to her hostility Mrs. Scorrier possessed a managing disposition, and an uncontrollable desire to show everyone, from Venetia down to the gardener's boy, a better way of performing any given task, whether it was the direction of a household or the preservation of geraniums. Even the cook, whose macaroons Mrs. Scorrier had declared to be as good as Gunter's, was to be given a recipe which would be found to be superior; and, as though the mental vision conjured up by this promise was not horrid enough, she further promised to furnish Venetia with the name of an excellent surgeon who, she had no doubt at all, would know just what to do to cure Aubrey's lameness. Venetia acquitted her of malice, but found no difficulty in understanding why it was that so many people had (according to herself) so frequently behaved disgracefully to her.

Once she was assured that the bedchamber prepared for Charlotte had been occupied by her predecessor she was pleased to approve of it; but when Venetia smiled at Charlotte, and said: "You will tell me, won't you, if you have not everything you need?" she shook a reproving finger, and said in a rallying tone: "No, no, Miss Lanyon, don't, I beg of you, encourage my lazy little puss to depend on you! I have been telling her that now she is a married lady and the mistress of her own house she must learn to give her own orders, and not rely upon me, or you, to manage for her."

When Venetia presently left her own room, and went downstairs again, she found Charlotte seated alone in the drawing-room. She was elegantly dressed in an evening-gown of silk with a demi-train, but she looked far more like a scared schoolgirl than a fashionable matron, and she instinctively rose to her feet as soon as she saw Venetia. Glad to have an opportunity of talking to her without the intervention of Mrs. Scorrier, Venetia exerted herself to put her at her ease. She was only partially successful, and soon realized that while Charlotte's pliant disposition and amiability of temper made her anxious to please, these meek attributes also made it impossible for her to withstand the domination of her strongminded mother. If she had put it into words (a feat of which she was wholly incapable) that Mrs. Scorrier had warned her to beware of her sister-in-law, that fact could not have been more evident; and since she had neither a sense of humour nor the habit of plain speaking, Venetia's smiling request that she might not be regarded as an ogress merely served to cast her into incoherent embarrassment. Only when she spoke of Conway did she become at all natural, and forget her shyness in hero-worship. He was a demi-god who had miraculously fallen in love with her; the very thought of his magnificence made her cheeks glow, and her soft eyes shine: and in recounting his daring deeds and sage utterances she grew quite animated.

Venetia might be amused by this unrecognizable portrait of her brother but she was also touched, and readily perceived what it was that had attracted Conway to this somewhat insipid girl. She said kindly: "It must have made you very unhappy to have been obliged to leave him. I do most sincerely feel for you!"

Tears sprang to Charlotte's eyes. "Oh, it was so dreadful! I didn't wish to go, but he thought it the only thing, because Colonel Skidby was uncivil to Mama, which made it so very awkward for Conway, because of course Mama wouldn't submit to being *insulted*, and so we couldn't invite the Colonel to our parties, which made it excessively uncomfortable for Conway! Only fancy! that horrid man spread the most untruthful tales about poor Mama, and a great many people believed him, and took his part, and behaved very unkindly, so that she was positively *obliged* to tell Lord Hill the whole story, which made Conway say that—which made him think that it would be best if we came back to England!" She ended this impulsive recital on an apprehensive note, and added hurriedly: "And, besides that, I was not very well!"

"I don't wonder at it!" said Venetia, a merry twinkle in her eye. "In your place I rather think I should have taken to my bed! I can conceive of nothing worse than finding oneself in the centre of a quarrel."

"Oh, it was so dreadful!" said Charlotte involuntarily, and shuddering at the recollection. "It made me quite hysterical, so of course Mama would not leave me—not that there was any question—for I am sure I could never bear to be parted from her, and particularly when I'm feeling poorly!" She began to pleat her handkerchief, and said haltingly: "Mama—Mama sometimes says things—but she doesn't mean them—and she has had a great deal to bear, because Papa was not wealthy, and his family behaved in such a disagreeable way, taking my Aunt Elizabeth's part when she was rude to poor Mama, and not making her beg pardon, so that there was nothing for Mama to do but to cut the connection. And then Papa died of fever, which he contracted in the Peninsula, for he was a military man, like Conway, you know, and so Mama had only my sister and me to live for."

"Have you just the one sister?" enquired Venetia, unable to think of a suitable comment to make on Mrs. Scorrier's trials.

"Yes, my sister Fanny. She is older than I am, but we were the greatest friends! It was so sad! She was married two years ago, and has a dear little baby, which I have never seen, because my brother-in-law, whom we had thought to be a most amiable man, has such a jealous disposition that he was quite unpleasant to Mama when we went to stay with him and Fanny, and said he would not have her *meddling and making trouble* in his house, only because she thought it her duty to advise my sister to turn off the housekeeper, who was quite shockingly extravagant, and even, Mama suspected, *dishonest!*"

Before Venetia had well recovered from the effects of this artless speech Mrs. Scorrier had entered the room, and the impulse to warn Charlotte that any attempt to rid Undershaw of its housekeeper could only lead to the discomfiture of her mama had to be abandoned.

Mrs. Scorrier came in all affability, and full of brisk plans for the future. She seemed to have extracted from the housemaid sent by Mrs. Gurnard to wait on her every detail of the organization of Undershaw, and she saw much room for improvement. What was very proper for an unmarried female living in retirement with her brother would by no means do for Lady Lanyon. In particular did her consequence require that there should be two uniformed menservants under the butler; but Miss Lanyon must not be thinking that this need mean any considerable increase in expenditure, for (if she might venture to say so) she believed that the number of females employed in the house was excessive. "Not that I mean to say that you have not managed very creditably, my dear Miss Lanyon," she assured Venetia kindly. "Indeed, I must own I am most agreeably surprised by all I have seen, and can truthfully say that you have no need to blush for your housekeeping."

"None at all!" agreed Venetia, amusement quivering in her voice. "Though I might blush to accept a compliment that is due to another! Mrs. Gurnard has been housekeeper at Undershaw since before I was born." She turned her head to address Charlotte, saying lightly: "I expect she will wish to conduct you through every department of the house tomorrow. Don't mind it if she should seem a trifle stiff! She will very soon take to you when she sees that you don't mean to upset all her economies and arrangements. Talk to her about Conway! She dotes on him, you know—even allows him to call her his dear old Gurney, which I should never dare to do. She will very likely present you with her keys. I've no need to warn you, I'm persuaded, that you must beg her to keep them!"

"Oh, no! I should not dream of—"

"Well, as to that, my love," interrupted Mrs. Scorrier. "I believe it is best to begin as you mean to continue. It is very natural that Miss Lanyon should be shy of asserting herself, having known the woman for so long, but for you it is another matter. It is always the same with old retainers! They are quick to take advantage, and become perfect tyrants. If you will be advised by me, my dear—"

"She'd do better to be advised by my sister," said Aubrey, who had entered the room in time to hear this interchange. "Lord, what a dust Conway would kick up if he came home to find Mrs. Gurnard had left Undershaw in a pelter!"

The thought of Conway's displeasure made Charlotte turn pale, and even seemed to give Mrs. Scorrier pause. She contented herself with saying: "Well, we shall see," but although the smile remained firmly pinned to her lips the glance she cast at Aubrey was by no means amiable. Venetia could only pray that she would not offer him any further provocation.

The prayer was not answered, and long before dinner came to an end it must have been apparent to anyone acquainted with Aubrey that he had decided to war. Upon entering the dining-room, and finding that she was expected to sit at the head of the table, Charlotte had hung back, stammering with instinctive good feeling: "Oh, pray—! That is where you are used to sit, Miss Lanyon, is it not? If you please, I would by far rather not take your place!"

"But I would far rather not take yours!" returned Venetia. "I wish, by the way, that you will call me Venetia!"

"Oh, yes! Thank you, I should be very happy! But *pray* won't you—"

"My dear Charlotte, Miss Lanyon will think you are quite gooseish if you don't take care!" said Mrs. Scorrier. "She is very right, and you need have no scruples, I assure you." She flashed a particularly wide smile at Venetia, and added; "It is the fate of sisters, is it not, to be obliged to take second place when their brothers marry?"

"Undoubtedly, ma'am."

"Doing it rather too brown, m'dear!" said Aubrey, a glint in his eye. "You'll still be first in consequence at Undershaw if you eat your dinner in the kitchen, and well you know it!"

"What a devoted brother!" remarked Mrs. Scorrier, with a slight titter.

"What a nonsensical one!" retorted Venetia. "Do you like to sit near the fire, ma'am, or will you—"

"Mrs. Scorrier ought to sit at the *bottom* of the table," said Aubrey positively.

"You mean the *foot* of the table; opposite to the *head*, you understand," said Mrs. Scorrier instructively.

"Yes, of course," replied Aubrey, looking surprised. "Did I say bottom? I wonder what made me do that?"

Venetia asked Charlotte if she had enjoyed her visit to Paris. It was the first of many hasty interventions she felt herself obliged to make during the course of what she afterwards bitterly described as a truly memorable dinner-party, for while Aubrey offered no unprovoked attacks he was swift to avenge any hint of aggression. Since he made it abundantly plain that he had constituted himself his sister's champion, and won every encounter with the foe, Venetia could only suppose that Mrs. Scorrier was either very stupid, or compelled by her evil genius to court discomfiture. She really seemed to be incapable of resisting the temptation to depress Venetia's imagined pretensions, so the dining-room rapidly became a battle-field on which (Venetia thought, with an irrepressible gleam of amusement) line inevitably demonstrated its superiority to column. Unable to counter Aubrey's elusive tactics, Mrs. Scorrier attempted to give him a heavy set-down. Bringing her determined smile to bear on him she told him that no one would ever take him and Conway for brothers, so unlike were they. What unflattering comparisons she meant to draw remained undisclosed, for Aubrey instantly said, with a touch of anxiety: "No, I don't think anyone *could*, do you, ma'am? He has the brawn of the family, I have the brain, and Venetia has the beauty."

After this it was scarcely surprising that Mrs. Scorrier rose from the table with her temper sadly exacerbated. When she disposed herself in a chair by the drawing-room fire there was a steely look in her eyes which made her daughter quake, but her evident intention of making herself extremely unpleasant was foiled by Venetia's saying that since it behoved her to write two urgent letters she hoped Charlotte would forgive her if she left her until tea-time to the comfort of a quiet evening with only her mama for company. She then left the room, and went to join Aubrey in the library, saying, with deep feeling, as she entered that haven: "*Devil!*"

He grinned at her. "What odds will you lay me that I don't rid the house of her within a se'ennight?"

"None! It would be robbing you, for you won't do it. And, indeed, love, you might consider Charlotte's feelings a trifle! She may be a ninnyhammer, but she can't help that, and her disposition, I am quite convinced, is perfectly amiable and obliging."

"*So sweetly mawkish and so smoothly dull,* is what you mean to say!"

"Well, at least the sweetness is something to be thankful for! Do you wish to use your desk? I must write to Aunt Hendred, and to Lady Denny; and I haven't had the fires lit in the saloon, or the morning-room."

"*You* haven't had them lit?" he said pointedly.

"If you don't wish to see me fall into strong hysterics, *be quiet!*" begged Venetia, seating herself at the big desk. "Oh, Aubrey, what a shocking pen! Do, pray, mend it for me!"

He took it from her, and picked up a small knife from the desk. As he pared the quill he said abruptly: "Are you writing to tell my aunt and the Dennys that Conway is married?"

"Of course, and I do so much hope that with Lady Denny at least I shall be beforehand. My aunt is bound to read it in the *Gazette*—may already have done so, for that detestable woman tells me she sent in the notice before she left London! You'd think she might have waited a few days longer, after having done so for three months!"

He gave the pen back to her. "Conway wasn't engaged to Clara Denny, was he?"

"No—that is, certainly not *openly!* Lady Denny told me at the time that they were both of them too young, and that Sir John wouldn't countenance an engagement until Conway was of age and Clara had come out, but there's no doubt that he would have welcomed the match, and no doubt either that Clara thinks herself promised to Conway."

"What fools girls are!" he exclaimed impatiently. "Conway might have sold out when my father died, had he wished to! She must have known that!"

Venetia sighed. "You'd think so, but from something she once said to me I very much fear that she believed he remained with the Army because he thought it to be his duty to do so."

"*Conway?* Even Clara Denny couldn't believe that moonshine!"

"I assure you she could. And you must own that anyone might who was not particularly acquainted with him, for besides believing it himself, and always being able to think of admirable reasons for doing precisely what suits him best, he *looks* noble!"

He agreed to this, but said after a thoughtful moment: "Do *I* do that, m'dear?"

"No, love," she replied cheerfully, opening the standish. "You merely do what suits you best, without troubling to look for a virtuous reason. That's because you're odiously conceited, and don't care a button for what anyone thinks of you. Conway does."

"Well, I'd a deal rather be conceited than a hypocrite," said Aubrey, accepting this interpretation of his character with equanimity. "I must say I look forward to hearing what the reason was for this havey-cavey marriage. Come to think of it, what *was* the reason? Why the deuce didn't he write to tell us? He knew he must tell us in the end! Too corkbrained by half!"

Venetia looked up from the letter she had begun to write. "Yes, that had me in a puzzle too," she admitted. "But I thought about it while I was dressing for dinner, and I fancy I have a pretty fair notion of how it was. And that is what makes me afraid that the news will come as a shocking blow to poor Clara. I think Conway did mean to offer for Clara. I don't mean to say that he was still in that idiotish state which made him such a bore when he was last at home, but fond enough of her to think she would make him a very agreeable wife. What's more, I should suppose that there had been an exchange of promises, however little the Dennys may have suspected it.

If Conway thought he was in honour bound to offer for Clara I see just why he never wrote to us."

"Well, I don't!"

"Good God, Aubrey, you know Conway! Whenever there's a difficult task to be performed he will put off doing anything about it for as long as he possibly can! Only think how difficult it must have been to write to tell me that in the space of one furlough he had met, fallen in love with, and married a girl he never saw before in his life, and had jilted Clara into the bargain!"

"Knew he'd made a cod's head of himself. Yes, he wouldn't like that," said Aubrey reflectively. "I suppose Charlotte was on the catch for him."

"Not she, but Mrs. Scorrier most certainly—and had no intention of letting him slip through her fingers! *She* was responsible for that hasty marriage, not Conway— and I give her credit for being shrewd enough to guess that if she did not tie the knot then, the chances were that he would forget Charlotte in a month! And when it was done, I daresay he meant to write to me—not *that* day, but the next! And so it went on, just as when he put off for the whole of one holiday breaking it to Papa that he wished him to buy him a pair of colours, instead of sending him up to Oxford—yes, and in the end *I* had to speak to Papa, for Conway had gone back to Eton! On *this* occasion there was no one to act for him, and I haven't the least doubt that he postponed writing until it must have seemed quite impossible to write at all. Perhaps he then persuaded himself that it would be better *not* to write, but to bring Charlotte home with him, trusting to chance or our pleasure of having him restored to us to make all right! Only Mrs. Scorrier scotched that scheme, by quarrelling with some Colonel or other, and making things so awkward for Conway that he saw nothing for it but to be rid of her on any terms. You can't doubt she would have kicked up a tremendous dust if he had tried to send her packing *without* Charlotte, and he would never face her doing that at Headquarters!"

"So he sent Charlotte home with her," said Aubrey, his lips beginning to curl. "You were wrong, stoopid! There *was* someone to break the news for him! What a contemptible fellow he is!"

With this he stretched out a hand for the book that was lying open on a table, and immediately became absorbed in it, while Venetia, amused by his detachment and a little envious of it, dipped her pen in the ink again, and resumed her letter to Mrs. Hendred.

Venetia awoke on the following morning conscious of a feeling of oppression which was not lightened by the discovery, presently, that her sole companion at the breakfast-table was Mrs. Scorrier, Charlotte being still in bed, and Aubrey having told Ribble to bring him some coffee and bread-and-butter to the library. Mrs. Scorrier greeted her with determined affability, but roused in her a surge of unaccustomed wrath by inviting her to say whether she liked cream in her coffee. For a moment she could not trust herself to answer, but she managed to overcome what she told herself was disproportionate fury, and replied that Mrs. Scorrier must not trouble to wait on her. Mrs. Scorrier, momentarily quelled by the sudden fire in those usually smiling eyes, did not persist, but embarked on an effusive panegyric which embraced the bed she had slept in, the view from her window, and the absence of all street noises. Venetia responded civilly enough, but when Mrs. Scorrier expressed astonishment that she should permit Aubrey to eat his breakfast when and where it pleased him, the tone in which she replied: "Indeed, ma'am?" was discouraging in the extreme.

"Perhaps I am old-fashioned," said Mrs. Scorrier, "but I believe in strict punctuality. However, I can well understand that you must have found the poor boy a difficult charge. When Sir Conway comes home, no doubt he will know how to manage him."

That made Venetia laugh. "My dear Mrs. Scorrier, you speak as if Aubrey were a child! He will soon be seventeen, and since he has managed himself for years it would be quite useless to interfere with him now. To do Conway justice, he wouldn't attempt to."

165

"As to that, Miss Lanyon, I shall venture to say that I should be greatly astonished if Sir Conway permitted Aubrey to order meals to be sent to him on trays without so much as a by your leave, now that Undershaw has a mistress, for it is not all the thing. You will forgive my plain speaking, I am sure!"

"Certainly I will, ma'am, for it enables me to do a little plain speaking myself!" promptly replied Venetia. "Pray abandon any notion you may have of trying to reform Aubrey, for neither you nor your daughter has the smallest right to meddle in his affairs! They are his own concern, and, to some extent, mine."

"Indeed! I seem to have been strangely misinformed, then, since I believed him to be Sir Conway's ward!"

"No, you have not been misinformed, but Conway would be the first to tell you to leave Aubrey to me. It is only right that I should warn you, ma'am, that while Conway deeply pities Aubrey for his physical disability he stands in absurd awe of his mental superiority. Furthermore, although he has many faults, he is not only excessively good natured, but has a sort of chivalry besides, which would make it impossible for him to be anything but indulgent—perhaps foolishly! were Aubrey ten times as vexatious as he is! That is all I have to say, ma'am, and I hope you will forgive my plain speaking as I have forgiven yours. Pray excuse me if I leave you now. I have a good deal to do this morning. I have desired Mrs. Gurnard to hold herself at Charlotte's disposal: will you be so good as to tell Charlotte that she has only to send a message to the housekeeper's room when she is ready?"

She left the parlour without giving Mrs. Scorrier time to answer her, but although she knew that Powick must already be awaiting her in the estate-room she did not join him there for some twenty minutes. She was dismayed to find herself so much shaken by her anger: before she could face the bailiff without betraying to him her agitation a period of quiet reflection was necessary. This enabled her to regain command over herself, but in no way helped her to regard the immediate future with anything but foreboding. She blamed herself for having allowed Mrs. Scorrier to goad her into retort, yet felt that sooner or later she must have been forced into taking a stand against a woman whose passion for mastery must, if unchecked, set the whole household by the ears. She entertained no hope that Mrs. Scorrier would not bear malice: she had seen implacable enmity in that lady's eyes, and knew that she would lose no opportunity now to hurt and to annoy.

It was past noon when she left Powick. A morning spent in the company of that dour and phlegmatic Yorkshireman did more to restore the balance of her mind than any amount of reflection, be it never so calm; and the study of accounts exercised over her much the same sobering effect as did the study of Plato over Aubrey.

There was no sign of Charlotte or her mother in the main part of the house, but Ribble, coming into the hall just as Venetia was about to go out into the garden, disclosed that both these ladies were inspecting the kitchenwing, under the guidance of Mrs. Gurnard. He gave Venetia a sealed billet, which the undergroom sent over to Ebbersley earlier in the day had brought back with him; and waited while Venetia read its message. It was short, a mere acknowledgement of her own letter, but written in affectionate terms. Lady Denny would not keep the messenger waiting, but begged Venetia to come to Ebbersley as soon as might be. She added in a postscript that she was busy packing for Oswald, who was leaving Ebbersley on the following day, to visit his uncle, in Rutlandshire.

Venetia looked up, and met Ribble's eyes, fixed anxiously on her countenance. For a moment she did not speak, but presently she said ruefully: "I know, Ribble, I know! We are in the suds—but we shall come about!"

"I trust so, miss," he said, with a deep sigh.

She smiled at him. "Have you fallen under her displeasure? So have I, I promise you!"

"Yes, miss—as I ventured to say to Mrs. Gurnard. If she had heard the things *I* have heard she would know where the blow has fallen hardest. If I may say so, it was as much as I could do, last night, to keep from boiling over! Oh, Miss Venetia, what can have come over Sir Conway? Undershaw won't ever be the same again!"

"Yes, it will, Ribble: indeed it will!" she said. "Only wait until Conway comes home! To *you* I needn't scruple to own that we are in bad loaf, and Mrs. Scorrier a detestable woman, but I believe—oh, I am *certain!*—that

167

you will very soon grow to be as fond of Lady Lanyon as—as you are of me!"

"No, miss, that couldn't be. Things will be very different at Undershaw, and I fancy her ladyship will be wishful to make changes. Very understandable, I'm sure. I'm not as young as I was, and I don't deny it, and if her ladyship feels that—"

She interrupted quickly; "She does not! Yes, I know exactly what you are about to tell me, and a great goose you are! How *can* you suppose that my brother could ever wish for another butler in place of our dear, kind Ribble?"

"Thank you, miss: you're very good!" he said, a little tremulously. "But we were hoping, Mrs. Gurnard and I, that if you are meaning to set up your own establishment, with Master Aubrey, like you always said you would, you might like us to go with you, which we would be very pleased to do."

She was a good deal moved, but she said in a rallying tone: "Oh, no, no! How could they manage at Undershaw without you? How could I be so shocking as to steal you from my brother? I won't think of such a thing! And however happy *I* might be in such circumstances, you would be wretched, away from Undershaw. I know that, and you know it too."

"Yes, miss, and indeed I never thought to leave it, nor Mrs. Gurnard neither, but we don't feel we could stay, not with Mrs. Scorrier. Nor we don't feel that—Well, miss, to speak plainly to you, if you'll pardon the liberty, anyone can see which way the wind's blowing, and we wouldn't wish to be turned off with a Scarborough warning, not at our time of life, and that's what might happen, before ever Sir Conway shows his front, as he would say. I'm too old to learn new ways, and when it comes to being told I'm not to take orders from Master Aubrey without her ladyship agrees to it—well, miss, one of these days I won't be able to keep the words from my tongue, and that, I know well, is just what that Mrs. Scorrier hopes for, so that she can work on her ladyship to send me packing!"

"Let her!" said Venetia, her eyes kindling. "I can assure you that she would catch cold at that! I don't think Lady Lanyon could be prevailed upon to do it and if she did I should be obliged to tell her that it is out of her power to dismiss you. Until Sir Conway comes home I shall continue as mistress here; and when he does come—I give Mrs. Scorrier one week before he sends her packing! Only be patient, Ribble!"

He began to look more cheerful, and when Venetia very improperly confided to him that Conway had already sent Mrs. Scorrier packing from Cambray he was wonderfully heartened, and went off chuckling to himself. He would certainly pass this titbit of news on to Mrs. Gurnard, and possibly to Nurse, but as it was unlikely that any of the younger servants would be deemed worthy to be taken into the confidence of their betters Venetia was untroubled by any qualm of conscience.

She went out into the garden, and was engaged in snipping the dead heads off a few late-flowering plants when she saw her sister-in-law come out of the house, and stand hesitating, looking about her in a timid way, as though she feared to be pounced on suddenly by some ogre. She waved to her, and, as Charlotte started towards her, strolled to meet her. Charlotte was wrapped in a shawl, and looked pale, and rather hagged. She said, with her nervous smile: "Oh, good-morning, Miss Lanyon!—Venetia, I mean! I thought I might take a turn in the garden, or—or perhaps just sit for awhile in the sun. I have the headache a little, and it was so hot in the kitchen, and I don't know how to cook, or—or any recipes, so I slipped away. Mama—Mama is telling your cook the French way of making veal into a ragout."

"How *very* wise you were to slip away!" said Venetia, laughing. "I can readily imagine the scene, and only hope the meat-axe may not be within reach!"

"Mama thinks she is a very good cook!" Charlotte said quickly. "She complimented her on her pastry, and—and—"

"My dear, I was only funning! Have you been conducted all over the house, and are you quite exhausted?"

"Oh, no!" Charlotte replied, sinking rather limply on to a rustic seat. "That is—it is so very large, and rambling, and I am so ignorant about managing a house! I know Mrs. Gurnard despised me dreadfully—though she was very civil! Oh, Miss—Oh, Venetia, I know it is silly to be afraid of a housekeeper, but I don't know what to say to her, because I can't ask her questions, like Mama! I wish Mama had made me learn those things!"

"Do you? Then I can tell you just what you should do!" said Venetia, in a heartening tone. "What's more, nothing would please Mrs. Gurnard more! One day, when you have an hour to spare, go to Mrs. Gurnard's room, and tell her just what you have told me. She knows, of course, that you have never managed a house, and she will take you the better for owning it. Ask her if she will teach you! You will find that you are soon on the most comfortable terms with her."

"Do you think so?" Charlotte said, rather doubtfully. "I would like to learn but perhaps Mama would not wish me to ask Mrs. Gurnard—"

"Perhaps she would not," agreed Venetia dryly. "But it is what Conway would wish you to do!"

She left this to sink in. Charlotte sat pondering it, and presently sighed. "Oh, if only Conway were here!" She turned her face away, and after a moment said in a trembling voice: "I never thought, you see, that I should have to come here without him! I don't mean—of course I like to be at Undershaw—and you have been so very—" Tears choked any further utterance.

"I know exactly what you mean," Venetia said, taking her hand, and patting it. "It was infamous of Conway to send you home in such a way! But, indeed, Charlotte, we are all very happy to have you, and we shall try to make *you* happy as well. And Conway will soon be with you again, won't he?"

"Oh, yes! You are so very good to me! I didn't mean to complain!" Charlotte said, hastily drying her eyes. "I beg your pardon! It was only not feeling very well, and then having to go with Mama and Mrs. Gurnard—But it is all nonsense! Nurse said—Oh, Venetia, Nurse is *very* kind, isn't she?"

"Ah, so you've made Nurse's acquaintance, have you? I am so glad—and that you like her!"

"Yes, indeed, she made me feel so comfortable! She was putting a hot brick in my bed when I went up last night, and she helped me to undress, and made me drink a posset, and told me about Conway, when he was a little boy! It was she who brought up my breakfast-tray, too."

Thankful that her thoughts had taken a more cheerful direction Venetia encouraged her to continue talking in this strain, and was presently helped by the arrival on the scene of Nurse herself, bringing a cup of hot milk to Charlotte. It was immediately made apparent to Venetia that Nurse had decided to admit Charlotte into the ranks of her charges, for she began scolding almost before she came within tongue-shot, demanding to know what was this that she had heard about her ladyship's not fancying her nuncheon? To Charlotte's faint excuse that she was not hungry she replied severly: "Never you mind whether you're hungry, my lady! You've two to feed now, and you'll just do what Nurse says, and no nonsense! Now, you drink this nice cup of milk!" As she put it into Charlotte's hand she looked sharply at her, and said: "Who's been upsetting you, my lady? Not Miss Venetia, I know!"

"Oh, no, no! I was silly—it's nothing!"

"She misses Conway," Venetia explained.

"To be sure she does, but crying won't bring him home any the sooner," said Nurse briskly. "There, now, my lady, drink up your milk, and you'll be better! What you want to do is to go with Miss Venetia for a walk in the park, instead of moping here. You'll have your Mama coming to find you before you know where you are, and you've had enough worriting for one day. You take her, Miss Venetia, but not too far, mind!"

"I will, and gladly," Venetia said, getting up. "Would you care for it, Charlotte?"

"Yes, please—only will it not be damp? Mama said—"

"Now, what did I tell you, my lady?" said Nurse. "There's no need for you to cosset yourself. It's what I don't hold with, and never have, and so I shall tell your Mama."

"Oh, Nurse, *pray*—!" gasped Charlotte imploringly.

"Don't you worry your pretty head, my lady!" advised Nurse, with a grim little laugh. "There, you go along with Miss Venetia, and no more nonsense!"

"I'll fetch the dogs: they need a run," said Venetia, unaware that she was striking dismay into Charlotte's heart.

"You won't do that, miss, for Master Aubrey took them with him," said Nurse, to Charlotte's great relief, "Yes, you may well stare! Gone off riding, he has, and not a bit of heed would he pay to me, except to say that if he didn't try whether it hurt him he wouldn't ever know. The next thing we know we shall have him abed again, for *he that*

171

hath a froward heart findeth no good, Miss Venetia, as I've told him often and often!"

"When Nurse becomes Biblical, it is a sign that she is much moved!" Venetia said, as she and Charlotte crossed the lawn together. "Aubrey had an accident a few weeks ago, and we are afraid his weak leg may not yet be fit for riding. However, I expect he won't persist, if he finds it pains him, and in any event it doesn't do to try to coddle him: he doesn't like to have his lameness mentioned, you see."

She led Charlotte into the park, chatting of such commonplaces as she hoped might set the girl more at her ease. Charlotte had already asked her if she was very bookish, and she had gathered that the epithet stood in her mind for all that was most alarming. She could not help thinking, as she recounted an anecdote of her childhood, that Charlotte would have little reason, after this session, for believing her to be very clever.

Charlotte seemed to enjoy her walk, but as she favoured a dawdling method of progression, and contributed nothing to the conversation but some rather trite observations on the scenery, a description of her wedding-dress, and several uninteresting stories about a school-friend, Venetia was soon heartily bored. She was about to suggest that it was perhaps time they made their way back to the house when the sound of cantering horses made her turn to look across a stretch of turf towards the avenue. She saw that the riders were Aubrey and Damerel, and at once waved to them, saying to Charlotte: "Shall we walk to meet them? The man with Aubrey is Lord Damerel, our nearest neighbour. I expect Aubrey brought him to pay his respects to you."

Charlotte assented, but in a scared voice which Venetia set down to shyness, and thought it best to ignore. Charlotte, however, was not thinking about the stranger she was to meet; she was hoping very much that the dreadful dogs bounding behind the horses were not savage. The horses were pulled up; Damerel drew his bridle over Crusader's head, and gave it into Aubrey's hand; and, to poor Charlotte's dismay, three of the dreadful dogs came racing towards her. She shrank instinctively, but was relieved to discover that so far from biting her the spaniels paid no heed to her at all, but fawned round Venetia with as much exuberant delight as if they had not seen her for weeks. Then a whistle from Aubrey made them all tear off again, and Charlotte was glad to see that he was riding on to the stables, and taking the dogs with him.

Damerel, coming towards the ladies with his easy stride, met Venetia's eyes for a pregnant moment before turning his own to the bride's countenance in a swiftly appraising glance. That second's interchange proved almost too much for Venetia's composure; there was a very slight tremor in her voice as she greeted him. "Good-morning! My odious little brother, I perceive, has stolen a march upon me, and told you our exciting news. All that is left for me to do is to present you to my sister-in-law, and although that is a very agreeable task I had hoped to have astonished you! This is Lord Damerel, Charlotte— our good friend and neighbour."

She saw with satisfaction, as Charlotte gave her hand to Damerel, and exchanged a few conventional words with him, that she showed no more shyness than was perfectly becoming. So nervous and so tongue-tied was she when trying to converse with her brother and sister-in-law that Venetia had begun to be afraid that she would make a poor impression on the neighbouring gentry. She was herself careless of appearances and knew little of the world but she was shrewd enough to guess that the secrecy in which Conway had seen fit to shroud his marriage would provide the *ton* of the North Riding with rich food for gossip and conjecture, and she thought it to be of the highest importance that Charlotte should give no one cause to say that she was so extraordinarily ill-at-ease that it was plain to be seen that something discreditable must lie behind the mystery of the strange marriage. But there was no fault to be found in her company-manners; she might be shy, she might utter nothing but platitudes, but Venetia was much inclined to think that such sharp-eyed critics as Lady Denny would pronounce her to be very pretty-behaved.

They walked back to the house with Damerel between them, and it was not long before Charlotte was prattling happily about Paris, and Cambray, of Sunday drives to Lonchamps, of parties at Lord Hill's Headquarters, of Lord Hill's kindness, and of what he had been so very obliging as to say to her about Conway. Venetia, at first astonished by this sudden blossoming, quickly realized that it was due not to any impulse of coquetry in Charlotte but to the adroit handling of an expert. She could only marvel, admire, and be at once amused and rueful. She had tried so hard to draw Charlotte out, and with so little success! Yet Damerel had done it within five minutes of making her acquaintance, and without apparent effort. He even made her laugh, for when she was talking about the delights of shopping in Paris he said: "And for hats of the first style of elegance, Phanie!" which surprised a little trill of mirth out of her. "Yes! How did you know?" she asked, looking innocently up at him.

Venetia choked, and saw a muscle quiver in the corner of Damerel's mouth. But he said gravely: "I fancy I must have heard the name on the lips of some lady of my acquaintance."

"Well, her hats are quite ravishing, but *shockingly* expensive!"

"They are indeed—if what I have been told is true!"

"Oh, yes, for my husband bought one for me there, and when I learned the price I declared I was ready to sink, and felt obliged to shake my head at him! But he bought it, for all that, and I wore it at the breakfast that was given for the Duke of Wellington, when he came to Headquarters."

In this artless style the conversation was maintained until they came within sight of the house. As they approached the arched gateway through which Venetia had led Charlotte into the park they were met by Aubrey, and Charlotte's confidences were at an end. She was absurdly nervous of Aubrey, and seemed to be embarrassed by his lameness, always looking away when he moved, in a manner too marked, Venetia knew, to escape his notice. His leg was dragging more than usual, as he came towards them, so it was to be inferred that his experimental ride had been premature.

He nodded at Charlotte, saying: "Puxton has just come back from York with your abigail, ma'am. No, I have that wrong: Your *dresser!* You should have sent William Coachman in with the carriage, Venetia: she ain't accustomed to driving in gigs with an undergroom."

This threw Charlotte into a flutter of apprehension; and after assuring Venetia incoherently that Mama had engaged Miss Trossell in London but would be the first to depress such pretension, she excused herself and hurried away to the house.

"Of all the ridiculous starts!" Venetia exclaimed. "What can Mrs. Scorrier have imagined Charlotte would want with a dresser at Undershaw?" She looked up at Damerel, mischief in her face. "As for you, sir, with your milliners, whose prices—you have *heard*—are so extortionate, how you could have the effrontery—!"

"Or *you* the impropriety, ma'am, to betray your understanding of the circumstances through which I became acquainted with Mlle. Phanie—!" he retorted.

She laughed, but said: "Yes, of course, I ought to have appeared unconscious—and so I would have done had it been anyone but you. How skilfully you contrived to set my sister-in-law at her ease, by the way!"

"But of course!" he murmured provocatively.

"What did you think of her?" interrupted Aubrey.

"Oh, your Pope quotation hits her off! A dead bore, but without guile or malice: she won't trouble your peace."

"No. Nor, I fancy," said Venetia thoughtfully, "was Conway *obliged* to marry her, though I did suspect it at the outset, when I heard she was breeding."

"Yes, so did I," remarked Aubrey. "But Nurse says she expects to be confined in May, so that don't fit. Nothing smoky about that."

"Well, don't sound as if you had rather there had been!" said Damerel, a good deal amused. "Am I to be privileged to meet Mama, or would that be unwise?"

"I should rather suppose it might be, if she *knows* about you," responded Venetia, seriously considering the matter. "Let us go into the library—though it may well be that she doesn't know, because although she is not *vulgar*—"

"She is excessively vulgar," interpolated Aubrey.

"Oh, she has a very vulgar mind!" agreed Venetia. "I meant that she is not underbred, in the style of poor Mrs. Huntspill, or that strange female I met when I visited Harrogate with Aunt Hendred, and who talked all the time of duchesses, and as if they had been her dearest friends, which my aunt assured me was not at all the case. Mrs. Scorrier doesn't boast in that fashion, and though

175

she is not sincere, and quite odiously overbearing, there is nothing in her manners to give one a disgust of her. But I don't believe she's a member of the *ton*."

"If she's the woman I rather fancy she must be, she's the daughter of some small country squire," said Damerel, following her into the library. "From what Aubrey tells me, I should say your sister-in-law must be Ned Scorrier's daughter—in which event you need not blush for the marriage. The Scorriers are well enough: not tonnish, but of good stock: a Staffordshire family. Ned Scorrier was one of the younger sons, and was at Eton in my time, though senior to me by a couple of years. I know he became a military man, and made a bad match when he was only twenty, but what happened after that I don't think I ever heard."

"He died of fever, in the Peninsula," said Venetia. "I should think he must be the same man, for Mrs. Scorrier did say something about her husband's family living in Staffordshire. She quarrelled with them." Her brow wrinkled. "At least, so I understood, from what Charlotte said, but it does seem an idiotish thing to have done, in her circumstances! She's not very beforehand with the world, you know: doesn't pretend to be; so one would have supposed that she would have taken care *not* to quarrel with her husband's family."

"One of the advantages of having led a sequestered life," said Damerel, smiling, "is that you've not until now encountered the sort of woman who can't refrain from quarreling with all who cross her path. She is for ever suffering slights, and is so unfortunate as to make friends only with such illnatured persons as soon or late treat her *abominably!* No quarrel is ever of her seeking; she is the most amiable of created beings, and the most long-suffering. It is her confiding disposition which renders her a prey to the malevolent, who, from no cause whatsoever, invariably impose upon her, or offer her such intolerable insult that she is *obliged* to cut the connection. Have I hit the mark?"

"Pretty well!" said Aubrey, grinning wryly.

"Add jealousy!" Venetia said. "Quite irrational, too! She took *me* in jealous dislike the instant she laid eyes on me, and I can't discover why she should have done so, for indeed I don't think I gave her cause!"

"But you give her great cause," Damerel said, the smile lingering in his eyes. "Had you been a dark beauty the case would have been different, for you might have served as a foil to that insipid blonde of hers. But you are fair, my dear, and you shine that girl down. Believe me, the gold casts the flax into dismal eclipse, which Mrs. Scorrier very well knows!"

"By Jupiter, I believe you're right!" exclaimed Aubrey, critically surveying his sister. "I suppose she *is* a remarkably handsome girl! People seem to think her so, at all events."

"And even *you* allow her to be tolerable! There can be no doubt!"

"Thank you! I am very much obliged to you both!" said Venetia, laughing. "I daresay you know how much I delight in the ridiculous. You will at least do Charlotte the justice to own that she is a very pretty girl!"

"Certainly—in the style of a puppet, without countenance."

"Well, I see nothing in her above the ordinary," declared Aubrey. "And unless he was castaway at the time I'm dashed if I know why Conway offered for her!"

"But they will deal charmingly!" said Venetia. "I know exactly why he offered for her! She is pretty, and gentle, she admires him excessively—indeed, I believe she worships him!—she hasn't two thoughts in her head to bother him, and she will always think he is as wise as he is handsome!"

"In that case he will become wholly insufferable," said Aubrey, dragging himself out of his chair. "I must go and attend to Bess; she picked up a thorn in one pad."

He limped out, and as the door closed behind him Damerel said: "I've no interest in the fair Charlotte, and less than none in her mama, but I own I have the liveliest curiosity in your brother Conway, my dear delight! What the devil's the meaning of this freak? What kind of a man is he to have served you such a trick?"

Venetia considered her brother Conway. "Well, he is large, and very handsome," she offered. "He looks as if he were strong-willed, but in fact he is excessively easy-going, and only now and then *obstinate*. He is kind, too, and I must say I think it is a great virtue in him that he doesn't take a pet when one roasts him. In fact whenever

177

Aubrey says one of his cutting things to him he is quite proud to think that however puny the poor little fellow may be he has a *devilish* clever tongue."

Damerel put up his brows. "But you are drawing the portrait of an estimable man, my dear!"

"So he is—in many ways," replied Venetia cordially. "Only he is selfish, and indolent, and for all his amiability it is of no use to suppose that he might put himself out for anyone, because without being so disobliging as to refuse outright he would either forget, or discover some excellent reason why it would be much better for everyone if he didn't bestir himself. He dislikes to be made uncomfortable, you see. And for the rest—oh, he is a bold rider to hounds, a first-rate fiddler, and a tolerable shot! He likes simple jokes, and laughs as heartily when he tells them for the tenth time as he did at the first."

"Aubrey's is not the only deadly tongue in the Lanyon family!" he remarked appreciatively. "Now, if you please, explain to me why this ease-loving fellow saddled himself with a termagant for his mama-in-law!"

"Oh, he wanted Charlotte, so he left the future to take care of itself! When Mrs. Scorrier made it uncomfortable for him at Cambray he got rid of her, I have no doubt at all, without a disagreeable scene, merely by encouraging Charlotte to fancy herself unwell, and then convincing her, and Mrs. Scorrier, and himself as well, that it was his duty to send her home to England. I daresay he would be glad if *I* would rid Undershaw of Mrs. Scorrier, and before he returns, but I doubt if I could, in the event, I don't mean to make the attempt. He must do it himself. He will, too—which is something I fancy she doesn't yet suspect!" Venetia gave a little chuckle. "Of course he would never quarrel with her at Cambray, where she would have made a great noise, and put him to the blush, but he won't care a button what noise she makes here! And I shouldn't wonder at it if he makes Charlotte tell her to go, and goes off hunting all day while she does it!"

Damerel laughed, but he said: "Meanwhile, she is cutting up your peace, confound her!"

"Yes," she acknowledged. "But it won't be for long, I trust, and perhaps if I can but persuade her that I haven't the least desire to usurp Charlotte's place, we may contrive to rub along tolerably well."

13

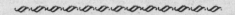

Venetia's optimism was soon found to have been misplaced. Within ten minutes of Damerel's departure hostilities had been resumed, Mrs. Scorrier, her eyes gleaming with righteous wrath, seeking her out to demand whether it was true that she had not only welcomed his lordship to Undershaw, but had actually presented him to Charlotte. She had been unable (she said) to credit her ears when Charlotte had informed her of this shocking incident; and while she had discovered already that Miss Lanyon behaved with what to her possibly outdated notions of propriety was unbecoming license, she had not supposed she was so lacking in prudence and delicacy as to permit a man of Lord Damerel's reputation to set foot within the grounds of Undershaw, much less to introduce him to her brother's innocent bride.

Whatever qualms Venetia might, upon sober reflection, have felt on the wisdom of making Damerel acquainted with Charlotte (since to be on calling terms with him could scarcely add to her credit in the district) vanished in a leaping flame of anger. She retorted swiftly: "Dear me, ma'am, do you consider Charlotte to be in danger of succumbing to his charms? I should have supposed her to be far too deep in love with my brother—but must bow to your better knowledge of her!"

"Miss—Lanyon!" ejaculated Mrs. Scorrier.

"Well?" said Venetia, deceptively cool.

Mrs. Scorrier drew an audible breath. "I ignore your impertinence. It is quite beneath my notice. But I would have you to know that for a modest female in my daughter's situation—a stranger to this part of the country, and coming to it without the protection of her husband—

to be receiving in her house a man of ill-repute would be grossly improper. Of the impropriety of a *single* female's claiming friendship with such a person I say nothing!"

"How should you, indeed? *My* credit won't suffer, after all! But for the rest you are very right: it was shockingly thoughtless of me, and I beg your pardon! In the circumstances, Charlotte cannot be too careful, of course. When one thinks how much scandal-broth must already be brewing—oh, have no fear, ma'am! I will tell Damerel he must on no account divulge to anyone that he has even clapped eyes on Charlotte!"

Unbecomingly flushed Mrs. Scorrier said in a voice tight with suppressed fury: "Indeed! *Indeed,* Miss Lanyon? So you fancy *your* credit won't suffer? You are strangely mistaken, let me tell you!" She paused, and Venetia waited, her brows slightly raised, a little contemptuous smile on he lips. It seemed to her that a struggle was taking place in Mrs. Scorrier's bosom; it certainly heaved alarmingly; but after a tense moment or two that lady turned abruptly on her heel, and stalked out of the room.

Venetia discovered that she was trembling, and was obliged to sit down. It was some time before she was able to recover her composure, and longer still before she could bring herself to acknowledge that the reproof, however offensively delivered, was not wholly without justification, and be sorry for her own loss of temper. She did at last realize it, and, after a struggle quite as severe as any Mrs. Scorrier had engaged in, went to offer the lady an apology. It was received with a cold bow, and closely folded lips.

"I ought not to have allowed my indignation to overpower me, ma'am," Venetia persevered. "I should rather have explained to you that Lord Damerel has been so good a friend to Aubrey that to hear him abused was rather too much for me to bear with patience."

"We will not discuss the matter, Miss Lanyon. I trust, however, that you will make it plain to Lord Damerel that his visits to Undershaw must cease."

"No," said Venetia gently. "I shall not do that, but you need be under no apprehension, ma'am; when he comes it will be to see Aubrey, not Charlotte."

To this Mrs. Scorrier vouchsafed no other answer than

a glance which assured Venetia that it would henceforward be war to the knife between them.

It was the prelude to a week more nearly resembling a nightmare than any Venetia had ever endured. Mrs. Scorrier, abandoning affability, spoke to her as seldom as need be, and then with formal civility; but while contriving largely to ignore her lost no opportunity that presented itself to vex her. If she could find no household custom to overset she discussed with Charlotte, in Venetia's presence, the changes that must be made in the management and economy of Undershaw. Charlotte, rendered acutely uncomfortable by these tactics, yet lacked the strength of character to combat them. She murmured a few feeble expostulations sometimes, but for the most part gave only monosyllabic answers, and looked miserable. On the rare occasions when Aubrey was present he used his deadly tongue with such excoriating effect that Venetia begged him to keep away from the drawing-room.

To make matters worse, the domestic staff, warmly espousing Venetia's cause, demonstrated a stubborn loyalty by referring to Venetia the most trivial order received from Mrs. Scorrier. "I will mention the matter to Miss Venetia, ma'am," was the invariable response she received; and when she imprudently commanded Fingle to bring the phaeton round to the house to take her ladyship for a gentle airing his answer was even more forthright. "I take my orders from Mr. Aubrey, ma'am," said the blunt Yorkshireman. Before Mrs. Scorrier could find Venetia, to lodge a complaint with her, she was herself sought out by Aubrey, who conveyed to her the unpalatable information that Fingle was his personal groom, and that he would be obliged to her if she would in future deliver her orders to William Coachman, whose business it was to drive the ladies of the establishment out, not in the phaeton, which again belonged to him and he would let none but Venetia drive, but in the barouche.

To all Venetia's protests her champions turned deaf ears; they had determined on their course, and they pursued it with enthusiasm. The better part of her time was consequently spent either in endorsing Mrs. Scorrier's commands, or in the hopeless attempt to reconcile bitter opponents.

For Mrs. Scorrier the situation was rendered the more

exacerbating by Nurse, who, while paying no heed to her at all, was rapidly acquiring a most undesirable influence over Charlotte. In this she was assisted by the superior Miss Trossell, who was so unfavourably impressed by the Yorkshire scene, and the lack of genteel society at Undershaw, that within twenty-four hours of her arrival she declared her inability to face the rigours of life in the country, adding a strong hint that she had been lured to Yorkshire under false pretences. There was just enough insolence in her tone to rouse Mrs. Scorrier to wrath, and after a stormy scene Miss Trossell departed incontinent, being conveyed to York in the degrading gig, and sped on her way by an assurance from Nurse that her loss would not be felt.

Nor was it; for infinitely preferable to Charlotte were the attentions of Nurse, who scolded, and bullied her, but took a warm interest in her well-being, knew just what to do for her when she felt queasy, and would spend hours talking about Conway, or discussing the future of Conway's son. Charlotte was never so happy as when resting in her room, with Nurse sewing beside the fire, and the door shut against intruders. Nurse had no sympathy to waste on nervous qualms, or fits of depression: she said: "Now, that's quite enough of that nonsense, my lady!" and: "You put your trust in the Almighty, my lady, and do what Nurse says, and you won't have any need to fidget yourself." But Nurse also unearthed Conway's christening robe, and as many of his caps and petticoats as had survived Aubrey's infancy; and made cosy plans for the redecoration of the nurseries. She told Charlotte not to fret about the alarming month-nurse interviewed by Mrs. Scorrier in London, because she knew of a very decent woman living in York; and as for accoucheurs, she wanted to hear no more talk about any Dr. Knightons (whoever he might be), because Dr. Cornworthy, also in York, had brought quite as many babies into the world as any grand London practitioner, and very likely more; and in any event her ladyship would trust Nurse to know what was best for her, and busy herself instead with stitching a cap for the Heir.

Under this bracing treatment Charlotte revived, only to be thrown back by the nervous strain imposed on her by her mama's determination to gain the upper hand of

Venetia. She lived in sick apprehension of just such a scene as she most dreaded; and after an evening of more than ordinary tension had to be scolded by Nurse out of a fit of mild hysterics. This episode led Nurse to take Mrs. Scorrier severely to task; and as her homily included the information that a dry morsel and quietness therewith was better than a house full of sacrifices and strife, it was hardly surprising that it resulted in a sharp skirmish. Mrs. Scorrier, already jealous of Nurse's influence over Charlotte, told her, with a smile more menacing than amiable, that she would be extremely sorry if she were obliged to recommend her daughter to send her away from Undershaw. She had no real intention of making such an attempt, for she knew very well that old and faithful retainers could not be dismissed, however irritatingly they behaved. She uttered the threat in the hope of intimidating Nurse, but its only effect was to afford Nurse with an opportunity to put her in possession of a fact which made it almost impossible for her to meet Venetia thereafter with even the appearance of complaisance.

"Well, and so I should think, ma'am!" said Nurse. "Where would be the sense in teasing her ladyship to do what she's got no power to do, and wouldn't do if she had?" She eyed Mrs. Scorrier's stiffening countenance with grim satisfaction, and delivered a leveller. "It's Miss Venetia as is mistress of Undershaw, ma'am, as even the scullery-maid is well aware of, and has a lawyer's piece with a seal on it, and signed by Sir Conway, to prove it."

Since Conway had omitted to tell his mother-in-law that he had given Venetia a power of attorney, and she, by some unaccountable oversight, had never considered the probability that he should have done so, this disclosure filled her with wrath which was none the less violent for being impotent. All she could think of to do by way of immediate revenge was to suggest to Charlotte at dinner that evening that she should adopt the library to her own use, since it was quite the best room in the house, and would, from its secluded position, sunny aspect, and door into the garden, provide any lady in delicate health with an admirable retreat. But this amiable scheme to enrage Aubrey (and through him Venetia) was foiled by Charlotte, who stood in even greater awe of Aubrey than of her mother, and hastily stammered out a repudiation of any desire to evict him from his stronghold. As she added that she much preferred even the smallest of the several parlours to it there was no more to be said, except by Aubrey, who cordially invited Mrs. Scorrier to come and try for herself how comfortable the room was.

Letters from Conway did nothing to improve matters, and gratified none but Charlotte, who received two whole sheets covered, and even crossed, with his sprawling writing, and went about the house for days in a glow of rapture. But as the letter, so far from containing a revocation of that infamous power of attorney, adjured Charlotte not to trouble her pretty head about anything whatsoever, but to leave everything to Venetia, whom he depended on to save his darling the least care or disagreeable exertion, it brought no pleasure to Mrs. Scorrier, but rather aggravated her annoyance, and confirmed her in her determination to rid her of a sister-in-law who enjoyed far too much of her brother's confidence.

Venetia also received a letter from Conway, which, as she told Damerel, would have put her in a towering passion had it not been so irresistibly funny. Exhausted by the labour of composing so handsome a letter to his bride Conway had confined himself to a single sheet in writing to his sister, excusing his brevity on the score of the press of work entailed by the imminent evacuation of the Army of Occupation. He neither explained his sudden marriage nor made the slightest apology for foisting a total stranger upon her without a word of warning. He knew that Venetia could not fail to be pleased with his Charlotte, and depended on her to take the greatest care of her. A dispassionate person, reading this missive, could scarcely have been blamed for supposing that Sir Conway had planned the whole affair with the object of giving his dearest sister a delightful surprise.

Venetia received another letter besides Conway's, but not through the medium of the post. It was brought over from Netherford by one of Edward Yardley's grooms, covered several sheets, and afforded her even less gratification than Conway's short note, since she found nothing in it that tickled her sense of humour. Though surprised and shocked by the news of Conway's marriage Edward was apparently deriving consolation from the conviction that Venetia must be happy in the companionship of her sister-in-law, and his own relief at the knowledge that in Mrs. Scorrier she had at last acquired an eligible chaperon. After moralizing for two pages on the evils of Venetia's previous situation, he covered two more with some very sensible advice to her (for he perfectly understood, he assured her, that she might find it difficult, at first, to accustom herself to the change in her circumstances) and an exact description of his own state of health. He ended by deploring that it was not in his power to visit Undershaw, to pay his compliments to Lady Lanyon, and to fortify Venetia with such guidance and counsel as he could give: not only was there still nearly a week to run before he could emerge from quarantine, but she would be sorry to learn that he had developed a cough, which, though slight, was occasioning some disquiet in his mother's mind. He begged Venetia not to be alarmed, however, since she might depend on him to incur no foolish risks. She would not be surprised to learn, he fancied, that the news that Conway must soon be at home again had done almost as much to hasten his recovery as any of Mr. Huntspill's excellent prescriptions.

Venetia rode over to Ebbersley to spend one day with Lady Denny, but although the respite from the frets and animosities at Undershaw did her good her visit was not one of unalloyed pleasure. One glance at Clara's face was enough to confirm her in the belief that more had passed between her and Conway than her parents had suspected. So indeed she had now confessed, as Lady Denny presently disclosed to her young friend, in reluctant answer to a blunt question. "Yes, my dear, I am afraid you were right," she said. "But as for thinking that Conway was in any way bound to Clara, pray put such a notion out of your head! I need not tell you what were my feelings when I learned that a daughter of mine had behaved with such impropriety, and as for Sir John, I promise you I never saw him more confounded in my life! For, you know, my love, to be exchanging promises with a man without the consent or knowledge of her parents shows such a want of conduct as I had not thought it possible I could discover in Clara! Indeed, it is even worse, for Sir John had expressly forbidden any such exchanges, not because he would not have been very well pleased with the match, but because he judged them both to be too young to enter upon an engagement. If poor Clara had but realized *then* that her papa knew best, how much pain she would have been spared *now!* She is very sensible of how deeply she erred, so we don't reproach her."

"Conway deserves to be *flogged!*" exclaimed Venetia.

"No, my dear, that fault was Clara's, though I don't deny that he did not behave just as he ought. But young men don't take such affairs as seriously as you perhaps suppose, and of *one* thing you may be sure! he neither suggested nor attempted to carry on a clandestine correspondence with Clara!"

"Oh, yes, I am very sure of *that!*" said Venetia. "Only to think I should live to be thankful he is an illiterate! I wish I might congratulate Clara upon her good fortune, but I collect she does not yet see what an escape she has had!"

"No, and we have agreed amongst ourselves that it is a case of the least said the soonest mended. We think that a change of scene would benefit her, and have planned to send her on a visit to her grandmama. Oh dear, if one knew the trouble one's children could be to one!" sighed Lady Denny. "First it was Oswald, and now it is Clara, and next, depend upon it, it will be Emily!"

"Dear ma'am, if you are imagining that there was anything more to Oswald's fancy for me than a fit of boy's nonsense I promise you there was not!" said Venetia, with her usual frankness. "He certainly made a great goose of himself, but wrote me a very handsome apology, so that I am in perfect charity with him."

"It is like your sweet nature to say so, my love," replied Lady Denny, blinking rather rapidly, "but I know very well that he must have behaved most improperly to you, besides vexing Lord Damerel, the very thought of which quite dismayed me!"

"Now, that I am very sure he did not!" declared Venetia.

"So Lord Damerel told Sir John," said her ladyship, with unabated gloom. "Sir John, chancing to meet him the other day, asked him to his head if Oswald had been causing him annoyance, and he replied immediately, *Not at all!* which convinced Sir John that it was only true."

Venetia could not help laughing at this, but she assured her old friend that Oswald had rather amused than annoyed Damerel. Lady Denny remarked with some feeling that it was small comfort to know that one's only son was setting up as a laughing-stock; but she did seem to derive some comfort from the knowledge, for she made a determined effort to overcome her despondency, and demanded from Venetia an account of the happenings at Undershaw. She was not deceived by the comical aspect which Venetia took care to stress, but expressed her opinion of Mrs. Scorrier's conduct in unusually forthright terms, and adjured Venetia not to hesitate, should that Creature become outrageous, to pack up her trunks and come at once to Ebbersley.

"I shall pay Lady Lanyon a bride-visit, of course," she said, with quiet dignity. "Pray, my dear, present my compliments to her, and explain to her that I am prevented at the moment from giving myself the pleasure of making her acquaintance by the illness in my house. Would you believe it, Venetia?—Cook has thrown out a rash this very day!"

On this calamitous note they parted; and it was not until she had waved goodbye to Venetia that Lady Denny realized that her more pressing troubles had driven all thought of Venetia's unfortunate *tendre* for Damerel out of her head. She now recalled that the look of radiance had disappeared from that lovely face, and although she was sorry for the cause she could not but hope that the infatuation which had set the girl in a glow had been as brief as it was violent. Much as she desired to alleviate Venetia's present unhappiness she would have been appalled by the knowledge that only the dangerous rake's presence in the district enabled Venetia to support her trials with smiling fortitude.

When she was with him the most galling vexation dwindled to a triviality; when she recounted to him Mrs. Scorrier's latest attack upon her position she perceived all at once that it was funny. She found it as natural to confide in him as in Aubrey, and, under her present circumstances, far less dangerous, since Aubrey was ripe for murder. There was no more need to warn Damerel not to betray, even to Aubrey, what she might have told him than there was to explain to him the thought that lay behind some ill-expressed utterance.

He found her, late one afternoon, seated alone in the

library, at Aubrey's desk. She was not writing, but sitting with her hands rather tightly clasped on the desk, and her frowning gaze fixed on them in deep abstraction. She paid no heed at first to the opening of the door, which seemed not to penetrate her reverie, but after a moment or two, as though aware of the searching scrutiny bent on her, she looked up, and, seeing Damerel on the threshold, uttered an exclamation of surprise, her brow clearing, and a smile lighting her eyes. She had not been expecting him, for in general he came to Undershaw before noon, and she said, as she rose, and went towards him: "You, my dear friend! Oh, I am *glad* to see you! I fell a prey to blue devils, and needed you so much, to laugh them away! What brings you to us? I didn't look for you today, for I recall that you told me you would be occupied with business."

He showed no disposition to laugh, but replied in rather a harsh tone; "*You* bring me! What is it, dear delight?"

She gave a tiny sigh, but shook her head, and looked up smilingly into his face. "Mere irritation of the nerves, perhaps. Never mind it! I'm better now."

"I do mind it." He had been holding both her hands, but he released one, and drew a finger lightly across her brow. "You mustn't frown, Venetia. Never in my presence, at all events!"

"Well, I won't!" she said obligingly. "Are you smoothing it away—*stoopid?*"

"I wish I might! What has happened to bring the blue devils upon you?"

"Nothing worth the trouble of mentioning to you, or that is not so commonplace as to be a dead bore! A battle royal with Mrs. Gurnard, from which I fled in quaking terror, the cause of the dispute being a complaint against the laundry-maid. Perfectly just, I daresay, but the wretched girl is none other than Mrs. Gurnard's own niece!"

"A Homeric encounter: you should have stayed to hymn it. *That* did not bring the frown to your brow."

"No. If I was frowning, it was in an effort to decide what were best for me to do. I don't think, you see, that we shall be able to remain here, Aubrey and I, until December, and there seems to be little hope that Conway will be free to return until then."

188

"I have never thought you could do so. Tell me the result of your deliberations!" He led her to the sofa as he spoke, and sat down beside her on it.

"None, alas! No sooner do I think of a scheme than objections rear their ugly heads, and I'm back in the suds again. Do you care to advise me? You always give me such good advice, dear friend!"

"If I do, I have the distinction of providing a living refutation of Dr. Johnson's maxim, that example is always more efficacious than precept," he said. "What's your problem? I'll do my best!"

"It is just the problem of where to go, if I should decide to do so—bearing in mind that Aubrey will go with me, and must not be removed from Mr. Appersett's tuition. I've always said that when Conway was married I should form an establishment of my own, and had he become engaged, in the ordinary mode, I should immediately have formed my own arrangements, so that I might have left Undershaw before ever he brought his wife to it. The very few friends I have were aware that that was my intention, and would not have wondered at it. But as things have turned out the case is altered—or so it seems to me. What do you think?"

"I agree that it is altered, in that if you were to leave Undershaw before your brother's return it would be generally assumed, since it must be widely known that he entrusted the management of his estate to you, that you were driven from your home. Which would be the plain truth."

"Exactly so! And that circumstance makes it impossible for me to hire a house in this district."

"True—if you think you owe it to your brother to preserve appearances which he does not seem to set much store by!"

"My dear friend, I have no such notion in my head, so don't curl your lip at me so contemptuously!"

"Not at you, simpleton!"

"At Conway? Oh, by all means, then! The truth is that I owe him nothing."

"On the contrary!"

"Not even that, if you mean that he owes anything to me. I accepted the charge he laid upon me because it suited me to do so. If I hadn't had Aubrey to think of I

189

shouldn't have done it, any more than I should have remained here one day after I came of age."

"Then are you bent on protecting the fair name of Lanyon?" he enquired.

"Stuff! No, be serious, Damerel! you must know I don't care a rush for fair names—witness my pleasure in *your* company! The scruple in my mind concerns Charlotte. Aubrey calls her *sweetly mawkish*, and so she is, but she doesn't deserve to be made any more uncomfortable than she is already, poor little creature! Conway has done all he can to prejudice people against her, and for me to add the finishing touch to his work would be the outside of enough! She has done me no harm—indeed, she is morbidly anxious to defer to me! To such an extent that if Mrs. Scorrier were *hors concours* I should infallibly take upon myself her role, and spend the better part of my time reminding Charlotte that *she* is now mistress at Undershaw! So if I leave Undershaw I must contrive to provide myself with an unexceptionable excuse for doing so, and I must not remain in this neighbourhood. I always meant to go to London, but that was looking ahead to when Aubrey will be at Cambridge. A whole year ahead, and what's to be done during that period has me in a sad puzzle. There must be excellent tutors to be found in London, yet I doubt whether Aubrey—"

"Leave Aubrey for a moment!" he interrupted. "Before I favour you with my opinion of your scheme of setting up an establishment in London—or York—or Timbuctu—tell me something!"

"Very well—but I haven't asked you to give me your opinion of *that!*" she objected.

"You will have it, nevertheless. What has happened since I saw you last, Venetia, to overset you, and make you regard your removal from this place as a matter of sudden urgency?" Her eyes lifted quickly to his; he smiled, in loving mockery, and added: "I don't want any stories about housekeepers or laundry-maids, my girl, and if you think you can hoax me you will have to learn that you are mistaken! What has that devil's daughter done?"

She shook her head. "Nothing more than I told you. I never thought of hoaxing you, but only that I was perhaps refining too much upon something that was said— very likely with no other purpose than to vex me!"

190

"And what *was* said?"

She hesitated for a moment, before replying: "It concerned Aubrey. Mrs. Scorrier dislikes him quite as much as she dislikes me, I fancy—and I must own that he gives her good reason to do so! He is like a particularly malevolent wasp, which, do what you will, continually eludes your efforts to slay it. She brought it on herself, by being spiteful to me, but I'm not excusing him: he should not do it—it is most improper conduct!"

"Oh, confound the boy!" Damerel exclaimed, in quick exasperation. "I hoped I had scotched that pastime!"

She looked at him in surprise. "Did you tell him he must not?"

"No: merely that what he regarded as an agreeable form of relaxation exposes you to the full blast of that woman's malice."

"Then that accounts for it! You did scotch it, and I am truly grateful! During these past two days he has scarcely opened his lips in her presence. But either the mischief is done, or she resents his shutting himself up in his room, and joining us only at dinner-time—with a Greek chorus ringing so loudly in his ears that you may speak his name half-a-dozen times before he hears you! She can't comprehend that, thinks he does it to be uncivil. Charlotte doesn't like him either, but that's because he says things she doesn't understand, which makes her afraid of him. Unfortunately—she is embarrassed by his lameness, and always looks away when he gets up from his chair, or walks across the room."

"I noticed that she did so when I met you in the park that day, and hoped she would speedily rid herself of the habit!"

"I think she tries to. But the thing is that it has provided Mrs. Scorrier with a pretext for saying what, I own, has quite sunk my spirits. She told me that Charlotte has a horror of *deformity*, which makes her wish that just now, when she is in a delicate situation, it might have been possible for Aubrey to visit friends. She did not phrase it as plainly as that and perhaps I have allowed myself to be stupidly apprehensive."

His countenance had darkened; he said in an altered voice; "No. Far from it! If she was capable of saying that to you I would not bet a groat on the chance that she won't say it to Aubrey himself, the first time he puts her in a rage."

"That is what I'm afraid of, but *could* anyone be so infamously cruel?"

"Oh, lord, yes! This vixen, I daresay, would not, in cold blood, but I told you before, my innocent, that you are unacquainted with her sort. Women of unbridled passions are *capable de tout!* Let them but lose their tempers and they will say, and afterwards find excuse for, what, on another's lips, they would condemn with sincere loathing!" He paused, scanning her face with eyes grown suddenly hard and frowning. "What else has she said to you?" he demanded abruptly. "You have much better tell me, you know!"

"Well, so I would, but surely you can't wish me to repeat to you a list of malicious *nothings?*"

"No: spare me! That fling at Aubrey was all?"

"It was enough! Damerel, if you knew what tortures of *self-hatred* have been endured—never mentioned, only to be guessed at!—the shrinking from strangers, the dread of pity or such revulsion as Charlotte tries to hide—"

He broke in on her agitation, saying: "I do know. I think it unlikely that this woman would sink so low, unless offered extraordinary provocation, but the boy is abnormally sensitive. Shall I take him off your hands? I've told him already that he may remove to the Priory whenever he chooses. His reply was inelegant, but certainly did him credit. He was much inclined to snap my nose off: demanded if I was in all seriousness inviting him *to run sly*, leaving you to *stand the shock!* It seemed scarcely the moment to suggest to him that the shock would be less if he *did* run sly, but I can still do so, and will, if you tell me to. The only difficulty will be to conceal from him the real cause, and I expect I could overcome that."

She put out her hand, almost unconsciously, saying playfully, to hide her deeper feelings: "What a *good* friend you are, Wicked Baron! Where 'should we be in this pass without you? I know I might, if the worst came to the worst, send Aubrey to you. *That* thought, I promise you, saved me from distraction! In emergency I shouldn't hesitate—were you ever before so scandalously imposed on?—but there's no emergency yet—may never be, if Aubrey will but shut his ears to the things that are said

192

merely to vex and sting. I don't mean to impose on you unless I must!"

His hand had closed on hers, and he was still holding it, but in a clasp that struck her as being curiously rigid. She glanced enquiringly at him, and saw a strange look in his eyes, and about his mouth the bitter sneer that mocked himself. She must have betrayed bewilderment in her face, for the sneer vanished, he smiled, and said lightly, as he released her hand: "I defy anyone to impose on me! I should be glad to have Aubrey at the Priory. I like the boy, and certainly don't consider him a charge, if that's what's in your mind. No one could accuse him of being a difficult guest to entertain! Let him come to me when you choose, and remain for as long as may suit you both!"

"Thus positively conferring a favour on you!" she said, laughing. "Thank you! It would not, I think, be for very long. Lady Denny tells me that Sir John has heard from Mr. Appersett that he means to return to us before the middle of next month. I suspect his cousin—who was so obliging as to offer exchange with him after his illness—has no great fancy to spend the winter in Yorkshire! Mr. Appersett told me years ago that if ever I should wish to go away for a time he would readily give Aubrey house-room."

"Then, Aubrey's affairs being satisfactorily arranged, we will turn to your own, *Admired Venetia!* Are you serious when you talk of setting up your own establishment?"

"Yes, of course I am!"

"Then it is time someone took order to you!" he said grimly "Leave nursery-dreams, and come to earth, my dear! It is not possible!"

"But it is perfectly possible! Don't you know that I'm mistress of what Mr. Mytchett—he is our lawyer, and one of my trustees—calls a considerable independence?"

"I still tell you that it is not possible!"

"Good God, Damerel, *you* don't mean to talk propriety to me, do you?" she exclaimed. "I warn you, you won't easily convince me that the least impropriety attaches to a woman of my years choosing rather to live in her own house than in her brother's! If I were a girl—"

"You are not only a girl, but a green girl!"

193

"Green I'll allow, girl I will not! I'm five-and-twenty, my friend. I know it would be thought improper if I were to live alone, and though I think it nonsensical I don't mean to outrage the conventions, I promise you. While Aubrey is at Cambridge I shall engage a chaperon. When he has taken his degree—well, I don't know yet, of course, but I expect he will next become a Fellow, and remain fixed in Cambridge, in which event the likeliest chance is that I shall keep house for him there, for I shouldn't think he would marry, should you?"

"God give me patience!" he ejaculated, springing up, and taking a hasty turn about the room. "Venetia, will you *stop* talking like a sapskull? Engage a chaperon! Keep house for Aubrey! Don't forget to buy a stock of caps suitable for a dowager, or an ageing spinster, I do beg you! Listen to me, you beautiful idiot! you've wasted six—seven—years of your life; don't waste any more! What, for heaven's sake, do you imagine would be the advantage in this house of yours? *Who* is to be your chaperon?"

"I don't know: how should I? I had supposed that it must be possible to hire, as one would a governess, some lady in impoverished circumstances—a widow, perhaps—who would answer the purpose."

"Then suppose it no longer! You might hire a score of widows, but not one to answer the purpose. I can picture this establishment! Where is it to be? In Kensington, I think, genteel and retired! Or perhaps in the wilds of Upper Grosvenor Place: just on the fringe of fashion! You will be dismally bored, my dear, I assure you!"

She looked a little amused. "Then I shall travel. I have always wanted to do that."

"What, with an impoverished widow for escort, no acquaintance anywhere but in Yorkshire, and rather less knowledge of the world than a chit out of boarding-school? My poor innocent, when I think of the only friendships you would be likely to form under such circumstances I promise you my blood runs cold! It won't do: Believe me, I know what I'm talking about! To carry off such an existence as you propose you must needs be fabulously wealthy, and eccentric into the bargain! Wealth, my dear delight, would excuse your eccentricity, and open most doors to you. You might hire a mansion in the best part of town, furnish it with oriental magnificence, force yourself on the notice of the *ton* by indulging in expensive freaks, boldly send out invitation cards—you would meet with some rebuffs, and not a few cuts-direct, but—"

"Be quiet, you absurd creature!" she interrupted, laughing. "That's not the life I want! How could you think I should?"

"I don't think it. Are you going to tell me that you want the life you would most certainly lead under your own scheme? You will be more bored and more lonely than ever in your life, for I assure you, Venetia, without acquaintance, without the correct background, you had as well live on a desert island as in London!"

"Oh, dear! Then what *am* I to do?"

"Go to your Aunt Hendred!" he replied.

"I mean to do so—but not to stay. I shouldn't like that—or she either, I fear. Nor would her house do for Aubrey."

"Aubrey, Aubrey! Think for once of *yourself!*"

"Well, and so I do! You know, Damerel, I never thought I could bear to stay at Undershaw with another woman as its mistress, and now I've discovered that it would fret me very much to live under such conditions anywhere! And to live with my aunt and uncle, submitting to their decrees, as I should be obliged to do, recognizing their authority, would be unendurable, like finding myself back again in the nursery! I've been my own mistress for too long, dear friend."

He looked at her, across the room, a wry smile on his lips. "You would not have to endure it for very long," he said.

"Too long for me!" she said firmly. "It will be five years at least, I imagine, before Aubrey will be ready to set up in a house of his own, and perhaps by then he won't wish it! Besides—"

"Greenhead! Oh, greenest of greenheads!" he said. "Go to your aunt, let her launch you into society—as she is well able to do!—and before Aubrey has gone up to Cambridge the notice of your engagement will be in the *Gazette!*"

She did not speak for a moment, but looked straitly at him, a little less colour in her cheeks, no lurking smile in her eyes. She could find no clue to his thoughts in his face, and was puzzled, but not alarmed. "No," she said at last. "It won't be. Did you think that my purpose in going to London was to find a husband?"

"Not your purpose. Your destiny—as it should be!"

"Ah! My *aunt's* purpose will be to find a husband for me?" He answered only with a shrug, and she got up, saying: "I'm glad you've warned me: is it allowable for an unmarried female to put up at an hotel? if she has a maid with her?"

"Venetia—!"

She smiled, putting up her eyebrows. "My dear friend, you are too *stoopid* today! Why must you picture me moped to tears, pining for company, bored because I shall be leading the life I'm accustomed to? Why, no! a much more entertaining life! Here, I've had books, and my garden, and, since my father died, the estate, to occupy me. In London, there will be museums, and picture-galleries, the theatre, the opera—oh, so much that to you seems commonplace, I daresay! And I shall have Aubrey during his vacations, and since I have an aunt who won't, I hope, cut my acquaintance, I don't *utterly* despair of forming a few agreeable friendships!"

"No, my God, *no!*" he exclaimed, as though the words had been wrenched out of him, and crossed the room in two hasty strides. "*Anything* were better than that!" He grasped her by the shoulders, so roughly that she was startled into uttering a protest. He paid no heed to it, but said harshly; "Look at me!"

She obeyed unhesitatingly, and endured with tranquillity a fierce scrutiny as keenly searching as a surgeon's lancet, only murmuring, a little mischievously: "I bruise *very* easily!"

His grip slackened, and slid down her arms to gather her hands together, and hold them, clasped strongly between his own. "What were you doing when you were nine years old, my dear love?" he asked.

It was so unexpected that she could only blink.

"Tell me!"

"I don't know! Learning lessons, and sewing samplers, I suppose—and what in the world has that to say to anything?"

"A great deal. Do you know what I was doing at that date?"

"No, how should I? I don't even know how old you were—at least, not without doing sums, which I abominate. Well, if you are eight-and-thirty now, and I am five-and-twenty—"

"I'll spare you the trouble: I was two-and-twenty, and seducing a married lady of quality."

"So you were!" she agreed affably.

A laugh shook him, but he said: "That was the first of my amorous adventures, and probably the most discreditable. So I hope! There is nothing whatsoever in my life to look back upon with pride, but until I met you, my lovely one, I could at least say that my depravity stopped short of tampering with the young and innocent. I never ruined any reputation but Sophia's—but don't account it a virtue in me! It's a dangerous game, seducing virgins, and, in general, they don't appeal to me. Then I met you, and, to be frank with you, my dear, I stayed in Yorkshire for no other purpose than to win you—on my own terms!"

"Yes, you told me as much, when we parted on that first day," she said, quite unperturbed. "I thought it a great piece of impertinence, too! Only then Aubrey had that fall, and we became such good friends—and everything was changed."

"Oh, no, not everything! You call me your friend, but I never called you mine, and never shall! You remained, and always will, *a beautiful, desirable creature*. Only my intentions were changed. I resolved to do you no hurt, but leave you I could not!"

"Why should you? It seems to me a foolish thing to do."

"Because you don't understand, my darling. If the gods would *annihilate but space and time*—but they won't, Venetia, they won't!"

"Pope," she said calmly. "*And make two lovers happy.* Aubrey's favourite amongst English poets, but not mine. I see no reason why two lovers should not be happy without any meddling with space and time."

He released her hands, but only to pull her into his arms. "When you smile at me like that, it's all holiday with me! O God, I love you to the edge of madness, Venetia, but I'm not mad yet—not so mad that I don't know how disastrous it might be to you—to us both! You don't realize what an advantage I should be taking of your innocence!" He broke off suddenly, jerking up his head as the door opening on to the passage from the ante-room slammed. The sound was followed by that of a dragging footstep. Damerel said quickly: "Aubrey. As well, perhaps! There's so much that must be said—but not today! Tomorrow, when we are both cooler!"

There was no time for more; he put her almost brusquely away from him, and turned, as the door was opened, to face Aubrey, who came into the room with his pointer-bitch at his heels.

14

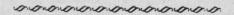

Damerel had placed himself between Venetia and the door, but it was immediately apparent that the precaution was unnecessary. Aubrey was looking stormy, his thin cheeks flushed, and his rather cold gray eyes full of sparks of light. His interest in his fellow-creatures was at the best of times perfunctory; when in the grip of anger he had none whatsoever, and would scarcely have noticed it had he found his sister in Damerel's arms. He said, in a brittle voice, as he shut the door: "You'll like to know, Venetia, that the Empress has issued a new ukase! The dogs—*my* dogs!—must in future be kept chained up! All but Bess here, who is too savage to be kept at all! Take care, Jasper; can't you see what an ugly-tempered bitch she is?"

Damerel, who was gently pulling the pointer's ears, while she stood with gracefully waving tail and an expression on her face of idiotic bliss, laughed, and said: "What's she been doing?"

"Endangering the succession!" Aubrey snapped. "She came into the house—looking for me, of course!—and Charlotte finding her lying at the foot of the stairs was so startled and appalled that she let out a screech, which made Bess lift up her head, and stare at her—as well she might!"

"Oh dear!" sighed Venetia. "I know Charlotte doesn't care for dogs, but if that's all that happened—"

"All! It was but the start of Bess's ferocious assault! Understand, m'dear, that her stare put Charlotte forcibly in mind of a wild beast! She knew not what to do, but decided on retreat—backwards, and stealthily! Whereupon Bess, not unnaturally intrigued, you may think, rose, and advanced towards her. Charlotte then screamed in good earnest, and ran behind a chair; Bess followed, Mrs. Scorrier burst out from the morning-room to discover what villain was attempting to rape her child, and started scolding Bess, and striking at her with the thing she had in her hand—what-d'ye call it? tambour frame? So Bess began to bark, Charlotte fell into hysterics, and—"

"Aubrey, how *could* you have allowed it?" exclaimed Venetia, between annoyance and amusement. "It was too bad of you!"

"You're mistaken: I wasn't there. What I'm recounting I had from the lips of the afflicted ladies." He grinned sardonically at his sister. "I was your *good* little brother, m'dear! I arrived in the arena to find Charlotte sunk in a chair, with Mrs. Scorrier waving her vinaigrette under her nose, and Bess baying the pair of them, but wagging her tail to show that though she wouldn't stomach being chased from her own house she was too well-bred to bite. I didn't think it of the least use to try sicking her on to the Empress, so I called her off. I even told that hen-hearted little ninny that she'd no need to be afraid, but all the thanks I got was abuse from the Empress. I brought Bess into the house on purpose to frighten Charlotte; my manners, character, and disposition all passed under unfavourable review, while Charlotte bleated *Oh, pray, Mama! Oh, no, Mama!* I think I bore it pretty well. Only when the Empress got to talking of Charlotte's delicate situation I couldn't resist! Not if I'd tried to, which I didn't. She said that perhaps I didn't *realise*, to which I replied that indeed I did, for Bess was in the same interesting condition. For one halcyon moment I thought she was going off in an apoplexy."

"Fiend!" Venetia said, trying not to laugh.

"Yes, and, what's worse, one who thinks because he is a cripple he may go his length," said Aubrey, in a silken tone. "Oh, don't look like that, stoopid! Do you imagine I haven't known from the outset how abhorrent my limp is to the pair of them? I'm sure I don't blame them for that—but Nurse did! By that time, you understand, she had come bustling downstairs to discover what was the reason for all the commotion. You missed a high treat, m'dear! She told the Empress to think shame on herself; she told Charlotte to stop kicking up such an uproar about nothing; and she told me to go away before I forgot that I at least had been taught better than to raise such a nasty, vulgar disturbance in a gentleman's establishment!"

"That was the most unkindest cut of all!" remarked Damerel. "I'd back your nurse against fifty Mrs. Scorriers!"

"Well, the issue was undecided when I left, but I daresay Nurse will come off the best," agreed Aubrey. "The cream of the jest is that she, who always cuts up stiff when even Conway brings his dogs into the house, flew up into the boughs when the Empress announced that she would not *allow* me to keep Bess unless kennelled, since she was clearly dangerous! She was so imprudent as to order me to chain her immediately, and to demand if I had not heard her, when I turned my back upon all that monstrous regiment, and brought Bess along the passage to my own room. The last I heard of the battle was a demand from Nurse to know what right the Empress quite falsely supposed she had to dictate to a *Lanyon born* in his own house."

"Oh dear!" Venetia sighed. She glanced at Damerel, a hint of shyness in her smile. "I must go, and do what I can to settle the dispute. Nurse will start quoting from the Book of Proverbs: she was doing so to me only yesterday, all about brawling and contentious women, and how much better it is to dwell in the corner of the housetop—not that I think she would consent to do so, if that means the attics!"

"Don't be a sapskull!" Aubrey interrupted sharply. "Let her say what she chooses to that virago! If she can rid us of her, so much the better!"

"Yes, if she *could*, but Mrs. Scorrier would never permit herself to be worsted by Nurse! And if Nurse becomes outrageous, only think how difficult it would be for us!"

"Do you mean to tell that woman the dogs shall be kept on chains?" he demanded, a still angrier flush staining his cheeks. "I give you fair warning, Venetia, that if you do that I'll shut Flurry into her bedchamber, with her best bonnet to worry!"

"Oh, love, don't *tempt* me!" she said mischievously. "Of course I don't mean to do any such thing! But I think it no more than just to promise her that you'll bring the dogs only into this room. It is nonsensical of Charlotte to be so much afraid of them, but—oh, Aubrey, we *must* remember that it is now *her* house, and not ours!"

"Remember it! When are we allowed to forget it?" he flung at her.

She said nothing, but turned to the door. Damerel moved to open it for her, and said, as she paused for a moment, looking up at him in the silent enquiry: "Decisive, I think! I shall see you tomorrow, but not, I fear, before noon. I was going to tell you—but it's no matter! My agent is at the Priory; I've been closeted with him most of the day, and I fancy shall be so again all the morning. It's important, or I'd let him go hang. As it is—" he paused, and smiled faintly, "—as it is, I must bear with him. Don't let that woman vex you to death!"

She shook her head, his smile reflected in her eyes, and hurried away, across the ante-room.

He shut the door, and turned, meditatively surveying Aubrey, who had gone over to the fire, and was savagely stirring the logs to a blaze. He did not look up from this task, but as though aware that he was being studied said pugnaciously: "It was no fault of mine!"

"Well, don't start ripping up at me!" replied Damerel. "I haven't said it was. Stop putting yourself into a passion for nothing more than a storm in a teacup!" Aubrey looked at him, his mouth hard shut, and two deep clefts between his brows. "Gudgeon!" Damerel said, friendly mockery in his eyes.

Aubrey gave a short laugh. "I'd give a monkey to be present when she tells Conway she won't have his dogs in the house! As for Charlotte, she'd do well to accustom herself to them, for she ain't likely ever to see him without as least three at his heels. What's more, Conway's dogs are the worst trained in the country, and infernal nuisances! He lets 'em jump on the chairs, and gives 'em scraps of meat at table. I don't make fools of *my* dogs! Oh, hell and the devil confound him, beef-witted Jack Pudding that he is!"

"Come back to the Priory, and we'll confound him in unison!" invited Damerel. "I have some worse epithets for him under *my* tongue!"

Aubrey grinned, but shook his head. "No, I'm not so paltry! I wish to God I *were* back at the Priory, but I've told you already I won't rub off."

202

"Well, I never try conclusions with mules, so I'll rub off myself," Damerel said, shrugging, and picking up his hat and his whip from the chair on which he had laid them. "*Hasta manana*, you testy pup!"

Aubrey glanced quickly at him, seemed to hesitate, and then said: "Are you out with me? I didn't mean—"

"No, I'm not out with you, chucklehead!" Damerel answered, laughing at him. "Stand buff, if you feel you must—I daresay I should do the same in your shoes."

He went away, and Aubrey, after a few minutes, sat down at the desk and expended his spleen on the composition of a venomous Latin epigram. After several unsatisfactory essays he achieved four neat and splendidly scurrilous lines, which pleased him so much that he sat down to dinner in a mood of almost bland complaisance. Informed by Mrs. Scorrier that until he expressed contrition for his behaviour she must decline to notice him, he merely bestowed a flickering smile upon her before applying himself with unusual appetite to his dinner.

Little conversation was exchanged, Mrs. Scorrier's loss of temper having been succeeded by majestic sulks, and Charlotte's hysterical fit by a nervous despondency which led her to reply to any remark addressed to her in a scared, breathless voice that discouraged further attempts to divert her mind from morbid self-contemplation. On rising from the table she excused herself, pleading a severe headache, and went upstairs to bed; and as Venetia accepted an invitation from Aubrey to play billiards Mrs. Scorrier was left to enjoy her sulks in solitude. Whether as a result of this treatment, or from the inescapable realization that in ostracizing the Lanyons she distressed no one but Charlotte, she appeared next morning with so firm a smile, and so inexhaustible a flow of amiable commonplaces, that she might have been supposed to have suffered a complete loss of memory. Venetia was not deceived, for the glitter in Mrs. Scorrier's eyes gave the lie to her smile, but she responded with absent civility to whatever was said to her, too preoccupied with her own affairs to perceive that her abstraction was causing Mrs. Scorrier to feel quite as much uneasiness as vexation. It had been forcibly brought home to Mrs. Scorrier that in her eagerness to ensure Charlotte's supremacy at Undershaw she had gone too far. She wanted to rid Undershaw of Venetia and Aubrey, but not under such circumstances as must render herself and Charlotte odious; and she had had the painful experience of seeing the daughter of whom, in her overbearing fashion, she was sincerely fond, turn not to the parent who was fighting her battles but to the detestable old woman who threatened to throw a jug of cold water over her if she did not instantly abate her hysterical tears. It had not previously occurred to Mrs. Scorrier that she might drive the Lanyons away only to find that Charlotte, instead of being grateful, and ready to convince Conway that she had been made wretched by their unkindness, was ranged on their side, and a great deal more likely to tell Conway that their eviction had been none of her doing.

Finding Venetia unresponsive even to compliment, she smiled more widely than before and forced her unwilling tongue to describe the irresistible prompting of maternal instinct to fly to the support of a beloved child. The result of this magnanimous gesture was disappointing, for after staring blankly at her for a minute, all Venetia said was: "Oh—Bess! Poor Charlotte! I do hope she will contrive to overcome her fear of dogs. Conway's are always so boisterous and unruly that I'm afraid her life will be a misery if she doesn't."

After that, she went away, and was next heard desiring Ribble to send a message to the stables that her mare was to be brought up to the house. From what Mrs. Scorrier presently overheard her saying to Aubrey she gathered that she was going to visit some tenant or retainer, who was the victim of an unnamed accident; and that at once deepened her resentment, because she felt that it was for Charlotte to enact the role of lady bountiful; and she would have liked very much to have accompanied her daughter in the carriage, dispensing comforts to the sick and indigent, giving good advice to the improvident, and in general showing all Conway's dependants how to contrive to the best advantage.

Had she but known it, neither charity nor advice would have been acceptable to the afflicted household, whose master was, in fact, a respectable farmer; and the accident which had befallen his youngest son, a lusty young man of some ten summers, was not one that called for jellies or sustaining broths, but rather (in the opinion of his incensed parent) for very different treatment, since all he had done was to break his arm, and that through an act of foolhardy disobedience. Venetia's visit was one merely of civility, and might not have been paid had she been feeling less restless, or more able to bear with patience the complaints of the various members of the domestic staff at Undershaw, who let no day pass without soliciting her aid against the encroachments of Mrs. Scorrier.

At the time, although she had wished her otherwhere, Aubrey's intrusion upon a scene that belonged to herself and Damerel alone had not greatly disturbed her. She had been obliged immediately to grapple with a crisis of a very different order, and it was not until much later that she had had the opportunity to think over all that had passed in the library, and to wonder what might have been the meaning behind some of the things Damerel had said to her. She no more doubted that she was loved than that the sun would rise on the morrow; yet, as she lay wakeful in her bed, her deep content, which neither the domestic brawl nor Mrs. Scorrier's sulks had the power to penetrate, became ruffled by a sense of misgiving, too inchoate to be at first recognizable, but gradually turning content to a vague disquiet. Nothing had been said that she could not attribute to some scruple of masculine honour, too frivolous not to be easily overcome; but even as she smiled at man's folly the fear that a different interpretation could be set upon Damerel's reluctance to commit himself peeped in her mind for a searing instant. It vanished as swiftly in the recollection of tenderness which instinct told her was far removed from the fleeting lust of a voluptuary; it was causeless, springing either from the irrational misgivings of a tired brain, or from mankind's superstitious dread of the unknown, malignant gods, whose sport was to ruin mortal happiness.

In the morning these fears abated. The night had been stormy; Venetia thought, as she looked from her window at the withered leaves blown in drifts across the lawn, that it had been the mournful howl of the wind and the flurries of rain beating against the windowpanes which had kept her awake and encouraged her to indulge morbidity. Damerel was coming to Undershaw, and the night's apprehensions had been nothing but lurid fancies imposed on weariness by the elements. Then she recalled that he had said he had business to attend to which would keep him at home all the morning, and was daunted again, until she remembered that he had told her that he had summoned his agent to the Priory. The agent was probably an attorney, and must certainly have come from London to wait upon him, and would as certainly be anxious to transact whatever the business was as speedily as might be. Damerel, too, would scarcely wish to keep him kicking his heels in Yorkshire for any longer than was necessary. So she argued away the thought that if Damerel were as lost in love as she believed him to be, no business, however important, would have kept him away from her for so many hours; but the serenity which had been like a warm cloak wrapped about her was disturbed; she found herself questioning what it had never before occurred to her to doubt; could not bring her mind to bear on any other problem than her own, harness her impatience, or tolerate the efforts of Mrs. Scorrier or Mrs. Gurnard to intrude upon her abstraction.

The farm she was to visit was in a distant part of the estate; the mare was fresh, and although the day was dull and a sharpness in the wind reminded her that the loveliest autumn within her memory was sliding into winter, the ride did much to lighten the unaccountable oppression of her spirits. She reached Undershaw again a few minutes before noon, knowing that today there was little chance that Aubrey would interrupt a tete-a-tete, since he had gone to one of the farther coverts, packing into the gig himself, his two spaniels, the gamekeeper, his treasured Mantons, and a large hamper containing such nuncheon as Mrs. Gurnard and Cook considered suitable for a delicate youth whose thin form they had for years been trying to fatten. No broken meats would be brought home to wound their sensibilities; and if either dame suspected that the game-pie, the galantine, the pigeon in jelly, and the Queen cakes, warm from the oven, would be much appreciated by the keeper and the spaniels, while Aubrey lunched on a morsel of cheese and an apple, she could be trusted to keep such dispiriting reflections to herself.

As Venetia slipped from the saddle, and gathered up the long skirt of her habit, Fingle came out of the harness-room, to take the mare's bridle. She saw at once that he was big with news, and so indeed it proved: he disclosed that she had not been gone from Undershaw above half an hour when a chaise-and-four had driven up to the house, and set down no less a person than Mr. Philip Hendred.

She was amazed, for so far from having had the least warning of this visit she had not yet received a reply to the letter she had written to her aunt, to announce the news of Conway's marriage. She exclaimed: "My uncle?" so incredulously, that Fingle was pleased with the sensation he had made, and confided to her that he too had been regularly sent to grass. "He come all the way in his own chaise, miss," he told her, apparently feeling that this circumstance added lustre to the unexpected visit, "*and* his own postilions, I suspicion, by the way he never offered to pay them, nor gave them the money for their board, but sent them on straight to the Red Lion."

"Sent them to the Red Lion!" she interrupted, quite shocked. "Good heavens, how did Ribble—or you—come to allow such a thing?"

But it appeared that Mr. Hendred had silenced every hospitable protest, which Fingle reminded Venetia, was to have been expected, seeing that when he had spent close on a se'ennight at Undershaw, when the master took and died, he would not for any persuasion suffer them to house his postilions, nor yet his cattle. "But he fetched his valet up with him that time, miss, which this time he hasn't."

This information, which was delivered in the voice of one reaching a climax, failed to astonish Venetia. She only said that she must go at once to greet her guest, and hurried away just as Fingle was preparing to describe to her in slow detail the several points and blemishes of the team of post-horses harnessed to the chaise.

She did not stay to change her riding-dress, but went immediately to the drawing-room, in which apartment Ribble informed her she would find Mr. Hendred being entertained by her ladyship and Mrs. Scorrier. Entering it, she paused for a moment on the threshold, still holding her whip in one hand, her cheeks becomingly flushed by the wind, and the tail of her habit cast over her arm. Then, as Mr. Hendred rose from a chair by the fire, and came

207

towards her, she let her skirt fall about her feet, cast aside her whip, and advanced to meet him with her hands held out: "My dear sir, of all the charming surprises! I am so happy to see you—but that, I give you warning, shan't stop me from plucking a crow with you! Let me tell you that we think ourselves insulted in Yorkshire when our guests send their servants and their horses to rack up at an inn!"

Before he could answer, Mrs. Scorrier broke in, saying archly: "Ah, did I not assure you, sir, that Miss Lanyon would cry out on you? But you must know, dear Miss Lanyon, that it has lately become the rule in many establishments far larger than this not to take in the horses of visitors, or more than one servant."

"That does not suit our northern notions of hospitality," said Venetia. "But tell me, sir, what brings you to Undershaw? I hope you mean to make a *respectable* stay with us on this occasion, and not post off in a great hurry before we have well realized that you have arrived!"

His rather severe countenance relaxed into a slight smile; he replied in a dry, precise voice: "My time, you know, my dear Venetia, is not as much my own as I could sometimes wish. The purpose of my visit concerns yourself, as I hope presently to explain to you."

She was a little surprised, but since he was her principal trustee supposed that he must have come to discuss some matter of business with her. She twinkled at him, and said: "If you are come to tell me that my fortune has vanished away on that mysterious thing called *Change*, wait until I have provided myself with a few burnt feathers and some sal volatile!"

He smiled again, but perfunctorily, because such a suggestion was too shocking to be humorous. Mrs. Scorrier again insinuated herself into the conversation. "It is too bad of you to keep her in suspense, Mr. Hendred, particularly when you have such a delightful treat in store for her! Don't fear, Miss Lanyon! You have my word for it that your uncle's errand is such as must be more likely to cast you into transports than into dismay!"

By this time two circumstances had been made plain to Venetia. From Mrs. Scorrier's effusive civility she gathered that she was well acquainted with Mr. Hendred's social and financial standing, and was determined to ingratiate herself with him; and from the cold glance with which her efforts were received that Mr. Hendred had taken her in strong dislike. Venetia thought it as well to remove him from her vicinity before he was provoked into giving her an acid setdown, so she invited him to go with her to the morning-room, since there were one or two matters of business she would like to discuss with him. Mrs. Scorrier took this in surprisingly good part, explaining her complaisance to her daughter, as soon as they were alone, by the simple announcement that Mr. Hendred was said to be worth every penny of £20,000 a year.

That made Charlotte stare, for there was nothing in Mr. Hendred's appearance to suggest opulence. But for the subtle distinction attaching to any coat, however plain, of Weston's making he might have passed for a lawyer in respectable but unassuming circumstances. He was a thin man, of rather less than medium height, with spindle-shanks, sparse gray hair, and a sharp-featured countenance which bore all the marks of chronic dyspepsia. He always dressed with neatness and propriety, but since any form of extravagances or display was abhorrent to him he wore no other jewellery than his signet-ring, and a modest gold pin securing the folds of his neck-cloth; never sported startling waistcoats or exaggerated shirt-points; and had inexorably transferred his patronage from Stulz to Weston when Mr. Stulz had been so unwise as to send home his new coat embellished with buttons designed according to the very latest fashion, and twice as large as Mr. Hendred considered seemly.

His avoidance of the extremes of fashion notwithstanding, Mr. Hendred was a gentleman of the first consequence, for besides possessing all the advantages of a very large fortune he was so well connected as to make it unwise to utter disparaging remarks in his presence about any member of the nobility, since the chances were that he was in some way related to that particular peer. He was a Member of Parliament, a Justice of the Peace, and, since his remarkable turn for business was allied to a rigid sense of duty, his was the first name that occurred to anyone needing a trustee or an executor.

Without being clutchfisted he liked to be beforehand with the world. He would tolerate no unnecessary expenditure in his household; and while he paid as much as £60 a year to a French cook, and never travelled with hired post-boys, his lady knew better than attempt to persuade him to engage one more footman than he thought necessary for the smooth running of the establishment. Besides a mansion in Cavendish Square he had a large estate in Berkshire, and two less important ones in different parts of the country; but, unlike the fifth Duke of Devonshire, who had maintained no fewer than ten houses fully staffed the year round, he kept his in good order with no more than skeleton staffs.

Venetia had first made his acquaintance when she had been invited by her aunt to spend a week at Harrogate. Mr. Hendred had been advised to try what the famous waters would do to cure him of his stomachic disorders, but unfortunately neither the waters nor the climate agreed with his constitution, and after ten days of miserable discomfort he beat a nauseated retreat. But in spite of his ailments he had been a kind and an attentive host, promoting every scheme for Venetia's entertainment, and contriving to make it plain to her, without committing the impropriety of uttering any criticism of his brother-in-law's eccentricity, that he strongly disapproved of the restricted life she was obliged to lead, and would be glad to rescue her from it. That had not been possible; and when, on Sir Francis Lanyon's death, he had renewed his offer of hospitality it had seemed to her no more possible than before. She had declined it; he had acquiesced in her decision; and as the matter had then been allowed to drop she had supposed that he had accepted her refusal as irrevocable. She was therefore a good deal startled to learn from him that his sole purpose in coming to Undershaw was to carry her off immediately to Cavendish Square, where he trusted she would believe herself to be a welcome addition to his family.

She was very much touched but he would not permit her to express the sense of her obligation. Setting the tips of his bony fingers together, and speaking with measured severity, he said: "You are aware, I don't doubt, my dear Venetia, of what my sentiments have always been. I hope it is not necessary for me to add that both your aunt and I hold you in affection and esteem. Hyperbole is foreign to my nature, but I don't hesitate to tell you that your conduct, distinguished as it has always been by good sense and upright principles, is such as must command respect. In fact, my dear niece," he added, warming to his theme, "you are a very good girl, and have been shabbily used by those who should have made your comfort their first concern! Let me assure you that it will give me a great deal of pleasure to do whatever may be in my power to recompense you for the years you have sacrificed to what you saw to be your duty!" She made a gesture of protest, but he merely frowned at her, and said with asperity: "Allow me to be plain with you, I beg! Reluctant as I am to open my lips to you on the subject of your late father's peculiarities I believe it to be proper for me to say that although I do not deny that he was in many ways an estimable man his behaviour upon the unhappy event which occurred during your childhood seemed to me to be as selfish as it was ill-judged. He was aware of my sentiments: more I will not say, except that I could not but acknowledge the propriety of a daughter's submitting to a parent's will. When, upon his sudden demise, you felt it to be your duty to remain here during the *then* unavoidable absence of your elder brother, I could not deny the force of your arguments, or think it right to press you. Nor did I renew my persuasions when it became apparent that Conway, instead of returning to set you free from the responsibilities you had been so unselfish as to have taken upon your own shoulders, had no notion of consulting anything but his own pleasure, for I was well aware that it would be useless, since you could be depended on to find excuses for him. When, however, I was made aware of the contents of the letter you wrote to your aunt—Venetia, I do not scruple to say that I have seldom been more shocked, or that I consider Conway's conduct in thrusting upon you in such a fashion not only his wife, but also her mother, is *outrageous*, and such as to release you from all obligation to continue at Undershaw!"

"Of course it is!" she agreed, a good deal amused. "I don't scruple to say so either! But I have never believed it to be my duty to stay here on his account, you know. I remained for Aubrey's sake—and pray don't imagine that the least sacrifice was entailed, my dear sir! He and I are the best of good friends, and have kept house very comfortably together, I assure you."

He regarded her with bleak approval, but said, in his dryest voice; "You will hardly do so now that Mrs. Scorrier has quartered herself upon you, however."

"No, indeed we shan't! I had already realized that the sooner I make other arrangements for us both the better it will be. I fancy Mrs. Scorrier had shown you her most conciliating face, so that you might find it impossible to believe how odious I find her!"

"My dear Venetia, you have no need to tell me, for I am well-acquainted with her sort! A very pushing, overbearing female, who wants both conduct and manner. Depend upon it, the unseemly haste of this marriage may be laid at her door! A very good match for her daughter she had contrived, upon my word! I am excessively displeased that Conway should have had no more sense than to shackle himself to such a dab of a girl, who has nothing to recommend her but a pretty face and an amiable temper. Her birth is no more than respectable, and as for fortune, I should doubt of her having above a thousand pounds settled upon her, and very likely less, for the Scorriers are not wealthy, and her father, besides, was a younger son."

This circumstance seemed to increase his disgust, and for several minutes he was unable to dismiss it from his mind. But when he had delivered himself of sundry pungent observations, and moralised briefly on the evils of impetuosity and improvidence he returned to the object of his visit, and in a manner that showed him to have formed the fixed resolve of removing Venetia from Undershaw immediately. "I do not wish to put you to inconvenience, Venetia, but it would be very agreeable to me if you could be ready to go with me tomorrow morning."

"But I could not! Even if— Dear sir, you must allow me time to think! There are so many considerations—Aubrey—Undershaw—Oh, sometimes I think I shall be obliged to remain here until Conway returns, for heaven

212

only knows what that woman might not do if she were left in command here!"

"As to that, it will not be in her power to overset your arrangements, my dear. I do not doubt that she has every disposition to do so, and so I thought it prudent to inform her that since Lady Lanyon has neither the authority nor the experience to assume the government of her husband's affairs, all such power will be left in Mytchett's hands. Indeed, I have already spoken to Mytchett, and all that remains to be done is for you to put him in possession of the necessary information, and to give him whatever directions you think right. I ventured to tell him that I hoped to bring you to his place of business tomorrow, on our way to London. For Aubrey, I should have explained to you that my invitation was naturally meant for him as well as for you."

She pressed a hand to her brow rather distractedly, for she really knew not what to say, or even what to do. To the objections she raised he returned calm answers that demolished them; and when she confided to him her scheme of setting up her own establishment he said, after a moment's silence, that he would be happy to discuss future plans with her when she was living under his roof. He then told her kindly that he regretted to be obliged to hurry her so uncomfortably, but was persuaded that when she had considered the matter for a little while her good sense would enable her to perceive the wisdom of withdrawing from Undershaw, and under his protection.

"I shall leave you now," he announced, rising to his feet. "I am, as you know, an indifferent traveller, and can never go above a short distance without bringing on my tic. Lady Lanyon will, I must hope, excuse me if I retire to my bed-chamber until dinner-time. No, do not put yourself to the trouble of accompanying me, my dear niece! I know my way, and have already desired your excellent housekeeper to send up a hot brick when I ring my bell. A hot brick to the feet, you know, will frequently alleviate cases of severe tic."

She knew him well enough not to persist, and he went away, leaving her to try to collect her scattered wits. It was no easy task, and after a very few moments the only clear thought in her head was that before trying to reach

213

a decision she must see Damerel. This put her in mind of his promise to visit her as near noon as might be, and made her look quickly at the clock. It wanted only a few minutes to one o'clock. She thought he might already be awaiting her in the library, and went there immediately. He was not there. She hesitated, and then, on a sudden resolve, left the house by the garden-door, and went swiftly back to the stables.

Nidd, who had served Damerel for almost as many years as had Marston, accepted the charge of Venetia's mare without betraying that he saw anything remarkable in the visit of an unattended lady to a bachelor's establishment. It was otherwise with Imber, admitting her to the house with reluctance, and exhibiting by every means short of actual speech the utmost disapproval. He ushered her into one of the saloons, and left her there while he went off to inform Damerel of her arrival.

She remained standing by one of the windows, but it was several minutes before Damerel came to her. The saloon seemed unfriendly, with no fire burning in the hearth, and the furniture primly arranged. They had never sat in it when Aubrey was at the Priory, but always in the library, and it still bore the appearance of a room that was never used. Venetia supposed that Imber must have led her to it either to emphasize his disapproval, or because Damerel had not yet finished his business with his agent. It was cheerless, and rather dark; but perhaps that was because heavy clouds were gathering in the sky, and it had started to mizzle.

She had begun to wonder whether she had missed Damerel, who might have set out for Undershaw by way of the road instead of taking the shorter way across country, when the door opened, and he came in, demanding: "Now, what in thunder has your Empress been doing to drive you from home, Admir'd Venetia?"

He spoke lightly, yet with a hint of roughness in his voice, as though her visit was an unwelcome interruption. She turned, trying to read his face, and said, with a faint smile: "Were you busy? You don't sound as though you were glad to see me!"

"I'm not glad to see you," he replied. "You shouldn't be here, you know."

"So Imber seemed to think—but I didn't care for that." She came slowly into the middle of the room, and paused by the table that stood there, drawing off her gloves. "I thought it best to come to you, rather than to wait for you to come to me. It might not be easy for us to be private, and I must consult you. Something quite unlooked-for has happened, and I need your advice, my dear friend. My uncle has come."

"Your uncle?" he repeated.

My Uncle Hendred—my uncle by marriage, I should say. Damerel, he wishes to take me to London, and at once!"

"I see," he said, after a moment's silence. "Well—thus ends a charming autumn idyll, eh?"

"Do you think that that is what I came to say to you?" she asked.

He glanced at her, his eyes a little narrowed. "Probably not. It is the truth, however. Unpleasant, I grant, but still the truth."

She felt as though the blood in her veins was slowly turning to ice. He had turned abruptly away, and walked over to the window; her eyes followed him, but she did not speak. He said harshly: "Yes, it's the end of an idyll. It has been a golden autumn, hasn't it? In another week there won't be a leaf left hanging to the trees, though. Your uncle timed his coming well. You don't think so, do you, my dear? But you will think it, believe me."

She still said nothing, because she could think of nothing it was possible to say. She found it difficult even to take in the sense of what Damerel, incredibly, had said, or to disentangle the wisps of thought that jostled and contradicted each other in her brain. It was like a bad dream, in which people one knew quite well behaved fantastically, and one was powerless to escape from some dreadful doom. She lifted one hand to rub her eyes, as though she had really been dreaming. In a voice that seemed to her to belong to nightmare, because it was so quiet, and in nightmares when one tried to scream one

216

was never able to speak above a whisper, she said: "Why shall I think it?"

He shrugged. "I could tell you, but not convince you. You'll find out for yourself—when you're less green, my dear, and know a little more of the world than what you have read."

"Will you think it?" she asked. A faint flush rose to her whitened cheeks; she added humbly: "I shouldn't ask you that, perhaps but I wish to understand, and I suppose I'm too green—unless things are explained to me."

"I think it would have been better if we had never met," he replied sombrely.

"For you, or for me?"

"Oh, for both of us! The end of the idyll was implicit in the beginning; I at least knew that, though you might not. And also that the more enchanted the idyll the greater must be the pain of its ending. That won't endure. Hearts don't really break, you know. No, of course you don't, but accept it as a truth, for I *do* know!"

"They can be wounded," she said simply.

"Many times—and be healed again, as I have proved!"

She knit her brows. "Why do you say that? It is as if you wished to hurt me, but that can't be so. I don't *feel* that it can be!"

"No, I don't wish to hurt you. I never wished to hurt you. The devil of it was, my dear delight, that you were too sweet, too adorable, and what should have been the lightest and gayest of flirtations turned to something more serious than I intended—or foresaw—or even desired! We allowed ourselves to be too much carried away, Venetia. Did you never feel you were living in a dream?"

"Not then. Now I do. *This* doesn't seem real to me."

"You are too romantic! We have been dwelling in Arcadia, my green girl: the rest of the world is not so golden as this retired spot! Only in fantasy does every circumstance conspire to make it inevitable that two people should fall in love! We should hardly have been more isolated had we been cast on a desert island together. Nothing happened to disturb our idyll, no person intruded on us: for one magical month we forgot—or I forgot—every worldly consideration, even that there are other things in real life than being sunk in love!"

217

"But it was real, for it happened, Damerel."

"Yes, it happened. Let us agree that it was a lovely interlude! It could never be more than that, you know: we must have come to earth—we might even have grown a little weary of each other. That's why I say that your uncle's arrival is well-timed: *parting is such sweet sorrow*—but to fall out of love—oh, no, what a drab and bitter ending that would be to our autumn idyll! We must be able to look back smilingly, my dear delight, not shuddering!"

"Tell me one thing!" she begged. "When you talk of worldly considerations are you thinking of your past life?"

"Why, yes—but of other considerations too! I don't think I should make a good husband, my dear, and nothing else is possible. To be frank with you, providence, in Aubrey's shape, intervened yesterday just in time to save us both from disaster."

She raised her eyes to his face. "You told me yesterday that you loved me—*to the edge of madness*, you said. Was that what you meant? that it was not real, and couldn't endure?"

"Yes, that's what I meant," he said brusquely. He came back to her, and grasped her wrists. "I told you also that we would talk of it when we were cooler: well, my love, the night brings counsel! And the day has brought your uncle—and there let us leave it, and say nothing more than *since there's no help, come let us kiss, and part!*"

She lifted her face in mute invitation; he kissed her, swiftly and roughly, and almost flung her away. "There! Now go, before I take still worse advantage of your innocence!" He strode over to the door, and wrenched it open, shouting to Imber to send a message to Nibb to bring Miss Lanyon's mare up to the house. He turned, and she saw the ugly, mocking sneer on his face, and involuntarily looked away from him. He gave a jeering little laugh, and said; "Don't look so tragic, my dear! I assure you it won't be very long before you will be thanking God to be well out of the devil's own scrape. You won't fall into another, so don't hate me: be grateful to me for opening your beautiful eyes a little! So very beautiful they are—*and about the eyelids much sweetness!* You'll make a hit in London: the young eagles will say

218

you are *something like*—a diamond of the first water—and so you are, my lovely one!"

The sense of struggling through the thickets of a nightmare again swept over her. There was a way out, so her heart's voice cried to her, and could she find it she would find also Damerel, her dear friend. But time was slipping away; in another minute it would be too late; and urgency acted not as a spur but as a creeping paralysis which clogged the mind, and weighted the tongue, and imposed on desperation a blanket of numb stupidity.

Suddenly Damerel spoke again, in his own voice, as it seemed to her, and abruptly: "Does Aubrey go with you?"

She looked blindly at him, and said, as though trying to recall to mind a name long-forgotten: "Aubrey..."

"To London!"

"To London," she repeated vaguely. She passed her hand across her eyes. "Yes, of course—how foolish! I had forgotten. I don't know. He went out. He went out shooting before my uncle came."

"I see. Does your uncle invite him?"

"Yes. But he won't go—I *think* he won't go."

"Do you wish for him?"

She frowned, trying to concentrate her mind. The thought of Aubrey steadied her. She pictured him in such a household as she guessed her uncle's to be, flayed by her aunt's well-meaning solicitude, bored by her attempts to entertain him, contemptuous of all that she believed to be at the first importance; and presently said in a decided tone: "No. Not in Cavendish Square. It wouldn't do for him. Later, when I shall have made arrangements—I told you, didn't I? I must hire a house—someone to lend me countenance—make a home for myself and Aubrey, for it is so *stupid* to say, as Edward does, that Aubrey ought to like what he detests, because other boys do. Aubrey is himself, and no one can alter him, so what is the use of saying *he ought*, when he won't?"

"No use at all. Let him come to me! Tell him he may bring his dogs, and his horses—whatever he chooses! I'll engage myself to see he comes to no harm, and hand him over to that grinder of his in good trim. If he were here you wouldn't fret yourself to flinders over him, would you?"

"No." Her smile went pitifully awry. "Oh, no, how could I? But—"

"That's all!" he interrupted harshly. "You won't be beholden to me, you know! I shall be glad of his company."

"But—you are remaining here?"

"Yes. I'm remaining here. Come! Nidd should have saddled up for you by now!"

She remembered that he had sent for his agent on business which he had said was important; and wondered if he had discovered his affairs to be in a worse state then he had guessed. She said diffidently: "I think you never meant to do so, and that makes me afraid that perhaps the business you have been engaged in hasn't prospered?"

The sneer that mocked himself returned to his face; he gave a short laugh, and replied: "Don't trouble your head over that, for it is not of the smallest consequence!"

He was holding open the door, a suggestion of impatience in his attitude. The second line of the sonnet he had quoted came into her mind: *Nay, I have done: you get no more of me.* He had not spoken those words; there was no need: a golden autumn had ended in storm and drizzling rain, an iridescent bubble had burst, and nothing was left to her but conduct, to help her to behave mannerly. She picked up her gloves and her whip, and walked out of the saloon, and across the flagged hall to the open entrance-door. Imber was standing by it, and through it she could see Nidd, holding her mare's bridle. She was going to say goodbye to Damerel, her friend and her love, watched by these two, and it did not seem to her as though she would be able to speak at all, because her throat was aching quite dreadfully. She stepped out into the open, and turned to him, drawing a painful breath.

He was not looking at her, but at a black cloud looming to the west. "The devil!" he exclaimed. "You'll never reach Undershaw before that comes down on you! What chance of its clearing, Nidd?"

Nidd shook his head. "Setting in wet, m'lord. Spitting already."

Damerel looked down at Venetia, not sneering now, but concerned, ruefully smiling. He said, lowering his voice to reach only her ears: "You must go immediately, my dear. I can't sent you home in my carriage; it wouldn't do! If that woman knew—!"

220

"It is of no consequence." She put out her hand; she was very pale, but the flicker of her sweet smile warmed her eyes. "Goodbye—my dear friend!"

He did not answer, but only kissed her hand, and holding it still, led her immediately to her mare. He tossed her up into the saddle, as he had done so many times when she had come to visit Aubrey, but today there was no lingering to make a plan for the morrow; he only said: "Take the short way, and don't dawdle! I only hope you may not be drenched! Off with you, my child!"

He stepped back as he spoke, and the mare, needing no urging to go home to her own stable, started forward. Damerel lifted a hand in farewell, but Venetia was not looking at him, and he let it fall, and turned sharply on his heel. His eyes fell on Imber; he said in a curt, hard voice: "Miss Lanyon is going to London. It's probable Mr. Aubrey will come here tomorrow, to stay for some few weeks. Tell Mrs. Imber to make his room ready!"

He strode away to the library, and the door shut with a snap behind him. Imber looked to see what Nidd made of this, not that he was likely to say, because he was as close as Marston, and dull as a beetle. Nidd was walking off to the stables, so there was nobody to gossip with but Mrs. Imber, and she was in a bad skin, because her dough hadn't risen, and only said: "Don't come fidgeting me!" and: "Get out of my way, do!" Imber wished himself at Undershaw, to see what they make of it there, when Miss Venetia came in looking like she'd seen a ghost. Proper set-about they'd be, and no wonder!

But only three people at Undershaw saw Venetia upon her return, and neither the undergroom nor the young house-maid who waited on her noticed more than her dripping habit, and the ruin of her hat, with its curled feather hanging sodden and straight beside her rain-washed face. She went up the backstairs to her room, and opened the door to find the maid there, with Nurse, and the room a welter of silver paper, and trunks, with gowns and cloaks laid out on the bed ready to be packed, the linen in which her furs had been stored all summer lying in a heap on the floor, and the sour apples which had kept the moth at bay scenting the air.

Nurse broke instantly into angry scolding, while Venetia stood on the threshold, her eyes, with that blind look in them, wandering around the disordered room.

Then, quite suddenly, Nurse rounded on Jenny, driving her out of the room with orders to fetch up a can of hot water, instead of standing there like a gowk, when anyone could see Miss Venetia was soaked to the skin, and likely to catch her death. She drew Venetia to the fire, still scolding, but differently, just as years ago she had fondly scolded a little girl, appalled by some catastrophe, until she stopped crying. The little girl had known that nothing dreadful could happen to her when Nurse was there; Venetia knew now that Nurse was powerless to help her, but still was a little comforted. Nurse stripped off her wet habit, and huddled her into a dressing-gown, and made her sit by the fire, while she herself bustled about, first trotting off to mix a cordial, which she made Venetia drink, then rubbing her chilled feet, tidying the room, laying out an evening-gown, and all the time talking, talking, but never waiting for answers, and only looking at Venetia out of the corners of her sharp old eyes. Let Miss Venetia sit quiet for a while: plenty of time before she need dress again! And no sitting up late, mind, with so much as there was to do, and Mr. Hendred wishful to make an early start! And no need to worry about Undershaw, either, not that she would do that for long, with all the exciting things she would be doing in London, and her aunt so kind, and new faces to see, and goodness only knew how many treats in store! It would seem strange, at first, and it stood to reason she would feel homesick, missing all the people she knew, but let her trust Nurse, and not fall into the dismals, because she would soon be better, never fear!

Venetia, understanding, tried to smile at her, and clasped her hand for a grateful moment.

"There, my poppet! there, my dove!" Nurse crooned, stroking her tumbled locks. "Don't cry, my pretty, don't cry!"

But it was Nurse who cried, not Venetia; and presently, seeing how calm she was, Nurse went away, hoping that she might drop off to sleep for a little while, so tired as she was.

When Nurse came back to help her to dress for dinner (for she would not let Jenny wait on Venetia tonight) she thought that she must have enjoyed a nap, for she had got a little colour back into her cheeks, and seemed more like herself, able to decide what must be packed to go to London, and what Nurse must store away in camphor and keep for her at Undershaw. She had made a list of the people she must see before she left, and the things she must attend to; and Nurse entered briskly into these matters, thinking: *Anything to take her mind off*, and *least said soonest mended*.

She had just fastened Venetia's dress when a knock fell on the door, and was followed by Aubrey's voice, demanding admittance. Venetia called to him to come in, but Nurse felt her stiffen under her hands, as she laid a gauze scarf over her shoulders, and said sharply, when he did come in: "Now, don't come worriting Miss Venetia, Master Aubrey, for she's tired, and has enough to think of without you adding to it!"

"I want to speak to you before you come downstairs," he said, paying no heed to Nurse.

Venetia's heart sank, for she knew by the look in his face that he was going to be difficult. She said, however: "Yes, love, to be sure! Did you have good sport? Were you caught in the rain? I was! Thank you, Nurse! I shall do now: no one ever dresses my hair as well as you do! Oh, Aubrey, my head is in such a whirl! I feel quite distracted, and can hardly believe it is true, and I am really going to London at last!"

She sat down at her dressing-table, so that she was not obliged to look at him, and began to select from her trinket-box the ornaments she wished to wear. As Nurse shut the door, he said: "You mean to go, then?"

"Yes, how can you ask me? It is exactly what will suit me best, and you, too."

"It won't suit me to stay with Aunt Hendred, if that's what you're thinking."

"No, not that, although— Have you seen my uncle?"

"Oh, yes, I've seen him! I told him I shouldn't go, unless you particularly wished for me."

"Aubrey, you weren't uncivil?" she exclaimed.

"No, no!" he answered impatiently. "I said what was proper, of course! I told him that Appersett having been away I was got behindhand, and must apply. He understood. At any rate, he didn't care. My aunt would as lief I didn't go, I know. That don't signify! But he said you had told him of your scheme to set up house—wished me

223

to promise I wouldn't encourage you, since it wouldn't do!"

"My dear, I hope you did no such thing! It's quite nonsensical! That's why I am so glad that this chance has come in my way. I had made up my mind to it that there can be no staying at Undershaw while Mrs. Scorrier remains fixed, and how can I find a house that will suit us unless I go to town? Do you dislike it? I won't drag you away from Mr. Appersett, if you do, but when you have gone up to Cambridge, there will be the vacations, and—"

"That's not it!" he interrupted. "There must be tutors to spare in London, or I could study alone. What I don't understand—Venetia, does Jasper know of this?"

"Yes, I rode over to tell him—thinking that very likely you wouldn't care to go to Cavendish Square, and wishing to be sure that—"

"What did he say to it?" Aubrey demanded, frowning.

"Need you ask? He said instantly that he would be glad to have you, and for as long as you choose to stay. Oh, and I was to tell you to bring your horses, and the dogs, and that reminds me, love, if you do that you must take Fingle as well. And make him understand that Nidd is head groom at the Priory: you know what he is!"

"Oh, for God's sake—" he broke in irritably. "I'll take care of all that! Is Jasper willing you should go? I thought— Venetia, are you going to marry him?"

"Good gracious, no! Oh, you are thinking of a silly talk we had once! I wish you will forget it, for I fancy I shall never marry anyone. I thought at one time I might marry Edward; then I wondered if Damerel might not suit me better; and now—well, now I can't think of anything but London, so it's plain I am a hopeless case!"

"I thought you were in love—both of you."

"Only flirting, stoopid!"

He stood looking at her for a minute. "Well, I still think it. I daresay I don't notice a great deal, but I know when you're shamming it!"

"But, Aubrey, indeed—"

"Oh, hold your tongue!" he snapped, his temper flaring up. "If you don't choose to tell me, it's all one to me, but stop pitching that gammon! I don't mean to meddle: I detest meddlers!"

"Don't be vexed with me! Pray don't!" she managed to say.

He had limped to the door, but he paused, and looked back. "I'm not vexed. Not with you—at least, I don't think so: I suppose you must know what you're about. Only I hoped you would have settled it between you. I like Jasper. Oh, well!" He pulled open the door, and went away, banishing her, she thought, from his mind.

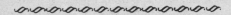

Three days later Venetia awoke, after a disturbed night, to the sound of a strident voice monotonously adjuring the residents in Cavendish Square to buy good silver-sand for their kitchen. Mrs. Hendred, installing her niece in the best spare bedchamber, overlooking the Square, had told her that she would find it wonderfully quiet, quite unlike rooms that looked on to a street. It was certainly quieter than the room Venetia had occupied in Newark, on the previous night, but to one accustomed to the stillness of the country it more nearly resembled Pandemonium than the quiet situation of the house-agents' advertisements. It seemed as though no one ever went to bed in London; and whenever, during a lull in the apparently endless flow of traffic, she dropped off to sleep, she was very soon jerked awake by the voice of the watchman, proclaiming the hour, and the state of the weather. She could only suppose that the ears of Londoners had been bludgeoned into insensitivity and trust that her own would soon grow accustomed to the ceaseless racket; and, being a well-mannered girl, presently assured her aunt that she had passed an excellent night, and was feeling perfectly restored from the effects of her journey.

Her heavy eyes belied her. She had, in fact, enjoyed little sleep during any of the past three nights; and, since she was wholly unused to travel, a journey of nearly two hundred miles had left her battered, exhausted, and unable to believe, when she lay in bed, that she was not still being rocked and jolted down an endless post-road.

The expedition, once so longed-for, would live in her memory, she thought, only as a nightmare. At the start all

226

had been bustle and distraction, with Powick to be interviewed, hurried arrangements to be made, keys, accounts, and memoranda to be handed over, warning reminders to be delivered; and a letter to be written to Lady Denny. Worst of all had been the leave-takings, for Nurse and Mrs. Gurnard and Ribble had wept, and had had to be comforted; and when, with her uncle standing by with his watch in his hand, she came to the final moment of parting with Aubrey she was so much overpowered that she dared not trust her voice, and could only hug him convulsively, unable to see his face for the tears that filled her eyes.

There had been no time for private reflection until she had left York, where an hour had had to be spent with Mr. Mytchett; but when she had signed the last of the documents spread before her, and answered the last of the careful questions put to her, there was too much. Mr. Hendred, resigning himself to an inevitable recurrence of his nervous tic, wrapped a shawl about his head, and leaned back in his corner of the chaise, resolutely closing his eyes; and his niece was consequently at leisure to indulge reflection. Her thoughts were not happy; unfortunately they were absorbing, so that instead of gazing eagerly upon an unknown countryside, and watching for landmarks of note, she looked at little but the bobbing forms of the postilions, and took only a faint interest in the various historic towns through which she passed. The first stage of the journey had been necessarily short, leaving a hundred and twenty miles still to be covered. She had acquiesced to her uncle's decision to halt but one night on the road; but when at last the chaise drew up in Cavendish Square she was so tired that she could reply to her aunt's solicitudes only with mechanical civility, and force herself to swallow no more than a few mouthfuls of the elegant supper provided for her refreshment. Nothing could have exceeded Mrs. Hendred's kindness, or the expressions of warm affection with which she greeted the niece she had not seen for seven years. She fondled her, and pressed every attention upon her, herself escorted her to her bedchamber, stayed while her dresser waited upon Venetia, and did not leave the room until she had tucked Venetia into bed with her own hands, kissing her,

227

and murmuring into her ear promises of much cosseting, and innumerable treats.

Mrs. Hendred was a very pretty woman of great good-nature and much less than commonsense. Her chief objects in life were to remain in the forefront of fashion, and to achieve advantageous marriages for her five daughters within the shortest possible time of having expensively launched each of these damsels, one after the other, into society. She had achieved an excellent match for Louisa that very year; and hoped to do no less well for Theresa in the following spring, provided that the treatment she was at present undergoing at the hands of the dentist proved successful, and she was not obliged to have three front teeth extracted, and false ones screwed to their stumps; and provided also that before the date of her presentation a husband could be found for her beautiful cousin. Theresa was a pretty girl, and would have a handsome portion, but Mrs. Hendred was under no illusion: Venetia might be handicapped by her five-and-twenty years, but she was not only so beautiful that people turned their heads in the street to stare at her, but she had more charm than all the Hendred girls put together. There were certain difficulties attached to the task of marrying her suitably, but that good lady's optimism encouraged her to hope that with the assets of beauty, charm, and a considerable independence she might be able to contrive a very respectable alliance for her. But she did think it a sad pity that Venetia had not accepted Edward Yardley's offer, for it would have been just the thing for her, since Mr. Yardley was a warm man, and had enjoyed her father's favour. Sir Francis, in writing, years ago, to decline his sister's offer to present Venetia, had informed her that Venetia's marriage was as good as settled. It was not long before she had told Venetia of this circumstance, and great was her shocked dismay when she learned that so far from entertaining any notion of marriage Venetia had come to town with the fixed resolve of establishing herself and Aubrey in a house in a quiet part of town, or even, perhaps, in the suburbs. She could not have been more aghast had Venetia announced her intention of entering a nunnery, and most earnestly did she beg her to banish all such schemes from her head. "Your uncle would never hear of it!" she said.

Venetia, who found her almost invariably comical, could not help laughing, but said affectionately: "Dear ma'am, I would not, for the world, distress you, but I'm of full age, you know, and I'm afraid it is not in my uncle's power to prevent me!"

The most that could be got from her was a half-promise not to think any more about houses and champerons until she had had time to grow accustomed to town life and customs. It would be churlish to make plans to leave her aunt's house almost as soon as she entered it, she thought: as churlish as it would be to betray how little she cared for the delightful schemes made for her entertainment. Mrs. Hendred, to whom country life was abhorrent, was so determined to make up to Venetia for the years she had spent in Yorkshire, and so sincerely anxious to do everything that might be supposed to give her pleasure, that gratitude as well as good manners made it impossible for Venetia even to hint to her that she longed only to be quiet, and alone. The least she could do, she felt, was to smile, and to appear at least to be happy.

She soon discovered that ease and enjoyment ranked only second in Mrs. Hendred's creed of fashion. Knowing her to be the mother of a numerous progeny, Venetia had supposed that she would have been continually busy with maternal cares, and was at first astonished to find that anyone so overflowing with soft affection should be content to surrender her children to governesses and nurse-maids. When she became better acquainted with her she was amused to perceive that although Mrs. Hendred had a kinder heart she was, in her own way, quite as selfish as had been her eccentric brother. While holding the members of her family and a large circle of friends in easy affection, her deepest feeling was reserved to herself. She was naturally indolent, so that half-an-hour spent amongst her children was as much as she could support without becoming exhausted by their chatter. Even Theresa, on the verge of coming-out, only appeared in the drawing-room, with her next sister, after dinner, when no company was being entertained, for Mrs. Hendred believed that there were few things more tiresome than households where girls not yet out were permitted to mingle with the guests. As for her three sons, the eldest was at Oxford, the second at Eton, and the youngest in the nursery.

Mr. Hendred, his ill-health notwithstanding, was seldom in Cavendish Square for many days together, but seemed to spend a large part of his time in posting about the country on errands either of private or of public business. It did not appear to Venetia that he took much part in the rearing of his offspring or in the management of his household, but he was held in great respect by everyone, his few commands being instantly and unquestioningly obeyed, and any of his reported utterances being accepted as clinchers to every dispute. Upon installing Venetia in his house, and telling her that she was to apply to him for such sums of money as she required, he left her to his wife to entertain, confining his attentions to the expression every now and then of his hope that she was enjoying herself.

To a certain extent she was enjoying herself. It would have been impossible for her not to have been diverted and interested on the occasion of her first visit to London, where everything was new to her, and so much was wonderful. Her aunt might wish that she could have taken her to the Opera, and to Almack's, and say a dozen times in a week; "If you had only been here during the season—!" but country-bred Venetia was in a puzzle to know how any more amusements could be squeezed into days already crammed with engagements. London was rather thin of company, but enough members of the *haut ton*, who shared Mrs. Hendred's opinion of country life, had flocked back to the metropolis at the beginning of October to constitute what to Venetia was a crowd; and a very respectable number of gilt-edged invitation-cards had been delivered to Cavendish Square. Even the shabbiest play was a treat to one who had never before been inside a theatre; a drive in Hyde Park could hardly be accomplished without Mrs. Hendred's pointing out to her some notable figure; and a walk down Bond Street, the most fashionable lounge in town, was fraught with interest and amusement, since while on the one hand one encountered there Pinks of astonishing elegance, there were also surely the finest shops in the world to be gazed at. Nor was Venetia's mind so elevated as to disdain fashion: she was possessed of natural good taste, and the dresses she brought with her from Yorkshire quite relieved Mrs. Hendred's mind of its fear that she might be a dowd, and had even drawn from her dresser a few words of rare praise; but she was perfectly ready to add to her wardrobe, and indeed, took a good deal of pleasure in rigging herself out in the first stare of the mode. In her aunt's company, too, she found endless amusement, for, having lived with selfish persons all her life, she was not in the least alienated by Mrs. Hendred's determination to let nothing interfere with her own comfort, but continued to think her comical, and to like her very well. But under her enjoyment there was a dull ache of unhappiness, never forgotten, and sometimes turning to acute anguish. She could not banish Damerel from her mind, or cease from thinking, involuntarily, of what she would tell him about St. Paul's Cathedral, or how he would laugh when he heard of Mrs. Hendred's conviction that by causing a plate of hard biscuits to be set at her elbow at every meal, while she partook of such delectable dishes as truffle pie and lobster patties, she was adhering to a strict and a reducing diet. Even as the mischievous smile quivered on her lips the recollection that she would never share a joke with him again, perhaps never see him again, would sweep over her, plunging her into such despair that she understood why people like poor Sir Samuel Romilly committed suicide, and envied them their escape from hopelessness. She lived for Aubrey's infrequent letters, but they brought her little comfort. He was a poor correspondent; and such news as he sent her was mostly concerned with Undershaw. When he mentioned Damerel it was only to say that he had been out shooting with him, or had beaten him three times in succession at chess.

Hers was not a demonstrative nature, and she indulged in no floods of tears, or fits of lethergic abstraction. Only the stricken look in her eyes sometimes betrayed her, and made her aunt uneasy.

On the whole, she dealt very agreeably with Mrs. Hendred, and Mrs. Hendred was well pleased with her. She was an attentive companion; she dressed in admirable taste; her manners were graceful; and instead of being awkward and tongue-tied amongst strangers, as might have been expected, she was perfectly assured, and could converse as easily with a clever man as with a stupid one.

Mrs. Hendred had only one fault to find with her behaviour, and that was her incurable independence. Nothing could persuade her that it was unbecoming in her to think she could manage her life without reference to her seniors, and positively improper of her to walk about London by herself. In almost every other respect Venetia was ready to oblige her, and even to defer to her judgment, but relinquish her freedom she would not. She went shopping alone; she walked alone in the parks; and no sooner did she discover that her aunt visited historic monuments only with extreme reluctance, and was interested in no pictures but those which were painted by fashionable artists, than she formed the appalling habit of sallying forth in the afternoon, while Mrs. Hendred recruited her forces with a peaceful nap on her bed, and driving off in a hack to such places as Westminster Abbey, or the Tower of London, or even to the British Museum.

"Which, setting aside every other consideration," said Mrs. Hendred tragically, "is enough to make everyone think you a blue-stocking! *Nothing* could be more fatal!"

This conversation took place at the nuncheon table, and Venetia, who had been watching in great astonishment the extraordinary grimaces her aunt made every time she took a sip of wine, exclaimed: "My dear ma'am, are you sure there is not something wrong with that sherry you are drinking?"

As she spoke she chanced to glance at the butler. He was a wooden-faced individual, but at Venetia's words he betrayed a quiver of emotion. This was immediately explained by Mrs. Hendred, who said, with a heavy sigh: "Not sherry, dearest: vinegar!"

"*Vinegar?*" repeated Venetia incredulously.

"Yes," nodded her aunt, eyeing it despondently. "Bradpole has been obliged to let out my lavender satin— the one with the French bodice, and the train with French double trimming, and lace net all round the neck—*two inches!* I am obliged to reduce, and there is nothing like vinegar for that. Vinegar and hard biscuits. Byron lived on that diet, you know, because he had a great tendency to put on flesh, and in that way he kept himself down."

"I wonder that he didn't kill himself! Aunt, he *cannot* have subsisted on such a diet!"

"You wouldn't think so," agreed Mrs. Hendred, "but I know it's what Rogers told me. The very first time he dined with Rogers he would partake of none of the dishes set before him, but only ate hard biscuits—or was it potatoes? I am not perfectly sure about that, but I know that he had vinegar."

"Not to drink!" protested Venetia.

"Well, he couldn't have *eaten* it, so he *must* have drunk it!" pointed out Mrs. Hendred reasonably.

"Perhaps he poured it over what he *did* eat. He would have been shockingly ill if he had drunk it by the glassful!"

"Do you think that is what I should do?" asked Mrs. Hendred, somewhat dubiously considering the ratafia cream on her plate.

"Most certainly I do not!" said Venetia, laughing. "Do, pray, let Worting take it away, ma'am!"

"I must say, I think it would quite ruin this cream. Perhaps it will do as well if I take care to eat a biscuit. Worting, you may hand me the cream again, and then you may go, for I shan't need anything more, except the macaroons, and those you may leave on the table. My love, I wish you will take one, for they are exceptionally good, and you have hardly eaten a morsel!"

To oblige her, Venetia took a macaroon and sat nibbling it while her aunt returned to the task of persuading her that solitary expeditions must never be undertaken by young ladies of *ton*. Venetia let her run on in her discursive way, for she could not tell he tell her that she went sightseeing in a dogged attempt to occupy her mind, any more than she could tell her that she was never alone, because a ghost walked beside her, soundless and invisible, yet so real that she felt sometimes that if she stretched out her hand it would find his.

"...and it is so particularly important, my love, that you should behave with the *utmost* propriety!" pursued Mrs. Hendred.

"Why?" asked Venetia.

"*Every* unmarried lady should do so, and in your situation, Venetia, you cannot be too careful what you do! My love, if you knew the world as I do, which of course you can't be expected to, and I daresay you haven't a notion how spiteful people can be, especially when a girl is so very handsome, and so exactly—I mean, so *striking!*"

"Well, I don't think anyone can say anything very

233

spiteful about me only because I go out alone," replied Venetia. "Nothing that I care for, at all events."

"Oh, Venetia, I do *beg* of you not to talk in that style! Only think how dreadful if you caused people to say you were *fast!* You may depend upon it they are on the watch for the least sign, and will be ready to *pounce* on you, and one can't wonder at it, after all! I daresay I should myself, not, of course, on *you*, dear child, but on another girl in your situation!"

"But what is there in my situation to make people ready to pounce on me?" asked Venetia.

"Oh dear, I wish you will not— You quite put me out! Your living with only Aubrey. I mean, with no chaperon, and—good gracious, Venetia, even you must know that it is not at all the thing!"

"I don't, but I know better than to argue with you on that head, ma'am! I daresay there may be many who would agree with you, but how should anyone in London know what my situation has been? I am persuaded *you* can never have divulged it!"

"No, no, indeed I never did! But—well, such things become known, I'm sure I don't know how, but you may believe that they *do!*"

But as Venetia found it impossible to believe that what happened at Undershaw could be known in London, she was quite unimpressed by her aunt's dark warnings. Fortunately it was not difficult to divert Mrs. Hendred's mind, so instead of arguing with her she seized the first opportunity that offered of introducing a fresh topic of conversation, and said that she had overheard someone saying, in Hookham's Library, that very morning, that he had had it on the best of authority that the Queen was not expected by her physicians to live out the week. As it was Mrs. Hendred's recurrent nightmare that her Majesty (whom everyone knew to be as tough as whitleather) would survive the winter, and ruin all Theresa's chances by dying in the middle of the next season, this gambit was very successful, and in hoping, doubting, and wondering for how long a period the Court (and of course the *ton*) would go into mourning, Mrs. Hendred forgot, for the time being, that she had failed to extract from her wilful niece any promise of conformity.

The Queen died at Kew, in the small hours of the

morning of the 17th November. Mr. Hendred brought the news to his wife, and it did much to raise her spirits, sunk very low by the outrageous behaviour of her dressmaker, who had delivered in Cavendish Square, instead of a promised promenade dress, a prevaricating note full of excuses for having been unable to fulfil her obligation.

The only fault Mrs. Hendred had to find in the news was that the Queen should have chosen to die on the 17th instead of the 18th November, for the 17th was the day fixed for the ball she was giving in Venetia's honour. Few things could have been more provoking, for all the preparations had been made, and after having been put to so much exertion, arranging with the French cook about the supper, speaking to Worting about the champagne, deciding what she should wear, and showing Venetia how to direct the cards of invitation, it was a great deal too bad that it should all have been for nothing. However, after wondering what was to be done with the creams and the aspics and the stuffed birds, she hit upon the happy notion of inviting a few of the guests bidden to the ball to come to dinner instead, quite informally, of course, and to spend a quiet, conversible evening, with perhaps a few rubbers of whist, but *no* music.

"No more than half-a-dozen persons; for any more would give it the appearance of a *party*," she told Venetia. "That would never do! My dear, that reminds me—black gloves! I daresay you have none, and they must be procured instantly! Black ribbons, too, and I think you should wear a high frock, not one cut low at the bosom—and I shall invite none of the *young* people. Just a few of my chiefest friends! What do you say to Sir Matthew Hallow? I daresay he would be charmed to dine here, and you like him, don't you, my love?"

"Yes, very much," replied Venetia absently.

"He is a most excellent person: I knew you would be pleased with him, and he with you! He admires you excessively: I saw *that* at a glance!"

"Well, as long as he doesn't take to paying me fulsome compliments—which I don't think he has the least intention of doing—he may admire me as much as he chooses," said Venetia depressingly.

Mrs. Hendred sighed, but said no more. Sir Matthew Hallow, though not quite the ideal man for Venetia, had

235

much to recommend him, and she had been very glad to see how friendly he and Venetia had become. He was rather too old for her, perhaps, and it was a pity that he should be a widower, but he seemed to have taken her fancy, and although he was popularly supposed to have buried his heart in his wife's grave there was no doubt that he was struck by Venetia's good looks, and found her company agreeable.

However, he was not the only possible husband Mrs. Hendred had found for her niece, so she was not unduly cast-down by Venetia's lack of enthusiasm. She decided that Mr. Armyn also should be invited to dine; he knew all about Roman remains, or something of the sort, and might just suit a girl who spent three hours at the British Museum, and selected from the shelves of the lending library a book about the Middle Ages.

Venetia seemed to like Mr. Armyn: she said that he had a well-informed mind. She liked two other eligible bachelors, agreeing that one had very good address, and that the other was extremely gentlemanlike. Mrs. Hendred felt a strong inclination to burst into tears, and would probably have done so had she known that Venetia had abandoned sightseeing, and was devoting each afternoon to house-hunting.

She found it an exhausting and dispiriting task, but she had been living for a full month with her aunt, and not only did she feel that a month constituted a very reasonable visit, but she was increasingly anxious to form her own establishment. Perhaps, if she could be busy all the time, as she meant to be, she might not feel so unhappy; perhaps, in household cares, she could forget her love, or grow at least accustomed to desolation, as Aubrey had grown accustomed to his limp.

She returned one afternoon from one of these expeditions to be informed by the footman who admitted her into the house that a gentleman had called to visit her, and was sitting with Mrs. Hendred in the drawing-room. She stood rooted, feeling her heart miss a beat.

"A Mr. Yardley, miss," said the footman.

Edward had come to London with a double purpose. He wished to consult a physician recommended to him by their good Huntspill—not that he believed there was any cause for alarm, but he could not deny that his cough still hung about him, which set his mother sadly on the fidgets; and so, upon Huntspill's saying, in his testy way, that if she fancied there might be more amiss than he could discover she had best call in a physician from York, he had taken the resolve to consult a London physician instead. "And I fancy, my dear Venetia, I have no need to tell you why I preferred to do so, or what was my *other* purpose in visiting the metropolis!" he said archly.

"I am sorry you should not be quite recovered yet," she replied. "Is Mrs. Yardley also in town?"

No, he had come without his mama. She had had a great mind to accompany him, but he had thought that the journey would be too fatiguing for her, and so she had remained at Netherfold. He was putting up at Reddish's, which had been recommended to him as a genteel hotel, though he had been surprised to find it so much larger than had been described to him. He feared the bill would make him open his eyes.

"However, I daresay it will not ruin me, and when one goes on holiday, you know, it is permissible to be a little extravagant."

When Mrs. Hendred left the room, which she very soon found an excuse to do, he told Venetia how happy he was to discover her in such comfortable circumstances. He had had no doubt of her aunt's being a most estimable female, but he had not been able to feel easy in his mind until he should have seen for himself how she went on. He now perceived that she was living in the first style of elegance, no doubt in a regular whirl of fashionable dissipation! "Your aunt, I daresay, has a large circle of acquaintances. She entertains a great deal, I believe. You will have been meeting quite a crowd of new faces!"

It was not difficult to see what was his real purpose in coming to London. Damerel he had not recognized to be a danger; but the unknown beaux and tulips of fashion, on whom he quizzed her, laughingly, yet watching her pretty sharply, might well dazzle the eyes of a country innocent.

She interrupted his attempts to discover if this had indeed been the case, by asking him if he had seen Aubrey. His countenance became grave at once; he replied: "Yes, I have seen him. I knew you would wish for news of him, and so I rode over to the Priory—a little against my inclination, I must own, for Damerel is not a man with whom I should wish to stand on terms of more than common civility. That was a very awkward business, Venetia: I was excessively vexed when I heard of it! I wonder your uncle should not have invited Aubrey to come with you to town."

"He did invite him, but Aubrey didn't wish to come. It wouldn't have answered, you know. Is he well? Pray tell me how—how you found everything at the Priory! Aubrey is the wretchedest correspondent!"

"Oh, he is very well! I need not tell you I found him with his nose in a book, and the desk all littered over with papers! I ventured to joke him about his *barricades*, as I called them. I assure you, if he had pulled one book from the shelves he had pulled a dozen. I told him that I wondered that anyone who cared as much as he does for books should leave them lying all over—on the floor, even! Does he *never* put away what he has done with?"

"No, never. Did you tell him you were coming to London?"

"Certainly—since that was my object in visiting him! I offered to be the bearer of any message, or letter, he might like to send you, but he was in one of his crotchety moods; you know his way whenever one tries just to give him a hint! He didn't like my reminding him that they were not his own books on the floor, and so he wouldn't entrust any message to me!"

"Aubrey doesn't recognize your authority, Edward. In fact, *you* are the only person to do so, and I wish you will remember that you have none."

"As to that—but it was no matter of *authority!* One would suppose that a boy of his age need not be above accepting a little friendly criticism!"

"Well, not if one knows Aubrey!" she retorted. "The truth is that you and he don't deal well together."

"I shall dare to contradict you, my dear Venetia!" he said, smiling. "The truth is that Master Aubrey is jealous, and hasn't yet learned to overcome it. He'll do so in time, particularly if one pays no heed to his miffs."

"You are wrong, Edward," she said, steadily regarding him. "Aubrey is not jealous. He knows he has no need to be—and I don't think he would be if there were! He is not much interested in *people*. I've told you that before, but you don't believe the things I tell you. I don't wish to give you pain, for we have been very good friends, and—and I am indebted to you for a great deal of kindness, but pray believe one thing at least!—I do not—"

"Now, if I were a young hot-head, like Aubrey, I should let you say what you would later regret!" he interposed, holding up a warning forefinger. "And then, no doubt, we should indulge ourselves with a stupid quarrel, when we might *both* of us be led into saying what we should regret! But I fancy I have rather more sense than you give me credit for, and also, my dear, that I know you a trifle better than you know yourself! You will tell me that I am impertinent, but so it is, little though you may think it! You are impetuous, your disposition is lively, you are enjoying your first taste of what is called *society*, and I daresay—indeed, I am sure!—that you have met with a great deal of admiration and flattery. It is very natural that you should be feeling a little giddy—I do not at all grudge you your treat, and you must not be thinking, you know, that when we are married you will not be granted a similar indulgence. I am not, myself, fond of town life, but I believe it may be of benefit to one to go about the world now and then, and certainly it is very diverting to study the manners and customs of persons whose way of life is

239

so far removed from one's own!"

"Edward, if I ever led you to suppose that I should marry you I am sorry for it, and I tell you now that I shall not!" she said earnestly.

She saw with dismay that her words had made no impression on him. He was still smiling, in a way that she found peculiarly irritating, and he said, in one of his rather ponderous essays in playfulness: "I fancy I must be growing a trifle *deaf!* But you have not told me, Venetia, how you like London, or what you have seen here! I can picture your astonishment when you first discovered its size, the variety of aspects of life which it offers to the enquiring gaze, its parks, and monuments, the handsome mansions of the affluent, the wretched hovels of the destitute, the crossing-sweeper in his rags, and the nobleman in his silk and purple!"

"I have never seen a nobleman dressed in silk and purple. I believe they only wear such things on State occasions."

But he only laughed heartily, saying how well he knew her literal mind, and promising to show her some places of interest which he ventured to think she might not yet have discovered. He himself had twice visited London, and although on the occasion of his first visit he had been too much amazed and bemused to do more than stare about him (for she must know that he had been no older than Aubrey at the time), when he came for the second time he provided himself with an excellent guide-book, which had not only acquainted him with what was most worth his notice, but had supplied him as well with such information as had greatly added to his appreciation of the various edifices to which it had directed him. He added that he had brought this valuable book with him, and had read it from cover to cover on the journey, to refresh his memory.

She could only marvel at him. She had never possessed the key to his mind, and what circumstance it was that made him now so calmly confident was beyond her power to fathom. She did not believe him to be desperately in love with her; she could only suppose that having once made up his mind that she was the wife that would best suit him he had either grown too accustomed to the idea to be able easily to relinquish it, or that the good opinion he had of himself made it impossible for him to believe that she could in all seriousness reject his offer. He did not appear to be put out by her blunt speech; he seemed rather to have decided that she must be humoured, and he adopted an attitude of kindly tolerance, such as a good-natured man might assume towards a spoiled child. He could not refrain from chiding her a little for having gone away from Undershaw without sending to inform him of her intention; he had heard the news from his mother, who, in her turn, had had it from Lady Denny, and a severe shock it had been to him. However, he forgave her, and did not mean to scold, for none could guess better than he how distracted she must have been. That led him to animadvert on Conway's marriage, and on that subject he spoke with a good deal proper feeling, and in more forthright language than it was his custom to employ when talking to Venetia of her brother. He owned that he had thought better of Conway; and in discussing the affair expressed himself so much like a sensible man that Venetia began to be in charity with him again. He had thought it right to take his mother to leave cards on Lady Lanyon; they had stayed no longer than twenty minutes, but half that space of time would have sufficed to provide him with a pretty fair notion of Mrs. Scorrier's character. She was an intolerable woman! He found no harm in Charlotte, but it had caused him a pang to see such a dab of a girl supplanting Venetia as mistress of Undershaw. He was sorry for her; he had formed the impression that her situation was not comfortable; and when Mrs. Scorrier had begun to talk of Aubrey's removal to the Priory, setting it down, of course, to *his* jealousy, and trying to persuade them that *she* had done all she could to reconcile him, she had looked as if she might burst into tears. A poor-spirited female! For his part he saw nothing to admire in her: Conway would have done better to have kept faith with Clara Denny.

"Poor Clara! If only she could bring herself to see how very well out of a bad bargain she is!"

He said gravely: "I fancy she does in part realize that she was mistaken in Conway, but it is too soon yet for her to derive consolation from the knowledge that he is unworthy. I am sincerely sorry for her: the consciousness of her own fault weighs very heavily on her spirits, but she behaves with great dignity and courage. I had some conversation with her, and trust I may have given her thoughts a more cheerful direction. The subject is not mentioned at Ebbersely, and that circumstance, you know, has deprived her of the benefit of such rational reflections on the affair as one would have supposed Sir John would have introduced to her mind."

"I am glad you were kind to her," Venetia said, her lip quivering involuntarily. "But tell me how it is at Undershaw! Do they go on fairly well? I don't mean Charlotte and Mrs. Scorrier, but our people!"

"Tolerably well, I think, but it was not to be expected that your people would be well-disposed towards Lady Lanyon when *her* coming meant *your* departure. From what Powick said to me, a se'ennight ago, they guess how it is, and resent it. You may be sure I said nothing to Powick to encourage such notions, but I could not but reflect, as I rode away from him, how much to blame—though unwittingly—*I* am for the awkwardness of the business."

"You?" she exclaimed. "My dear Edward, what can you mean? Only one person is blameworthy, and that is Conway! You had nothing to do with it!"

"I had nothing to do with Conway's marriage, nor could I have prevented it: that was not my meaning. But his conduct has shown me that the scruples which forbade me to urge you to consent to *our* marriage, after Sir Francis's death, have resulted in an unfortunate situation which, had you been already established at Netherfold, would not have arisen. The present arrangement is on all counts to be lamented. I say nothing of the undesirable gossip it must give rise to—for although Aubrey might naturally have come with you to London, it cannot be thought natural that he should have chosen rather to remove no more than a few miles from Undershaw—but while he is within reach, and, indeed, frequently sees Powick, and your keeper, your people won't render allegiance to Conway's wife. I cannot think that right, and I suspect, moreover, that they are falling into the way of applying to *him* in any little difficulty."

242

"I wonder what advice he gives them?" she said. "One never knows with Aubrey! He *might* give very good advice—if he happened to be in an amiable mood!"

"He should not give *any*. And however much cause he has to feel obliged to Lord Damerel he ought not to be living under his roof. I do not deny his lordship's good-nature, but his influence I must think most undesirable, particularly for Aubrey. He is a man of few morals, and the tone of his mind must render him a most unfit companion for a lad of Aubrey's age and disposition."

It was a struggle to suppress the indignation which surged up in her, but she managed to say with tolerable composure: "You are mistaken if you imagine that Aubrey stands in danger of being corrupted by his association with Damerel. Damerel would no more dream of such a thing than you would yourself, even if it were possible, which I very much doubt! Aubrey is not easily influenced!"

His smile was one of conscious superiority. He said: "I am afraid that is a subject on which you must allow me to be a better judge than you, Venetia. We won't argue about it, however—indeed, I should be sorry to engage in any sort of discussion with you on a matter that is not only beyond the female comprehension, but which one could not wish to see *within* it!"

"Then you were ill-advised to mention it!"

He returned no other answer than a slightly ironical bow, and immediately began to talk of something else. She was thankful that her aunt just then came back into the room, affording her a chance to escape, which she instantly seized, saying that she had a letter she must finish writing before dinner, and must therefore bid her visitor goodbye.

For how long he meant to remain in London she had been unable to discover, but from the evasive nature of his reply to that question she feared he contemplated a visit of indefinite duration. How to bear his company with patience, or how to convince him that his was a sleeveless errand, were problems not made easier to solve by Mrs. Herdred's well-meaning efforts to further his suit.

Venetia soon discovered that during the period he had spent alone with her aunt he had made an excellent impression on her. In her view he was the stuff of which good husbands were made, for he was kind, dependable, of reasonable consequence, and comfortably circumstanced. He had succeeded in persuading her to the belief that his tardiness in bringing Venetia to the point was due to no lack of ardour, but to the nicety of his principles. Mrs. Hendred, herself a high stickler, perfectly understood his patience, and honoured him for it. He rapidly became established in her mind as a figure of unselfish devotion, and she thought it all very noble and touching, and spared no pains to bring this Jacob's labours to a happy conclusion. She promoted his plans for Venetia's entertainment and instruction, included him in her own schemes, and invited him so many times to take what she inaccurately called his pot-luck in Cavendish Square that Venetia was forced to protest, and to disclose that so far from having abandoned her intention of setting up her own establishment she was the more confirmed in it, and had inspected a house in Hans Town which she thought might be made into a comfortable home for herself and Aubrey.

She had not meant to make this announcement, which she knew would meet with much opposition, until she had signed the lease, and engaged a chaperon; but when she found that her aunt had accepted an invitation from Edward to bring her to dine with him at the Clarendon Hotel, and afterwards to go to the theatre at his expense, she was so indignant (having herself declined the invitation) that she could no longer restrain her annoyance.

Mrs. Hendred received the news with horrified incredulity. From her first disjointed ejaculations it was hard to decide whether it was her niece's determination to embrace a life of spinsterhood that most shocked her, or the deplorably dowdy locality she had chosen for her asylum. The repulsive accents in which she repeated the words, *Hans Town?* could scarcely have held more disgust had she been speaking of a back-slum; and she several times reiterated the disgusting syllables, interjecting them between assurances that Venetia's uncle would never countenance so improper a scheme. But she presently saw that although Venetia was listening to her with civility her mind was made up, and she exclaimed, with a sudden change of tone: "Oh, my dearest child, indeed, indeed you must not do it! You would regret it all your life—you can have no notion—you are still young, but only think what it would be like when you are growing old—the loneliness—the mortification of—" She broke off as a quiver ran over Venetia's face, and leaned forward in her chair to lay one of her plump little hands on Venetia's. "My dear, marry Mr. Yardley!" she said urgently. "I am persuaded you would be happy, for he is so kind and good, and in every way so eligible!"

The slim hand under hers was rigid: Venetia said in a constricted voice: "Pray do not say any more, ma'am! I don't love Edward and that must be the end of the matter."

"But, dearest, I assure you you are mistaken! It is not in the least necessary that you should love him, for the happiest marriages *frequently* start with only the most moderate degree of affection! Indeed, I have known several where the couples were barely acquainted, but were content to let their parents arrange the match. You know, my love, girls *cannot* be better able to judge of what will suit them than their parents!"

"But I am not a girl, ma'am, and I have no parents."

"No, but— Oh, Venetia, you don't know what a mistake you would be making!" exclaimed Mrs. Hendred despairingly. "It would be better to marry a man one positively disliked than to remain a spinster! And how are you to make a respectable match if you go to live in Hans Town, and in such a *peculiar* style? For, after all, even with a disagreeable husband, though of course it would have grave drawbacks to be married to a disagreeable man, you would be a woman of consequence, and you would have all the comfort of your children, which, you know, is a female's *greatest* interest—and, in any event, Mr. Yardley is *not* disagreeable! He is a most amiable person, values you just as he should, and, I daresay, would do everything in his power to make you happy! To be sure, he is not a *lively* man, but what husband *is*, after all! If you had fancied Sir Matthew, or Mr. Armyn, or even Mr. Foxcott, though I very much doubt whether *he*—But I can't help feeling, dear child, that Mr. Yardley is the very man for you! He understands you so well, and
245

knows what your circumstances are, so that there wouldn't be any difficulty or awkwardness—and you would be living near your brother, and your friends, and in just the style to which you are accustomed, only not, of course, at Undershaw, but, still, in the country you *know!* You would feel yourself to be *going home!*"

"I don't wish to go home!" The words were wrung from Venetia, and although quietly spoken were charged with anguish. She got up quickly, saying: "I beg your pardon—pray excuse me! There are circumstances—I can't explain, but I beg you, ma'am, not to say any more! Only believe that I do know what must be the—the disadvantages of the course I am determined to pursue! I'm not so green that—" Her voice failed; she turned, and went with hurried steps to the door.

She was arrested by the sound of a convulsive sob, and looked back in startled dismay to see that her aunt had burst into tears.

Mrs. Hendred did not like the people around her to be unhappy. Even the sight of a housemaid crying with the pain of the toothache made her feel low, for misery had no place in her comfortable existence; and when it obtruded itself on her notice it dimmed the warm sunshine in which she basked, and quite ruined her belief in a world where everyone was contented, and affluent, and cheerful. What she had seen in Venetia's face overset her completely, and, since she had grown very fond of her niece, really pierced her to the heart. Her pretty features were crumpled: tears rolled down her cheeks; and she uttered in a sort of soft wail: "Oh, my dearest child, don't, *don't* look like that? I cannot bear to see you so wretched! Oh, Venetia, you must not take it so much to heart, *indeed* you must not! It makes me feel so dreadfully low, for I do most sincerely pity you, but it would not *do*—I *assure* you it would not!"

Venetia had started solicitously towards her, but at these words she checked, and stiffened. "What would not *do?*" she asked, keeping her eyes fixed on Mrs. Hendred's face in a compelling way which set the final touch to the poor lady's agitation.

"That man! Oh, don't ask me! I didn't mean— Only when I see you in such affliction how can I help but—

Oh, my dear Venetia, I can't endure that you should think I don't feel for you, for I *exactly* enter into your sentiments! Oh dear, it brings it all back to me, but I promise you I haven't thought of him for *years*, which just *shows* how soon you will forget, and be *perfectly* happy again!"

Very pale, Venetia said: "I don't know how you should be aware of it—but what you have said I can't have misunderstood! You are speaking of Damerel, aren't you, ma'am?"

Mrs. Hendred's tears flowed faster. She dabbed ineffectively at her eyes. "Oh, dear, I ought never—Your uncle would be so vexed!"

"Who told you, ma'am, that Damerel and I—had become acquainted?"

"*Pray* don't ask me!" begged Mrs. Hendred. "I should not have mentioned it—your uncle particularly charged me—oh, I believe I am going to have one of my spasms!"

"If my uncle charged you not to speak, of course I won't press you to do so, but will apply to him instead," said Venetia. "I am glad I've learnt of this in time to see him before he sets out to Berkshire. I believe he has not yet left the house. Excuse me, aunt! I must go at once to find him, or it will be too late!"

"Venetia, *no!*" almost shrieked her aunt. "I implore you—besides, it wouldn't be any use, and everything is so uncomfortable when he is displeased! Venetia, it was Lady Denny, but promise me you won't say a word to your uncle!"

"If you'll be frank with me, there is no reason that I know of why I should. Don't cry! Lady Denny! Yes, I see. Did she write to you?"

"Yes, though I never met her in my life, for I was married before Sir John, but it was a very proper letter, and showed her to be a woman of excellent feeling, your uncle said. Though it was very disturbing, and upset me so much that I could scarcely swallow a mouthful of food all that day for thinking about it. For, you know, my dear, *Damerel*—! Not that you could possibly know, poor child, and I am not in the *least* surprised you should have fallen in love with him, because he is *fatally* attractive, though I am not, of course, acquainted with him! Still, one sees him at parties, and in the park, and at the opera, and—

Well, my dear, *scores* of females— But to think of *marrying* him—! Which your uncle said was in the highest degree improbable—that such a notion should cross his mind, I mean! Only what to do I didn't know, because your uncle thought it useless to invite you to come to town, and your being of age made it so very difficult besides that he was persuaded your principles were too high to allow of your—your accepting a *carte blanche*, as they say!"

"None was offered me!" Venetia said, standing very straight and still in the middle of the room.

"No, my love, I know, but although it seems a dreadful thing to say, to have married him would have been *worse!* At least, I don't precisely mean—"

"Don't distress yourself, ma'am! Lady Denny was mistaken. Lord Damerel's affections—were not so deeply engaged as she supposed. There was nothing more between us than—a little flirtation. He made me no offer—of any kind!"

"Oh, my poor, poor child, *don't!*" cried Mrs. Hendred. "No wonder you should be so wretched! There is *nothing* so mortifying as to fall in love with someone who does not share one's sentiments, but *that* pain you need not be made to suffer, whatever your uncle says, for gentlemen don't understand anything, however wise they may be, and even he owned to me that he had been mistaken in Lord Damerel, so he may just as easily be mistaken in *you!*"

"Mistaken in Lord Damerel?" Venetia interrupted. "Then—Aunt, are you telling me that uncle *saw* Damerel when he came to Undershaw?"

"Well, my love, he—he thought it his duty, when you have no father to protect you! He considered it *most* carefully, not at first perceiving how he might be able— But then you wrote me the news of Conway's marriage, and it was the most providential thing that ever happened, though I was never more shocked in my life, for it furnished your uncle with an excellent excuse to remove you from Undershaw, which he saw in a flash, because he is very clever, as I daresay anyone would tell you."

"Good God!" Venetia said blankly. She pressed a hand to her brow. "But if he saw him— Yes, it must have been

248

before he reached Undershaw—before *I* saw— Aunt, what passed between them? You must tell me, if you please! If you will not I shall ask my uncle, and if he will not I'll ask Damerel himself!"

"Venetia, don't talk in that dreadful way! Your uncle was most agreeably surprised, I promise you! You must not think that they quarrelled, or that there was the least unpleasantness! Indeed, your uncle told me that he felt most sincerely for Lord Damerel, and in general, you know, he never does so. He even said to me that it was a great pity that it should be out of the question—the marriage, I mean—because he was bound to acknowledge that he might have been very— But it *is* out of the question, my dear, and so Lord Damerel *himself* acknowledged. Your uncle says that nothing could have done him greater credit than the open way he spoke, even saying that he had done very ill in not going away from Yorkshire, which your uncle had not accused him of, though of course it is perfectly true. Your uncle was not obliged even to point out to him, which he had expected would have been the case, and a very disagreeable task it would have been, and I'm sure I don't know how—but that doesn't signify, because Lord Damerel said that he knew well that it would be *infamous* to take advantage of you, when you knew nothing about the world, and had never been beyond Yorkshire, or met any other men—well, only Mr. Yardley!—so that you were almost *bound* to have fallen in love with him, and how *could* you understand what it would mean to be married to a man of his reputation? And you *don't* understand, dear child, but indeed, indeed it would be *ruinous!*" She paused, largely for want of breath, and was relieved to see that the colour was back in Venetia's cheeks, and that her eyes were full of light. She heaved a thankful sigh, and said: "I *knew* you would not feel so badly if you didn't think yourself slighted! How glad I am that I've told you! For you are not so unhappy now, are you, my love?"

"Unhappy?" Venetia repeated. "Oh, no, no! Not *unhappy!* If I had only known—! But I did know! I *did!*"

Mrs. Hendred did not quite understand what was meant by that, nor did she greatly care. All that signified was that the haunted look which made her so uncomfortable had vanished from Venetia's eyes. She gave a final wipe to her own, and beamed upon her suddenly radiant niece, saying with satisfaction; "*One* thing you may plume yourself on, though, of course, it will not do to *say* so, for that would not be at all becoming. But to have captivated such a man as Damerel into actually *wishing* to offer for you is a triumph indeed! For he must have meant to reform his way of life, you know! There was never anything like it, and I don't scruple to own to you, my love, that if it had been one of my daughters I should be as proud as a peacock—not that I mean to say I think any of them could, though I fancy Marianne may grow to be a very handsome girl—and, of course, I should never *dream* of letting him come in their way!"

Venetia, who had been paying no attention, exclaimed: "The wretch! The *idiotish* wretch! How could he think I should care a jot for such nonsense? Oh, how angry I am with the pair of them! How dared they make me so unhappy! Behaving as though I were seventeen, and a stupid little innocent! My dear aunt—my dear, *dear* aunt, *thank* you!"

Mrs. Hendred, emerging from an impulsive embrace, and instinctively putting up a hand to straighten her cap, began to be uneasy again, for not even her optimism could ascribe the joy throbbing in Venetia's voice to mere pride of conquest. "Yes, dear child, but you are not thinking— I mean, it cannot *alter* anything! Such a marriage would utterly *ruin* you!"

Venetia looked down at her in a little amusement. "Would it indeed? Well, ma'am, when Damerel came north it was to escape the efforts of his aunts to marry him to a lady of respectable birth and fortune, so that he might become re-established in the eyes of the world. I don't see how that was to be achieved if marriage to him meant her social ruin, and I can't believe that the plot was being hatched without the knowledge and approval of Miss Ubley's parents!"

"*What?*" cried Mrs. Hendred, momentarily diverted. "Amelia Ubley? You don't mean it!"

"But I do mean it, so now, ma'am, will you explain to me how it comes about that though *her* credit would survive that marriage mine would not?"

Mrs. Hendred's brief period of relief was over. She stared at her niece with an expression on her face of absurd chagrin, fidgeted with her shawl, started several sentences, and finished none, and finally answered lamely: "The cases are not the same. Oh dear, now I wish—Venetia, you don't understand these matters! Miss Ubley's situation—the circumstances— Well, they are quite *different!*"

"In what way?"

"Oh—oh, in a hundred ways! Good gracious, for one thing she's more than thirty years old, with a deplorable figure, besides a pug-nose, and she has a way of poking herself forward when she walks, and—oh, she was at her prayers *years* ago! No one could blame Latchford for being thankful to accept *any* offer for her, particularly if the Damerel ladies mean to make him their heir, which wouldn't surprise me in the least, now I come to think of it. And although I don't mean to say Miss Ubley is not respectable, for she is *dowdily* respectable, naturally she cannot be thought an innocent, at her age, and having always lived in town, so that she *must* be up to snuff, as they say! But in your case, my dear, everyone knows what your circumstances have been, and how you cannot possibly have had any experience! And," she added with a flash of inspiration, "if Damerel were to marry you, everyone would say that it was the wickedest thing imaginable, and the most shocking take-in! I assure you, my love, there is something particularly repugnant in the marriage of a rake to a beautiful girl, years younger than himself, and perfectly innocent, as you are, my dear, whatever you may choose to say!"

At the start of this speech a disquietingly confident smile glinted in Venetia's eyes, but by the time Mrs. Hendred reached her triumphant conclusion it had faded. Anxiously observing her, Mrs. Hendred was thankful to see that she was now looking thoughtful, slightly frowning.

Mrs. Hendred decided to pursue her advantage. "*You,* dear child, are not aware of the way such things are looked upon—indeed, I don't know how you should be, any more than a *nun!*—but you may depend on it that *he* is!"

Venetia glanced at her. "Yes," she said slowly, remembering that interrupted scene in the library at Undershaw, and how troubled she had afterwards been by Damerel's reluctance. *You don't realize what an advantage I should be taking of your innocence?* he had said. "Yes," she repeated. "I begin to see now..."

"I was persuaded you must, for you have such excellent good sense, my love!" said Mrs. Hendred, much heartened. "I know how it seems to you *now*, but you may believe me when I tell you that these things don't endure. Oh, dear! I thought I should have died of despair when Mama—your grandmama, my dear—and Francis made me give up poor Sebastian! I cried for three days without ceasing, but in the end, you know, I was married to your uncle, and I am sure nothing could have been more comfortable!"

"Did you never regret, ma'am?" asked Venetia, looking curiously at her.

"Never!" declared Mrs. Hendred emphatically. "It would have been a shockingly bad match: he had no fortune—hardly a feather to fly with! Only think how disagreeable that would have been! Yes, and that puts me in mind of another thing, my love! Everyone says that Lord Damerel has brought a noble to ninepence with his extravagant ways, which makes him *quite* ineligible! Naturally, had he been wealthy the case might have been different, for, after all, a handsome fortune— But he has brought his to a nutshell, so there is nothing whatsoever to recommend him, and so he knows, for he says so to your uncle. You would be throwing yourself away, and though I myself very much doubt whether it can be brought about, he and your uncle are both of the opinion that you will make a splended marriage. And no one, my dear niece, would be more pleased than I should be if you did!"

"No one, however, would be less pleased than myself, ma'am."

"It is very proper you should say so," said Mrs. Hendred approvingly. "Nothing is more unbecoming in a girl than to appear mercenary, or on the catch! For my part, I should be happy to see you married to a respectable man, of sufficient consequence, of course, and affluent enough to be able to provide you with the elegancies without which, I do assure you, life would be insupport-able!"

Venetia, who had paced over to the window, and back again, said; "It is going to be difficult. Yes, I see that now."

"No, no, dearest child! Not the least difficulty in the world! I only meant—"

"To whistle happiness down the wind for a scruple!" Venetia said, unheeding. "To me that seems so absurd— so *addle-brained*—! But that's what he did, and if he has made up his mind to be idiotishly noble— Yes, it is going to be very difficult. I must think!"

Quite forgetful of her aunt, she went quickly out of the room, leaving that harassed lady to reflections which were as uneasy as they were puzzled.

Venturing, rather later, to renew her protests against the hiring of a house in Hans Town, Mrs. Hendred was at first thankful to discover that Venetia had abandoned her fell purpose, and then, when she had thought it over, apprehensive. She could not bring herself to believe that any representations of hers had brought about this sudden change; and the more she considered the matter the less did she like her niece's readiness to relinquish a scheme to which she had all but committed herself. It had seemed almost as though she had forgotten the house in Hans Town, for upon the subject's being broached she had stared for a moment, and then had said: "Oh—! *That!* No, no, ma'am, don't be in a worry! I daresay you are quite right, and I shouldn't like to live there at all."

Mrs. Hendred, with every reason to be satisfied with this answer, felt vaguely alarmed. It seemed to her not only that Venetia's thoughts were far away, but that she was weaving some new plan. An attempt to discover what this might be failed: Venetia merely smiled, and shook her head, which made it seem unpleasantly probable that the new plan would prove to be quite as shocking as the old. Mrs. Hendred began to wish that her austere spouse had not gone into Berkshire; and during an unusually wakeful night even reached the stage of wondering whether it would not be as well to send a letter to him express. In the morning this desperate resolve seemed as foolish as it was imprudent, for what, after all, could Venetia be contemplating that would justify a summons to her uncle? Such a summons would displease him quite as much as the inevitable disclosure that his wife had told Venetia precisely what he had thought it best she should never know for he had gone into Berkshire to attend the

Quarter Sessions, which, since he was *Custos Rotulorum* and punctilious in the performance of his duty, he always made a point of doing, generally remaining for a full week. On this occasion, however, he had told his wife that she might expect to see him again within four or, at the most, five days, since he had engaged himself to attend a Party Meeting. Nothing, she thought, could happen in so short a period: in fact, it was hard to see how anything cataclysmic could happen at all. Venetia might be ready to count the world well lost for love, but she could hardly tell Damerel so. And even if she did tell him—not that Mrs. Hendred supposed that she would dream of behaving with such gross impropriety, however unconventional she might be—Damerel knew that for a young female of quality the world would not be at all well lost; and he had given Mr. Hendred his word as a gentleman that he would not propose marriage to Venetia. So there was really no danger threatening Mrs. Hendred's peace of mind, and the night's forebodings were possibly to be ascribed to the goose and turkey pie, of which she had partaken a little too freely at supper. Or perhaps it had been a mistake to have eaten mushroom fritters: mushrooms had never agreed with her delicate constitution, so she must remember to send a message to the artist ruling over her kitchens that they must in future be excluded from his luscious recipes.

While Mrs. Hendred's mind was drifting into gastronomy Venetia's was employed in forming and discarding schemes for achieving social ruin. Quite as quickly as her aunt she had decided to tell Damerel how little she cared for the world, or its opinion, would serve no useful purpose. He had from the start called her his green girl; instinct warned her that he would not think her matured by one month's sojourn in London. She thought, but tenderly, that for all his wide experience of women he was as stupid as Edward Yardley, or her clever uncle. Because she had her knowledge of the world at secondhand he believed she knew her own heart no better, and had apparently convinced himself that within a measurable time of being plunged into fashionable circles she would not only be thankful to have escaped from—what had he called it?—*the devil's own scrape*, but would be happily engaged to some virtuous young gentleman of birth, for-

255

tune, and consequence. That was bad enough: far worse—or, at any rate, more difficult to overcome—was the aspect put before her by her aunt. A worldly man, he knew what the world's opinion would be of his marriage to herself: not only knew it, but shared it. He had told her that his depravity had stopped short of tampering with the young and innocent: marriage had not been his context, but she guessed that in just such a light did he regard it. He had placed her above his touch, and how to demonstrate that she was well within it was a problem that she could see no way of solving. She remembered that it was her plan of setting up house with Aubrey which had so nearly broken down his resolution. *Anything were better than that!* he had exclaimed. For a little while she played with the idea of immediately hiring the house in Hans Town, and writing off to tell Aubrey that she had done it. But that scheme was soon discarded with all the others, because she could not be quite sure that it was out of his power to scotch it. He had more influence over Aubrey than she had chosen to admit to Edward; moreover, since he seemed to have discussed her future with her uncle, he might rely on Mr. Hendred to scotch it for him. In course of time he could be made to realize that she preferred spinsterhood to the brilliant match he apparently believed to be her destiny, but she neither wished to languish until public opinion placed her on the shelf, nor did she cherish illusions about her love; not for him the life of a celibate, mourning his lost bride: he was very much more likely to seak forgetfulness in excess, and would probably be next heard of flaunting some dazzling lightskirt all over Europe. For the moment he was tied to Yorkshire by Aubrey's presence in his house; but any day now Aubrey would leave the Priory, and then, Venetia thought, he would be lost to her indeed.

Her fears and schemes left little room in her mind for minor considerations. She responded mechanically to her aunt's suggestions for the day's pleasures; accompanied her dutifully on a shopping expedition, and to a concert; her brain in a ferment while her lips uttered inane civilities. Mrs. Hendred, finding her in so complaisant a mood, brought up the subject of Edward's projected party again, and was delighted to meet with no opposition. She suspected that Venetia hardly realized what had been said to her, but she was determined to hold her to the word she had given so abstractedly. Edward had invited them to dine at the Clarendon Hotel, and in Mrs. Hendred's opinion this lavish gesture could not fail to recommend him to Venetia. The best and most expensive dinner in town was to be laid there, for the cook was a Frenchman, and not less than £4 was the cost of quite a simple repast. Edward had invited Mr. Hendred too, but seldom had that dyspeptic gentleman refused an invitation with less regret. French dishes were no treat to him, and he had taken Edward in aversion. He said that a man who was prosy before he reached his thirtieth year would be intolerable long before he attained his fortieth; and that Venetia could do very much better for herself. So the party numbered three persons only, Edward having no acquaintance in town, and Mrs. Hendred not choosing to fill her husband's place from her own large circle of friends. Even quite elderly gentlemen were more than likely to put forth their best efforts to captivate Venetia, and she wanted to introduce no rival to Edward into his party.

The evening began well. No sooner did the *maitre d'hotel* realize that the gentleman from the country was entertaining that well-known epicure and leader of the *ton*, Mrs. Philip Hendred, and a perfectly ravishing young female, dressed in the first style of elegance, than he revised his previous plan, and bowed the party not to a secluded table in one corner of the room, but to one reserved for the most respected patrons, and himself presented Mr. Yardley with a large bill of fare. Between them, he and Mrs. Hendred selected a most succulent meal, which Mrs. Hendred was able to partake of without the smallest misgiving, because she had met Mr. Rogers that very day, and he had set her right about Lord Byron's reducing diet: his lordship had not drunk vinegar, but soda-water, and what regimen could be easier to follow, when one was not particularly partial to wine? So the dinner passed off very successfully, and if Venetia contributed little to the conversation at least she responded with her lovely smile to any remark that was addressed to her. Probably Mr. Yardley was satisfied, for he had so much to impart to his guests about the various places of historic interest which he had been visiting that neither lady had much opportunity to say more than; "Indeed!" or: "How interesting, to be sure!"

Mrs. Hendred's town coach conveyed them to the theatre. Edward had procured a box, and Mrs. Hendred was glad to see that Venetia accepted with sweet, if slightly absent, complaisance all his solicitous efforts to secure her comfort. Venetia was, in fact, considering a new and extremely daring scheme, and thoughout the first act of the play she sat wondering whether she could summon up the courage to present herself boldly to the eldest of Damerel's aunts, disclosing all her story, and begging for her support. It was a desperate plan, and by the time the curtain fell a great many objections to it had presented themselves to her. She came out of her deep reverie to find that Edward was asking her how she liked the play. She returned a civil answer, and then sat looking idly round the house while he delivered himself of his own considered opinion.

Her attention was almost immediately attracted to a box on the opposite side of the theatre. It had been empty until after the curtain had risen, but it was now occupied by a lady and gentleman of such modish appearance that many more eyes than Venetia's were turned towards them. Neither was in the first blush of youth, the gentleman, indeed, bearing a strong resemblance to the Prince Regent. He had very much the same protuberant blue eyes, and florid complexion; he wore a coat of exaggerated cut, a splendid waistcoat, and his pantaloons were smoothly stretched across a stomach of noble proportions. He had levelled his quizzing-glass at Venetia, but after one cursory glance at him she had transferred her gaze to his companion.

If the gentleman was magnificent, the lady was the more striking of the two. A hint of brass in the colour of her exquisitely dressed curls might betray the hand of an expert *coiffeur*, the delicate blush on her cheeks might have issued from an expensive jar of rouge, but her figure, tantalizingly revealed by a very low cut gown of silk so soft and diaphanous that it clung like a cobweb to her form, owed no more to art than did her large, brilliant eyes, her classically straight nose, or the lovely line of her jaw. Diamonds hung from the lobes of her ears, flashed on her white bosom, and on her arms; an ermine cloak had been flung carelessly over the back of her chair, and she was leaning a little forward, her gaze, like her companion's, directed towards Venetia. There was a slightly amused smile on her tinted lips; she was slowly waving to and fro a fan spangled with diamond chips, but as Venetia stared at her she lifted the other hand in a tiny gesture of salute.

Mrs. Hendred, somnolent after her sumptuous repast, had dozed peacefully through the first act of the play, and was now listening sleepily to Edward's measured discourse, and wishing that the curtain would rise on the second act, and so allow her to drop off again. Edward's voice was monotonous enough to make it hard for her to remain awake, but she was saved from sliding back into sleep by Venetia's saying suddenly. "Aunt, who is that lady in the box over there?"

There was a sharpened note in her voice which startled Mrs. Hendred enough to rouse her, and drive away the fog of drowsiness. She straightened herself, giving her plump shoulders a little twitch, and said. "Which lady, my love?" in a slightly thickened voice, but with an assumption of bright interest.

"Almost directly opposite, ma'am! I can't point to her, because she is watching me. She has been doing so these past ten minutes, and I—Aunt Hendred, who is she?"

"My dear, I'm sure I don't know, for I saw no one in any of the boxes with whom I am acquainted. Which box do you say—" She stopped with a gasp, and ejaculated in a stunned tone: "Good God!"

Venetia's hands were tightly clasped over her folded fan; she said: "You know her, don't you, ma'am?"

"No, no!" declared Mrs. Hendred. "Good gracious, no! As though I should know any female who wore such a dress! The most indecent— Dear child, don't seem to notice them! Such impertinence, staring at you like— Hush, my love, the curtain is going up and we must not talk any more! Dear me, how I long to discover what will happen in this act! An excellent first act, was it not? I don't know when I have enjoyed a play more! Ah, here is the comical man, and his valet! We mustn't talk, or we shall miss the diverting things they say!"

"Only tell me, ma'am—"

"'Sh," uttered Mrs. Hendred.

As this sibilant command was endorsed by the party in the adjoining box, in an even more menacing manner, Venetia relapsed into silence. Mrs. Hendred was agitatedly fanning herself; and instead of joining in the burst of laughter which greeted one of the diverting things that was said on the stage she seized the opportunity to tweak Edward's sleeve, and, upon his bending towards her, to whisper something in his ear. Venetia, who had not joined in the laughter either, but who was sitting bolt upright, an expression on her face compounded of incredulity and bewilderment, did not hear what was said; but in another minute or two Edward whispered to her: "Venetia, your aunt is feeling faint! You will not object to removing from this box? It is very stuffy—I am conscious of it myself, and believe Mrs. Hendred will revive if she can but be got into the air!"

Venetia rose with alacrity, and, while Edward led the afflicted lady out, she flung her own cloak over her shoulders, caught up her aunt's, and slipped out of the box, to find two of the attendants solicitously reviving Mrs. Hendred with smelling-salts, vigorous fanning, and drops of water sprinkled on her brow. Her colour seemed a trifle high for a lady on the brink of a swoon, but when Edward, who was looking very grave, told Venetia, in a lowered voice, that he thought they should take her home as soon as she was a little recovered, Venetia at once agreed to it, and recommended him (since Mrs. Hendred's coachman would not bring her carriage to the theatre for another hour) to go at once to summon a hackney. He went off immediately, to confer with the door-keeper; and Mrs. Hendred, allowing herself to be supported by the two box-attendants to the stairway, said, in failing accents, that she feared her unfortunate indisposition was due to the evil effect upon her system of woodcock a la Royale. "Or, perhaps, it was the *croque enbouche aux pistaches*, but I would not for the world say so to Mr. Yardley!"

Venetia replied to this with remarkable calm, making no attempt, either then or when she sat beside her aunt in the somewhat malodorous vehicle procured for their conveyance, to repeat the question which had played so large a part in throwing Mrs. Hendred into queer stirrups. But when Mrs. Hendred, upon arrival in Cavendish Square, announced her intention of instantly retiring to bed, she said, with more amusement than concern; "Yes, if you wish, ma'am, but I warn you I am not to be so easily fobbed off! I'll go with you!"

"No, no, dear child! I can feel one of my spasms coming on! That is, I can't imagine what you can possibly— Worting, why do you not send to fetch Miss Bradpole to me, when you can see how unwell I am?"

Before Worting could remind his mistress that she had granted her dresser leave of absence until eleven o'clock, Edward, who had accompanied the ladies into the house, intervened, saying heavily: "I believe, ma'am, upon consideration, that the wisest course *now* will be for you to inform your niece of the circumstance which made it unhappily necessary for us to quit the theatre before the end of the act."

"You may depend upon it that it will be!" said Venetia. "Do take my aunt upstairs to the drawing room, while I mix a dose of hartshorn and water for her! That will make you feel very much more the thing, dear ma'am!"

She ran lightly up the stairs, as she spoke, heedless of the protesting moan that pursued her.

When she presently entered the drawing-room, it was to find her aunt sunk into an armchair, her expression that of one resigned to the worst bludgeonings of fate. Edward, his countenance preternaturally solemn, was standing on the hearth-rug; and Worting, having lit the candles and made up the fire, was preparing to take his reluctant departure.

Mrs. Hendred distastefully eyed the potion her niece had prepared, but accepted the glass with faint thanks. Venetia glanced over her shoulder to be sure the door was firmly shut behind Worting; and then said, without preamble: "Who was that lady, ma'am?"

Mrs. Hendred shuddered; but Edward, who had apparently taken the conduct of the affair on himself, replied with deliberation: "She is Lady Steeple, my dear Venetia. She was accompanied, Mrs. Hendred informs me, by her husband, Sir Lambert Steeple. I am aware, however, that these names can convey but little to you."

"An understatement, Edward!" Venetia interrupted. "They convey nothing whatsoever to me, and I wish very much that you will allow my aunt to answer for herself! Ma'am, when I first caught sight of her I had the oddest

261

feeling— But I knew it to be impossible, and thought it was just one of those resemblances for which there is no accounting. Only she stared at me so hard, and directed her husband's attention to me, and lifted her hand, not quite waving to me, but—but as though she meant it as a sign of recognition! It cannot be so, of course, but the most fantastic notion shot into my brain! I—I thought she was my mother!"

Mrs. Hendred moaned, and took a sip of hartshorn and water. "Oh, my dear child!"

"Your quickness of wit, Venetia, has made it easier for me to discharge the unpleasant duty—for such I feel it to be under these unforeseen circumstances—of divulging to you that she *is*, in fact, your mother," said Edward.

"But my mother is dead!" exclaimed Venetia. "She has been dead for years!"

"Oh, if only she *had* been!" Mrs. Hendred set down the glass she was holding, and added bitterly; "I said it at the time, and I shall always say it! I *knew* she would never cease to afflict us! And just *now*, when we thought she was fixed in Paris—! I shouldn't wonder at it if she came back on purpose to ruin you, my poor child, for what has she ever done but make trouble, besides being the most *unnatural* parent!"

"But how is this possible?" demanded Venetia, looking, and, indeed, feeling, quite stunned. "Mama—*Lady Steeple?* Then—"

"I don't wonder that you should find it difficult to understand," said Edward kindly. "Yet I fancy that a moment's reflection will inform you of how it must have been. Let me suggest to you, my dear Venetia, that you sit down in this chair, while I procure a glass of water for you. This has been a shock to you. It could not be otherwise, and although the truth must have been divulged to you it has been my earnest hope that this need not have been until you had become established in life."

"Well, of course it has been a shock to me! But I don't wish for any water, thank you! Only to have the whole truth told me, and *not*, Edward, such portions of it as you consider suitable! I collect my parents were divorced. Good God, was it the same as— Did my mother elope with that man?"

"I think, Venetia, that it is unnecessary for you to know

262

more than the bare fact," said Edward repressively. "Indeed, I am confident that when you have a little recovered the tone of your mind you will not wish to know more. The subject is not an edifying one, nor is it one which I can venture to enlighten you. You must remember that at the time of that very unhappy event I was myself still at school."

"Oh, for heaven's sake, Edward, *must* you be so Gothic?" she demanded indignantly. "Aunt, *did* she elope?"

Mrs. Hendred, now that the news was out, had begun to revive. She sat up, straightening her elegant cap, and replied with tolerable calm: "Well, no, my love! No, she didn't *elope*, precisely. In some ways, one can't help wishing—not that I mean—only it wasn't the first time, which seemed to make it worse, because people had been talking for *years*, which made everything so disagreeable, though she was so discreet to begin with that I'm sure I had not the least guess—not, that is, until the affair with— Well, never mind that! It is not at all to the purpose, for the General was alive then, poor man, and he persuaded Francis to condone it, for he *doted* on her! There was never anything like it, for I don't believe she cared the snap of her fingers for him, or anyone! A more heartless—"

"Wait, ma'am, wait! *What* General?"

"Good gracious, Venetia, her father, of course your grandfather, though naturally you can't remember him! General Chiltoe, such an amiable, delightful man! Everyone liked him: I did myself. She was his only child, and he thought nothing too good for her, for his wife died when she was quite an infant, which I daresay accounted for it. She was so spoiled and indulged that anyone might have foretold how it would be, and I can assure you that poor Mama—your dear grandmama, my love—begged and implored Francis not to offer for her, but all to no purpose! He was utterly out of his senses, and in general, you know, his understanding was most superior, and I assure you that if Mama introduced *one* eligible female to his notice she must have introduced a score! His affections were never in the least animated—and, you know, my dear, though I should not say so to you, his disposition was *not* warm!—But no sooner did he clap eyes on Aurelia than he fell violently in love with her,

263

and wouldn't listen to a word anyone said to him!" She heaved a gusty sigh, and shook her head. "I never liked her, never! I daresay she was very beautiful—everyone thought her *ravishing!*—but there was always something about her that I couldn't quite like. And I wasn't the only one, I promise you! A great many of my friends thought the fuss and to-do that was made over her was positively nonsensical, but of course none of the gentlemen could see the least thing amiss with her! She had them all dangling after her in the most absurd way—and no fortune, mind you! That was what made it so particularly— However, I must own that it was a great triumph for your father to have won her, though heaven knows he would have done better to have married Georgiana Denny—Sir John's sister, my love, that afterwards married Appledore's eldest son—for you know what he was, dear child, not *hard-fisted*, but *careful*, and from the very start there was trouble, because she hadn't the smallest notion of economy, besides being *fatally* addicted to gaming! The dresses she used to have made for her! The jewels she coaxed out of Francis!—My dear, those diamonds she was wearing tonight! I never saw anything so *vulgar*— And that gown, with not a stitch under it but one invisible petticoat! I wish I might know how she has contrived to keep her figure! Not but what she looked exactly like—" She broke off in some confusion, as Edward cleared his throat warningly, and added hastily: "I'm sure I don't know *what* she looked like, except that it was not at all the thing!"

"Like a Bird of Paradise," supplied Venetia obligingly. "I thought so myself. But—"

"Venetia," interposed Edward, in a tone of grave reproof, "do not let your sportive tongue betray you into saying what is not at all becoming, believe me!"

"How did it come about, ma'am, that Papa divorced her?" demanded Venetia, ignoring this interruption.

"That," declared Mrs. Hendred, with a shudder, "nothing shall ever prevail upon me to discuss! If only Francis had not allowed the General to reconcile him to her, after the Yattenden affair! But so it was—and the way Aurelia could twist men round her thumb—! Well, it would have been better for everyone if he had remained adamant, but he let her coax and cajole him, and then Aubrey was born, and such a pet as she fell into when she found she was

264

increasing again—! And then that dreadful Sir Lambert Steeple began to cast out lures, so that anyone could have known how it would be! His father had just died, and left him that *immense* fortune, and of course he was excessively handsome, but the most shocking profligate, besides being— Well, never mind that, but he wore the Prince's button—for he wasn't the Prince Regent *then*— and a more *improper* set than the Prince's people I daresay never existed! And don't, I beg of you, my dear niece, ask me to tell you how it was that your father was obliged to divorce her, for it makes me feel vapourish only to think of the scandal, and the way even one's closest friends—I am quite overpowered! My smelling-salts!— Oh, I have them here!"

Venetia, who had listened to this in amazement, said slowly: "So that was why Papa shut himself up at Undershaw, and wouldn't let anyone mention her! Of all the *mutton-headed* things to have done— But how like him! how very like him!"

"Hush, Venetia!" said Edward sternly. "Remember of whom you are speaking!"

"I shall not hush!" she retorted. "You know perfectly well that I never held him in affection, and if you think that this is a suitable moment for me to pretend I loved him you must have windmills in your head! Was there ever such a selfish folly? Pray, how much affection had he for me when, instead of taking care I should be brought up as other girls so that everyone might have been well-acquainted with me, he buried me alive? Why, for anything that is known of me I might be as like Mama in disposition as I'm held to be like her in appearance!"

"*Exactly* so, my love!" corroborated Mrs. Hendred, replacing the stopper of her vinaigrette. "It is why I am for ever telling you that you cannot be too careful not to give people the smallest cause to say you *are* like her! Not but what I for one couldn't blame your poor papa, though your uncle, of course, did his utmost to persuade him that he would be making the greatest mistake, for he is very strong-minded, and never pays the least heed to gossip. But Francis was always such a high stickler, never passing the line, and holding himself so very much up! He could not bear to be so mortified, and I'm sure it wasn't to be wondered at, for instead of hiding herself from the world, as one might have supposed she would, Aurelia—your mama, I mean, and how very dreadful to be speaking to you of her in such terms, but I do feel, dear child, that you should know the truth!—well, she positively *flaunted* herself all over town, though not, of course, *received*, and only think how degrading for Francis it would have been! No sooner did Sir Lambert marry her—and the wonder is that he did marry her, when it was an open secret that she was his mistress, and costing him a fortune, too!—no sooner did he marry her than she became perfectly outrageous! Nothing would do for her but to put us all to the blush, and set everyone staring at her! She used to drive a high-perch phaeton every afternoon in the park, with four cream-coloured horses in blue and silver harness, which they say Sir Lambert bought from Astley, just as though she had not been his wife at all, but something very different!"

"Good heavens!" said Venetia, on a tiny choke of laughter. "How—how very dashing of her! I see, of course, that that would never have done for Papa. Poor man! the last in the world to be set dancing to the tune of *cuckolds All Awry!*"

"Well, yes, my dear, though I do beg you won't use such improper language! But you do perceive how awkward it was? And particularly when it was time for you to be brought out, which your uncle insisted I must urge your papa to consent to. And no one can say I didn't offer to present you, but when your papa declined it—well, only think what a quake I should have been in, for they were then living in Brook Street—the Steeples, I mean—and Aurelia was always so capricious that heaven only knows what she might not have taken it into her head to do! Why, she had the effrontery to wave her hand to you this very evening! I shall never cease to be thankful that there was no one I'm acquainted with to see her! Oh, dear, what in he world has brought them back to England, I wonder?"

"They don't live here now, ma'am?"

"No, no, not for years, though I fancy Sir Lambert comes every now and then, for he has a very large property in Staffordshire. It's my belief Aurelia thought that because she entertained the Prince Regent, and *that* set, the *ton* would receive her again, but of course it was no such thing, and so Sir Lambert sold the London house—oh, six or seven years ago!—and I believe they went to Lisbon, or some such place. Lately—since the Peace, I mean—they have been living in Paris. Why they must needs come to London at this moment—and your uncle away from home, so that what's to be done I cannot think!"

"My dear ma'am, nothing!" said Venetia. "Even my uncle can't be expected to drive them out of the country!" She got up from her chair, and began to walk about the room. "My head is in a perfect whirl!" she said, pressing her hands to her temples. "How is it *possible* that I should never have heard so much as a whisper of this? Surely they must have known—? Everyone at home—Miss Poddemore, Nurse—the villagers!"

"Your papa forbade anyone to speak of it, my dear. Besides, it is not to be supposed that they knew the whole at Undershaw, for it was very much hushed up—your uncle saw to that!—and in any event I am persuaded Miss Poddemore—such an excellent woman!—would never have opened her lips on the subject to a soul!"

"No. Or Nurse, or— But the maids— No, they all held Papa in such awe: they wouldn't have dared, I suppose. But later, when I grew up—"

"You forget that until Sir Francis's death you were acquainted only with the Dennys, and with my mother and myself," said Edward. "By then, moreover, several years had passed. I do not say that the scandal was *forgotten*, but it was too old to be much thought about in Yorkshire any longer. It was not at all likely that you would ever hear it mentioned."

"I never did. Good God, why could not Papa have told me? Of all the infamous—Does Conway know?"

"Yes, but Conway is a man, dear child! And of course he had to know, when he was sent to Eton, but Papa forbade him *ever* to speak of it!"

"Gothic! perfectly Gothic!" said Venetia. Her eyes went to Edward. "So *that* is why Mrs. Yardley doesn't like me!" she exclaimed.

He lifted his hand. "I assure you, my dear Venetia, you are mistaken! My mother has frequently told me that she likes you very well. That she did not, for some time, wish for the connection is—I know you must agree—*understandable*, for her principles are high; and anything in

267

the nature of scandal is repugnant to her—as, indeed, it must be to anyone of propriety."

"Such as yourself?" she asked.

He replied weightily; "I do not deny that it is not what I like. Indeed, I struggle to overcome what I felt was an attachment I ought never to have allowed myself to form. It would not do, however. I became persuaded that there was nothing in your character, or your disposition, that made you unworthy to succeed my dear mother as mistress of Netherfold. You have sometimes a trifle too much volatility, as I have had occasion now and then to hint to you, but of your *virtue* I have no doubt."

"Edward, this encomium un—*unwomans* me!" said Venetia faintly, sinking into a chair, and covering her eyes with one hand.

"You are upset," he told her kindly. "It is not to be wondered at. It has been painful for you to learn what cannot but cause you to feel great affliction, but you must not allow your spirits to become too much oppressed."

"I will put forth my best endeavours not to fall into flat despair," promised Venetia, in a shaking voice. "Perhaps you had better go now, Edward! I don't think I can talk about it any more without becoming hysterical!"

"Yes, it is very natural that you should wish to be alone, to reflect upon all you have heard. I shall leave you, and in good hands," he added, bowing slightly to Mrs. Hendred. "One thing, which occurs to me, I will say before I go. It may be that—er—Lady Steeple will seek an interview with you. You will not, of course, grant such a request, but if she should send a message to you, do not reply to it until you have seen me again! It will be an awkward business, but I shall think it over carefully, and don't doubt that by tomorrow I shall be able to advise you in what terms your reply should be couched. Now, do not think you must ring for your butler to show me out, ma'am, I beg! I know my way!"

He then shook hands with his hostess, patted Venetia reassuringly on the shoulder, and took himself off. Slightly affronted, Mrs. Hendred said: "Well, if anybody should advise you how to reply to Aurelia I should have thought—however, I am sure he meant it kindly! Poor child, you are quite overset! I wish to heaven—"

"I am quite in *stitches!*" retorted Venetia, letting her

hand drop, and showing her astonished aunt a countenance alive with laughter. "Oh, my dear ma'am, *don't*
look so shocked, I do beg of you! Can't you see how
absurd— No, I see you can't! But if he had stayed another
instant I must have been in whoops! *Painful* news? I
never was more overjoyed in my life!"

"*Venetia!*" gasped Mrs. Hendred. "My dearest niece,
you *are* hysterical!"

"I promise you I am not, dear ma'am—though when
I think of all the nonsense that has been talked about *my*
reputation, and *my* prospects I wonder I am not lying
rigid on the floor and drumming my heels! Damerel must
have known the truth! He *must* have known it! In fact,
I daresay he is very well acquainted with my mama, for
she looked to me precisely the sort of female he *would*
be acquainted with! Yes, and now I come to think of it
he said something to me once that proves he knows her!
Only he was in one of his funning moods, and I thought
nothing of it. But—but why, if he knew about my mother,
did he think it would ruin me to marry him? It is quite
idiotish!"

Mrs. Hendred, reeling under this fresh shock, said:
"Venetia, I *do implore* you—! It is precisely what makes
it of the very first importance that you should *not* marry
him! Good gracious, child, only think what would be said!
Like mother, like daughter! How many times have I impressed upon you that your circumstances make it *imperative* that you should conduct yourself with the greatest propriety! Heaven knows it is difficult enough—
though your uncle says that he is confident you will receive very eligible offers, for he holds, and Lord Damerel
too, I make no doubt, that when you are seen to be an
unexceptionable girl—not at all like your mother, however much you may resemble her, which, I must own, it
is a thousand pities you do—no man of sense will hesitate—though the more I think of Mr. Foxcott, the more
doubtful I feel about him, because—"

"Don't waste a thought on him!" said Venetia. "Don't
waste a thought on any of the eligible suitors you've found
for me, dear ma'am! There is more of my mama in me
than you have the least idea of, and the only eligible
husband for me is a rake!"

When she was in London, Mrs. Hendred's breakfast was
invariably carried up to her bedchamber on a tray, but it
was Venetia's custom, like that of many other ladies of
more energetic habit than Mrs. Hendred, to rise betimes,
and sally forth, either to do a little hum-drum shopping,
or to walk in one of the parks. Breakfast was served on
her return in a parlour at the back of the house, and such
was the esteem in which she was held in the household
that it was Worting's practice to wait on her himself, instead of deputing this office to the under-butler. Worting,
like Miss Bradpole, had recognized at a glance that Mrs.
Hendred's niece from Yorkshire was no country miss on
her probation, or indigent hanger-on unexpectant of any
extraordinary civility. Miss Lanyon was Quality; and it
was easy to see that she was accustomed to rule over a
genteel establishment. Moreover, she was a very agreeable young lady, on whom it was quite a pleasure to wait,
for she was neither familiar nor high in the instep. She
could depress a pert London housemaid with no more
than a look, but many was the chat Worting had enjoyed
with her in the breakfast-parlour. They discussed such
interesting topics as Domestic Economy, Town Life as
contrasted with Country Life, and the Changes that had
taken place since Worting had first embarked on his distinguished career. It was he who was Venetia's chief
guide to London, for she did not at all disdain to ask his
advice. He told her what places were considered worthy
of being visited, how they were to be reached, and what
it was proper to bestow on chairmen, or the drivers of
hacks.

On the morning following Edward Yardley's unlucky theatre-party she did not go out before breakfast, nor did she wish for information about any historic monument. She wanted to know which were the most elegant hotels in town, and she could scarcely have applied to anyone more knowledgeable. Worting could tell her something about them all, and he was only too happy to do so, reciting, with a wealth of detail, a formidable list ranging from such hostelries as Osborne's Hotel, in Adam Street (genteel accommodation for families, and single gentlemen), to such establishments as the Grand, in Covent Garden (superior), and (if one of the First Houses was required) Grillon's, the Royal, the Clarendon, the Bath, and the Pulteney, all of which (and a great many others besides) catered exclusively for the Nobility and the Gentry. He was himself inclined to favour the Bath, on the south side of Piccadilly, by Arlington Street; a rambling house, conducted on old-fashioned lines, and patronized by persons of taste and refinement, but if Miss had in mind something generally considered to stand at the height of the mode, he would recommend her to enquire for her friends at the Pulteney.

Miss had; and after learning that during the somewhat premature Peace Celebrations held in London in 1814 the Pulteney had housed no less a personage than the Tsar of Russia (not to mention his impressive sister, the Grand Duchess of Oldenburg), she decided to place it at the head of her list of hotels where she was most likely to discover Sir Lambert and Lady Steeple. Charging Worting with a message for his mistress that she had been obliged to go out on an urgent shopping expedition, she presently set forth, charmingly attired in a blue velvet pelisse trimmed with chinchilla, and fetching velvet hat with three curled ostrich plumes, and a high poke lined with gathered silk. She carried a large chinchilla muff, and altogether presented so delightful a picture that when she reached the hackney coach stand in Oxford Street the competition for her custom amongst the assembled Jehus was fierce, and extremely noisy.

Arrived at the Pulteney, which stood on the north side of Piccadilly, and overlooked the Green Park, she found that her instinct had not erred: Sir Lambert and Lady

271

Steeple were occupying the very suite allotted, four years earlier, to his Imperial Majesty.

Venetia sent up her card; and in a very short space of time was being ushered into an ornate saloon upon the first floor, where Sir Lambert, gorgeously arrayed in a befrogged dressing-gown, had just (and rather hastily) swallowed the last mouthful of a large and varied breakfast.

Nothing could have been more gratifying than the affibility with which he received her. It might even have been considered to be a trifle excessive, for after rapidly running over her the eye of a connoisseur he claimed the right of a father-in-law to greet her with a kiss. Venetia accepted this demurely, repressed a strong inclination to remove herself from the circle of his arm, and smiled upon him with dazzling sweetness.

He was delighted. He gave her waist a little squeeze, saying: "Well, well, well, who would have thought such a dull, gray morning would bring such a beautiful surprise? I declare the sun has come out after all! and so you are my daughter! Let me look at you!" He then held her at arms' length, scanning her up and down appreciatively, and in a way that gave her the uncomfortable feeling that she had ventured forth far too lightly clad. "Upon my word, I never thought to have such a lovely gal for my daughter!" he told her. "Aha, that makes you blush, and devilish pretty you look, flying your colours, my dear! But you have no need to colour up, you know! If your papa-in-law may not pay you a compliment I wish you will tell me who may! And so you have come to see us! I am not astonished. No, I said last night to Aurelia that you looked like a sweet gal, and so you are! When she saw you with Maria Hendred she guessed at once who you was, but 'depend upon it,' she said, 'Maria will take care not to let her come within tongue-shot of me!'"

"Did—did my mother wish to see me?" asked Venetia.

"Who wouldn't wish to see you, my dear? Yes, yes, I'll venture to say she'll be devilish glad you came. She don't speak of it, you know, but I fancy she didn't above half like it when that brother of yours never came to call. A fine young man, but holds himself too much up!"

"Conway?" she exclaimed. "Where was this, sir? In Paris?"

"No, no, in Lisbon! Silly young jackanapes would do no more than bow—as top-lofty as his father! Ay, and a pretty mess he's made of his marriage, eh? Lord, my dear, what made him fall into that snare? 'Well,' I said, when I heard the Widow had snabbled him, 'here's a come-down from his high ropes!' And what brings you to town, my pretty little daughter?"

She told him she was on a visit to her aunt, and when he learned that it was her first, he exclaimed that he wished he might take her to see all the lions.

After about twenty minutes a smart French maid came into the room, announcing that miladi was now ready to receive mademoiselle; and Venetia was led through a smaller saloon and an ante-room and ushered into a large and opulent bedchamber. It was redolent of a subtle scent, which brought Venetia up short on the threshold, exclaiming involuntarily: "Oh, your scent! I remember it! I remember it so well!"

A laugh like a peal of bells greeted this. "Do you? I've always used it—*always!* Oh, you used to sit and watch me when I dressed to go to a party, didn't you? Such a quaint little creature you were, but I thought very likely you would grow to be pretty!"

Recalled from her sudden nostalgia, Venetia stammered, as she dropped a curtsy; "Oh, I *beg* your pardon, ma'am! How—how do you do?"

Lady Steeple laughed again, and rose from her chair before a dressing-table loaded with jars, bottles, and trinket-boxes, and came towards her daughter, holding out her hands. "Isn't it *absurd?*" she said, offering Venetia a delicately tinted and powdered cheek to kiss. "I don't feel it to be possible that I *can* have a grown-up daughter!"

Obedient to a nudge from her good angel, Venetia responded: "Nor could anyone, ma'am—I don't myself!"

"Darling! What did they tell you about me—Francis and Maria, and all their *stuffy* set?"

"Nothing, ma'am, except that I should never be as beautiful as you, and that I had from Nurse! Until yesterday I believed you had died when you left us."

"Oh, no, did you? Did Francis tell you so? Yes, I'm sure he did, for it would be *so* like him! Poor man, I was *such* a trial to him! Were you fond of him?"

"No, not at all," replied Venetia calmly.

273

This made her ladyship laugh again. She waved Venetia to a chair, and herself sat down again before the dressing-table, looking her daughter over critically. Venetia now had leisure to observe that the foam of lace and gauze in which she was wrapped was in reality a dressing-gown. It was not at all the sort of garment one would have expected one's mama to wear, for it was as improper as it was pretty. Venetia wondered whether Damerel would like the sight of his bride in just such a transparent cloud of gauze, and was strongly of the opinion that he would like it very much.

"Well, tell me all about yourself!" invited Lady Steeple, picking up her hand mirror, and earnestly studying her profile. "You are excessively like me, but your nose is not as straight as mine, and I fancy your face is not *quite* a perfect oval. And I do think, dearest, that you are a *fraction* too tall. Still, you have turned out remarkably well. Conway is very handsome too, but so stiff and stupid that it put me in mind of his father, and I couldn't but take him in dislike. *What* a mull he made of it in Paris! Should you have liked it if I had upset the Widow's scheme? I daresay I might have, for she is such a respectable creature that it is an object with her to pretend she doesn't know I exist! I had that from someone who knew it for a *fact!* I had a great mind to pay her a visit—to make the acquaintance of my future daughter-in-law, you know! It would have been *so* diverting! I forget why I didn't go after all: I expect I was busy, or perhaps the Lamb—oh, no, I remember now! It was so hot in Paris that we removed to the *chateau*—my Trianon! The Lamb bought it, and gave it to me for a surprise-present on my birthday: the sweetest place imaginable! Oh, well, if Conway finds himself leg-shackled to an insipid little *nigaude* he is very well-served! Why aren't *you* married, Venetia? How old are you? It is so stupid not to be able to remember dates, but I never can!"

"More than five-and-twenty, ma'am!" replied Venetia, a rather mischievous twinkle in her eye.

"Five-and-twenty!" Lady Steeple seemed for a moment to shrink, and did actually put up her hand as though to thrust something ugly away. "Five-and-twenty!" she repeated, glancing instinctively at the mirror with searching, narrowed eyes. What she saw seemed to reassure her, for she said lightly: "Oh, impossible! I was the merest *child* when you were born, of course! But what in the world have you been doing with yourself to be left positively on the shelf?"

"Nothing whatsoever, ma'am," said Venetia, smiling at her. "You see, until I came to London a month ago, I had never seen a larger town than York, nor been farther from Undershaw than Harrogate!"

"Good God, you can't be serious?" cried Lady Steeple, staring at her. "I never heard of anything so appalling in my life! Tell me!"

Venetia did tell her, and although the thought of Sir Francis as a recluse made her break into her delicious laugh she really was horrified by the story, and exclaimed at the end of it: "Oh, your poor little thing! Do you hate me for it?"

"No, of course I don't!" replied Venetia reassuringly.

"You see, I never *wished* for children!" explained her ladyship. "They quite ruin one's figure, and when one is in the straw one looks positively *hideous*, and *they* look hideous, too, all red and crumpled, though I must say you and Conway were very pretty babies. But my last—what did Francis insist on naming him? Oh, Aubrey, wasn't it, after one of his stupid ancestors? Yes, Aubrey! Well, he looked like a sick monkey—*horrid!* Of course Francis thought it was my *duty* to nurse him myself, as though I had been a farmwench! I can't think how he came by such a vulgar notion, for I *do* know that old Lady Lanyon *always* hired a wet-nurse! But it didn't answer, for it made me perfectly ill to look at such a wizened creature. Besides, he was so fretful that it made me nervous. I never thought he would survive, but he did, didn't he?"

Within the shelter of her muff Venetia's hands clenched till the nails dug into her palms, but she answered coolly: "Oh, yes! Perhaps he was fretful because of his hip. He had a diseased joint, you see. It is better now, but he suffered a great deal when he was younger, and he will always limp."

"Poor boy!" said her ladyship compassionately. "Did he come with you to London?"

"No, he is in Yorkshire. I don't think he would care for London. In fact, he cares for nothing much but his books. He's a scholar—a *brilliant* scholar!"

"Good gracious, what a horrid bore!" remarked Lady Steeple, with simple sincerity. "To think of being shut up with a recluse and a scholar makes me feel quite low! You poor child! Oh, you were the Sleeping Beauty! What a touching thing! But there should have been a Prince Charming to kiss you awake! It is too bad!"

"There was," said Venetia. She flushed faintly. "Only he has it fixed in his head that he isn't a Prince, but a usurper, dressed in the Prince's clothes."

Lady Steeple was rather amused. "Oh, but that spoils the story!" she protested. "Besides, why should he think himself a usurper? It is not at all likely!"

"No, but you know what that Prince in the fairy tale is like, ma'am! Young, and handsome, and virtuous! And probably a dead bore," she added thoughtfully. "Well, my usurper is not very young, and not handsome, and certainly not virtuous: quite the reverse, in fact. On the other hand, he is not a bore."

"You have clearly fallen in love with a rake! But how intriguing! Tell me all about him!"

"I think perhaps you know him, ma'am."

"Oh, no, do I? Who is he?"

"He is Damerel," replied Venetia.

Lady Steeple jumped. "*What?* Nonsense! Oh, you're shamming it! You must be!" She broke off, knitting her brows. "I remember now—they have a place there, haven't they? The Damerels—only they were hardly ever there. So you *have* met him—and of course he came round you—and you lost your heart to him, devil that he is! Well, my dear, I daresay he has broken a score of hearts besides yours, so dry your tears, and set about breaking a few hearts yourself! It is by far more amusing, I promise you!"

"I shouldn't think anything could be as amusing as to be married to Damerel," said Venetia.

"*Married* to him! Heavens, don't be so gooseish! Damerel never wanted to marry anyone in all his scandalous career!"

"Oh, yes, he did, ma'am! He wanted once to marry Lady Sophia Vobster, only *most* fortunately she fell in love with someone else; and now he wants to marry me."

"Deluded girl! He's been hoaxing you!"

"Yes, he tried to hoax me into thinking he had only been trifling with me, and if it hadn't been for my aunt's

276

letting the truth slip out he would have succeeded! That—that is why I've come to see you, ma'am! *You* could help me—if you would!"

"I help you?" Lady Steeple laughed, not this time so musically. "Don't you know better than that? I could more easily ruin you, let me tell you!"

"I know you could," said Venetia frankly. "I'm very much obliged to you for saying that, because it makes it much less awkward for me to explain it to you. You see, ma'am, Damerel believes that if he proposed marriage to me he would be doing me a great injury, because between them he and my Uncle Hendred have decided that I should otherwise make a brilliant match, while if I married him I should very likely be shunned by the *ton*, and become a vagabond, like himself. I should like that excessively, so what I must do is to convince him that instead of contracting a brilliant match I am on the verge of utter social ruin. I've racked my brains to discover how it can be done, but I couldn't find any way—at least, none that would answer the purpose!—and I was in such flat despair—oh, in such *misery!* And then, last night, when my aunt told me—she thought I should be aghast, but I was overjoyed, because I saw in a flash that you were the one person who could help me!"

"To social ruin! Well, upon my word!" cried her ladyship. "And all to marry you to Rake Damerel—which I don't believe! No, I *don't* believe it!"

But when she had heard the story of that autumn idyll she did believe it. She looked oddly at her daughter, and then began to fidget with the pots on the dressing-table, arranging and rearranging them. "You and Damerel!" she said, after a long silence. "Do you imagine he would be faithful to you?"

"I don't know," said Venetia. "I think he will always love me. You see, we are such dear friends."

Lady Steeple's eyes lifted quickly, staring at Venetia. "You're a strange girl," she said abruptly. "You don't know what it means, though, to be—a social outcast!"

Venetia smiled. "But thanks to you and to Papa, ma'am, that's what I have been, all my life."

"I suppose you blame me for that, but how should I have guessed—"

"No, indeed I don't blame you, but you will allow,

ma'am, that you haven't given me cause to be grateful to you," Venetia said bluntly.

Lady Steeple shrugged, saying with a pettish note in her voice: "Well, I never wished for children! I told you so."

"But I can't believe that you wished us to be made unhappy."

"Of course I did not! But as for—"

"*I* am unhappy," Venetia said, her gaze steady on that lovely, petulant countenance. "You could do a very little thing for me—such a *tiny* thing—and I might be happy again, and grateful to you from the bottom of my heart!"

"It is too bad of you!" exclaimed Lady Steeple. "I might have known you would only try to cut up my peace— throw me into an irritation of nerves— What do you imagine I can do to help you?"

Sir Lambert, venturing to peep into the room half an hour later, found his daughter-in-law preparing to take her leave, and his wife in an uncertain temper, poised between laughter and vexation. He was not surprised; he had been afraid that she might find this meeting with her lovely daughter a little upsetting. Fortunately he was the bearer of tidings that were bound to raise her spirits.

"Oh, is it you, Lamb?" she called out. "Come in, and tell me how you like my daughter! I daresay you have been flirting with her already, for she is so pretty! Isn't she? Don't you think so?"

He knew that voice, rather higher-pitched than usual, full of brittle gaiety. He said; "Yes, that she is! Upon my soul, it's devilish hard to tell you apart! I fancy you have the advantage, however—ay, you ain't quite the equal of your mama, my dear—and you won't mind my saying it, because she has perfect features, you know. Yes, yes, that was what Lawrence said, when he painted her likeness! Perfect features!"

Lady Steeple was seated at a small writing-table, but she got up, and came with a hasty step to stand beside Venetia, pulling her round to face a long looking-glass. For a minute she stared at the two mirrored faces, and then, to Venetia's dismay, cast herself upon Sir Lambert's burly form, crying: "She is five-and-twenty, Lamb! *five-and-twenty!*"

"Now, my pretty! now, now!" he responded, patting her soothingly. "Plenty of time for her to grow to be a beauty like her mama! There, now!"

She gave a hysterical little laugh, and tore herself away "Oh, you are too absurd! Take her away! I must dress! I *abominate* morning callers! I look *hagged!*"

"Well, I can tell you that you don't," said Venetia, tucking a sealed letter into her reticule. "I was used to think, you know, when I was a little girl, that you were like a fairy, and so you are. I never was made to feel so clumsy in my life! I *wish* I knew how to walk as if I were floating "

"Flattering creature! There, kiss me, and be off to seek your fortune! I wish you may find it! You won't, of course, but don't blame me for it!"

"Going to seek her fortune, is she?" said Sir Lambert. "So you have set up a secret between you? But here is your woman, my pretty, on the fret to make you ready to receive I know not how many people sent round from Roberts's!"

"Oh, my new riding-habit!" exclaimed Lady Steeple, her face lighting up. "Send Louise in to me directly, Lamb! Dear child, I must bid you goodbye—I positively must! *No* Frenchman can make a riding-habit: Roberts has made mine ever since I came out! That's why I came with the Lamb! I *hate* London—and in November, too!"

Once more Venetia was given a soft, scented check to kiss; she said: "Goodbye, ma'am—and *thank you!* You have been very, very kind to me!"

She curtsied as Lady Steeple made a wry mouth at her, and then Sir Lambert ushered her out of the room, saying as he closed the door: "That's a good gal! I'm glad you said that to her! She feels it, you know—gets into the dumps! Not as young as she was! You didn't object to my saying you wasn't her equal?"

Venetia reassured him; he then said that he would take her downstairs to her maid, and, upon her disclosing that she had come alone, declared his resolve to escort her back to Cavendish Square. She begged him not to put himself out, saying that she was used to walk alone, and meant to do a little shopping in Bond Street, but to no avail.

"No, no, it will not do! I wonder at Maria Hendred, upon my word, I do! A lovely gal walking by herself! Ay, and all the Bond Street beaux ogling you, the rascals! You must give me the pleasure of escorting you, and no need to be in a worry that your mama might not like me to go with you. I promise you she won't take a pet, for," said Sir Lambert simply, "I shan't mention the matter to her."

So, as soon as Sir Lambert's man had eased his master into his overcoat, handed him his hat, his gloves, and his walking-cane, Venetia sallied forth in his company, not ill-pleased to demonstrate to as many of her aunt's acquaintances as she might be fortunate enough to meet that she stood on the best of terms with her disreputable stepfather. Sir Lambert's was an impressive figure, and since his corpulence made rapid movement impossible to him their progress was slow. By the time they had turned into Bond Street they were fast friends, and Sir Lambert, besides behaving in a very gallant manner to his fair companion, had regaled her with several anecdotes of his youth, which made her laugh in a way that delighted him very much, and encouraged him to confide several rather warmer anecdotes to her. He accompanied her into a linendraper's shop, and was of the greatest assistance to her in choosing muslin for a dress; and when they came out would have carried the parcel for her had she not tucked it into her muff, telling him that she had never yet seen a Pink of the *Ton* carrying anything so dowdy as a parcel tied up with string.

There were a good many carriages in the road, and quite a number of modish-looking strollers, but it was not until Grosvenor Street was reached that Venetia had the satisfaction of seeing anyone with whom she was acquainted. She then recognized in an astonished countenance a lady whom she had met in Cavendish Square, and bowed slightly. Sir Lambert, always very polite, raised the beaver from his pomaded locks, and bowed too. The Cumberland corset which he wore creaked protestingly, but Venetia was quite amazed to see with what majestic grace so portly a man could perform his courtesy.

By this time they were abreast a jeweller's shop, and Sir Lambert, struck by a happy thought, said: "You know, my dear, I think, if you should not dislike it, we will take a look in here. Poor Aurelia is subject to fits of dejection, and there's no doubt she was a trifle overset. You shall help me to choose some little thing to divert her mind!"

She was very willing, and considerably entertained to discover that his interpretation of "some little thing" proved to be a diamond pendant. Aurelia, he said, was partial to diamonds. It did not seem to Venetia that he stood in much need of guidance from her in making his choice, but she soon found that he liked to have his taste approved, so she stopped preferring any of the pendants which did not take his fancy, and dutifully admired each one of the three which obviously appealed to him. The choice at last made, he demanded to be shown some brooches, and here Venetia was allowed to have her way. She could not prefer an opulent brooch made up of sapphires and diamonds to a very pretty one of aquamarines. He did his best to persuade her that the aquamarines were mere trumpery, but when she laughed at him, and insisted that they were charming, he said: "Well, well, if you think so indeed I will buy it, for you have excellent taste, my dear, and I daresay you know best!"

They emerged from the shop to find Edward Yardley standing with his hands behind his back, closely studying a tray of rings set out in one of the windows. He turned his head just as Venetia tucked her hand in Sir Lambert's proffered arm, and ejaculated in a voice loud enough to make a passer-by look over his shoulder at him: *"Venetia!"*

"Good-morning, Edward!" she said, with what he felt to be brazen calm. "I am very glad to see you, but pray don't make the whole street a present of my name! Sir, will you allow me to present Mr. Yardley to you? He is an old friend of mine, from Yorkshire. Edward, you are not acquainted, I fancy, with my father-in-law—Sir Lambert Steeple!"

"How-de-do?" said Sir Lambert, giving Edward two fingers. "Aha, you wish me at Jericho, don't you? Well, I don't blame you, but I don't give up my prize! No, no, you may glare as much as you choose, but this little hand shall stay where it is!"

Edward might be said to have been taking full advantage of the permission so genially accorded him. As he spoke Sir Lambert patted the little hand on his arm in a fatherly way, and smiled down into Venetia's merry eyes

281

in a manner so far removed from fatherly that Edward was quite unable to contain himself, but said with a good deal less than his usual grave deliberation: "I am on my way to Cavendish Square, sir, and will escort Miss Lanyon!"

Sir Lambert was amused. His prominent blue eyes took Edward in from top to toe, missing no detail that marked him as the country squire of comfortable fortune but no touch of town bronze. This, then, was the inevitable *pretendant*, and, judging by the familiarity with which Venetia addressed him, he enjoyed her favour. Sir Lambert thought she might have done better for herself, but he wasn't an ill-looking young fellow, and no doubt she knew her own business best. He looked down at her, a roguish gleam in his eyes. "Shall we let him go along with us, my dear, or shall we give him the go-by? What do you say?"

This was too much for Edward. His countenance was already unbecomingly flushed, for not only had his wrath been aroused by the sight of Venetia with her hand in Sir Lambert's arm, but his self-esteem was smarting under that experienced roue's jovial but faintly contemptuous scrutiny. Sir Lambert might be nearly double Edward's age, but Edward resented his lazy assurance, and still more did he resent being regarded by Sir Lambert as a jealous stripling. He glared more fiercely than ever, and said with awful civility: "Miss Lanyon is obliged to you, sir, but will not put you to the trouble of escorting her farther!"

Sir Lambert chuckled. "Yes, yes, I see how it is! You would like to have it out with me at dawn! That's the dandy! I like to see a young fellow ready to sport his canvas! Lord, I was the devil of a fire-eater myself in my day, but that was before you were born, my boy! You can't call me out, you know! Well, well, it's too bad of me to roast you! Do go along with us to the top of the street, and then, if my pretty little daughter likes, you may take her the rest of the way by yourself."

Edward nearly choked. Before he could utter whatever rash words surged to his tongue Venetia intervened, saying in a tone of cool amusement: "Oswald Denny to the life! My dear Edward, do not *you* make a cake of yourself, I beg!"

"And who," demanded Sir Lambert, pleasantly intrigued, "is Oswald Denny, eh? Oh, you may look demurely, but you don't bamboozle me, puss! Yes, yes, *I* can see what a twinkle you have in your eye! I'll be bound you have all the cockerels in Yorkshire squaring up to each other!"

She laughed, but turned it off, directing the conversation into channels less exacerbating to Edward. He, determined not to leave her with Sir Lambert and unable to wrest her forcibly away from that elderly buck, had nothing to do but to fall in beside her, and to reply, in stiff monosyllables, to such remarks as were from time to time addressed to him.

Arrived at the top of the street, Venetia stopped, and, withdrawing her hand from Sir Lambert's arm, turned to face him, saying, with friendliest smile; "Thank you, sir. You are a great deal too good to have come so far with me, and it would be quite infamous of me to drag you any farther. I am so very much obliged to you—and you were *perfectly* right: the Indian muslin will make up much better than the sprig!"

She held out her hand to him, and he clasped it warmly, sweeping off his curly-brimmed and shining beaver with an air many a budding dandy would have envied. She found that he was pressing into her hand the smaller of the two jeweller's cases, and was for a moment bewildered. "But, sir—!"

He closed her fingers over the little box. "There, it's nothing! A trumpery thing, but you seemed to like it the best! You will let me give you a little present—a trifle from your father-in-law!"

"Oh, *no!*" she exclaimed. "Indeed, sir, you mustn't! *Pray—!*"

"No, no, take it, my dear! You will oblige me very much by taking it! I never had a daughter, you know, but if I had I should have wished for one like you, with your sweet face, and your pretty ways!"

She was very much touched, and regardless alike of the passers-by and Edward's speechless anger stood on tiptoe to kiss Sir Lambert's cheek, one hand on his broad shoulder. "And *I* wish very much that you *had* been my father, sir," she said. "I should have loved you much more than ever I loved my own, for you are a great deal kinder!

Thank you! indeed I will take it, and remember you whenever I wear it, I promise you!"

He returned her embrace, putting his arm round her, and giving her a hug. "That's a good gal!" he said. He then dug Edward in the ribs with the head of his cane, and said, with a slight lapse from his parental mood: "Well, you young dog, you may take her now, but if I were ten years younger damned if I wouldn't cut you out!".

After that he executed another of his practised bows, settled the beaver on his head again, and sauntered off down the street, keeping a weather eye cocked for any personable female who might come within his orbit.

"You know, he may be a sad rip, but he's the dearest creature!" Venetia said, forgetting that Edward's mood was scarcely in harmony with hers.

"I can only suppose you to have taken leave of your senses!" he said.

She had been watching, with a little smile of appreciative amusement, Sir Lambert's progress down the street, but she turned her head at this, and said with considerable asperity: "I certainly supposed you to have taken leave of yours! What can have possessed you to behave with such a want of conduct? I was never more mortified!"

"*You* were never more mortified!" he said. "I do not know how you can stand there, Venetia, speaking in such a manner!"

"I don't mean to stand here speaking in any manner at all," she interrupted, stepping off the flagway in the wake of the urchin who was zealously sweeping the crossing for her. "Stop looking as sulky as a bear, and give that boy a penny!"

He caught up with her as she reached the opposite side of Oxford Street. "How came you to be in that old court-card's company?" he demanded roughly.

"Pray remember that you are speaking of my father-in-law!" she replied coldly. "I have been visiting my mother, and he was so obliging as to escort me home."

"*Visiting your mother?*" he repeated, as though unable to believe his ears.

"Certainly. Pray, have you any objection?"

He replied in a resolutely controlled voice: "I have

284

every objection, and you shall presently learn what they are! I do not choose to bandy words with you in public! We will be silent, if you please!"

She returned no answer, but walked on, her countenance untroubled. He kept step beside her, his brow frowning, and his mouth grimly set. She made no attempt to speak to him until they stood on the steps of her uncle's house, when, glancing thoughtfully at him, she said: "You may come in with me, if you wish, but don't show the porter that face, if you please! You have advertized your displeasure to enough people already."

As she spoke, the door was opened, and she stepped into the house. It was the under-butler who had admitted her, and she paused to ask him if his mistress was in. On learning that Mrs. Hendred, having suffered a disturbed night, had not yet left her bedchamber, she took Edward up to the drawing-room, and said, as she began to strip off her gloves: "Now say what you will, but try to recollect, Edward, that I am my own mistress! You appear to believe that you have authority over me, but you have not, and so I have told you very many times!"

He stood looking at her gloomily, and at length replied: "I have been mistaken in your character. I allowed myself to believe that the levity of which I have frequently had cause to complain sprang from a natural liveliness rather than from any want of disposition in you. My eyes have been opened indeed!"

"I am extremely glad to hear it, for it was certainly time they should be. Don't accuse me, however, of deceiving you! You deceived yourself, for you would never believe that I mean the things I say. The truth is, Edward, that we are poles apart. I have a great respect for you—"

"I wish I might say the same of you!"

"How very uncivil of you! Come, let us shake hands, and say no more, except to wish each other happy!"

He made no movement to take the hand stretched out to him, but said heavily: "My mother was right!"

Her ready sense of the ridiculous overcame her annoyance; her eyes began to dance; she said cordially: "To be sure, she was!"

"She begged me not to allow my judgment to be overborne by my infatuation. I wish that I had heeded her. I might then have been spared the mortification of discovering that the female whom I had intended to make my wife had neither heart nor delicacy!"

"Well, I wish you had, too, but all's well that ends well, you know! In future you will do as your mother bids you, and I expect she will find the very wife to make you comfortable. I'm sure I hope she will."

"I should have known what to expect when you did not scruple, in spite of my representations, to visit the Priory daily. You appear to have a preference for libertines!"

The smile swept over her face, transfiguring it. "It's very true, Edward: I have indeed! Now I think you had better go. You have rung a fine peal over me, and it is time I went up to see how my aunt does."

"I shall leave London by the first coach tomorrow morning!" he announced, and on this valedictory line stalked from the room.

Hardly had his step died away on the stair than the door opened again, this time to admit Mrs. Hendred, who came in looking very much startled, and instantly exclaimed; "My love, what has happened, to send Mr. Yardley off in such a pucker? I was coming downstairs when he rushed out of this room with such a countenance that I declare I was quite alarmed! I spoke to him, as you may suppose, asking if anything was amiss, but he wouldn't stop—said only that you would tell me, and was gone before I could fetch my breath! Oh, Venetia, *don't* tell me you have quarrelled?"

"Well, I won't tell you, if you had rather I didn't, dear aunt, but it is the truth, for all that!" replied Venetia, laughing. "Oh, dear, *what* a goose he did make of himself! I could almost forgive him for it! I'm afraid you will be quite as shocked as he was, ma'am: I have been to call on Mama, and Edward met me in New Bond Street, coming home on Sir Lambert's arm!"

She was obliged to repeat this confession before Mrs. Hendred could at all take it in, and then to support the poor lady to her favourite chair. This second disaster, following on the shock of the previous evening's encounter, proved too much for Mrs. Hendred's shattered nerves: she burst into tears, and between her painful sobs delivered herself of a disjointed monologue which was at once a jeremiad and a diatribe. Venetia made no attempt to defend herself against the various charges levelled at her, but devoted herself to the task of soothing and petting her afflicted relative into comparative calm. Exhausted by her emotions, Mrs. Hendred at last lay back in her chair with her eyes shut, merely moaning faintly, and feebly repulsing her ungrateful niece. Venetia looked doubtfully at her, decided against making any further announcement, and went away to summon Miss Bradpole. Consigning Mrs. Hendred to her competent care, she once more left the house, and made her way to the hackney stand. "To Lombard Street, if you please!" she told the jarvey. "The General Post Office!"

The afternoon was considerably advanced when she again returned to Cavendish Square. She learned from Miss Bradpole that Mrs. Hendred had retired to bed, but had declined all offers to summon the doctor to her side. She had been coaxed to toy with a light nuncheon—just a cup of broth, a morsel of chicken, and some ratafia cream—and now seemed a trifle easier, and inclined to sleep. Venetia, showing a proper concern, favoured Miss Bradpole with a glib explanation of her aunt's collapse, and went away to her own room.

It was not until much later that she ventured to tap gently on Mrs. Hendred's door. A failing voice bade her come in, and she entered to find her aunt reclining against a mountain of pillows, a very pretty nightcap tied under her chin, her handkerchief in one hand, her vinaigrette in the other, and on the table beside the bed a battery of sedatives and restoratives. Upon hearing Venetia's voice, she turned reproachful eyes towards the door, and uttered a heart-rending sigh. Then she perceived that Venetia was wearing a travelling dress under a thick pelisse, and her demeanour underwent an abrupt change. She sat up with a jerk, and demanded in far from moribund accents: "Why are you dressed like that? Where are you going?"

Venetia came to the bedside, and bent over her aunt, kissing her cheek affectionately: "Dearest aunt, I'm going home!"

"No, no!" cried Mrs. Hendred, clutching her sleeve. "Oh, dear, I shall become perfectly distracted! I didn't mean it! Heaven knows what's to be done, but your uncle will think of something, depend upon it! Venetia, if I said anything—"

"Of course you didn't, ma'am!" Venetia said, smiling at her, and patting her shoulder caressingly. "But you cannot hope to re-establish my credit, and I would so much rather you didn't make the attempt. You have been too kind to me already, and I'm a wretch to make you so uncomfortable. But, you see, it's my whole life I'm fighting for, and I can't be sure that even now it's not too late! Pray try to forgive me, my dear aunt, and—and understand a little!"

"Venetia, only *consider!*" implored Mrs. Hendred "Good God, you *cannot* throw yourself at that man's head! What would he *think* of you?"

"I have considered. It does seem quite shocking, doesn't it? I hope my courage won't fail! No, I don't think it will, because there's nothing I couldn't say to him, or he not understand. Don't be distressed! I wish I need not have disturbed you again, but I couldn't go without bidding you goodbye, and thanking you for being so very kind to me. I've told Bradpole and Worting that Edward brought me bad news of Aubrey, and is to accompany me to York by the mail, so you mustn't fret over what any of the servants will think. And I have packed my trunk, and desired Betty to cord it, and to sent it to me by the carrier—when I write to tell you my direction. I can't take more than a portmanteau on the mail, you know."

"Listen, Venetia, only wait until we can consult your uncle!" said Mrs. Hendred feverishly. "He will be at home by breakfast-time tomorrow—why, he may even arrive this very evening! Now, do, do—"

"Not for the world!" said Venetia, with a quiver of laughter. "I am very much obliged to my uncle, but the thought that he might find another way of rescuing me from my dear rake puts me in the liveliest dread!"

"Wait, dear child! I have had a very good notion! If you find your affections don't change when you have had time to see more of the world—no, no, do but listen!—won't say a word against this dreadful marriage! But Lord Damerel would tell you *himself* that it's far too soon for you to commit yourself! Your uncle shall think of a way to overcome what happened today, and I shall put off Theresa's coming-out in the spring, and bring *you* out instead!"

"Oh, poor Theresa!" exclaimed Venetia, laughing outright. "When she is counting the days!"

"She may very well wait for another year," said Mrs. Hendred resolutely. "Indeed, I am much inclined to think she should, for I noticed a spot on her face the other evening, and you know, my dear, if she is going to fall into that vexatious way young girls have of throwing out a spot whenever one particularly wishes them to be in their best looks, it would be *useless* to bring her out next year! Now, what do you say to that?"

"Horrid!" replied Venetia, rubbing her cheek tightly against her aunt's before disengaging herself from the clutch on her sleeve, and going to the door. "Long before the season ended—if not before it started!—Damerel would be heaven knows where, strewing roseleaves about for some abandoned female to tread on! Well, one thing at least I'm determined on! If he *must* indulge in such wasteful habits he shall strew his rose-leaves for me to tread upon, not one of his ridiculous Paphians!" She blew a kiss to her aunt, and the next instant was gone.

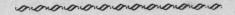

Venetia reached York midway through the afternoon of the following day, the mail having been considerably delayed by fog in and around London. If she was in very much better spirits than on her previous journey she was far more exhausted. She alighted from the coach feeling battered and tousled, and instead of immediately hiring a chaise and pair to convey her to the Priory, which had been her intention, bespoke a bedchamber, some hot water, and some tea. Anxious to reach her journey's end though she might be she had no desire to arrive at the Priory in a crumpled dress, her face unwashed, and her hair unbrushed. When the chambermaid at the inn led her up to an empty bedchamber, one glance at the looking-glass was enough to confirm her in the belief that no lady, however handsome, could drive for two hundred miles in a mail-coach carrying its full complement of six inside passengers without emerging at her destination in an unbecomingly travel-worn condition.

She had been fortunate to have succeeded in booking a seat at such short notice; it was naturally not one of the corner seats; and she had very soon discovered that between a private post-chaise and a mail-chaise there was a world of difference. Unlike two of her fellow passengers, who snored hideously throughout the night, she was quite unable to sleep; and when a respite of twenty minutes was allowed the travellers at breakfast-time she was able only to swallow two sips of scalding coffee before being summoned to resume her place in the coach, because she was obliged to wait for fifteen minutes before the over-driven waiter slapped the coffee-pot down on the table in front of her.

A wash and a cup of tea revived her a little; and she thought that if she lay down on the large fourposter bed for half an hour her headache might go off. That was her undoing, for hardly had she drawn the coverlet over herself than she fell asleep.

She awoke in darkness, and to hear the Minster clock chiming the threequarters, and started up in dismay, groping for the bell-rope that hung beside the bed. When the chambermaid appeared, bearing a candle, she was somewhat relieved to learn that the hour was not quite so far advanced as she had feared. It wanted ten minutes to seven. The chambermaid, a kindly soul, said that she had taken a look-in at her at four o'clock, but had thought it would be a shame to rouse her. She suggested that Miss must be ready for her dinner, which was now being served in the coffee-room; but Venetia, though ravenously hungry, merely begged her, as she scrambled into the clean dress she had earlier unpacked from her portmanteau, to run downstairs to the landlord, and to bespeak on her behalf a chaise-and-pair, or any other available vehicle, to convey her immediately to Elliston Priory.

It had been her intention, after the refreshment of half an hour on that treacherous bed, to have stepped round to Mr. Mytchett's place of business, for after buying her ticket on the mail, paying for the breakfast she had had no time to eat, and tipping the guard, her resources had dwindled to no more than would enable her to defray the charges at the inn. She was just able to do that; and presently climbed up into the job-chaise in reduced circumstances, but heartened by the reflection that someone at the Priory—Aubrey, or Damerel, or Imber—could defray the postboy's charges.

But Imber, opening the door to this wholly unexpected visitor shortly after half-past eight, merely goggled more than ever at an airy request to pay off the postboy, and repeated in such stunned accents: "Pay off the postboy, miss?" that Venetia said, impatiently of further delay: "Oh, never mind! His lordship will give you the money! Where shall I find him? Is he in the library?"

Still staring at her with dropped jaw Imber slowly shook his head. A numbing fear clutched her heart; she stammered: "G-gone? Imber, has he l-left Yorkshire?

291

Don't stand there gaping at me! do you take me for a ghost? Where is his lordship?"

He swallowed, and replied: "He's in the dining-room, miss, but—but he's eaten Hull cheese, Miss Venetia! You hadn't ought—*Miss—!*"

But as this excursion into the vernacular was quite incomprehensible to Venetia, she paid no heed to the note of urgent entreaty in Imber's voice, but went quickly down the hall towards the dining-room. Opening the door, she stepped into the room, and stood on the threshold, hesitating a moment, because suddenly, mingled with the longing to see her love again, she was aware of shyness.

All the way north she had pictured this meeting, wondering what Damerel would say, and how he would look, what she herself would say to him. It had not occurred to her that he would neither speak nor look at her, or that their actual meeting would be so wholly unlike anything she had imagined.

He was alone, sprawling in the carved armchair at the head of the table, one arm resting on the table, and the fingers of that hand crooked round the stem of a wine glass. The covers had been removed, and a half-empty decanter stood at his elbow, its stopper lying beside it. He was always rather careless of his appearance, but never had Venetia seen him so untidy. He had loosened his neck-cloth, and his waistcoat hung open, and his black hair looked as if he had been in a high wind. He sat immobile, his shoulders against the high chair-back, his legs stretched out, and his brooding gaze fixed. The harsh lines of his face seemed to be accentuated, and his sneer was strongly marked. As Venetia moved softly forward into the candlelight he at last turned his eyes and looked at her. She stood still, shyness and mischief in her smile, and a hint of enquiry. He stared uncomprehendingly at her, and then, startling her, lifted his hand to his eyes, to shut her from his sight, ejaculating in a thickened voice of repulsion: "O God! *No!*"

This entirely unexpected reaction to her arrival might well have daunted Venetia, but as she had by this time realized that his lordship was, in the common phrase, extremely well to live, she was undismayed, and even rather amused. She exclaimed: "Oh Damerel, *must* yo be foxed just at this moment? How *odious* you are, my dear friend!"

His hand fell; for one instant he gazed at her incredulously, then he was on his feet, knocking over his wineglass, "Venetia!" he uttered. *"Venetia!"*

Two hasty, uncertain strides brought him round the corner of the table; she moved towards him, and melted into his arms as he seized her.

He held her in a crushing embrace, fiercely kissing her, uttering disjointedly; "My love—my heart—oh, my dear delight! It *is* you!"

She had flung one arm round his neck, and as he raised his head to devour her face with his eyes she tenderly smoothed back the dishevelled lock of hair from his brow. Whatever qualms or doubts had assailed her had vanished; she smiled lovingly up at him, and said, turning the word into a caress: *"Stoopid!"*

He gave a laugh like a groan, kissing her again, tightening his arms round her until she could scarcely breathe. Then he seemed to recollect himself a little, and slackened his hold, exclaiming shakily: "I must reek of brandy!"

"You do!" she told him frankly. "Never mind it! I daresay I shall soon grow accustomed to it."

He released her, pressing his hands over his eyes. "Hell and the devil! I'm jug-bitten—drunk as a wheelbarrow! I can't—" His hands dropped, he demanded almost angrily: "What brings you here? O God, why did you come?"

"The mail-coach brought me, love, and I'll tell you why presently. Oh, my dear friend, I have so *much* to tell you! But first we must pay off the chaise. Imber seems not to have any money, so will you let him have your purse, if you please?"

"What chaise?"

"The one I hired in York to bring me here. I hadn't enough of my money left—in fact, I am run quite off my legs, and must now hang on your sleeve! Damerel, do, pray, give me your purse!"

He dived a hand mechanically into his pocket, but apparently he was not carrying his purse, for he brought it out again empty. His love, apostrophizing him affectionately as a castaway pea-goose, turned from him to go in search of Aubrey, and found that Imber was standing in the doorway, his face a study in disapproval, curiosity, and astonishment.

"Marston is paying the postboy, miss," he said. "But, begging your pardon, if he's to be sent back to York—Miss Venetia, you don't mean to *stay* here?"

"Yes, I do," she responded. "Tell Marston to send the chaise away, if you please!"

This seemed to penetrate to Damerel's somewhat clouded brain. "No!" he said forcefully, if a little huskily.

"No, my lord," agreed Imber, relieved. "Shall I tell him to rack up for a while, or—"

"Pay no heed to his lordship!" said Venetia. "Surely you must be able to see that he is *not* himself! Send the chaise off, and then, if you don't wish me to drop into a swoon, do, I implore you, fetch me some supper! All I've eaten since yesterday is one slice of bread-and-butter, and I am *famished!* Tell Mrs. Imber I beg her pardon for being so troublesome, and that some cold meat will do very well!"

Imber looked for guidance towards his master, but as Damerel was occupied in an attempt to marshal his disordered wits, and paid no attention to him, he went reluctantly away to carry out Venetia's orders.

"Venetia!" said Damerel, raising his head from between his hands, and speaking with painstaking clarity. "You can't remain here. I won't let you. Out of the question. Not so top-heavy I don't know that."

"Nonsense, my dear friend! Aubrey is all the chaperon I need. Where is he, by the by?"

He shook his head. "Not here. Gone—forgot the fellow's name—some parson! Grinder."

"What, is Mr. Appersett home again?" she exclaimed. "I *knew* I dared not wait another hour! Has Aubrey left you already? Oh, well! It can't be helped, and, to own the truth, I don't care a rush!"

He frowned. "Not left me. Gone to dine at the Parsonage. Appersett. Yes, that's right! He came home yesterday—or the day before. Can't remember. But it doesn't signify. You can't remain here."

She regarded him with a sapient eye. "Yes, I see how it is," she remarked. "I daresay it is the same with every man, for I recall that whenever Conway was in the least disguised he would take some notion into his head, in general an *idiotish* one, and hold to it buckle and thong!"

He repeated, very creditably: "'Idiotish'!" A laugh shook him. "I thought I should never hear you say that again!"

"Do I say it a great deal?" she asked, and then, as he nodded: "Oh dear, how very tiresome of me! I must take care!"

"No. Not tiresome. But," said his lordship, sticking to his guns, "you can't remain here."

"Well, I warn you, love, that if you cast me out I shall build me a willow cabin at your gates—and very likely die of an inflammation of the lungs, for November is *not* the month for building willow cabins! On, good-evening, Marston! Have you paid the postboy for me? I am very much obliged to you!"

"Good-evening, ma'am," said the valet, with one of his rare smiles. "May I say how very happy I am to see you here again?"

"Thank you—I am very happy to be here!" she replied warmly. "But what is to be done? Here is his lordship threatening to turn me out of doors: not at all happy to see me!"

"Just so, ma'am," said Marston, casting an experienced glance at Damerel. "Perhaps if you would care to step up to Mr. Aubrey's room, to take off your bonnet and pelisse—? There is a nice fire burning there, and I have instructed the housemaid to carry up a can of hot water, if you should wish to wash your hands. Also your portmanteau, ma'am."

She nodded, and crossed the room to the door.

"*No!*" said Damerel obstinately. "Listen to me!"

"Yes, my lord, in one moment!" replied Marston, ushering Venetia, out of the room, and pulling the door to behind him. "The room next to Mr. Aubrey's shall be prepared for you, ma'am. I should perhaps explain that Mr. Aubrey has driven over to dine at the Parsonage: but he will be back presently." He added, in a reassuring tone: "His lordship will very soon be himself again, ma'am."

"Marston, has he been getting foxed often?" Venetia asked bluntly.

"Oh, no, ma'am! He has been dipping rather deep,

perhaps, but only when Mr. Aubrey has gone up to bed."
He hesitated, and then added, in his expressionless way:
"It is always a sign of trouble with his lordship when he
makes indentures, if you will pardon my saying so,
ma'am."

She looked frankly into his impassive countenance.
"Has he been in trouble, Marston?"

"Yes, ma'am. In worse trouble than I have ever known
him to suffer."

She nodded, and said with a little smile: "We must see
what can be done to cure that."

"Yes, ma'am: I should be extremely glad," said Marston, bowing slightly. "May I suggest supper in—about
half an hour?"

She was so hungry that it took considerable resolution
to enable her to suppress an instinctive protest; but she
managed to do it, and even to acquiesce graciously, since
it was evident that he wished her to keep out of the way.
She went upstairs, and was rewarded for her docility as
soon as she caught sight of her reflection in the looking-
glass in Aubrey's bedchamber. In the indifferent light
provided by the one candle brought in by the chambermaid at the inn she had dressed by guess, and had done
no more than drag a comb hastily through her curls before
tieing on her hat; but Marston had caused two branches
of candles to be set on the dressing-table, and in their
relentless light Venetia saw with horror that she presented almost as dishevelled an appearance as did her
castaway host. All thought of supper forgotten, she ripped
off her hat, flung her pelisse on the bed, and set about
the urgent task of making herself once more fit to be seen.
By the time this had been accomplished rather more than
half an hour had elapsed. She disposed a very handsome
zephyr shawl across her elbows, in the approved mode,
took a last, critical look at her reflection, blew out the
candles, and went downstairs again to the dining-room.

Here she found matters much improved, all traces of
debauch having been removed, the table freshly laid, the
fire made up, and Damerel, his disordered attire set severely to rights, miraculously sobered. He was in the act
of draining a tankard when Venetia entered the room. She
looked a little doubtfully at it, but whatever its contents
had been they seemed to have exercised a beneficial ef-

fect upon his system, for he said in a perfectly clear voice, as he handed the empty tankard to Marston: "That's better! Bread-and-cheese, and I shall do." He turned, and smiled at Venetia, saying lightly, but with a glow in his eyes that warmed her heart: "Quite starving, my poor child? You shall be served immediately! Come and sit down—and let me set your anxious mind at rest! I won't drive you from my roof: we have hit on a better scheme—or, to be honest, Marston has done so! *My* head isn't yet capable of devising schemes. You have come here to consult with Aubrey on some important matter—don't forget that!—and *I* am going to remove to the Red Lion. Thus we observe the proprieties!" He pushed in her chair, as she seated herself at the table, and added, still in that light tone: "You are doing your hair in a new way: very smart!"

She realized that he was going to be difficult, but she was not much perturbed. Whatever his tongue might utter, his eyes betrayed him. She said chattily: "Do you like it? I hope you do, for I'm assured that it's all the crack!"

He had moved to his own chair, and he now lifted his quizzing-glass to one eye. "Yes, excellent! *A la Sappho*, I fancy."

"Wretch!" she said, with her infectious chuckle. "Do you know the names of *all* the styles of female coiffure?"

"Most of 'em, I think," he replied brazenly. He sat down, letting his quizzing-glass fall on the end of its long ribbon. "What has brought you here, Venetia?"

"The mail coach—and excessively uncomfortable it was!"

"Don't quibble, girl!"

She smiled at him, saying softly: "Stoopid!"

She won no answering smile; he was looking pale, and rather grim; and after a tiny pause, he said: "I wish to God you had not come!"

"Oh! That's—that's a horrid set-down, particularly when it seemed to me that you were glad to see me."

"I was badly foxed—I'm still a trifle concerned, but no longer out of my senses!"

"Oh, dear, do you mean to kiss me only when you're foxed?"

"I don't mean to kiss you at all!" he said harshly.

"Then of course I won't press you to," she replied.

297

"Nothing is more detestable than to be pressed to do what one hasn't the smallest wish to do! I have lately had a great deal of experience of that. I know of only one worse thing, and that is to be beset by well-meaning but perfectly mutton-headed persons who can't keep themselves from meddling with what doesn't concern them."

"Venetia—" He checked himself, as Imber came in, and sat in frowning silence while a bowl of soup was set before her.

"How very good it smells!" said Venetia, picking up her spoon. "Oh, Imber, fresh bannocks? Yes, indeed I'll take one! Now I *know* I'm at home again!" She turned her head to address Damerel. "My aunt, I must tell you, has a French cook. He contrives the most delectable dishes, but I couldn't help yearning sometimes for plain Yorkshire food."

"How do you like London?" he asked, as Imber filled Venetia's glass with lemonade.

"Not at all. Well, perhaps that is being unjust to it! Under different conditions I think I might have liked it very well." She added, as Imber left the room: "I was too unhappy, and too lonely to be entertained. I had no one to laugh with, you see."

He said in a constricted voice: "You felt strange, of course. Were they kind to you, your uncle and aunt?"

"Very kind. Only—well, never mind! I don't think I can explain it to you."

"Explain it to me? Do you think I don't know? Do you think I haven't missed you every day—every minute?" he demanded impetuously. "And pictured you, sitting just where you are now, as you sat on that first evening, with that smile in your eyes—" He broke off. "Well, you need not explain it to me! I know! But believe me, *believe* me, my dear delight, it will pass!"

"Yes, so you told me, when you said goodbye to me," she agreed. "My aunt told me so too, and I've no doubt my uncle would, for I'm sure he told *you* it would. But what none of you has made at all plain to me is why you should think it a—a *consummation devoutly to be wished!* However, I don't mean to be troublesome, so I won't tease you with questions. Oh, dear, I can hear Imber coming back! I think it would be better if I don't tell you what brought me here until we can be safe from interruption. I have so many other things to tell you, too! Oh, Damerel,

I have seen your cousin! He was at a rout-party, and I heard his name spoken, and nearly disgraced myself by laughing! He is a *splendid* quiz!"

He smiled, but with an effort. "A *quiz*? Good God, what can you be thinking of? Top-of-the-Trees is Alfred! You should see him when he goes upon the strut! Who is in town? Not many people yet, I fear, but I hope you made a few agreeable acquaintances?"

She responded readily, and continued to chat in an easy, cheerful way, while she ate her supper. Damerel did not say very much, but sat watching her, a queer smile in his eyes which made her long to put her arms round him, because she thought that just so would he smile at a dear memory.

When Imber set apples and nuts on the table, and finally withdrew from the room, Damerel said: "And now, Venetia, tell me what happened to make you take this crazy step!"

"I will," she replied. "But first, my dear friend, *I* have a question to put to *you!* Why did you never tell me that my mother wasn't dead, but very much alive?"

He was cracking a walnut between his long fingers, but he looked up at that, and said: "So you've found that out, have you?"

"That," said Venetia severely, "is not an answer!"

He shrugged. "It wasn't for me to tell you what you were evidently not meant to know. Who did tell you? Your aunt? Very wise of her! I hoped she would, for you might otherwise have discovered it in a way that could have shocked you."

"Well, that is precisely how I did discover it! It was certainly a *surprise* to me—but I had almost guessed it before poor Aunt Hendred was compelled to tell me the whole. I saw her at the play, the day before yesterday."

"The devil!" he exclaimed, frowning. "I thought she was fixed in Paris!"

"So she is," Venetia answered, holding out her hand for the nut he had just peeled. "Thank you! She was obliged to come to London to have a new riding-habit made. She tells me that no Frenchman can make them as well as an English tailor."

There was suddenly an arrested look on his face. "She *tells* you? You spoke to her?"

"Spoke to her? Why, of course! I visited her at the

Pulteney, and I can't describe to you how kind she was—
and Sir Lambert, who, I must say, is the greatest dear!
Only fancy! He walked all the way to the top of Bond
Street with me, and as though that were not enough he
bought this charming brooch for me! Wasn't it touching
of him? He told me that he wished I *was* his daughter,
and—"

"I've no doubt!" Damerel interrupted wrathfully.

"—and so do I wish it," continued Venetia serenely,
"for my own father I didn't like half as well!"

"Do you mean to tell me," demanded Damerel, "that
your aunt had no more gumption than to permit you to
do what any but a greenhead would have known was
enough to set every gossiping tongue wagging? Oh, my
God!"

"You must meet my aunt," said Venetia. "I am persuaded you would deal wonderfully together, for I see
you have exactly the same notions! Do you know, it had
me quite in a puzzle—before I knew about my mother,
I mean—to understand why Aunt was for ever telling me
that I must be excessively correct and prim, because of
my *circumstances*? And though she was bent on finding
me a respectable husband I could see that she thought
it would be a very hard task. It seemed odd to me, for I'm
not an *antidote*, and I'm not by any means penniless. I
saw how it was, of course, when I learned the truth about
Mama. I must own, Damerel, that I wish you had been
frank with me—but I daresay you felt you could not." She
added reflectively: "No, to be sure you couldn't! It was
a most awkward fix to be in!"

"What the *devil* do you mean by that?" Damerel shot
at her, in a voice ominous enough to cause any female to
quail.

Venetia showed him a face of sweet innocence. "Why,
only that I *do* understand how very difficult—quite impossible, in fact!—it was for you to explain that for a Damerel to marry a daughter of Lady Steeple would *never* do.
I think now that you did try, once or twice, to give me a
hint, but—"

"Tried to—How dare you?" he said furiously. "How
dare you, Venetia? If you imagine that I let you go because I thought you beneath my touch—"

"But that must have been the reason!" she objected.

300

"I know you bamboozled me into believing that it was you who were beneath *my* touch, and that was kind, and very like you, my dear friend—but perfectly absurd, now that I know how shockingly ineligible I am!"

He half started up from his chair. She thought she was going to be seized, and, probably, well shaken, and waited hopefully. But he sank back again, and although he eyed her bodingly she saw that the wrath had vanished from his eyes. "You don't think anything of the sort, my girl," he said dryly. "Whether your aunt—who sounds to me to be a confirmed ninny-hammer!—put it into your head that your parents' divorce makes you ineligible, or whether it's a notion you've hatched for my benefit, I know not, but you may now listen to me—and believe that I am speaking the truth! There's no man worthy to be called a man at all, who, knowing you, and loving you, would care a tinker's damn for that fustian nonsense! Ask your uncle, if you think I'm lying to you! He'll tell you the same. Good God, do you imagine that no one was ever divorced before? Anyone would suppose your mother to have joined the muslin company who heard you talk such moonshine, instead of which she has been married to Steeple these fifteen years!"

"Well, I must say that that takes quite a load from my mind," Venetia told him gratefully. "And it brings me to the reason why I came home. I *knew* you would be able to advise me! Of course, Aubrey is the chief person I must consult, but he isn't old enough to be able to *advise* me. Damerel, I have received an offer, and I am not perfectly sure whether I should accept it, or not. It's not what I wish for, but I think I should prefer it to living alone— wasting my life, you called that, and perhaps you were right."

He said in a hard voice, and rather hastily: "If this offer comes from Yardley, I can't advise you! I should have said—the last man alive to—But you know best what will suit you!"

"From Edward? Good gracious, no! How could you think it possible I should want advice about an offer from him?"

"I don't—that is, I know he followed you to London. He came here to tell Aubrey. I didn't see him."

"He did follow me to London," agreed Venetia. She
301

heaved a mournful sigh. "He has been mistaken in my character, however, and I daresay he is even now on his way back to Netherfold. It is a *very* lowering thought, but I've been as good as *jilted*, Damerel! I expect, in the end, he will offer for Clara Denny."

"Is this another attempt to hoax me?"

"No, no! You see, he *does* care about divorce, and although, after struggling against his judgment for several years, he yielded to his infatuation, believing me to have delicacy, under my levity—"

"Venetia, even Yardley *could* not talk like that!" he protested, his lip quivering.

Her laughter bubbled over. "But he did, I promise you! He was strongly of the opinion that I should give my mama the go-by, you see, and—and he took the most unaccountable dislike to Sir Lambert!"

"Oh, he did, did he?" retorted Damerel, regarding her with grim appreciation. "He's an insufferable coxcomb, but as for you, fair torment—!"

"Well, I see nothing to take exception to in Sir Lambert!" she declared. "Only wait until you learn how *very* kind he is! You see, the offer I spoke of was from *Mama!*"

"What?"

"I don't wonder you are astonished: I was myself—but so very much touched! Only think, Damerel! She invites me to go back with them both to Paris, and to remain with them for as long as I like—and with Sir Lambert's *full* approval! I own, I can't help but be tempted: I have always longed to travel, you know, and Mama talks of going to Italy in the spring. *Italy!* I don't think I can resist!"

"Venetia, you are doing it very much too brown!" he said, breaking in on this without ceremony. "I know your mama! She would no more invite you to take up residence in her hotel than she would shave off her eyebrows!"

Quite prepared for this scepticism, Venetia said anxiously: "Oh, Damerel, do you think she didn't mean it after all?"

"I think she never so much as dreamed of inviting you to visit her, my love!"

"But she *did!*" Venetia assured him. "It was because I told her of my scheme to set up house with Aubrey. She was quite as horrified as ever you were, and said I might as well bury myself. She says it wouldn't do for me to live with her in England, but that abroad people are not so strait-laced, so that—But read her letter for yourself!"

Looking thunderstruck, he took the letter she had extracted from her reticule, and spread it open. He cast her a suspicious glance, and then lowered his eyes to Lady Steeple's charmingly written missive. He read it, heavily frowning, twice, before he again looked at Venetia. He was still suspicious, but she could see that he was shaken. "Venetia, how the *devil* did you persuade her to write this?" he asked.

"Well, you *see* what persuaded her to write it!"

"That is exactly what I do *not* see! Aurelia Steeple in a fret because you told her—Oh, for the Lord's sake, Venetia, don't ask me to swallow *that* fling! I don't know what you've been doing, but if this isn't a hoax I hope you know that under no circumstances must you join *that* menage!"

She said apologetically: "No, I fear I don't. I see that it wouldn't be a wise thing to do if my ambition were to become one of those tonnish females whom my aunt describes as being *of the first consideration*, but as it isn't—"

"Stop talking like the greenhead you are!" he said sternly. "You know nothing about the Steeples' world! Well, I do know—none better!—and if I thought that this was anything but a hum—" He stopped abruptly, raising his head a little.

"Well?" she prompted.

He lifted his finger, and she too heard the sound that had reached his ears. A carriage was approaching the house. "Aubrey!" Damerel said. His eyes went back to her face. "What reason do you mean to give him for being here? You won't regale him with this!" He handed back Lady Steeple's letter to her as he spoke.

She was wishing Aubrey a hundred miles away, and could have screamed with vexation, but she replied with seeming calm: "But, my dear friend, I couldn't take such a step without first discovering what his sentiments are!"

"If that is all—"

She smiled. "His *sentiments*, Damerel, not his *opinions!* For anything I know he might prefer to lodge with the Appersetts than to join me in London." Her smile wavered. "I don't think I am very necessary to him either," she said.

He was on his feet now, standing over her, grasping her wrists, and almost jerking her up out of her chair. "Venetia, I would give my life to spare you pain—disillusionment—all the things you don't realize—have no knowledge of!—My life! What an empty, fustian thing to say! I could scarcely have hit upon a more worthless sacrifice!" he said bitterly.

There was a murmur of voices in the hall, footsteps were approaching. "*Damn* Aubrey!" Damerel said under his breath, releasing Venetia's wrists.

But it was not Aubrey. Setting the door wide, Imber announced in a voice of doom: "Mr. Hendred, my lord!"

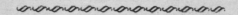

Mr. Hendred walked into the room. He was looking pale, tired, and very angry; and after bestowing one brief glance on Venetia he addressed himself stiffly to Damerel. "Good-evening! You must allow me to apologize for making so belated an arrival! I do not doubt, however, that you were expecting to see me!"

"Well, I suppose I ought to have done so, at all events," replied Damerel. "You have quite a knack of arriving in what might be called the nick of time, haven't you? Have you dined?"

Mr. Hendred shuddered, momentarily closing his eyes. "No, sir. I have *not* dined! Nor, I may add—"

"Then you must be devilish sharp-set!" said Damerel curtly. "See to it, Imber!"

An expression of acute nausea crossed Mr. Hendred's countenance, but before he could master his spleen enough to decline, with civility, this offer of hospitality, Venetia, less charitable emotions vanquished by compassion, started forward, saying: "No, no! My uncle can never eat when he has been travelling all day! Oh, my dear sir, what can have *possessed* you to have come chasing after me in this imprudent way? I wouldn't have had you do such a thing for the world! So unnecessary! so *foolish!* You will be quite knocked-up!"

"*Foolish?*" repeated Mr. Hendred. "I reached London last night, Venetia, to be met with the intelligence that you had left town by the mail-coach, with the expressed intention of coming to this house—where, indeed, I find you! So far as I can discover, you took this disastrous step because of a quarrel with your aunt—and I must say, Venetia, that I credited you with too much sense to refine anything whatsoever on what your aunt may have said in a distempered freak!"

"My dear, dear uncle, of course I didn't!" Venetia said remorsefully, coaxing him to a chair. "Do, pray, sit down, for I know very well you are fagged to death, and have that horrid tic! There was no quarrel, I promise you! My poor aunt was quite overset by first seeing my mother at the theatre, and then discovering that I had been so ungrateful as to make a mull of her efforts to bring me into fashion by walking on my father-in-law's arm all the way from the Pulteney Hotel to Oxford Street. She gave me a rare scold, and I didn't blame her in the least; I knew she would! But as for leaving town because of it, or parting from her in anger—Sir, she *cannot* have told you that! She knew what my reason was; I made no secret of it to her!"

"Your aunt," said Mr. Hendred, expressing himself with determined restraint, "is a woman of great sensibility, and is subject, as you must be aware, to irritation of the nerves! When her spirits become overpowered, it is hard for her to compose herself sufficiently to render a coherent or even a rational account of whatever may have occurred to cast her into affliction. In fact," he ended, with asperity, "you cannot make head or tail of anything she says! As for knowing what your reason was, I don't know what you may have seen fit to tell her, Venetia, but so far as I understand it you could think of nothing better to do than to beguile her with some farrago about wishing Damerel to strew rose-leaves for you to walk on!"

Damerel, who had resumed his seat, had been staring moodily into the fire, but at these words he looked up quickly. "Rose-leaves?" he repeated. *"Rose-leaves?"* His eyes went to Venetia's face, wickedly quizzing her. "But, my dear girl, at *this* season?"

"Be quiet, you wretch!" she said, blushing.

"Exactly so!" said Mr. Hendred. Scrupulously exact, he added: "Or her purpose *may* have been to discourage you from indulging in such wasteful habits. I was unable to discover which—not that it signifies, for a more foolish story I never heard! What you told your aunt is of no consequence. What is of the first consequence to me is that you, my dear niece, a girl—and do not tell me that you are of age, I beg of you!—a girl, I say, residing in my house, under my protection, should have been allowed to run off, unattended, and with the expressed intention of seeking shelter under this of all imaginable roofs! And you call it *foolish* and *unnecessary* of me to exert myself to prevent *your* ruin and my own mortification?"

"No, no!" she said soothingly. "But are you not forgetting that I have a brother living under this roof, sir? I told your servants that I had been sent for because he was ill, and *surely*—"

"I have neither forgotten Aubrey, nor am I here to lend you countenance!" he interposed sternly. "I am here, as well you must know, to save you from committing an act of irremediable folly! I make no excuse, Damerel, for speaking thus plainly, for you already know my mind!"

"By all means say what you choose," shrugged Damerel. "We are perfectly in accord, after all!"

Venetia, watching her uncle press his finger-tips to one temple, rose, and went quietly out of the room. She was not absent for many minutes, but when she returned her uncle told her that he had been discussing with Damerel her visit to the Steeples. "I have no hesitation in assuring you, my dear niece, that what his lordship has already told you is perfectly true. No stigma whatsoever attaches to *you*, and although any *regular* intercourse between you and Sir Lambert and Lady Steeple would be most undesirable, nothing could be more unbecoming—I may say *improper*—than for a daughter to cut her mother's acquaintance! I do not conceal from you that on that painful subject I have never found myself in agreement, either with your aunt, or with your late parent. In my opinion, the policy of secrecy which was insisted on was as ill-judged as it was absurd!"

"Very true!" said Venetia. She looked from one to the other, a smile in her eyes. "What else have you discussed? Have you settled between you what my future is to be? Or shall I tell you what *I* have settled?"

Mr. Hendred, seeing that smile reflected in Damerel's eyes, said quickly: "Venetia, I beg you will consider before you do what I gravely fear you cannot but regret! You think me unfeeling, but believe me, it is not so! I think it my duty to tell you, however—and I trust your lordship will forgive me!—that no more unsuitable marriage than the one you contemplate could well be imagined!"

"My dear uncle, how *can* you talk in such an exaggerated fashion?" Venetia protested. "Do but recollect a little! Damerel may be a *rake*, but at least he won't turn out to be my *father!*"

"Turn out to be your father?" repeated Mr. Hendred, in a stupefied tone. "What, in heaven's name—?"

Damerel's shoulders had begun to shake. "Oedipus," he said. "At least, so I apprehend, but she has become a trifle confused. What she means is that *she* won't turn out to be *my* mother."

"Well, it is the same thing, Damerel!" said Venetia, impatient of such pedantry. "*Just* as unsuitable!"

"You will oblige me, Venetia," said Mr. Hendred acidly, "by abandoning a subject which I consider to be extremely improper. I may say that I am excessively shocked to think that Aubrey—for I collect it was he!—should have sullied his sister's ears with such a story!"

"But you must surely see, sir, that Damerel isn't in the least shocked!" she pointed out. "Doesn't that circumstance help you to understand why he would be the most *suitable* of all imaginable husbands for me?"

"No, it does not!" replied Mr. Hendred roundly. "Upon my word, I don't know how to bring you to your senses! You appear to me to be living in a—in a—"

"Soap-bubble," supplied Damerel.

"Yes, very well! a soap-bubble!" snapped Mr. Hendred. "You have fallen in love for the first time in your life, Venetia, and in your eyes Damerel is some sort of a hero out of a fairy-tale!"

She went into a peal of laughter. "Oh, no, he is not!" she exclaimed. "Dear sir, how can you suppose me to be such a goose? If that pretty soap-bubble image was meant to signify that a dreadful disillusionment is in store for me, I can assure you that you may be easy!"

"You compel me to be blunt—and a very distasteful task it is! Damerel may have the intention of reforming his way of life, but habits of long standing—the trend of a man's character—are not easily altered! I have a considerable regard for you, Venetia, and it would cause me distress and self-blame if I saw you made unhappy!"

She looked at Damerel. "Well, my dear friend?"

"Well, my dear delight?" he returned, a glint in his eyes.

"Do you think you will make me unhappy?"

"I don't—but I will offer you no promises!"

"No, pray don't!" she said seriously. "As soon as one promises not to do something it becomes the one thing above all others that one most wishes to do!" She turned her head towards her uncle again. "You mean to warn me that he may continue to have mistresses, and orgies, and—and so-on, don't you sir?"

"*Particularly* so-on!" interpolated Damerel.

"Well, how should I know all the shocking things you do? The thing is, uncle, that I don't think I ever should know."

"You'd know about my orgies!" objected Damerel.

"Yes, but I shouldn't care about them, once in a while. After all, it would be quite unreasonable to wish you to change *all* your habits, and I can always retire to bed, can't I?

"Oh, won't you preside over them?" he said, much disappointed.

"Yes, love, if you wish me to," she replied, smiling at him. "Should I enjoy them?"

He stretched out his hand, and when she laid her own in it, held it very tightly. "You shall have a splendid orgy, my dear delight, and you will enjoy it very much indeed!"

Fortunately, since the much-tired Mr. Hendred was showing alarming signs of having reached the end of his endurance, the door opened at that moment, and Imber came in with the tea-tray. He set this down before Venetia, who at once poured out a cup, and gave it to her uncle, saying: "I know you won't venture to eat anything, sir, but tea always does you good, doesn't it?"

He could not deny it, and it did indeed exercise a beneficial effect upon him, for by the time he had finished his second cup he had so far accepted the marriage as inevitable as to demand of Damerel whether he had any notion how his affairs stood, to what tune he was in debt, and in what style he proposed to support his wife.

These pregnant questions were posed in a tone of withering irony, but Damerel's answer was in the nature of a doubter. "I know exactly how my affairs stand: what my debts amount to, and what my disposable assets will bring in. I shan't be able to support my wife in luxury, but I trust to support her in comfort. I have been into all this with my man of business—a month since! He merely awaits my instructions to act in the manner agreed upon at that time."

Driven against the ropes, Mr. Hendred was still full of pluck, and rattled in again, game as a pebble. "And a settlement?" he demanded.

He was thrown in the close. "Naturally!" said Damerel, raising his brows with unaccustomed haughtiness.

At this point Venetia entered the ring. "I may not know much about orgies, but you are now talking of what I do understand!" she announced. "And in a perfectly idiotish way! *Disposable assets* means your race-horses, and your yacht, and the post-horses, you stable all over England, and I know not how many other things! There is not the smallest need for you to dispose of them, and as for making a settlement on me, why the—the *devil* should you, when I have a great deal of money of my own? I must own, I should myself choose to pay off the debts, but if you prefer to live in debt, it is quite your own affair! As for making all these sacrifices—Damerel, it would end in regret for *you*, not for me!"

"Live in debt?" exclaimed Mr. Hendred, regarding her with an expression not far removed from revulsion. *"Prefer* to live in debt?"

"Yes, we'll discuss all these matters, sir—in our idiotish way—at some future date!" said Damerel. "Don't distress yourself, my sweet! My happiness doesn't hang on my disposable assets, but on one green girl."

"Stop!" commanded Mr. Hendred. "You are going a great deal too fast! This will not do!"

"Well, at least it will do better than for her to join the Steeples' set!" retorted Damerel. "Yes, you may stare, but that is the pistol what has been held to *my* head!"

"Nonsense!" said Mr. Hendred testily. "Aurelia wouldn't entertain such a notion for an instant! Aurelia with a daughter taking the shine out of her? Ha!"

310

"Yes, that's what I think, but although I haven't yet discovered how she did it, Venetia has wrung an invitation out of her: I've been privileged to read it!"

"Good God!" said Mr. Hendred blankly.

"So," continued Damerel, "we will now devote our energies not to the hopeless task of convincing my green girl that she is making a mistake, but to the problem of how to ensure that she shall *not* find herself ostracized by the *ton*."

"I assure you it won't trouble me in the least to be ostracized!" interpolated Venetia.

"It would trouble me, however." Damerel turned his head, and looked thoughtfully at Mr. Hendred. "With your support, sir, and my Aunt Stoborough's, I think we may contrive to brush through it. I rather fancy you are acquainted with my aunt?"

"I have been acquainted with Lady Stoborough these twenty years," replied Mr. Hendred, with a thin, triumphant smile. "And the only heed she would pay to any persuasion of mine, or of anyone, would be to do precisely the opposite to what was desired."

"Just so!" said Damerel. "I see that you will know to a nicety how to bring her round your thumb."

There was silence. Mr. Hendred, on whom this speech seemed to have exercised a powerful effect, sat gazing at a picture invisible to his companions. Under Venetia's fascinated eyes, the skin round his mouth began slowly to stretch, and while his thin lips remained a little pursed two deep creases appeared in his cheeks: Mr. Hendred was enjoying a private joke, too rare to be imparted to his companions. Emerging from this reverie, he surveyed them with disfavour, and declared his inability to discuss the matter on hand any more that evening. He then asked his niece if she meant to accompany him to York, where he meant to spend the night, but not as though he expected to receive an assenting answer.

This gave her the opportunity for which she had been waiting. She said: "No, dear sir, not another yard will I travel this day, and nor, I must break it to you, do you! Don't eat me! but I directed Imber to send your chaise on to the Red Lion some time ago. I know that is what you like, and indeed, we are so very shorthanded—I mean, Damerel is so short-handed here at present that the postilions could hardly be housed without putting the servants to a great deal of work they really have no time to undertake! And Damerel's valet, a most excellent man, will have seen that a room is prepared for you by now, and will have unpacked your portmanteau. I ventured to direct him to find the pastilles you always burn when you have the headache, upon hearing which he said that he would immediately prepare a *tisane* for you to drink when you go to bed."

This programme was so attractive that Mr. Hendred succumbed, though not without warning his host that his complaisance must not be taken to mean that he gave his consent to a marriage of which he strongly disapproved, much less that he was prepared to promote it in any way whatsoever.

Accepting this blighting announcement with equanimity, Damerel then rang the bell for Marston, at which moment Aubrey, having driven into the stableyard, and entered the house by way of a sidedoor, came into the room. He was looking faintly surprised, and said as he entered: "Well, I wondered who the deuce you could be talking to, Jasper! How d'ye do, sir? Well, m'dear, how are you? I'm glad you've come: I've missed you."

He limped across the room to Venetia as he spoke, and much moved by his greeting she embraced him warmly. "And I have missed you, love—you don't know how much!"

"Stoopid!" he said, with his twisted smile. "Why didn't you send warning that you were coming? What's brought you, by the way?"

"*I* will tell you what brought your sister here!" said Mr. Hendred. "You are of an age to be thought capable of forming an opinion, and I am told you are considered to have a superior understanding! It may be that Venetia will be more willing to attend to you than to me. Let me tell you, young man, that she has announced her intention of accepting an offer from Lord Damerel!"

"Oh, good!" said Aubrey, his face lighting up. "I hoped you would, m'dear: Jasper is just the man for you! Besides, I like him. I shall be able to spend my vacations with you, and I could never have stood Edward, you know. By the by, did he come boring for ever in London?"

"Is that all you have to say, boy?" demanded Mr. Hendred, pardonably incensed. "Do you *wish* your only sister to marry a man of Lord Damerel's reputation?"

"Yes, I told her I thought she should an age since. I never paid much heed to all the gossip about Jasper's reputation myself, and if she don't care for it why should I?"

"I suppose," said Mr. Hendred bitterly, "that such sentiments might have been expected from a boy who does not scruple to recount grossly immoral and indelicate stories to his sister!"

Aubrey looked astonished. "What the deuce has she been saying sir?" he enquired. "If she's been telling warm stories she must have had 'em from Jasper, for Edward wouldn't tell her any, and I don't *know* any!"

"*Oedipus Rex*, cawker!" said Damerel.

"*Oedipus Rex?* I don't recall telling Venetia about him, but I daresay I may have, and in any event, to apply such epithets as *immoral* and *indelicate* to the works of Sophocles is the most shocking thing I've ever heard said—even by Edward!"

At this point, Marston, who had been standing on the threshold for some minutes, intervened, saying: "You rang, my lord?"

"Yes, I did," said Damerel. "Will you take Mr. Hendred up to his room? Ask Marston for anything you may need, sir; I've never yet known him at a loss!"

So Mr. Hendred, bidding a grudging goodnight to the company, allowed himself to be shepherded out of the room. Damerel said softly, just as Marston was preparing to follow his jaundiced charge: "Marston!"

Marston paused. "My Lord?"

Damerel grinned at him. "Wish me happy!"

Marston's impassive countenance relaxed. "If I may, my lord, I wish you both happy. I should like to say that there are others who will be happy with you."

"Lord, I ought to have wished you happy, oughtn't I?" said Aubrey, as the door closed behind the valet. "I do, of course—but you know that without my saying it! Well, I think I'll go up to bed too: I'm sleepy."

"Aubrey, don't go for a moment!" begged Venetia.

313

"There is something I want to say to you, and I'd as lief do so at once. I hope you won't mind it: I don't think you will. I discovered two days ago that Mama—isn't dead, as we thought."

"No, I know she isn't," replied Aubrey. "Of course I don't mind it, stoopid! Why should I?"

Well as she knew him, she gasped. "Aubrey! You mean to say—Did Papa tell you?"

"No, Conway did."

"Conway! When?"

"Oh, the last time he was at home! Just before he went off to Belgium. He said I ought to know, in case he was killed."

"Well, of all the ramshackle things to do!" she exclaimed indignantly. "Why could he not have told *me?* If he could have told a fourteen-year-old boy—!"

"I don't know. I suppose he thought Papa would be angry, if he found you knew. Anyway, he told me not to speak of it."

"You might have told me later—after Papa died! Why on earth didn't you?" she demanded.

"I don't think I thought of it," he replied. "Well, why should I? I wasn't particularly interested. I daresay I should have been if I'd ever known Mama, but, dash it, Venetia, you can't be interested in what happened when you were only a few months old!" He yawned. "Lord, I am sleepy! 'Night, m'dear! 'Night, Jasper!"

He limped out, and Venetia turned to find her love smiling at her in affectionate mockery. "Let that be a lesson to you, Admir'd Venetia!" he said. He came across the room to her, and took her in his arms. She did not resist, but she held him off a little, with her hands against his chest.

"Damerel, there is something I must say to you!"

His smile faded; he looked searchingly down at her. "What is it, my dear delight?" he said.

"It is—you see, my aunt said—I couldn't throw myself at your head! It seemed as though I could, and I *did*, but when my uncle began to talk about your debts, and settlements, I suddenly saw how right she was! Oh, my love—my *friend!*—I don't wish you to marry me if perhaps you had rather *not* be married!"

"Then you are by far more unselfish than I am, my

dear heart, for I wish to marry you whatever your sentiments may be!" he replied promptly. "You may regret
this day: I could not! What I regret I can never undo, for
the gods don't annihilate space, or time, or transform such
a man as I am into one worthy to be your husband."

She clasped him tightly. "Stoopid, stoopid! You know
I found my *worthy* suitor a dead bore, and as for the rest,
does it not occur to you, love, that if you hadn't run off
with that fat woman—"

"She was not fat!" he protested.

"No, not then, but she is now! Well, if you hadn't behaved so badly you would probably have married some
eligible girl, and by now would have been comfortably
settled for *years*, with a wife and six or seven children!"

"No, not the children! The caterpillar would have had
them," he reminded her. "Does it occur to *you*, Miss Lanyon, that although I have twice been on the verge of it,
I have not yet offered for you? Being now safe from interruption, will you do me the honour, ma'am—"

"Good! You haven't gone to bed yet," said Aubrey,
suddenly re-entering the room. "I have had a most excellent notion!"

"This," said Damerel wrathfully, "is the second time
you have walked in just as I am about to propose to your
sister!"

"I should have thought you must have done that hours
ago. In any event, this is something important. You can
spend your honeymoon in Greece, and I'll come with
you!"

Still standing within the circle of Damerel's arm, Venetia choked, and turned her face into his shoulder.

"Greece in the middle of winter? We shall do no such
thing!" said Damerel.

"But why be married so soon? If you were to settle on
a date in the spring—"

"We have settled on a day in January—if not December!"

"Oh!" said Aubrey, rather dashed. "Then I suppose it
had better be Rome. It's a pity, because I'd prefer Greece.
However, we can go there later on, and it's your honeymoon, after all, not mine. I daresay Venetia will like
Rome, too."

"We must remember to ask her some time—not that

315

it signifies! Go to bed, you repulsive whelp!"

"Oh, you want to propose to Venetia, don't you? Very well—though you needn't mind me, you know! Good-night!"

He limped out, and Damerel strode to the door, and locked it. "And now, my love," he said, returning to Venetia, "for the *fourth* time...!"